MW00892734

THE BOOK OF
RUTH

A Novel

Russell Clarke

PAGE PUBLISHING, INC.
Conneaut Lake, PA

First originally published by Page Publishing 2020

ISBN 978-1-6624-0950-9 (hc)
ISBN 978-1-6624-0949-3 (digital)

Printed in the United States of America

"I dedicate this book to my mother, Ruth Matilda Sprick, born on August 8, 1920, a woman who always faced the hardships of life with grace and dignity, even to the end."

Part 1

At this they wept again. Then Orpah kissed her mother-in-law goodbye, but Ruth clung to her. "Look," said Naomi, "your sister-in-law is going back to her people and her gods. Go back with her." But Ruth replied, "Don't urge me to leave you or to turn back from you. Where you go I will go, and where you stay I will stay. Your people will be my people and your God my God."

—Ruth 1:14–16

1

As Ruth Clarkson walked down the large open staircase at the front of the funeral home, she stopped on the midway landing and looked out across the familiar old viewing parlor that had been such a big part of her life for the past thirty-plus years. She was amazed by the large number of sympathy plants, floral baskets, and funeral arrangements that flanked each side of the bier at the front of the room, and her heart fluttered a beat as she heard the muted sound of a piano and acoustic cello arrangement playing softly in the background, sounds she had heard a thousand times before, but never quite so clearly. Her attempts to appear in control, to face the day like any other, were betrayed only by her eyes, which always seemed to announce her mood from any distance, always gave portal to the innermost workings of her mind. She clenched her hands tightly as she thought about what would surely be the "worst" day of her life, as she had worded it to her brother the day before, and continued her descent down the grand old stairway. When she reached the bottom, she paused and took a breath, reaching out for the predictable, and then went about her usual task of inspecting the place, adjusting the flowers, and straightening the chairs, anything to keep her busy. She desperately hoped the comfort and reassurance of routine, the mindless intimacy of the customary, could occupy her intellect, could carry her through the day.

The Clarkson Funeral Home, although having gone through several major renovations over the years, as well as several name changes, was still representative of a much earlier time and place. The building that currently housed the funeral home had also, in the past, doubled as a furniture store. When the sole proprietorship first opened in the spring of 1888, the scarce commodity of skilled craftsmen made building furniture for the living, as well as the dead, a common occurrence in rural areas, and out of necessity, the business had opened its doors with both *furniture* and *funeral* proudly displayed on its signage. As the years passed and specialists took over the construction of ornate metal caskets with custom, tailored design features and secured vaults, the dual-business model was simply adjusted to accommodate the changing times, becoming more of a financial partnership and less of a production necessity. The separate income streams that had kept the fledgling enterprise going in the early years continued to give the business a more balanced cash flow and had enabled the proprietors to "keep the doors open," as Mr. Werner Clarkson, the second owner of the business, had recounted at numerous chamber meetings and loan reviews. For years, the main furniture showroom, with its atrium opening to the second floor at the front of the building, could, with surprising speed and efficiency, be converted into a grand viewing parlor that could accommodate up to fifty mourners at a single time, if such a viewing space was requisite.

The three-story brick building in Ox Bend, Missouri, an architectural achievement in its day, had originally been built in 1888 by a wealthy German immigrant, Alfred Sprick, and his wife Edna. It had remained in their immediate family until 1932, when Mr. Werner Clarkson bought the business, the building, and all the furniture and fixtures for the colossal sum of twenty-five thousand dollars. A large addition in 1933 that more than doubled the square footage on the ground level had been accomplished by taking over an attached building vacated by a local bank. It had been rumored for years that Werner Clarkson, always a shrewd businessman, had "stolen" the vacated bank building through surreptitious financial maneuvers, but nothing had ever been proven, and the old man simply rode out the storm by refusing to confirm, or deny, any disreputable activity in the business transaction.

A huge four-bedroom third-floor apartment, where Alfred and Edna Sprick had originally lived, as well as all the subsequent owners of the funeral home at one time or another, had also been renovated on numerous occasions and had even been compelled into service when additional viewing rooms were needed. In February of 1957, when a nursing home fire killed seventy-two residents and brought the small Missouri town unwanted national attention, the entire upstairs apartment, as well as parts of the lower basement area, had been pressed into service to accommodate such an unprecedented event.

In the spring of 1958, a large storage room that had originally housed buckboards and horse-drawn funeral wagons at the back of the building was structurally reinforced and remodeled to allow the Clarksons to warehouse a larger furniture inventory. But as the years had passed and the large national furniture retailers started to flourish—and the automobile made access to the nearby city of St. Louis much more of a possibility—the furniture business, which had at its zenith accounted for 65 percent of the profit base, had become much less of a viable entity and had been gradually downsized to take up less and less of the building's total square footage. When a category 3 tornado went through Ox Bend in 1963 and blew down the somewhat-dilapidated "Clarkson Furniture & Funeral" sign, a truncated "Clarkson Funeral" sign, refashioned from the original, had been hung in its place, and the furniture sales part of the ledger was phased out completely. Despite the renaming, and the weekly advertisements in the local *Ox Bend Journal,* many of the older locals still referred to the location as the Sprick Building, a custom that was reinforced by a small bronze placard embedded in the foundation at the front corner footing of the building that read, "Sprick Building—1888," and for several years after the transition, rural neighbors occasionally still stopped in to look for furniture!

When Werner Clarkson died unexpectedly of colon cancer in the spring of 1972, his only son, Richard Clarkson, took over the business with the assistance of his mother. Initially, he had attempted to keep the business and the then-eighty-four-year-old building, a viable enterprise with periodic cosmetic improvements, but in the spring of 1989, he gave the building a "much-needed face-lift" as his wife, Ruth, had phrased it to her local Dorcas Society. A plush, new, commercial-grade carpet with three-inch padding had been installed throughout the first two floors of the building, aesthetically covering up a great deal of the unfortunate "irregularities," as Mrs. Clarkson had worded it, that invariably lurked below the surface of any edifice built in the nineteenth century. Luxurious, new curtains, remodeled bathrooms, new showing room furniture, new double-hung windows, and various other aesthetic improvements had been added, and the electrical and plumbing had been brought up to current code. A whole new reinforced, pitched roof had been installed, putting an end to the constant leaking issues that had plagued the owners for years, and the floorplan on the main ground level was revamped. New interior walls were constructed, allowing for two reappointed viewing parlors that could accommodate funerals concurrently, and a much-needed, new central air-conditioning system was installed. Two separate, leasable office spaces were created on the second floor to boost the cash flow, and the back of the building, which had been used as furniture warehouse space, was reappointed. The embalming area that had been in the basement since the business opened in 1888 was moved up to the main floor, allowing for easier access to a newly constructed docking platform that exited to the alley.

At a financial outlay that Richard Clarkson had initially called highway robbery, an Otis elevator was installed at the back corner of the building, a capital improvement that sanctioned a substantial increase in the monthly rentals of the second-floor office spaces and had added direct access to the third-floor apartment, an improvement that Mrs. Clarkson had been demanding since she first moved into the residence; and Mr. Clarkson quickly started calling his new addition the best investment he'd ever made! New lighting systems with specific dimming capabilities, state-of-the-art speakers, and a small refurbished church organ were also added to put the finishing touches on a remodel that had given the place a touch of modernity that the Clarksons' daughter, Regina, who had shown an early interest in interior design, had always said it needed.

As Ruth Clarkson finished aligning the chairs and adjusting the volume on the sound system, she finally looked up at the imposing wall of flowers and foliage that surrounded the scene, the scent almost overwhelming, and then walked up to the coffin and looked down lovingly at the young man, barely thirty years old, lying in repose. She nervously glanced at her watch, expecting her husband to arrive at any moment, and then stood back and closely examined the massive funeral spray of cascading gladiolas, roses, and carnations that covered the foot of the half-couch coffin. She leaned in and gently touched the crimson satin ribbon with the words *dearest son* embossed in bright gold lettering, then meticulously adjusted a drooping lily that was partially covering the letter *d*. She stood back, examined the spray again, and then noticed a flowerpot to the left of the bier that needed adjusting.

She was a small-framed woman with thinning light-blond hair who, in the pinnacle of her youth, had stood five foot seven but had almost imperceptibly shrunk to five foot five, a setback that she simply corrected by always wearing two-inch heels. Her weight, a problem that she had battled for years, had deposited a few extra inches around her waist, and her arms, at one time strong and firm, had started a process of "inevitable graceful sagging," as she always playfully worded it to her grandchildren, who as babies could never resist grabbing at them whenever they sat on her lap. But despite the predestined foibles of a woman of fifty-five, her large green eyes, which had always been her most prominent feature, still sparkled, and her complexion was remarkably clear and unwrinkled and gave her the appearance, at least at first glance, of someone ten years younger.

Mrs. Clarkson had been born Ruth Matilda Saroh, a baptismal name that had great family significance, on August 8, 1935, in St. Louis, Missouri, to a well-to-do couple in the finance industry. Based on an echoed ancestral legend that had been passed down from mother to daughter, the name Ruth had been used for many generations on Ruth's mother's side of the family. As Emma, Ruth's mother, had heard it from her mother, in 1819, Ruth Peteresmeyer, of Detmold, Germany, the great-great-great-great-grandmother of Emma, had experienced a celestial deathbed visitation from Ruth the Moabite, the scriptural great-grandmother of King David. Although many in the family were skeptical about the actuality of the biblical visitation, the story proved to be one with staying power, and the fact that the name meant "companion" and "vision of beauty" in Hebrew only added to the popularity of the name. Ruth's grandmother, Ruth Mildred Petersmeyer Schmidt, a citizen of Germany, would often visit the Saroh family during the summer months and affectionately started calling her little granddaughter "klein Rutie" based on her petite size, a nickname that was picked up and copied by other members of the family as well. Her middle name, which she had always despised, had been given to her in homage of an elderly aunt who had spent the last few months of her life living with the Saroh family in what had been at that time Ruth's childhood bedroom, requiring Ruth to temporarily share quarters with her younger brother. Ironically, despite being named after her aunt, Ruth had often related that the only memory she had of her namesake was the poor old woman lying in her childhood bed, her mouth flopping open and shut as she gasped for air, a memory that had been recounted, and relived, in numerous dreams and nightmares.

Ruth and her two siblings had initially been raised in a one-time-affluent neighborhood just off downtown St. Louis called Lafayette Square. The large architecturally significant Victorian homes in the area, vestiges of an age when St. Louis was the toast of the world, had slowly become almost impossible to maintain financially, and as new highways were cut across the area, making automobile transportation a more feasible option, more and more of the local residents had made their way westward, finding the cost of new construction much more financially prudent than pouring money into ancient, aging brick structures. In keeping with this trend, after Ruth's thirteenth birthday, the Saroh family relocated to Webster Groves, a suburban area outside the congested footprint of downtown St. Louis.

Just as Ruth was bending down to reposition the flowerpot to the right of the bier, her husband of thirty-three years walked into the main viewing parlor, another late-arriving flower arrangement in hand. Richard Dean Clarkson, who had managed to maintain many of the accoutrements of youth, looked exceptionally fit for a man just shy of his fifty-sixth birthday, and he still carried himself with that unjustified gift of confidence and assuredness that exceptionally good-looking men typically possess, however unmerited it might have been. He stood six foot two, had salt-and-pepper hair that he kept combed straight back, deep-set blue eyes, and a squared-off chin with a small dimple in the middle, a feature that been passed down from his grandfather. He had been born in the upstairs apartment of the funeral home in November of 1934, had worked in the family business as a young child and teenager, had comanaged the business with his parents after he had graduated from college, and then had taken over the funeral home when his father died suddenly of cancer in 1972. Although he had at one time, in the rebellious jurisdictions of youth, voiced that he wanted to "test the waters," as he had positioned it to his father, and look at other career options, his indoctrination into the family business had been too complete, the dye much too indelible, and he had quietly followed the path that his parents had orchestrated for him, and had never looked back, had never again questioned or agonized over the direction of his life. He possessed that uniquely male ability to simply forge ahead in life with his own somewhat-myopic point of view, seemingly unaware of a world filled with opposing ideas and philosophies, and had never worried about the consequences or ramifications that his limited philosophical view might have on others, an ability that had both amazed and infuriated his wife. His visceral physicality and his perfectly formed features had filled most of the women he met in his life with admiration—and even desire—and most men with envy, an advantage that he had parlayed into a very successful public image.

An initial outside glimpse of the couple might have given an impression of emotional connection and stability, a stalwart example of small-town values and marital harmony, but a closer examination would have revealed a relationship crippled by years of neglect. Like most couples in small-town America, they had gone to great lengths to keep up the outward image, to portray a unified front to the residents of the small community, an almost-necessary component of a successful business in those days. But secrets in any environment are hard to maintain, especially in the fertile soil of a small town like Ox Bend, and the local rumor mill had, on more than one occasion, whispered about Richard's infidelities and unfortunate dalliances with women from the nearby urban city of St. Louis; but it seemed their indignation went no further than the small town's city limits. Based on his position in the community, and his affable persona, they had approached his shortcoming with an "out of sight, out of mind" mentality, and such rumors had been quickly dispatched. His wife, a devoutly religious woman who had entered the marriage with great hopes and aspirations, had simply chosen, for the benefit of their children, to "turn the other cheek" when her husband's actions triggered the next round of rumors, and always chose to "think the best," no matter how many times he gave evidence of the worst.

They had initially met when both were attending an expensive Jesuit-run university just off the downtown corridor of St. Louis that bore the city's name. Richard, who had attended on a scholarship in business and finance, had been immediately drawn to the youthful-looking blonde, an English literature major, and wasted no time in pursuing his attraction. And in what Ruth's mother had termed an ardent involvement, the inseparable young couple had dated throughout their remaining college years and were married in 1956, just three weeks after Richard's graduation. Although they had talked about Ruth, who was a semester behind her husband in total credits, completing her degree as well, she had never been able to finish, despite a great love and aptitude for the subject matter. It seemed the educational concerns of a woman in 1950s mid-America, were much less pressing than those of a man, and she had left the university just fifteen credits short of a degree of her own, an outcome that she would later come to regret.

The fact that they had come from such opposing upbringings— Ruth had been raised in an urban area her entire life, and Richard in a small rural community—caused some concern, especially in the conservative realm of the Saroh fraternity. One of the family aunts from New York who Ruth always considered her favorite had even discreetly proclaimed "It's doomed" at one of the three showers that were thrown for the young bride-to-be. But the young twosome, like most couples of that age, had come under the influence of a more primal inclination and had chosen to completely ignore any advice that might countermand their plans, and they both, at least initially, believed that they were destined to be together. Ruth had even girlishly penned in her daily journal that she had found the love of her life, however cliché she thought the phrase might have sounded, and after a honeymoon week in New York City at the invitation of her favorite aunt, the young bride left the familiarity and bustle of her urban home and came to live in the third-story apartment of the Clarkson Funeral Home. Richard's parents, who had vacated the apartment some years earlier for a larger place in the country, had the entire dwelling freshened up with a new coat of paint, new wall-to-wall carpeting, and a completely refurbished, new kitchen, wedding presents for the young newlyweds.

The transition to a bucolic lifestyle and the day-to-day commitments of a family business had initially been difficult for the young bride, as her family had so fittingly predicted, and she soon came to realize that the seemingly unlimited love and devotion that her husband had initially dispensed during their college courtship were more of a restricted commodity. She only managed to "survive," a term her mother kept using, the first three years of the union. As the excitement of physical exploration and new sensual experiences faded, so did the primary bond that seemed to hold them together. As Ruth wrote to her mother in the winter of 1958, "He offers no consistency in the relationship and seems unable to provide any true intimacy," a theme that had been repeated in numerous following correspondences over the years. It seemed that the simple act of signing a marriage decree had dramatically, almost overnight, decreased the amount of affection that the young groom afforded his wife, a change that did not go unnoticed in the young bride's family. When Ruth's father, Cole Saroh, who had strongly opposed the union from the start, first heard of the situation, he coldly remarked, "She's his property now. Of course he's changed!" And her mother, who seemed to subserviently agree with her husband's parochial take on the matter, had told her daughter in no uncertain terms that the die was set, and the young bride came to accept the situation as it was and convinced herself that such was the bane of married life. But as the children came and her expectations were tempered, she came to accept her new environment, became engrossed in the family business, and had gracefully accepted her role as the "doting wife of a civic leader," a description that had been published in the town's local newspaper in a twenty-fifth-wedding-anniversary article. As the years went by and Richard's parents passed and their own children approached adulthood, the full influence and responsibility of the business fell to the couple. They settled into a gentle rhythm and structure, a subconscious inertia that seemed to propel them forward. Ruth, an avid reader and lover of poetry, had often thought of Donald Hall's prophetic words whenever she had contemplated her life with Richard in the small rural community: "Then we row for years on the midsummer pond, ignorant and content."

"Where do you want me to put this one?" Richard asked, brushing a lock of salt-and-pepper hair off his brow as he entered the room with his typical air of self-assurance and confidence. The interruption startled Ruth, and she turned and looked at her husband, dressed in his tight-fitting, tailored gray business suit and newly polished wingtip oxfords.

"Oh! Over there, I guess." She waved, with an air of detachment. "Put it next to that red one there," she added, pointing to other side of the viewing area.

"Have you ever seen so many flowers?" Richard commented as he slipped his reading glasses on the end of his nose, his voice filled with childlike astonishment. He dutifully placed the small arrangement exactly where Ruth had suggested and then backed off and admired his handiwork. "I must say, it's been a while since we had this kind of outpouring!" he added on before his wife could respond. He took a last glance at the positioning of the plant and then picked up a loose flower petal from the floor.

"You're probably right," Ruth replied, with counterfeit sincerity, "and they're still coming in—I got two more this morning—and there's probably more to come." She made a final adjustment to a small ivy palm and dracaena potted plant and then took a seat on one of the two Ballard Designs ivory herringbone viewing couches that sat directly opposite the casket. As she sat down, she let out a noticeable sigh, folded her hands on her lap, and lowered her head.

"You never thought of him as disabled, did you?" she asked her husband without looking up. "I just never thought of him that way," she went on before he could answer. "I mean, I knew he had limitations, but I just never saw him that way."

Richard, who was bending over, reading a card on a large arrangement of carnations, daisies, and calla lilies, was surprised by the question, and he stopped and looked back over his shoulder at his wife. "I guess I just always saw him the way you did," he replied, not knowing exactly what to say. "He was definitely a mama's boy, and you're the one who always encouraged his development." He paused and took a hurried breath. "More than I ever did," he confessed with a hint of regret.

"I know, I know," Ruth muttered to herself, her voice laced with emotion. She looked down and crossed her arms and seemed to be visibly shaking. "How am I going to make it through this?" she mumbled under her breath. "How can I possibly find the strength?" She sat back into the couch and sighed heavily, as the waves of anxiety and sorrow that she had been trying to suppress came rushing back to the surface.

Richard nervously tucked the loose flower petal in his coat pocket and then walked to the casket and adjusted a gladiola bloom that had started to tilt. "I don't know, Ruth," he answered and then paused a moment, as if searching for just the right words. "But we have to do it. We don't have any other choice," he finally offered in a very matter-of-fact way. He glanced back over his shoulder at his wife sitting behind him. "We just have to," he repeated. He picked up another fallen petal from the carpet, slipped it into his pocket, and then came back and stood in front of his seated wife.

"Choice!" Ruth yelled as she looked up at her husband towering over her. "There is no choice here. And it's just not right that a mother should have to do so much for her own son's funeral. How am I going to stand in that greeting line and shake all those hands when I can barely—"

She stopped all of a sudden and let out another low moan. "Stand to think of him without falling apart."

"I'll be right by your side the whole way," Richard responded with a sincerity that Ruth was not used to hearing. He sat down on the couch next to his wife, took off his reading glasses, and placed them in his coat pocket. "And if you get tired, or you need to sit down, we'll have the stools up there." He paused and looked back up toward the coffin. "It's going to be all right," he added, sounding surprisingly sympathetic.

"Oh, that's not it, Richard!" Ruth fired back anxiously. "I'm not worried about that. That's not it! What if I can't do it? What if I fall apart? What if I just mentally can't do it?" She paused and theatrically pointed at the casket and the rows of flowers that flanked it on each side. "Look around! Look at all the flowers! Everyone in town will be here!" she added, almost in a panic. "I've been working here all these years, and I've seen countless mothers bury their children, and they all did it, they all made it through it one way or another, but I just don't know if I can. I just don't know if I have the strength!" She stopped abruptly, looked down, and clenched her hands together.

"Look, Ruth, I know what you're saying," Richard replied after a few moments of silence, his voice indecisive. "And you're right, parents shouldn't have to bury their children. But we have to do this. We have to give Aaron a decent burial, a decent service." He stopped talking again and looked back at his wife. "He deserves that," he added as he awkwardly placed his arm around his wife's shoulders, attempting to comfort her.

"You do it then," Ruth spoke up. She turned and looked her husband in the eye. "You do it and tell them that I'm sick. Tell them the doctors told me that the funeral and the grave site and the luncheon, it would all just be too much for me. Tell them—"

She stopped abruptly, her breathing short and labored.

"Tell them anything. I just don't care," she added, lowering her head into her hands.

Richard placed his hand under his wife's chin and pulled her head toward him. "What's going on? There has to be something else going on here. For a woman, for a mother, to not want to attend her own son's funeral."

"My son?" Ruth retorted, then looked keenly at her husband. "My son?" she snapped again.

"Yes, Ruth, *your* son," Richard responded with pronounced clarity.

"I know," Ruth said with a tone of regret as she nervously wrung her hands on her lap again. "I know he's my son. I don't know what I'm saying. Don't listen to me," she added, repentance etched in each and every word.

Richard took his arm from around Ruth's shoulders and clasped his hands together and leaned forward, his elbows resting on his knees.

"What's going on with you?" he asked as he turned his head and looked back at his wife. "Why are you feeling this way?"

Ruth suddenly stood and walked to the casket and placed her right hand on the folded hands of her son. She looked down at his peaceful face and noticed the curly brown hair around his temples and the perfect dimple in his squared-off chin. After several minutes of absolute silence, she looked back at her husband still sitting forward on the couch. "Because she'll probably be there," she whispered and then turned again to look at her son. "She hasn't been out to see him for years!" She paused and looked at the long row of flowers to the right of the casket. "And I just don't know if I'm ready for that yet."

"Ah, so that's the thing," Richard commented. "That's what's going on here." He quickly got up and stood next to his wife and looked down at Aaron lying in the coffin. "Don't you think she has a right to be here?" he asked, brushing a lock of hair away from his son's forehead.

"I don't know what rights she has," Ruth shot back. "I'd say she gave up her rights years ago." Ruth paused and looked up at a small heart-shaped flower arrangement pinned to the inside of the coffin. "And I don't want to share him now."

"Yes, yes, she did give up her rights," Richard replied with a firm tone as he glanced to his right at his wife standing rigidly in front of the coffin. "But she is the boy's biological mother," he added, very matter-of-factly, and then looked back down at his son again. "She is the boy's mother."

"Oh, I don't want to talk about this anymore," Ruth replied. She placed both of her hands on the rim of the open coffin and started to sob uncontrollably.

B y six thirty that evening, the line to get into the funeral home was at least fifty people deep as it wound its way down the side of the building and then around to the front. Because such a large crowd was expected, the entire funeral home staff was on hand to help marshal the assembly, and four of the ladies from Mrs. Clarkson's Dorcas Society had volunteered to assist as well. Once those wanting to express their condolences survived the twenty-minute wait to get into the building, there was another, even longer wait inside, as each guest stopped and signed a leather-bound guest book that had a picture of Aaron embossed on the cover, a keepsake that was typically boxed up with the flower cards, letters, and notes that the home received during the course of the funeral. Clyde and Ruth Kaermor, longtime friends of the Clarksons, had volunteered to serve as greeters at the entranceway, a job that was typically done by the Clarksons themselves; but the Kaermors had done the job on several prior occasions. They knew the procedure quite well and were intimately acquainted with the majority of the townspeople and were more than capable of welcoming, greeting, and engaging the visitors in small talk and issuing the perfunctory "Yes, I know" and "They're doing as good as can be expected" response as questions and expressions of sympathy arose.

Ruth and Richard had positioned themselves in front of a row of stools just to the left of the casket, and their three surviving children, Regina, the eldest; Charles, a deputy sheriff and part-time farmer, who lived in adjacent Lincoln County; and Richard Jr., the youngest, were positioned just to the left of them. Richard and Ruth had initially started the visitation standing side by side as they greeted the parade of mourners, but that plan was soon abridged when Richard started walking away and visiting with guests and business acquaintances throughout the viewing parlor, leaving Ruth alone with the burdensome responsibility of greeting each mourner as they stopped in front of the body, a familiar process of subtle abandonment that had started to take place only a few years after the couple were first married.

As their years together had rolled by, Richard became more and more involved in the community and less and less committed to his marriage, serving on countless boards and civic committees. He had a social grace and affability that seemed to draw people toward him and make them consider him a friend. Although in truth, no one really knew him beyond his surface persona, his physical veneer, and he had thrived in the realm of public service, where sound bites and handshakes were all that were needed for perceived success. He had served as president of the local chamber of commerce for fifteen years, had been an active Rotarian, had served on the policy board of the National Funeral Directors Association, and had even unsuccessfully run for mayor, and the "billable hours," an idiom that Ruth's brother had often used when referring to the actual time that the couple spent together, became fewer and fewer as the years went by. The financial success of the business, bolstered by several cash injections over the years from the Saroh family, sanctioned Richard to hire competent assistants to take over more of the day-to-day business operations and had allowed him to take regular monthly business trips, an expenditure that he had couched as "qualified education expense" on his annual tax filings.

As Richard's traveling took up more and more of his time, Ruth had been left with the daily responsibilities of running the business and parenting the couple's four children, and she had finally come to accept that the actual partnership that she shared with her husband was a part-time commission, unlike her role in the business, which had become a full-time obligation. The couple simply "rowed forward," as she had worded it to her best friend, heading in the same direction, but on separate, parallel paths. Although Richard Clarkson had never been able to provide his wife with the level of intimacy that she had so longed for—a commodity that he simply did not possess—he had quite effectively assumed the role of figurehead of the business, a position that was all but mandatory in the patriarchal mindset of small-town America. He had become a sort of benign roommate to his wife, a business partner, a monetary arrangement that had allowed them to socially and economically coexist very comfortably.

But despite all of Ruth's earlier trepidation about surviving the long line of mourners, she did quite well and surprised even herself in her ability to power through the evening. She had found some way to mentally disconnect herself from the deep pathos that lay just beneath her breast and went on a sort of "autopilot" that allowed her to almost mechanically greet everyone, express some representation of her feelings, and then thank the guest for being there without revealing "the else-betrayed, too-human heart," as she remembered the poet had so aptly put it. And even Richard, who had always excelled at superficial public encounters and dispassionate, surface exchanges with acquaintances, had ultimately, as Ruth later told her daughter, performed better than she ever expected.

She did, however, have a few breakdowns at the beginning of the evening. The first one came when her longtime friend, Ruth Kaermor, first arrived at the funeral home about an hour before the viewing officially started, to assume her role as official "greeter" at the main entrance. The two women had been close friends since Ruth and Richard had first moved into the apartment above the funeral home back in 1957. At that time, Clyde and Ruth Kaermor, married for only four months, were renting a small efficiency apartment above the dry cleaners that was located just down the street, a propinquity that initially triggered the friendship. The commonality of their lives in the small town proved to be a link that the years had been unable to break, and they had come to rely on each other for camaraderie and support for over thirty years. The fact that the two young girls shared the same first name had originally provided a great deal of confusion, but as time went on and the friendship grew, Ruth Kaermor, assumed the role of "Ruthie," an affectionate moniker that stuck with her for the rest of her life.

Ruthie had frequently assisted her friend with taking care of the four Clarkson children when a funeral had been in progress, and had often accompanied Ruth on her frequent trips back to the city for doctor's appointments or to visit her family, a process that had gone a long way in solidifying their enduring friendship. As Ruth struggled with the initial truths and the exacting actualities of married life, Ruthie had become a compassionate listener and afforded her friend an unfiltered voice to the many emotions she experienced. She had become a sort of unofficial therapist, with a keen ability to simply listen, a skill that seemed beyond the grasp of her insensitive husband. Ruthie had also, more than anyone else, understood the challenges of raising a child with special limitations, and she had stood at Ruth's side from the very beginning as the exacting realities of Aaron's development became clear. She had a deep, uncompromising love for the young man that now lay in the coffin.

Ruthie, unlike her more-urbane friend, had been raised on a farm and was the seventh of eight children. She had lived her entire life in Ox Bend and had rarely traveled beyond the small town's geographic border, but her loving and giving temperament—and the lonely realities that often plague young married women—had gone a long way in leveling the playing field, and the two women had become the best of friends within a year of meeting.

When Ruthie walked into the viewing room and looked at her friend, Ruth's mental wall of protection disappeared, and she immediately broke down. As the tears streamed down her face, she just kept repeating, "Thank you so much for being here," and, "I couldn't make it through this without you." And Ruthie, familiar with the rules of grief, said little to her lifelong friend, just let her cry, and held her hand before assuming her duties at the front entrance.

The second breakdown came when Ruth's younger brother entered the main viewing room about thirty minutes before the doors were first opened to the public. Lawrence Harrison Saroh, who had always been close to his sister throughout his life, had been involved in a devastating auto accident that had taken the life of his wife and his three-year-old son in the winter of 1978 and caused a spinal column injury that had left him confined to a wheelchair. At the time of the accident, the thirty-two-year-old had been working for his father's investment company for over ten years, a position that he had been able to maintain after the accident, but with very different expectations; and the collision had caused more than just a physical alteration to the young father. He had gone through what he himself would later call an existential metamorphosis as he struggled to comprehend the new limitations in his life and accept the overwhelming loss of his wife and young son. Lawrence's preaccident approach to living had been one centered on unending corporate progression, a path that had been met with unremitting praise and a fast-tracked road to advancement by his corporate-minded father, a process that had also started to innocently compromise his homelife. He had started an almost-subconscious, gradual process of assuming a lot of the harsh business practices and long nights at the office that his father had so often modeled, and he had begun to put his family in a secondary position to his job and career. But the view of life from a seated position, without the affection of wife and son, had transformed the young man's interpretation of the world, and he had developed a keen affection for his disabled young nephew and had even established a trust fund to ensure the young boy's financial protection into the future. It seemed that the common reality of perceived societal limitations, however different they might have been, created a bond between the two, and Aaron, who had never really developed past a fifth-grade ability, had on many occasions unequivocally stated, "Lawrence is my favorite uncle."

As Ruth reached down and placed her arms around her brother, he grabbed her hand, pulled her in close, and started to whisper in her ear, a sense of urgency in his voice. "What happened?" he implored, his hands shaking as thoughts of his own three-year-old son lying in a coffin appeared in his mind. "My god, I thought he was doing better."

"I thought so too," Ruth whispered, picking up on her brother's fragile emotional state. "I thought so too," she repeated mournfully.

Lawrence looked around at the rows of flowers surrounding the casket and then lowered his head into his hands, the scene almost more than he could bear. "So how did all this start anyway?" he asked distraughtly as he looked back up at his sister, his eyes filled with sorrow.

"Just a few weeks ago," Ruth started out, her own emotions getting the better of her, "he was playing out on the loading dock, and somehow he slipped and fell off and landed on the concrete. I didn't think that much of it at that time, and he didn't seem to be in a lot pain. But he had fallen about five feet, and he had scratched up both of his knees, so I took him to the doctor, just to be on the safe side. The doctor cleaned the wounds and bandaged them up, and he even took some x-rays and said that nothing was broken, that Aaron just needed some time to heal and recuperate." Ruth paused and shook her head, as if she still couldn't believe what all had happened, and Lawrence bowed his head again, as if the weight of the world had been placed upon him. "But then about a week ago, he just stopped talking and became totally noncommunicative."

"Well, that was a bad sign," Lawrence interjected. "That's not like Aaron at all."

"I know!" Ruth concurred. "I could just tell that something was wrong, so I called Dr. Lenzenhuber, and he came to the house for an examination, but he really didn't know what to think about it either. He said to just keep an eye on Aaron and let him know if anything else changed." Ruth paused and looked back at the coffin. "And then four days ago, I said good night to him before he went to bed, like I always did." She hesitated again, and an intensity entered her voice. "I actually thought he was getting better because he had started to eat a little more that day, and it just seemed like he was improving. It seemed like he was getting back to his old self." She stopped and looked back at her brother, her face filled with a kind of horror. "I was the one that found him that next morning. I tried to wake him up, but his body was…" She stopped and started to cry again. "His arms were cold, and I knew then that he was gone," she finally added as she regained her composure.

Lawrence finally raised his head and glanced back over at the coffin again.

"Well, at least the battle is done now," he responded. "I guess that's the only way to look at it."

25

"I know," Ruth replied, her voice filled with regret. "The doctors did tell me that he probably wouldn't have a normal life expectancy, but they were wrong about so many things, and I just never thought that he would be gone at thirty-three."

"Is that how old he was?" Lawrence asked, trying to corral his runaway emotions.

"Yes. He would have been thirty-four this coming November."

"Well, they were thirty-three great years!" Lawrence proclaimed as he regained his composure. "I guess we just have to be thankful we had him as long as we did."

"But how are you doing, Lawrence?" Ruth asked, attempting to lift the somber mood. She bent down and adjusted his necktie. "You look a little tired."

"Oh, don't you worry about me," he answered, his emotions drained. "I guess I'm doing as good as can be expected from down here," he added half-heartedly. "I just feel like this is all some kind of terrible dream," he uttered with a broken voice. He lowered his head again and rubbed his temples. "You know something?" he whispered, looking back up quickly. "If truth be told, I think Aaron was my best friend."

Ruth felt the immense depth of her brother's comment, and it resonated in her response. "That's a wonderful thing to say about Aaron, but you have tons of friends, Lawrence." She grabbed a tissue from her dress pocket and dabbed her nose. "Everyone loves you."

"But none of them saw me the way *he* did," Lawrence responded passionately. He paused and rubbed his hand over his forehead and brushed his curly brown hair off his brow. "You know, he never did see me as some invalid like everybody else does. I think he just saw me, if that makes any sense. He was the only one who seemed to be able to look past this wheelchair." Lawrence stopped and looked down at his legs, weakened from years of atrophy. "And I don't know what I'll do now," he added despondently. He suddenly looked up as an almost-frantic look came over his face, his emotions rising again. "And I worry about you. And then there's the trust we'll have to deal with. I had most everything set up for his protection if anything happened to me."

"Don't even think about all that now," Ruth countered lovingly as she slipped the tissue back into her pocket. She reached down and pinched her brother's lips shut with her right hand. "Just think about the good times with Aaron. You know how much he loved you, don't you?"

Lawrence looked up at his sister, and his face reddened. "I know. But not as much as I loved him," he replied as tears started to well up around his eyes.

"Don't you dare start crying," Ruth whispered. She looked away and attempted to cage her emotions. "You'll have me falling apart before we even get the doors opened."

Lawrence pulled himself up straight, wiped the tears from his eyes, and then turned his wheelchair around to face the coffin, seemingly ready to face the abyss. "So how is Richard taking it?" he asked as he pushed his emotions aside and looked at the rows of flowers on each side of the bier.

"Ah, you know how he is," Ruth whispered, shaking her head. "I don't know if he's even taken the time to really let it all sink in yet. He's been so busy with the arrangements and everything."

"Well, he is consistent, I'll give him that," Lawrence replied, shaking his head.

"Oh, I think all men just have a different way of dealing with things, especially death," Ruth replied very philosophically. "Present a man with an emotional problem and he immediately wants some job to do, something to keep him busy, so he doesn't have to really deal with any true feelings."

"Well, you may be right," Lawrence concurred, his mind racing. "I did read once that we men were more fragile than our counterparts in certain arenas," he added with a subtle grin.

"And Richard is just like his father, Werner. And Lord knows Daddy was the same way too."

"Oh, I think Father was worse than Richard!" Lawrence responded emphatically as memories of his distant father entered his mind. "That old man rarely showed any emotion at all!"

Ruth looked closely at her brother, as if some past memory had just resurfaced in her mind as well. "I know I shouldn't say this," she said, flushing, "but the only emotion I ever really remember Daddy showing was anger."

"Oh, I think you've summed it up accurately. He was always angry about one thing or another as far as I can remember, especially around women." Lawrence paused, and his brow took on a philosophical angle. "I don't think he ever looked at women as equal in any way, shape, or form. And yet he would have been lost without them!"

"And poor Mother!" Ruth exclaimed. "How did she ever survive it all?"

"And I don't think we really know the half of what all she went through, especially in those early years."

"You're probably right," Ruth agreed, her voice falling off.

"Well, speaking of Mother, is she going to make it?" Lawrence quizzed, attempting to change the subject and lighten the mood.

"Oh, no. I talked to her this morning, and they think now that Daddy has pneumonia. She thinks he'll end up back in the hospital before it's all over." Ruth paused and took a breath. "So they're not coming, and I think that's the best. And she really has no business making the trip out here anyway."

"What about Cora?" Lawrence asked tepidly. "I know she's thinking about it, because last night she called me out of the blue."

"I haven't talked to her since Grandma Elsie's funeral," Ruth responded with a trace of regret. "So you know more about that subject than I do."

Lawrence grabbed his sister's hand and looked up at her. "I just wish you two got along better and that you could end this *thing* that's between you." He paused, glanced over at the coffin, then back at his sister. "Life is short, as you well know." Ruth pursed her lips and said nothing. "Whatever happened between you two?" Lawrence finally asked boldly. "You were inseparable when you were kids. I know she's a bit unconventional, but she's still your sister," he added with just a hint of judgment.

"Oh, don't talk to me about my sister now," Ruth replied, her voice filled with exasperation. "Not now. I haven't seen her for over six years! The only thing we get from her are birthday cards and Christmas presents for Aaron!"

"Okay, Kleine Ruthie," Lawrence replied teasingly with a German accent, regretting the timing of his questions around Cora. He reached over and grabbed his sister by the hand again. "I didn't mean to upset you. I just wish that you and Cora could reconcile. I hate having my two sisters not speaking to each other." Lawrence paused, and his voice seemed to have some new purpose as he went on. "You know, she's not like she used to be. She's changed in a lot of ways." He paused and squeezed his sister's hand tightly. "She really has," he added, with an extra dose of sincerity. "And I guess I just want you both to be happy, that's all."

"Don't worry about me," Ruth replied, her feelings softened by her brother's words. "If I can just make it through the next forty-eight hours, I think I'll be okay."

"So what can I do to help you?" Lawrence asked.

"See! All you men *are* just alike!" Ruth responded ironically with a smile. "You don't need to do a thing. Your just being here is helping me more than you'll ever know."

"Well, if you change your mind or you think of something..." He paused and grimaced a little. "You may be right, a man does need something to do," he added playfully.

"Well, if Cora comes, just run interference for me," Ruth replied and then let out a small forced chuckle. "Now, you are going to join us at the church after the service tomorrow, aren't you?" Ruth asked. "The ladies are preparing a wonderful lunch."

"I wouldn't miss it," Lawrence replied optimistically, "and I plan on going to the grave site too!" Then he added, "Chair or no chair," patting the armrests on his wheelchair.

CHAPTER

3

The morning of October 10, 1990, started out cold and overcast, but at around ten o'clock, the clouds lifted and a bright sun flooded the area. Many of the worries about the grave site service that had kept Ruth awake through most of the night had disappeared, and the overpowering headache that she woke up with had somehow completely vanished. She went to her third-floor bedroom window that looked out over the side of the funeral home and saw the large black hearse and stretch limousine lined up at the side door in preparation for the upcoming service. She could see John Green, one of the company's longtime employees and Richard's second-in-charge, putting up the parking ropes at the entrance to the side drive. Richard was nowhere to be found, and she assumed that he, always worried about the last-minute details of a well-planned funeral service, had gotten up early in the morning and was already down in the viewing area.

As Ruth left the window, she stopped at a large American Drew cherry chest of drawers that had been handed down from Richard's parents, to rummage through the catchall drawer. As she sifted through the miscellaneous pictures, letters, and mementos, she found a black-and-white portrait mounted in a gold-inlaid walnut frame of Aaron as a baby sitting on the lap of his aunt Cora. She grabbed the keepsake and sat down on one of two overstuffed dressing chairs across from the bed and rubbed the dust from the frame and started to recount the unusual circumstances that had first brought the young child into her home.

In the fall of 1957, after only a few months of marriage, Ruth had received a call from her mother, Emma Saroh, with some distressing family news. The mother had reported that her younger sister, Cora, had been feeling sick for several weeks and that she had been having trouble sleeping and had been experiencing spontaneous bouts of nausea, and at the urging of her mother, Cora had made an appointment with the family physician. As the details of the doctor's visit unfolded, Ruth had learned that her younger sister was two months pregnant, and the family was looking for an "acceptable" solution, as her mother, Emma, had so delicately couched it, to a most embarrassing problem. The family had approached Richard with a plan to spare themselves the unnecessary shame that would inevitably come from the pregnancy of an unmarried woman of Cora's age. The solution that they had proposed was to send Cora off to New York as soon as possible to stay with Emma's sister, Jewel, until the baby could be delivered, and then, to assure the child's position, Richard and Ruth would adopt the baby and raise it as their own.

Ruth's acceptance of the information came in subtle phases over the next few days as she grappled with the idea of raising her sister's child and keeping the baby's true parentage a secret. At first, it seemed almost too much to ask, much less accept, and it had only been her own desire for the unconditional love of a child, and her own naivete, that had eventually opened her mind to the possibility of following through with such a furtive plan. As the days passed and her sense of filial responsibility started to increase, and after much cajoling from her mother, Ruth finally, surprising even herself, had consented to the arrangement. With utmost discretion, Cora had been shipped off to New York by the end of the week, saving the family from any further embarrassment. This unusual adoption, cloaked in family subterfuge, had marked a significant change in the young couple's relationship and had started an ever-growing detachment between them that only increased as time went on.

Ruth had also felt a keen sense of betrayal as it pertained to her sister. Before her pregnancy, the two siblings had been on fairly good terms, and Cora had even come out and stayed with the young couple only a few days after they had returned from their honeymoon trip to New York, to help Ruth set up the third-floor apartment in Ox Bend. It was also during this stay that a terrible nursing home fire had killed over seventy residents in Ox Bend, and the small town was flooded with newsmen from all over the country. As she gazed at the picture, she could remember clearly, as if it were only yesterday, making her way across town to watch the horrific scene play itself out as firemen, volunteers, and employees of the facility tried desperately to save as many lives as they could. But throughout the entire visit, Cora at no point had ever given any indication that she had been dating someone casually or that she had been seeing someone of any significance, so the announcement of her pregnancy had come as quite a shock. When Ruth had questioned her directly about the identity of the father, Cora skirted around the issue, and her ability to obfuscate any conversation around the child's parentage had left the immediate family members as confused as Cora herself seemed to be on the matter. But all those concerns and thoughts had vanished once Ruth had held the small baby in her arms.

As Ruth continued to sit and stare at the photo of Aaron and Cora, she remembered fondly the first day the child had arrived. Richard had announced at a local chamber meeting that he and his wife were actively attempting to adopt and very convincingly had reported that an infant boy had been identified in Upstate New York and that he would be arriving within a week. Ruth signed the adoption papers that her husband had brought home without question, and the process, like so much of her life with Richard, simply moved forward. Local tongues had secretively battered around the usual reasons that surround an adoption announcement, but after the child had arrived and the next big "thing" to consume the small town took its place, the close-knit community had wholeheartedly embraced the new Clarkson addition.

It wasn't until almost a year later that Ruth first noticed certain deficiencies in the child's development, and after months of testing and trips to specialists in St. Louis, the young couple had learned that the child was developmentally challenged, as the doctors had first put it. They were later told that the child was not expected to advance mentally much further than a first-grade level, a disclosure that only increased Ruth's devotion to the child. They had learned that the cause of such a condition was often impossible to determine, and the family had been warned that upcoming problems might include seizures, mood disorders, motor-skill impairment, vision problems, and even autism. It had been initially proposed that oxygen deprivation might have been the cause of the issue, or some trauma during the pregnancy, but the real cause remained a mystery. When Cora and her aunt had been asked questions about the maternity and the actual birth of the child, both seemed to close ranks on the subject and insisted that the process had been uneventful or, as her aunt Jewel would always respond, "quite ordinary." Although the news had rocked the young couple to the core, Ruth's love and instantaneous parental connection had already been set, and she had embraced the young child with all the love and affection she could give; and the child, although far from "normal" by society's standards, had far exceeded the doctor's initial predictions in health, wellness, and development.

As Ruth tucked the picture back into the top drawer and then made her way down to the main viewing parlor, she found most of the immediate Clarkson family already gathered for the funeral. Ruth's firstborn and only daughter, Regina Battenhorst, a striking-looking brunette who had inherited her father's dark hair, chiseled facial features, and piercing blue eyes, had been the first to arrive. She was standing with her husband, Scott, and their three children and had even brought an additional flower spray that a local neighbor had brought to them the night before.

Charles, the second born, who had the facial features of his mother, with light blond hair that he wore in a flat top, and the physical strength and presence of his father, was standing near the main entranceway next to wife, Allison, and their two children, Clifford, ten, and Eli, nine. He was an assistant deputy sheriff and part-time farmer in adjoining Lincoln County, and he lived on a tract of land that had been surveyed off and given to the couple as a wedding present from Allison's parents.

When Ruth entered the main viewing parlor, she caught the eye of her son Charles, and she was relieved to see him there in full police uniform, with his two young sons, dressed in matching blue suits, standing at his side. Charles's relationship with his father, Richard, had been an inconstant one, and since his marriage to Allison, the two men had only exchanged perfunctory "grunts" at each other at the occasional family gathering, funeral, or wedding, a problem that Ruth had simply accepted as inevitable after unending attempts to reconcile the two had proved hopeless. Her daughter, Regina, had finally concluded, with tongue in cheek, that they were "simply too much alike," both of them telling the other exactly what they thought in no uncertain terms, and although Regina never made her feelings on the subject known, she secretly envied her brother's ability to tell her father what he thought, a talent that she had not yet developed.

A further scan of the room discovered Richard Jr., Ruth's youngest son, standing quietly beside the coffin, peering down at his deceased brother, and it was her son Richie, as she often affectionately called him, whom Ruth had bonded with around their common interest in literature, an awareness that Ruth had developed during her years at St. Louis University. He often jokingly represented himself as Richard II, the historical son of Edward the Black Prince, and often secretively referred to his father as the Black Prince, remarks that, when brought to the attention of the father, were not so easily accepted. Richard Jr. had left the small town as soon as he had graduated from high school and had attended St. Louis University, just as his father had done so many years earlier, and although Richard was at first delighted when his son chose his alma mater, he soon withdrew his support when the boy decided to major in philosophy and religious studies, a decision that he had called utter lunacy, and his financial support was soon withdrawn as well. In a letter home to his mother during his sophomore year, Richard Jr. jokingly wrote, "I never expected to be primogeniture, but I could certainly use at least some financial assistance," a request that Ruth took most seriously and dealt with in a surprisingly bold fashion. In direct opposition to her husband's wishes—something she had never done before—for the remainder of his college years, it had been Ruth who personally wrote out the checks for Richard Jr.'s expenditures, and after numerous battles on the subject, and with a newfound determination in Ruth, Richard Jr. was finally reinstated into the family hierarchy. As Ruth had later explained to her dear friend Ruthie, the whole process proved to be a turning point in the financial trench warfare between husband and wife, with some major ground being gained by the latter.

Besides his choice of study, Richard did not like the fact that his namesake had yet to take a bride, a fact that only created a further chasm between father and son, a split that started out as loud shouting matches and confrontations and then slowly evolved into a subtle, voiceless indifference between the two men. When Richard Jr., in one of their battles on the subject, asked his father why he thought marriage was so important when he had all but bailed on his own, the gloves were removed, and the distance between the opposing energies had become impenetrable. At first, Ruth felt pulled between the divergent forces, but as the years went on, she finally gave up on all attempts at reconciliation and usually backed her son when forced to choose a side, a decision that only exacerbated the strained relationship between the couple.

Ruth walked up to Richard Jr., dressed in a tailored black suit with a white shirt and light-gray tie, stood beside him, and gently grabbed his hand in her own. They looked at each other somberly and then looked back down at Aaron.

"So how did you sleep last night?" Ruth asked, her motherly instincts taking over. "I hope that bed wasn't too uncomfortable."

"No, no," Richard Jr. answered. "It was fine. I always sleep good out here."

"Well, I didn't get to ask you yesterday, but how do you think he looks?" Ruth questioned as she looked down at Aaron's face, her voice trembling as she squeezed her son's hand tightly.

"I think he looks great, Mom," Richard Jr. responded. "John did a great job on him." He looked closely at his brother's face and touched the lapel of his coat jacket, then glanced back over at his mother. "Dad didn't help with it, did he?" he questioned. "I just think that would be awfully difficult," he added before she could respond.

"No, no, I don't think so," Ruth replied as she shook her head. "These past years he's been turning more and more responsibilities over to John." She paused and took a deep breath. "And he's traveling more than ever now. And I think this whole thing has affected him more than he likes to let on. You know how he is—that stiff upper lip. But I think this has really shaken him."

"Richard the Black Prince, shaken? Oh, say it ain't so," Richard Jr. retorted with a smirk on his face.

"Believe it or not, I think he is," Ruth replied as a subtle smile of her own appeared.

Richard Jr. looked closely at his mother's still-youthful face and smiled affectionately. "Well, I'm more worried about you than him," he said tenderly. "I know what Aaron meant to you."

"I'm just so glad you're here, Richie," Ruth exclaimed as she grabbed her son's hand again. "Yesterday was tough, and I never would have made it without you and Ruthie," she went on, giving her son's hand another extra squeeze. She paused and looked down at her son lying in the coffin, and a wave of anxiety came over her. "I'm really going to miss him," she whispered despondently. "He's been with me for so long, and I just can't imagine life without him, without his spirit. There was just this innocence about him—that's what I'm going to miss the most."

"We're all going to miss that," Richard Jr. concurred as he, too, looked down at his brother again, and thoughts of their childhood together started running through his mind.

"I remember all the doctors—when we first took him to the specialists—telling me about all the things that could end up being wrong with him, about all the problems that he could cause." Ruth leaned in and placed her hand on her son's head. "But none ever said a word about all the things he could accomplish, about all the gifts that he would give us!"

"What the hell do doctors, know anyway?" Richard Jr. quipped playfully.

"Boy, isn't that the truth," Ruth answered. She paused and took a deep breath, as if some deep pain had just resurfaced, and she stood up straight again. "What are we going to do without him, Richie? What am I going to do?" she repeated again, sounding almost desperate. She looked back up at her son, and tears started to stream down her face.

"Mom, it's going to be all right," Richard Jr. replied with a positive tone. "Come here," he said, placing his arm around her shoulders and pulling her toward him in embrace. "I am going to get you through this. I promise," he added.

Ruth continued to cry and grabbed for a tissue from her dress pocket. "I'm a mess, aren't I?" she asked as she dabbed her eyes, attempting to rein in her emotions.

Richard Jr. gave his mother another tight squeeze and then looked her in the eye. "Ah, when to the heart of man, was it ever less than a treason to…bow and accept the end of a love or a season?" he whispered.

"Ah, Frost," Ruth uttered as she slipped the tissue in her dress pocket. "He always did say the right things, didn't he?" Ruth stood up straight and looked back down at her dead son, as if Frost's words had somehow given her a new sense of courage. "You know I had him thirty-three years," she continued with a hint of forced optimism. "Thirty-three wonderful years," she repeated affectionately. "I just wonder where all that time went. It just seems like only yesterday he was placed on my lap." She paused and looked up into her son's face again. "He was a good brother, wasn't he?' she asked imploringly.

"Oh, he was the best," Richard Jr. replied as he seemed to think back to his childhood. "You know, my first memory of him must have been when I was around three, I guess. I was in this little red wagon, and I just remember him pulling me down the sidewalk in front of the building."

"Oh, I remember that wagon," Ruth chimed in. "And he would pull you around in that thing for hours." She stopped and looked down closely at her son lying in the coffin again. "He sure loved you, you know that, don't you?"

"I know, Mother. And I loved him too."

"Maybe—and I know that I shouldn't feel this way—but maybe this was God's plan for him," Ruth uttered half under her breath after a few moments of silence. "You know, I have been so worried about who would take care of him if anything happened to me." She looked up at her son, who had turned again and was looking directly at her.

"At least I know he's safe now." She paused and looked back down at the casket. "Am I wrong to feel that way?"

"Oh, Mother, you shouldn't have been worried about that. You know that Lawrence and I would have always taken care of him," he added, regret imprinted on every word. "I should have told you that. I should have known that you were worrying about that."

"Then you don't think I'm terrible?" she half-jokingly asked her son.

"Well, maybe a little," Richard Jr. joked, letting out a small laugh, and giving his mother another big hug.

Ruth pulled out her tissue again and dabbed at her nose. "Well, I can live with that," she added. "I must look a fright," she said as she brushed her hair back off her face and slipped the tissue back in her pocket. "Now, you're going to read Edna, right?" she asked, changing the subject completely. "The 'Dirge Without Music' poem?"

"Yes, if that's what you want," Richard Jr. assured her, a trace of uncertainty stamped in his voice. "I don't know if it's exactly appropriate for a Christian funeral, but I'm like you, I just think there aren't any better words."

"What do you mean not appropriate?" Ruth shot back, sounding a little agitated.

"Well, it is a pretty profound existential statement!" Richard Jr. countered. "Some might say the ultimate existential statement. At least that's the way I see it."

"Oh, phooey on all that." Ruth retorted. "The best words in the best order. Isn't that what you always say?

"Yes, Mother," Richard Jr. responded with a huge smile on his face. "The best words in the best order!"

4

The actual funeral service was held inside the large viewing chamber at the front of the funeral home rather than at a church, a decision that was being opted for more and more as the years had passed. Initially, during the early years of the funeral home business, most of the actual services were held at a local church, and the funeral home and church had acted in tandem to meet the wishes of the families involved. The typical complete ceremony consisted of two to three days of "showing" at the funeral home, a time for friends to visit and pay their respects, followed by a service that would be performed at a local church. The four-day event gave family members who lived out of the area time to make the appropriate travel arrangements, and although the lengthy process had been hard on the immediate family, it was a custom that had been carried over from as far back as when funerals were held in the home. As travel options improved, the mourning time had been cut dramatically, and the typical small-town funeral was abridged to consist of a one- or two-night viewing, followed by a midday funeral service the following day. Some had even shortened the event to a single day, a two-hour viewing time starting at ten o'clock, followed by a service, with interment immediately thereafter, and as the process was condensed over time, the inconvenience of a service at a separate church had become less and less of an option.

The large viewing parlor had been staged with rows of chairs, with a main aisle down the middle to accommodate what Richard and his staff had thought would be an exceptionally large turnout. Extra folding chairs that were typically stored in the basement had been brought up, and a retractable wall that could divide the large viewing parlor into two smaller rooms was opened to accommodate the large crowd. The first three rows of the seating were reserved for immediate family members, with six of those seats specifically designated for the pallbearers. The stereo system that had just recently been updated had been checked for tone and volume and was turned on, ready for use.

All of Ruth and Richard's children were there, along with some of their children and a few cousins from the Saroh side of the family that had made their way out of St. Louis. Richard's uncle Louis, the youngest brother of his father, Werner, now ninety-seven years old, and one of the few surviving veterans of World War I, had also made it and was seated in a wheelchair in the center aisle. Louis's wife had been confined to a nursing home for the past four years with Alzheimer's, and his daughter Olivia, who had taken on the monumental task of transporting the old man, sat in the end seat next to her father to give him any assistance that might be necessary. Olivia had told Ruth that he probably wouldn't be able to hear a word that was spoken but that he wanted to be there nonetheless, a request that the doting daughter could not refuse. Ruth's bother Lawrence, who had actually stayed overnight in the third-floor-apartment guest suite, was seated in his wheelchair next to the front row, and Ruth and Richard were seated in the front row couch next to Lawrence.

As the crowd continued to file in and all the existing rows were filled, several of the funeral home workers were sent scuttling to the basement to bring up additional chairs, and they quickly added six more rows to the fifteen that had already been set up. The unwelcomed clanging of chairs at the back of the room had almost unnerved Richard, who expected clockwork perfection in any ceremony at the Clarkson Funeral Home, and he turned around and gave his workers one of his trademark "looks" of disapproval, then glanced at his wife with the same intense glare, a look that she completely ignored.

Richard glanced at his watch and saw that it was fifteen minutes to eleven, and promptly waved to Vickie, one of the home's assistants, to start the music. Almost immediately, the soft tones of a cello composition started to flow across the room, and most of the side conversations that had been taking place were suddenly hushed as everyone looked to the front in expectation. Ruth had just picked up a small rubber ball that little Eli had dropped in the seats behind her, and just as she looked back up, she spotted her sister Cora Undine Lasciter coming through the main entrance door on her right.

She hadn't seen her sister since their grandmother's funeral in St. Louis over six years earlier, and even though the years had somewhat altered her sister's appearance, her personal style and graceful identity were unmistakable. Much like Ruth's, her face had changed very little over the years, and her emerald-green eyes were still as striking as ever, and her skin looked surprisingly young for a woman just over a half-century. Her hair, dyed a rich auburn red, was pulled back off her face and fashioned into a small bun in the back. She wore an expensive-looking black dress that showed off her still-youthful physique, and her matching shoes, purse, and diamond accessories gave her the appearance of someone who had grown accustomed to the finer things in life.

At her side was her fourth husband, Henry William Lasciter, a rotund-looking man with a rubicund complexion, outfitted in an expensive Kenneth Cole dress suit that went a long way in "compensating" for the disproportion of his body. He was an executive vice president at Boatman's Investments, a St. Louis-based wealth management company, and a majority stockholder, who had risen to the top of the enterprise on his keen business acumen and the very deep pockets of his father, who had originally made his fortune in the coal mines of Kentucky. As this was Cora's fourth bite at the wedding apple, her expectations had changed dramatically from the young girl who had first married an unemployed high school football star, and her expectations from her later husbands had become increasingly more ledger-based. As she herself had admitted to her brother, what her later husbands lacked in physical appearance had been more than compensated for by their checkbooks. Harry, as he was referred to by his immediate family, was holding a flower arrangement in his left hand, and his right was gently placed on his wife's back as he led her into the viewing room.

The Lasciters spied two vacant seats at the end of the second row that were positioned directly behind Ruth and Richard, and they quickly made their way to the unoccupied chairs. Cora glanced to her right as she walked past Ruth, and even though Ruth could feel her sister's eyes upon her, she kept her gaze straight forward. She nervously squeezed Eli's small rubber ball as she felt her sister slip by. As the couple approached their seats, Vickie quickly came forward and unburdened Henry of the flowerpot he was holding, and as they were sitting down, Cora reached her right hand forward and placed it lightly on Ruth's shoulder. She left it there for no more than a moment, and Ruth, unable to move, simply sat silently as a shudder ran through her body.

Cora had always been called Daddy's little girl by her demanding father, Cole Saroh, who had taken over his family's business in the late sixties after his father had died from an unexpected heart attack. The company, Diversified General Plastics, had originally been started in 1931 by Cole's father, Frederich Wilhelm Saroh, a hard-nosed businessman with an iron fist and a short temper, and had been grown into a very successful enterprise despite some turbulent years in the foreign marketplace. The strong-willed approach of the son, who had adopted his father's merciless business methodology and his willingness to do whatever it took to succeed, however cutthroat it might have been, increased the production capabilities many times over and grew the bottom line to profits that the older Saroh could have only dreamed about. When the opportunity to cash out presented itself, he sold the company to a national conglomerate that literally made him a multimillionaire overnight. During his time at the helm of his company, Cole Saroh had earned the reputation of a stern taskmaster who expected complete dedication and propriety from all his employees, a philosophy that was applied to his own family as well, except for his second daughter, Cora, who, for reasons not completely known to consanguine parties, was sanctioned liberties and freedoms that the older two siblings were never allowed. Those closest to the family, who had the opportunity to peer in on the Sarohs' family dynamic, chalked it up to parental regret and felt the old man was attempting to make up for the harshness of his approach with his older children, Ruth and Lawrence, while others argued that he simply liked his youngest daughter better than the others and felt no compulsion to hide the fact. Whatever the reason, it seemed the rough, almost-militaristic approach that held sway with his first two children had somehow been softened the third time around, and he had lavished the youngest Saroh with whatever she wanted, a change that did not go unnoticed by the two older siblings, or his wife.

As the service started, Ruth's mind drifted in and out of the present as thoughts of Aaron and the unusual way he was brought into her life swirled through her mind. She thought back on the deliberate choosing of his name, Aaron, in honor of the biblical older brother of Moses, and how she had hoped that he, too, might assist his younger brothers if Providence should bring them forth. She remembered the first time she held the young baby and could see the gentle smile that appeared across his face as she whispered to him in baby talk, and she could hear the soft coo that he made when he was content, and his cry when he was hungry. She remembered his first awkward step, his first word, the long trips to the specialist, the harsh realities of his diagnosis, his first day of school, and a hundred other day-to-day occurrences that stretched out over a lifetime. She wondered if she had done enough, if the love and commitment that she had given the child was sufficient, and if he could have developed more if only she, herself, had done more. She questioned if subconsciously she had loved him less than she did her own three children because she had not given birth to him.

She was brought back to the present when her granddaughters, Anna and Abby, rose and started to sing "The Lord's Prayer." The quality of the young girls' voices, and the heaviness in her heart, unleashed a flow of tears, and she bowed her head in utter despair. As the two young girls were taking their seats and Richard Jr. stepped up in front of the crowd, she pulled herself together, and silently chanted, *Stop it*, in her mind as she attempted to regain her composure.

After a few introductory remarks, just as Ruth and her son had planned, Richard Jr. eloquently started to recite Edna St. Vincent Millay's somber dirge:

"I am not resigned to the shutting away of loving hearts in the hard ground. So it is, and so it will be, for so it has been, time out of mind. Into the darkness they go, the wise, and the lovely. Crowned with lilies and with laurel they go; but I am not resigned."

Ruth looked up and gazed around the gathering as Richard Jr. continued his recitation. She could smell the subtle scent of florets and blossoms that lined the walls, an evasive, familiar aroma that had filled the rooms of the old funeral home her entire adult life. But somehow, now, the saccharine, portending scent seemed almost unbearable, seemed to be closing in around her, suffocating her. She could feel her husband of thirty-three years sitting next to her, distant and remote, she could see the casket draped in floral display, she could see the tender face of Aaron lying all alone, and she lowered her head and closed her eyes. She could sense her own mortality, the finite element of her own corporeal being, and for just a moment, she imagined herself lying in a casket, free from the manacles and anguishes of living, free from the pain of loss, lilies and laurel at her side.

"Lovers and thinkers, into the earth with you," Richard Jr. continued. "Be one with the dull, the indiscriminate dust. A fragment of what you felt, of what you knew. A formula, a phrase remains, but the best is lost."

Suddenly she felt a touch, like an olive branch from the past reaching out to her, beckoning her to return, and she quickly glanced to her left and could see her sister's hand placed softly on her shoulder. Memories of Cora came flooding back into her consciousness, and she wondered if it was possible that she might have finally changed, as Lawrence had alluded, had somehow come to regret the wild impetuosity of her youth; and Ruth wondered if this was her awkward way of reaching out, attempting to bridge the years of neglect that had so thoroughly separated them. Maybe Cora, too, was suffering, Ruth thought, was filled with regret and remorse, could remember the unforgiving pain of giving up a baby, and could feel the utter despair of the death of a child. Had she thought of him through the years? Had giving up her child haunted her throughout her life? Had her callous, carefree approach to living only been a thin veneer, a cover for true feeling of hopeless anguish?

"Down, down, down into the darkness of the grave," Richard Jr. spoke out, his voice starting to break up. "Gently they go, the beautiful, the tender, the kind; quietly they go, the intelligent, the witty, the brave. I know. But I do not approve. And I am not resigned."

CHAPTER
5

T he short service at the grave site, which both Ruth and Richard had worried about the most, started off without incident. The actual digging of the grave, done two days before, was a process that Werner and Marcella Clarkson, Richard's parents, had started to outsource years ago, finding it much more cost-effective to bring in an outside vendor. A funeral tent had been erected next to the grave, green Astroturf was used to line the floor, and lightweight folding chairs were lined up under the canopy facing the site. Ruth had personally selected a Wellington-brand solid-walnut wood casket, with almond velvet interior fabric, spindled corners, and swing bar handle hardware, and it had been placed on a lowering device: a metal frame with straps that straddled the top and grave that would be used to lower the casket. The large funeral wreath with the words *dearest son* embossed on its ribbon had been placed on top of the closed walnut chest, and many of the flowers that had adorned the funeral home were positioned around the base of the lowering device. The heavy rains the day before had left the grounds soggy and moist, and long strips of particle board were used to create a bridge from the gravel road that circled the small church yard to the grave site, and large sheets of plywood were placed around the funeral tent to keep the mourners' feet dry during the short grave site ceremony.

Aaron was being interred into a large plot of reserved graves toward the far front of the cemetery that Werner Clarkson had purchased when his mother had died in 1929, hoping to create a true family resting plot for his parents, his family, and all their offspring. The actual graveyard was part of an old Evangelical Church that had been built in 1877 but had since been merged into a larger church in 1951. The original congregants who formed in 1853 found that the dwindling congregation could no longer substantiate a full-time pastor, and most of them joined the Ox Bend Evangelical Church, a congregation that Ruth and Richard had attended since they were first married. Ruth had always loved the pastoral setting of the small redbrick church, and Richard had even served on the cemetery association that had been formed to take over the perpetual care and maintenance of the property. But what most intrigued Ruth about the small country church, what had endeared her to it irrevocably, had been the origin of the church name. Almost unbelievably, the church had been named Lippstadt, after a province in Germany called Lippe, the exact same area in Germany that her own mother had emigrated from at age nine, a discovery that Ruth had seen as something much more than pure coincidence.

As Ruth sat under the tent, waiting for the long line of cars to unload their cargo and make their way to the site, she glanced to her right and could see the headstone of Werner and Marcella Clarkson, and the harsh realities of the finiteness of life again closed in around her. She looked back at the small brick church in the distance, its metal steeple reaching toward the sky, and remembered the bell service that was held annually in recognition of all those who had been interred during the preceding year.

"Have you ever been to the annual memorial service they have here?" Ruth whispered to Ruthie, who was sitting on her right, as thoughts of the ceremony filled her mind. "Every spring they have a small service to honor all those buried during the year, and they ring the bell for them."

"Yes, once," Ruthie whispered after giving it some thought. "When Clyde's aunt died. She was buried here. But that was years ago. She's over there," Ruthie went on, pointing off to the side of the tent. "Over on the other side of the church."

"Well, you're going to have to come with me when they have the next one," Ruth whispered. She turned and looked back anxiously toward the road. "I do hope that they can get Lawrence's wheelchair out here. He said yesterday that he really wanted to come."

"Oh, I'm sure the men can handle that," Ruthie assured her as she, too, turned and looked back toward the road. "And I talked to Cora. She said that she and Henry—I think that's what she said her husband's name was—are going to come out too. And they're also going to the church for the luncheon."

"What!" Ruth exclaimed as she turned back around and faced her friend. "When did you talk to her?"

"She came up to me as I was getting into the car to come out here," Ruthie answered defensively.

"Oh," Ruth uttered to herself with a tone of despair.

"And she just seems different now somehow," Ruthie went on. "It's hard to explain. She looks about the same—she looks great, in fact—but she just didn't seem as harsh as she used to be." Ruthie paused and rethought her comment. "Well, maybe *harsh* isn't the right word, but something has changed about her. It's just hard to put in words."

"Lawrence said that same thing," Ruth concurred as she looked back at her friend. "But she hasn't been out here for years. And I rarely even talk to her on the phone, so I have no idea what she's like now."

"Didn't she ever check in and see how Aaron was getting along?" Ruthie, who was the only outsider who knew that Cora was Aaron's birth mother, asked without thinking. "I mean, if it were my child," she whispered, afraid someone would overhear her, "I think I would want to keep up with how he was doing."

Ruth pulled her jacket closed, as if a chill had just come over her. "She used to, in the beginning. And I think that was the original purpose of leaving the child with me and Richard, so she could at least be a small part of his life. And she did come out a lot at first. But then after Jasper, her second husband, was killed in Korea, we didn't see her for a long time after that. And then she married that Brian Teasdale on the rebound."

"Did I ever meet him?" Ruthie asked, her curiosity getting the better of her.

"Oh, I doubt it. I only met him once myself, and that was at the wedding."

"Why in the world did she ever marry him?" Ruthie whispered.

"He had a lot of money, and I think that's what got Cora's attention in the beginning, but he was an abusive man, treated Cora terribly." Ruth paused and glanced back toward the road. "She just went through a lot with those two, and as time went on, we heard less and less from her." Ruth looked back and grabbed Ruthie's hand. "And Aaron had become such a wonderful part of our lives. I mean, he really was *my* son. And I was his mother. And she could see that. Maybe she couldn't handle it all. Maybe she felt completely left out." Ruth paused as Reverend Vollbrecht walked by and took his place next to the coffin. "She did always send him a birthday card and Christmas present every year, though," she started up again in hushed voice. "But she just finally stopped coming out, and as I said, she always seemed to be embroiled in some drama with a husband or an ex-husband." Ruth stopped talking and looked up at the large funeral wreath draped over the casket. "I just think that after Jasper was killed, she never really was the same. That just seemed to change her."

"Yeah, I remember that," Ruthie responded emotionally. "That must have been terrible."

"And I think that she really loved him," Ruth said sincerely. "And he was a great guy. Of all of them, I think I liked him the best!"

"She told me something else too," Ruthie stated and then took an uneasy breath. "She said she needs to talk to you." Ruthie continued to look closely at her friend for some type of reaction.

"Did she say about what?" Ruth whispered as memories of their childhood together started to form in her mind.

"No. She just said that she needed to talk to you." Ruthie paused again and sensed that Ruth wanted more of an explanation. "Yes, those were her exact words: 'I need to talk to her,'" Ruthie enunciated for clarity. "That's all she said!" Just as Ruthie finished her comment, Richard walked up and took a seat on the other side of his wife.

"Oh my," Ruth moaned as her husband placed his arm around her shoulders. "I wonder what she wants now."

As the short service was ending, Ruth sat quietly and tried to suppress the mound of anguish that she felt building up inside. She realized that after over thirty years of loving, nurturing, and mothering the young man in countless ways, this would be the final thing she would do for Aaron, this would be her final glimpse at the earthly connection to her dear lost son, and the thought of leaving her loved one alone at the cold, deserted graveyard was almost more than she could bear. She realized that after the short service, everyone would leave the grave site, would go to the church, would eat and talk and drink, and life, as it always did, would go on without her son. And she shuddered at the economy of human memory. *Others would forget,* she thought, but not me. *My connection is too deep, too indelible to be severed, even by the exacting finality of the grave.* It almost seemed too much, and tears started to pour from her eyes, and she buried her head in her hands.

"Peace I leave with you," Reverend Vollbrecht said, reading John 14:27. "My peace I give you. I do not give to you as the world gives. Do not let your hearts be troubled and do not be afraid."

CHAPTER

6

The seemingly incongruous idea of a celebratory lunch after something as emotional as a funeral was a practice that had been done as far back as any of the residents of Ox Bend could remember. It symbolized a process of healing and the ultimate "letting go" of the loved one and the nurturing progression of moving forward and returning to the "daily business of life," as Ruth's mother-in-law, Marcella Clarkson, had so aptly worded it; and the Ox Bend Evangelical Church had entertained countless funeral lunches over its lengthy history. The Women's Society had been challenged with the task of preparing the meal, a process that they, through trial and error and a strong sense of fellowship, had almost turned into an art form. Based on a rotating schedule that involved volunteers from the congregation, many of the local church members had dropped by casseroles, salads, breads, pies, and desserts of all kind to accommodate what was thought to be a large turnout. Portable round tables were set up and covered with red checkered oilcloth, and each was adorned with condiments, napkins, and plastic flower centerpieces that had graced the tables on many such occasions. A large bank of folding chairs, usually stowed on rolling frames at the back of the basement, had been brought out and placed around each table; and a long row of rectangular tables, the length of the entire room, was placed just outside the kitchen, where the food could be set up, and a coffee and dessert stand, with a fifty-cup coffee maker, was placed just to the right of that.

As Ruth and the immediate family made their way into the dining area, they were greeted by a large number of family, friends, and acquaintances, many who hadn't seen one another, or visited, since the last funeral gathering, and the somber mood from the earlier services was replaced by the steady roar of multiple conversations, muted laughter, and the noise of children banging on an old piano at the back of the room. Old Louis Clarkson, the sole surviving brother of Werner Clarkson, who had attended the funeral service in his wheelchair, had been carried down the steps that led to the dining area, in his chair, by Scott Battenhorst, Ruth's son-in-law, and Victor Vollbrecht, son of Reverend Vollbrecht, a task that they performed for Lawrence Saroh as well.

The vast majority of the attendees were local townspeople: a group of ladies from the Dorcas Society had staked out a table in the back of the room; six employees, including the president, from the local People's Bank were there; a large contingent from the county courts building had found a table near the front of the serving line; and a large number of prior customers who had used the Clarkson Funeral Home over the years were all gathered, in hopes of talking to Ruth and the bereaved family members. As Ruth was making her way among the tables, she made a point to stop and talk to Louis Clarkson, who had rolled his wheelchair up to a table at the back of the dining room. His daughter, Olivia, had just made her way to the back of the serving line, and he was sitting by himself. Ruth bent down and hugged the old man around the neck from behind.

"Louis! How are you doing?" she yelled out, knowing his hearing was all but gone.

"Right as rain," the old man retorted absentmindedly. He cupped his arthritic left hand behind his ear. "Who goes there?" he spouted as he looked around, his eyes surprisingly bright and clear for a man of his age.

"It's me, Ruth Clarkson," Ruth confirmed buoyantly. She walked around to the side of his wheelchair, took a seat to his left, and patted him on the arm. "I'm so glad that you could make it, Uncle Louis! I was hoping you'd be here. How is Flora doing?"

The old man looked down as he thought of his wife and slowly started shaking his head. "Not so good anymore. I go and visit when I can, but she doesn't know me anymore—she doesn't know anybody, really."

"Oh, I hate to hear that," Ruth replied compassionately. "But it looks like you're doing pretty good. I hear that you're at the Harbor Pines place now."

"Where?"

"Harbor Pines!" Ruth yelled. "I hear you're at Harbor Pines now!"

"Yes, they have me there now. But it's nothing but a bunch of old people!" he roared, unable to hear his own volume. "They don't know what to do with us, I guess," he added, then let out large, self-deprecating laugh. He took his right hand, which shook constantly, and patted himself on the chest. "As long as this thing keeps ticking, I guess I'll be here. I just wish I could hear better. Can't even really watch TV anymore—can't hear what they're saying."

"Do you have a hearing aid?" Ruth asked.

"What?"

"Do you have a hearing aid?" Ruth all but yelled, temporarily stopping the children who were banging on the piano, who looked around in surprise.

"Oh, they don't work!" the old man countered once he understood the question. "Too much background noise." He paused, and his face took on a more philosophical ken. "Most of what's said these days ain't worth hearing anyway!" he added, and he then chuckled to himself. He took his left hand and placed it on Ruth's forearm and gave it a gentle squeeze. "Ruth, I'm so sorry about all this," he started out intently. "You have my deepest sympathies, dear. Such a tragedy to be gone at such an early age." He paused and gave her arm another quick embrace. "He was a good boy, wasn't he?"

"Yes, he was," Ruth answered solemnly. "He was no problem at all, and we're certainly going to miss him. It's going to be so different without him around the house." Ruth stopped and looked down at the old man's purple hand resting on her arm. "I just don't know what I'm going to do without him," she lamented as the all-too-familiar feelings of anguish started to surface again.

"It's just not the way of things, children going before the parents," the old man stated, picking up on Ruth's sudden feelings of melancholy. "He's gone way too early, and here I am, hanging on way too late!"

"Oh, you do all right, don't you, Louis?" Ruth asked with a great sense of sincerity that seemed to somehow affect the old man.

"There are still a few good days," he started out quite seriously, "and that brings me a little joy, I guess, but they are few and far between anymore. This old-age business is far worse than I ever imagined!" He paused and patted Ruth on the arm. "You know, when you turn sixty you start to disappear, people start to look right past you. You get to my age and you're totally invisible!"

"Oh, nonsense, Uncle Louis! I still see you. In fact, my grandmother Mildred told me that after you turn eighty, you get cute again."

"Well, I should be damn good-looking then!" the old man roared. After a few moments, Louis leaned forward in his wheelchair and reached over and grabbed ahold of Ruth's forearm again. "You've been a great wife to Richard—better than he ever deserved—and an even better mother to Aaron, and that was wrong, the way they handled all that business back then. Richard should have told you the truth from the start. I told him you had a right to know," he added irritably.

"Told me what, Louis?" Ruth asked, unsure of just what the old man was referring to.

"The truth!" the old man shouted back. "The truth!" he repeated again with added force.

Just as Ruth attempted to question the old man further, Olivia walked up with two plates of food and placed them on the table. "Here you go, Dad!" she yelled into his good ear and then took a seat to his right, placing his plate in front of him. "Ruth, he hasn't been going on about that 'reunification of Germany' stuff, has he?" she asked as she placed a napkin and some silverware in front of her father. "That's all he's been talking about for the past two weeks!" she added with a laugh. "Isn't it, Daddy?" she questioned the old man in baby talk.

"You read that, didn't you, Ruth?" the old man chimed in right on cue. "You heard that East Germany and West Germany just reunited! They're now the Federal Republic of Germany! I read it in the paper."

"Oh, she doesn't care about that," Olivia retorted, regretting her decision to bring the topic up again.

"She's got German blood, same as me," he defended. "Her mother even emigrated from there!"

"I did read that, Louis," Ruth responded, getting up from the table. "The world is changing, isn't it?" she added rhetorically.

The old man grabbed his fork and started to eat. "I was over there, you know. I was there!" he repeated with his mouth half-full.

"Well, you take care of yourself, Louis, and I'll talk to you both later." Ruth got up and kissed the old man on the head. "And I want you to take one of the small plants with you when you go. You can put it in your room at Harbor Pines."

"Oh, that's nice of you, Ruth," Olivia answered for the old man. She leaned over toward her father. "She wants you to take one of the small plants! Isn't that nice, Daddy?" she hollered in baby talk.

The rest of the luncheon was a blur of activity as over seventy-five people came through the line and filled the small dining room to overflowing. Most the original dishes were soon consumed, and Harlan Wolff, who ran a small grocery just three doors down, brought in a large ham and some prepackaged potato salad to cover the shortage, and after about an hour, most of the remaining crowd consisted of only close friends and family members. Regina and Scott Battenhorst were still there with all three of their children. Charles Clarkson and his wife, Allison, and their two little boys were there, Charles boasting about a new patrol cruiser that he had just acquired, and Richard Jr. was still there, too, seated at a table with his brother Charles and his family. Clyde and Ruthie Kaermor were still there with three of their six grandchildren, who were mostly accountable for the unwelcomed piano playing that was eventually brought to an end by Reverend Vollbrecht himself, and Ruthie was helping with the long process of cleaning up the large kitchen area, seeing that everything was put back exactly the way it was found.

Worn out by the full schedule of the morning, Ruth had set up camp at one of the large round tables in the middle of the dining room with her daughter Regina and Regina's two girls, Anna, eleven years old, and Abby, just a few weeks shy of her tenth birthday. Richard had assumed a position near the main exit and was thanking guests and bidding best wishes as the remaining crowd slowly made its way out of the building. Henry Lasciter, who didn't know a soul at the event except for his wife, Cora, had found a comfortable seat in the back near the now-quiet piano and was thumbing through the financial section of *The Wall Street Journal* that he had sneaked in under his suit coat. Regina had just brought the last two surviving slices of cherry pie and had set them down on the table.

"Oh my god, I can't eat anything!" Ruth exclaimed, pushing one of the pieces of cherry pie in front of her granddaughter Abby. "I don't have a fork anyway," she threw out as a secondary excuse.

"Well, I can fix that!" Regina chimed in, jumping up and heading for the kitchen.

"Don't give it to me!" Abby exclaimed in a high-pitched voice, her eyes filled with mischief. "I need that like I need a hole in my head," she clowned and then let out a small nasal giggle that sounded just like her mother's.

Ruth looked at her nine-year-old granddaughter, who was a carbon copy of Regina, with long black hair and piercing blue eyes. "You're not worried about your weight already, are you?" she asked with grandmotherly concern.

"She better be!" Anna chimed in, poking her sister in the stomach. "She has a boyfriend now!"

"I do not!" Abby blustered, her face turning red. "And so what if I did?" she yelled back at her sister, after giving it a second thought.

Ruth was just about to start a lecture on the pitfalls of growing up too fast when Regina came rushing back to the table with several forks in hand. "Don't look now, but here she comes," Regina whispered to her mother as she slid into her seat beside her. Ruth knew immediately whom her daughter was talking about, and she sat back in her chair and folded her hands on the table, as if praying for some type of heavenly intervention.

"Ruth," Cora said softly as she walked up behind her sister and placed her hands on her shoulders. "It was a wonderful service, and the graveyard out at Lippstadt was just lovely. I know now why you like it out there so much. It was a beautiful tribute to Aaron." She paused awkwardly, and Anna and Abby gathered up the two untouched pieces of pie and darted across the dining room.

"Oh, thank you, Cora," Ruth replied cordially. She turned and looked up at her sister towering over her, and she could see immediately what Ruthie had been talking about at the grave site. Even at first glance, she seemed very different, in some inexpressible way. "And those two young ladies—I guess that's the right term—running across the dining room are my granddaughters, Anna and Abby," Ruth put forward with a slight embarrassed undertone. "And Alex is around here somewhere too," she added nervously as she looked around the room, attempting to locate him. "Those are Regina's three."

"Yes, I remember them as children," Cora acknowledged, her voice filled with an uneasy tension, "but they certainly have grown up since I last saw them. I think I can see a little Saroh in all of them." She paused and turned her head and looked directly at Ruth's daughter. "And you must be Regina. I definitely remember you." She reached down and awkwardly attempted to shake hands with her niece. "You probably don't remember this, but you used to love to play with my makeup and jewelry when you were little!"

Regina blushed, not knowing exactly how to respond, and just smiled up at her estranged aunt. "My two girls are the same way!" she finally countered. She stood up and gave her aunt a hug and then invited Cora to have a seat with them.

"Yes, here, have a seat here by me," Ruth suggested. "Ruthie told me that you needed to talk to me."

"Yes, if you don't mind," Cora replied timidly.

"No, no, please have a seat. It's been too long as it is," Ruth responded, pulling out a chair for her sister.

"I'll let you two catch up," Regina jumped in. She hopped up and gave her mother a subtle wink as she passed by. "I'll go see if Ruthie needs help in the kitchen."

Cora gracefully took her seat next to Ruth and placed her Louis Vuitton handbag on top of the table. Cora was four years younger than her older sister, and the age difference showed vividly between the two women. Although both had been blessed with the genetic staying power of youthful-looking faces, Cora was more youthful-looking in her appearance and carriage, and her hands and arms had not yet started to suffer the unfortunate consequences of time. She had always had an "air of indifference" about her, as her mother, Emma, had expressed on many occasions, and she seemed to approach the world as if there might not have been a great deal of thought or deliberation behind the decisions she seemed to make so capriciously. It was an approach that had provided a great deal of excitement in her life but had also led to some regrettable outcomes, a combination that many men found initially exciting. While Ruth had applied herself assiduously in high school, had walked within the predefined lines of communal acceptance and societal expectation, and had worn the heavy yoke of conformity, Cora had taken a much-less-defined, more-circuitous path, lived each day as if it might have been her last, and preferred to take life's teachings on the learn-as-you-go basis, a very counterintuitive approach to her staid and traditionalist family. When Cora had returned from New York after giving birth, she had resumed her life as if nothing had happened, her absence explained as a loving niece assisting an ailing aunt through a difficult time, a fiction that had never been questioned by nosy neighbors or acquaintances. The deception had been so successful that Cora had been crowned homecoming queen her senior year and married the captain of the football team just two months after her high school graduation, a marriage that lasted four months and three days. As Lawrence had written in a letter to his nephew Richard Jr., "The process of attracting husbands has always come easy to my sister, but keeping them has proved more of a challenge!"

"I mean it, Ruth," Cora started out as she positioned herself next to her sister. "The service was absolutely beautiful, and the cemetery out there is lovely. Everything was just perfect."

"Well, thank you, that means a lot to me," Ruth responded, surprised by her sister's kind words. She looked closely at Cora sitting next to her and again was struck by how different she seemed to be now. The aura of strong-willed remoteness and distance that had always seemed to surround her was gone, and she looked almost vulnerable, exposed. "There were times that I didn't know if I was going to make it through it all," Ruth went on as she felt herself relaxing a little, "but I've made it this far. Unfortunately, I hear that worst is yet to come."

"Yes, I can only imagine," Cora replied thoughtfully. She looked down and started to nervously spin a large ill-fitting diamond ring on her wedding finger. "But you've always been the strong one. I know you'll make it through it all."

"I wish I had your confidence," Ruth batted back. "You know, I've seen countless mothers go through this over the years, and they all made it somehow." Ruth paused and seemed to focus on some distant point across the room. "I guess I will too," she added, with a hollow tone of optimism, as she looked back at her sister. Cora only looked up briefly and then looked back down and said nothing, and Ruth started to think about the last time they saw each other. "Remember when Grandma died?" she finally asked, much to the surprise of her sister. "I think that was the last time I saw you."

"Yes," Cora answered as she, too, seemed to relax a little. "That seems like so long ago now."

"It appears that the only time we see each anymore is at funerals!" Ruth quipped with a chuckle.

"Yes, that seems to be the way of the world once you turn fifty! And I think you're right. The last time we saw each other was at Elsie's funeral—it was in the fall of the year, wasn't it?" Cora paused and let out a short sigh and seemed to drift back to her past. "You know what I miss the most about Grandma Elsie?" she stated, finally looking back up at her sister. "I miss those peach coffee cakes she used to make all the time," she added, then smiled for the first time.

"Oh my god, I do remember those!" Ruth rejoined excitedly. "And I loved the cinnamon ones too, and I tried on many occasions to make them myself, but they were never the same. Why we didn't get her recipe for those is beyond me!"

"She'd never give it out!" Cora retorted with a muted laugh. "I asked her for it on several occasions, but she always avoided giving it up in one way or another."

"Yeah, that sounds like her! I remember she used to bring them over on Sunday afternoons and we'd have them finished off before she even left!"

"Well, I blame most of that on Lawrence," Cora retorted. "My god, the way that boy could eat!" she added and then let out an artificial laugh.

"Oh, I remember," Ruth confirmed with a nostalgic tone.

Cora looked down and crossed her arms tightly, and her mood seemed to change dramatically. "That all seems so long ago now," she sighed, as if the weight of the world had suddenly settled upon her. "When I heard the news that Aaron was gone, I just couldn't believe it. And I wanted to reach out to you, but after all that's transpired, I just didn't know if you wanted to hear from me or not." She took a deep breath, and her voice quivered slightly as she went on. "I know how much you loved him. And I guess I just didn't know if seeing me would be a good thing or a bad thing. But I was definitely thinking about you, about Aaron, and wondering how you were."

"I appreciate that," Ruth responded warmly, amazed by Cora's genuine comments. "And I was fine through the showing and the funeral, but I'm worried about tomorrow and the next few days. I just feel this overwhelming..." Ruth paused, as if looking for just the right term. "This pressure, if that's the right word. There were a few times last night when I woke up and I almost felt like I physically couldn't breathe."

Surprised by her sister's heartfelt disclosure, Cora unexpectedly reached over and grabbed Ruth's right hand. "You really loved him, didn't you?" she asked with a depth of sincerity that Ruth was not used to seeing in her sister.

"Oh, more than you will ever know," Ruth answered, placing her left hand on top of Cora's.

"I want to thank you," Cora started out as she looked down again, her hands trembling, her voice resonant with sincerity. "No, I *need* to thank you for stepping forward back then and taking care of Aaron all these years." Ruth attempted to respond, but Cora cut her off. "No, don't say anything. Please let me say this. Let me get this out. I know what you and your brother think of me, and believe me, I don't blame you at all. I haven't exactly made the right choices in my life, and God knows I'll probably make more mistakes as time goes on, but as I've gotten older, I've come to really appreciate the amazing thing you did for me all those years ago when you agreed to adopt Aaron."

Ruth said nothing, but her face displayed every emotion she was feeling.

"And I didn't really understand it at that time," Cora went on, finally looking up at her sister. "As you know only too well, I was this stupid little girl who thought she knew everything, who only thought of herself, and I really had no idea the sacrifice that you made. I just wish there were some way that I could pay you back for all that you've done." She paused and took a large gulp of air. "You know, Ruth, you've done more for me than anyone, and that goes far beyond just taking care of Aaron." Cora stopped and looked down again and started nervously spinning the wedding ring again.

"Oh, Cora," Ruth responded warmly, "I'm glad to hear you say that. It's been so long since we really talked, and I've missed that. I've missed having a sister in my life. But it's really not necessary to thank me." She reached forward and clutched her sister's hands in her own. "And I think sometimes I forget about all that you gave up back then, the price you paid, all that you went through. And I've tried to put myself in your shoes, having to give up a child at such an early age, and I can only imagine how painful that must have been. And now to have to attend his funeral."

Cora said nothing, but she looked up at her sister, seemingly touched by Ruth's keen awareness of her own feelings.

"So thanking me is really not necessary. Not anymore." Ruth paused and tightened her grip on Cora's hands. "Don't you see? Aaron wasn't a burden. I didn't sacrifice anything. He was a gift. He was the most wonderful gift that I ever received. And I loved him from the moment I first held him in my arms. And he gave me more than I ever gave him. And he taught me more than I ever taught him!" Ruth paused again, and a solemnity came over her as she went on. "Don't you see what a child like him can give? Regina and Charles and Richie, I love them with all my heart, I always will, but they went on with their lives as they grew older. That's the way of it. But Aaron, a gift like Aaron, he was forever. He saw the world from a different perspective, he trusted everyone, he loved everyone."

The women sat quietly, until Abby started to play "Clair De Lune" on the old piano behind them and seemed to startle them out of their trance. Ruth looked closely at Cora, whose eyes were filled with sorrow and regret, and she reached across and wiped a tear from her cheek. "Now that we're talking again, can I ask you something, Cora?"

"Yes, ask me anything you want. I think you've earned that right."

"Why didn't you ever have any more children?" she asked and then paused for an answer, afraid she might have overstepped her bounds.

Cora thought for a minute before she spoke, as if really analyzing the question closely. "Ah, that's a good question. Do you think I would have made a good mother?" She was evading.

"Oh, I don't know. Who knows such things until they're thrust into the fire? But I'd like to think that if you were given the chance, you'd be a good one."

"Even with my track record with men and husbands?" Cora replied half-jokingly as she reached for a handkerchief from her purse.

"Well, you do certainly seem to favor quantity over quality," Ruth replied and then blushed with a trace of regret. "I guess you just never found the right one," she augmented as a hint of a smile appeared on her face.

"Too many *right* ones," Cora fired back sarcastically, picking up on Ruth's subtle smile as she dabbed her eyes. "And you're right, I haven't exactly been focused on quality." She stopped and flashed a playful grin that Ruth hadn't seen on her sister's face for years. "Maybe I need to re-read *Zen and the Art of Motorcycle Maintenance*," she added as Ruth's mouth fell open.

"I had no idea you read that book!" Ruth exclaimed, her mind drifting back. "That was always one of my favorites!"

"Don't you remember giving it to me?" Cora asked. "It had to be back in the midseventies. Mom and I had come out to visit, and you were sitting out on the steps at the back of the building, sunning yourself, reading it." Cora paused and thought for a moment. "I remember you said it was a metaphysical examination of quality!"

"Oh my!" Ruth gushed. "I don't remember saying that or giving it to you, but I did love that book." Ruth paused and let out a short sigh. "Oh, I do miss the seventies sometimes!" she added, letting out a small laugh of her own.

"Well, I should have read it more closely, because I've come to realize that my problems don't reside in the men I choose, it's more… how should I say this…closely rooted." Cora paused and let out a subtle, self-conscious sigh. "And to get back to your question, I have on occasion thought about children, but the men I marry aren't necessarily interested in that kind of thing."

"Well, you are a mother, Cora. I mean, it was you who gave birth to Aaron."

"No, no, Ruth," Cora repeated adamantly. "You were Aaron's mother in any way that really matters, and that was the best thing that could have happened to him." Cora hesitated, and a subtle smile came across her face. "Could you imagine me raising a child at age sixteen?"

Ruth looked carefully at her sister, and she could again sense some vulnerability lurking behind her self-deprecating remarks. "Cora, are you all right?" she asked as she leaned forward, looked her sister in the eye, and reclasped her trembling hands in her own. "I just sense that something is wrong. Does Aaron's death upset you that much?"

"It does upset me, but not in the way you think," Cora answered cryptically. "And you're right, I'm not okay. In fact, I started to see a psychiatrist a couple of years ago."

"Oh," Ruth uttered. "I'm sorry."

"No, don't be. In fact, it's probably been one of the best things I've ever done. He actually has me examining my life for the first time. Imagine that!" She chuckled ironically. "And he has me looking back at the past, and he's trying to get me to deal with a lot of the issues that I simply chose to ignore at the time." Cora paused and took a deep, exaggerated breath. "It's hard to drag it all up again, but

I guess I'm going to have to. You have to bring it up and then walk through it—that's what Dr. Whitman says, anyway." She stopped and looked at Ruth as if she were thinking seriously and analyzing what she wanted to say next. "And lately we've been talking about you," she finally got out.

"Me?" Ruth replied with a shocked look on her face.

"I meant it when I said that you've been the most important person in my life, and Dr. Whitman is helping me see that now. He's trying to help me overcome all those things that happened in my childhood." Cora stopped talking abruptly, as if she might have said something that she regretted, and she pulled her hands back and seemed to somehow disconnect.

"What do you mean by all the things that happened in your childhood?" Ruth asked. "What are you talking about? Are you talking about Aaron?"

"No, no," Cora replied, then looked painfully at her sister. "When we were children, did you feel safe?" she asked with a depth of sincerity that Ruth had not seen before.

"What do you mean?"

"I always just felt so afraid as a child," Cora began as tears started to roll down her face. "I think Mom tried to protect me, and I guess she did the best she could." Cora stopped and looked out across the large dining room at the rows of empty tables. "I guess she tried to protect me," she uttered again, half under her breath, and then looked back down at her trembling hands.

"Protect you from what?" Ruth asked, feeling as if some missing part of the puzzle was being omitted.

"Oh, everything," Cora replied, wiping the tears from her face. She looked back up at her sister. "It's all water under the bridge now, anyway. Isn't that what Daddy would always say, water under the bridge? That's water under the bridge now," she repeated mockingly.

"Ugh, I can still hear him saying it!" Ruth chimed in. "That, and failure's not an option!" she added with a short laugh.

"Oh yes," Cora rejoined. "Failure is *not* an option," she repeated jokingly.

"And remember, he always called you *Daddy's* little girl," Ruth stated as she relaxed again, feeling that her sister's mood was lifting.

"Oh god, don't remind me!" Cora volleyed back. "If I never hear that phrase again, it'll be too soon."

"But you really were his favorite, you know," Ruth replied with a more serious tone in her voice. "Lawrence and I always noticed that. Believe me, you got away with a lot more than we ever did!"

"Well, being *Daddy's* little girl is not always such a good thing," Cora responded, sounding a little cryptic.

"What do you mean by that?" Ruth asked, again feeling that her sister was being deliberately evasive and leaving something out.

"Oh, it doesn't matter now. It's way too late." Cora bowed her head again, as if all the wind had been taken out of her. "Water under the bridge! Water under the bridge," she repeated as tears continued to roll down her cheeks.

Suddenly, Ruth felt an overpowering sense of closeness to her sister that she had not felt for years, and all the trivial worries and petty thoughts over the past few days seemed like a thing of the past. As she gazed at her sister sitting by her side, she wanted to say something, wanted to express exactly how she felt, but the words would not come forth, the chasm brought on by years of separation too large to forge, and the two of them just sat silently.

"Mom," Regina said as she walked back up to the table. "Mom!" she repeated a little louder. "I need the check for the minister, and the ladies are ready to get out of here." She was standing behind the two women and was peering down on them. "What have you all been talking about over here?" she asked playfully. "You two look like you've seen a ghost!"

"Oh, we've just been catching up," Ruth replied. She turned her head and looked up at her daughter. "And maybe, just maybe, chasing a few ghosts away in the process too."

Part 2

And Ruth the Moabitess said to Naomi, "Let me go the fields and pick up the leftover grain behind anyone in whose eyes I find favor." Naomi said to her, "Go ahead my daughter." So she went out and began to glean in the fields behind the harvesters.

—Ruth 2:2–3

CHAPTER

7

The sun was shining through the back windows of the three-story Victorian home that Peniscott Whitman and his wife, Flora, had owned for over twenty years, and although they had poured a great deal of money into the "aging beauty," as Flora always affectionately called it, the top floor was still in its original 1870 form; but the rest of the home in the old Lafayette Square area had been painstakingly renovated to bring it back to its original grandeur, with the addition of all the modern-day conveniences. The ground where the house sat had originally been a common pasture for village livestock outside the city of St. Louis and had been put up for sale in 1835 to force out encampments of criminals who would rob and attack local travelers. The newly formed neighborhood had been named after the famous Marquis de La Fayette, who had visited the city on his famous tour of the United States in 1824. The Whitman house was on a cul-de-sac on Benton Place, a street named after the state's famous senator, Thomas Hart Benton, and was in easy walking distance to Lafayette Park, which had the honor of being the oldest park west of the Mississippi.

"I'm looking at the paper right now!" Dr. Whitman bellowed into the telephone. "There's a picture of Highway 40 just disappearing into what looks like a gigantic lake," he went on with great enthusiasm. The doctor had just opened the morning *Post Dispatch* and had read the headline, 'Flood of '93 Continues—Valmeyer Underwater,' and was perusing a series of local pictures from around the two-state area that gave absolute documentation to the flood's unprecedented devastation.

"Yes," the doctor went on, his voice rising a half-octave, "and Valmeyer is where Alfred and Thale would stop and rest on their

69

rides over there. I even went over there with them one time. And from what I can tell from these pictures, even parts of the main bluff road are under!"

A long pause occurred as the doctor continued to page through the *Post*.

"Well, the worst is still yet to come, because from what I've read, the thaw's not even done up north," he finally responded, taking off his rather-thick reading glasses. "So what's the latest on my brother's case?" he asked as he tucked the readers into his shirt pocket and rubbed the red spots on the bridge of his nose. "So you have no leads at all, then?" the doctor asked, unhappy with the response. Dr. Whitman grabbed his crutches, got up, and went to look out the back window, as if he might have heard something that needed his attention, the phone precariously pinched under his chin. "He's back in the hospital. They had to redo his hip replacement, and he's in physical therapy, but no timeline yet on when he can go back to work." The doctor paused and switched his weight to under his arms and grabbed the phone with his right hand.

"And I think he's still severely depressed over the death of Thale. What a tragic thing this has all turned out to be." Dr. Whitman continued to stare out the window and just nodded. "Okay," he finally replied, "just keep me abreast of any changes. I keep getting calls from people asking if I know anything. And you guys need to find Thale's killer!" he added dramatically. "Okay, bye now," he ended and then hobbled back and sat down in his reading chair again.

Just as the doctor was picking the paper back up, his wife, Flora, came in from the backyard, a pair of dirty garden gloves in her hand. "Who was that on the phone?" she asked, stomping her feet on the doormat.

"It was Detective Rich. She was giving me my annual update on Thale's case."

"And?" Flora chimed in.

"The same old story. I'm sure the investigation is colder than ever."

"Oh, that reminds me," Flora chirped as she raised a finger in the air. "I want to stop and get some snacks to take over to Alfred when we visit tomorrow. He called and said he was thoroughly sick of the hospital food," she added and then laughed. Dr. Whitman glanced at his watch and then frantically started grabbing for his crutches. "Dear Lord, I have to go! I have Cora Lasciter coming in at ten!"

Dr. Whitman's office was only a ten-minute drive from his home on Benton Place, and it lay just outside the Lafayette Square boundaries, in an older strip mall that had been recently renovated. Although he had wanted to have a home office, the historical guide-lines that had been imposed on the Victorian neighborhood specifi-cally restricted in-home businesses, a constraint that his wife secretly embraced wholeheartedly. His office was neatly decorated with a dark-wood wainscoting around the entire room, with a light-blue striped wallpaper above that, and a composition drop ceiling that somehow didn't seem to fit the aesthetic of the rest of the workplace. A large aquarium, which put out a soothing "gurgle" across the space, had been positioned to the side of the couch where patients would sit, an addition that seemed to somehow calm the nerves of anxious clients who found themselves sitting across from the doctor.

Dr. Whitman was seated in his brown leather chair, with his crutches propped up against the arm, when Cora Lasciter walked into the office. She was dressed in a navy-blue suit with a matching pillbox hat, with a light-colored silk blouse. Her face, which was typ-ically flawlessly made up, looked tired, and small bags had started to form under her emerald-green eyes; and for the first time in her life, her appearance might have actually matched the age on her driver's license, a thought that entered the doctor's mind as he first glanced up as she entered the room.

"Ah, Cora, good to see you again," Dr. Whitman started out as he keenly watched his patient take a seat on the office couch. "You've missed the last couple of sessions, and I was beginning to worry about you," he added and then jotted a few notes in a leather-bound notebook that he used during all his sessions.

Cora placed her purse on the floor in front of the couch and crossed her legs uneasily. "I know," she responded self-consciously. "But I did remember my journal!" she chimed in girlishly, hoping to move past the fact that she had missed her last two sessions. She reached down and pulled a small loose-leaf binder from her purse, showed it to the doctor, and then placed it on the couch next to her.

"That's good, and we'll get to your journaling exercise," the doctor responded, looking up from his notebook, "but I want to talk about what's been going on first. I was worried about you." He leaned back and slipped his reading glasses on the end of his nose.

"I know, I know," Cora responded, sounding almost like a misbehaved child. "I've been out in Ox Bend with my sister for the past few weeks."

"Is this the same sister who raised your baby?" the doctor asked, cocking his head to the right, something he always did when he changed the direction of the dialogue.

Cora locked her fingers and restlessly placed them around her crossed legs. "Yes," she answered nervously. "That's my only sister, Ruth."

"How have things been going between you two?" the doctor asked, peering over the top of his glasses. "Talk a little about that."

"Actually, much better than I ever thought possible, considering all that's happened," she replied as she nervously started swinging her crossed leg. "And we've actually been keeping in touch a lot, and I really think we're starting to rebuild our relationship again." She paused and placed her hand on her journal. "And I've been writing about it a lot in my journal too," she interjected. "I'm trying to show her in my actions, like you suggested, how sorry I am for the way things transpired, and I really think she's starting to see me differently, to forgive me."

"Well, giving up your child was not an easy thing for you either," Dr. Whitman reminded her.

"Oh, I know," Cora replied quickly. "And Ruth is aware of that. In fact, when Aaron died, I think she was more worried about me than herself." Cora paused and looked off to the side of the room. "I just feel like she understands what I had to go through, more than anybody else."

"What makes you feel that way?"

"Well, I think she loved Aaron more than anything in the world, and she was devastated when he died. And yet with all that she was going through, she still seemed more concerned about me than her-self." Cora paused again and looked back at the doctor. "That's kind of the way she's always been. She always seems to put others before herself."

"So you've been keeping in touch with her regularly?"

"Yes. In fact, I've been going out there every other weekend." Cora stopped and pulled out a cigarette from her purse and just ner-vously held it between her fingers. "Did I tell you that our mother is staying out there now with her?"

"No. I remember you telling me about the house fire, but not that she had been moved. How do you feel about that change?"

"Well, I knew that it was inevitable. I knew that she couldn't be there in that big house by herself anymore." Cora paused and leaned forward, her elbows resting on her crossed legs. "But I hate that my sister, Ruth, has once again stepped in and taken responsibility for everything."

"And what do you think you could have done?"

"I don't know. I wanted to put her in the same home with my father—I thought it might be good that they would at least be closer together again—but Ruth didn't want to do that. She wanted to try to take care of her herself."

"And you didn't want her to take care of your mother?"

"Well, no. That's not it," Cora answered, sounding a little frus-trated. "I just didn't want her to have to take on that responsibility as well." Cora paused and looked at Dr. Whitman and frowned. "I was just trying to protect *her.*"

"Protect her from what?"

"From once again having to shoulder all the responsibility of everything," Cora fired back as she leaned back into the couch and looked up at the ceiling.

"And what did your mother want?"

"Oh, I think she was happy to go out there and stay with Ruth. She pushed back a little at first about leaving her home, but I think that she's very comfortable out there—and she made it clear to me that she didn't really want to be around Daddy anymore—and in some ways I can understand that." Cora looked back down at the doctor. "And Ruth has this huge third-floor apartment above the funeral home that has a large guest suite. So Mom has her own bathroom and everything. And Ruth has two grown children out there, and I guess they help out too." Cora stopped and grabbed her lighter and finally lit her cigarette. "Nasty habit," she added nervously as she got up and grabbed an ashtray and then placed it on her lap as she sat back down. "I keep trying to quit, but I can't give up all my corruptions at once," she added, smoke exhaling on each syllable.

"So it bothers you that your sister is the one taking care of your mother?" Dr. Whitman asked, hoping to keep the conversation going.

"No." Cora paused and took a long drag off her cigarette and then tilted her head back and blew the smoke into the air. "Maybe a little," she qualified. "She always seems to do the right thing, and me...well, I seem to always do the wrong thing." She stopped talking and looked back down at the doctor. "Why am I always the bad one? Why can't I be more like my sister?"

"So you're upset with yourself because you didn't want to take care of your mother?"

"Yes!" Cora replied sharply.

"Well, let me ask you this, Have you ever taken care of an older person or an invalid before?"

"No," Cora responded.

"And so what makes you think that you'd be able to do it now?"

"But I didn't even try," Cora responded with a tone of disgust. "And Ruth, she just took it on without giving it a thought."

"So you want to be like your sister, then?"

"Yes!" Cora yelled. "Yes," she repeated. "Why can't I be more like her? Why can't I...I don't know...see the world the way she sees it?" Dr. Whitman leaned forward in his chair and looked closely at Cora sitting nervously across from him. "Why do you want to be like your sister?" he asked with an inquisitive look on his face. "Why can't you just be you? Why can't you just be the best version of you that you can be?" Cora's shoulders slumped, and she crushed out her cigarette and leaned back into the couch and stared up at the ceiling again, as if she had completely disconnected from the conversation. "Everyone has their own personal strengths and weaknesses," the doctor continued, "and the goal is to find out what yours are, not your sister's. You need to look for ways to help your mother in your own way." Cora sat motionless and said nothing, and the doctor just leaned back into his chair and didn't say a word either.

After a few minutes, Cora sat up and looked at the doctor, and her eyes started to fill with tears.

"What's going on, Cora?" the doctor finally asked, breaking the silence and sensing that something was going on. "What aren't you telling me?"

"Ruth's husband, Richard..." Cora stopped, as if she didn't want to go on. "He died yesterday morning."

The doctor took off his readers and placed them on his lap and leaned forward again. "I am so sorry to hear that, Cora," he responded sympathetically. "What was the cause of death?"

"He was diagnosed with pancreatic cancer around the first of the year, and he just went downhill almost immediately. And by the time they discovered what it was, it had already metastasized throughout his body, and it was too late. So the only thing that Ruth could do was to try and keep him comfortable, help him through the process." Cora paused and crossed her arms tightly. "And I've just been trying to help her through it the best I can."

"Well, I sure do hate to hear that," the doctor repeated in condolence.

"And now she has to bury her husband, and just barely three years since she buried Aaron!" Cora exclaimed, shaking her head.

Dr. Whitman cocked his head to the right again and looked closely at Cora. "Why didn't you tell me about Richard's death when we first started the session?"

"I don't know," Cora answered quickly. She stopped for a moment, as if thinking of exactly what to say next. "I guess I just didn't want to talk about him," she finally confessed.

"Not even now?" Dr. Whitman questioned back.

"Especially now!" Cora fired back.

"You have this pattern of trying to avoid any discussion about Richard, even when I deliberately bring up the topic."

Cora uncrossed her legs and nervously placed her hands rigidly on the couch at her side and looked over at the aquarium. "I know," she whispered.

"Have you ever told your sister about Richard?" the doctor probed.

"No," Cora replied, looking back at the doctor.

"So how do you feel about that?"

"I feel terrible," Cora started out, sounding panicked. "I feel terrible about it. But what good is it going to do to bring it all up now?" Cora stopped abruptly, as if some overpowering realization had just taken ahold of her, and she looked back at the fish tank. "What if it ruins all the progress that we've made these past few years?"

"You don't think she would forgive you?"

"Would you?" Cora shot back, sounding half-angered and half-disgusted. "It's all my fault, anyway. I'm the bad one. I'm the one to blame for it all!" she cried, tears starting to run down her face.

"Cora," the doctor started out with a distinct focus, "we always end up here, with you blaming yourself for everything. And blame is not going to change anything or help you in any way. You carry all this burden and guilt around with you. You blame yourself for everything, and you think that all your problems are going to go away by just ignoring them. But despite popular myth, time doesn't heal anything! And until you unburden yourself with all this, until you finally just lay everything down and just tell the truth, you're never going to get past it. You're never going to heal emotionally."

Cora said nothing and just turned her head and stared at the fish tank.

"You're like those fish in that tank," the doctor went on. "Stuck in some little self-contained world. You've imprisoned yourself in your own world of guilt."

"Oh, I know, I know," Cora responded with emotions that didn't seem to quite match the words. "But how do I just let it all go? All these masks that I've been carrying around, all these lies, how can I just let it go?" She paused, and an intense sincerity came over her, and she looked back at the doctor. "What if all I am is my secrets? What if the mask is really me?" she added as she bowed her head and reached for another cigarette.

CHAPTER 8

Ruth and her lifelong friend, Ruthie, were standing in the main bedroom suite of the third-floor apartment of the Clarkson Funeral Home, and Ruthie was attempting to zip up the back of a black dress, made of cotton challis rayon, that Ruth hadn't worn since her son's funeral three years earlier. The bright sunlight that was pouring in the back windows revealed a thin layer of dust over the usually spotless bedroom furniture, and half-empty pill bottles, extra towels, buckets, and boxes of rubber gloves were scattered haphazardly around the perimeter of the room, mute remnants of the isolated world of advancing age and unforgiving illness. The couple's five-foot-high cherry headboard, which they had acquired at an estate sale during the 1989 renovation, had been dismantled and stored in the basement along with the mattress, springs, and frame, and an Invacare adjustable hospital bed had been parked in its spot, next to a portable toilet and oxygen machine. One of the small twin beds that Ruth's grandchildren would often use when they stayed overnight had been taken from the middle guest room and had been placed alongside the hospital bed for Ruth to use during the final days of Richard's battle. As she had told one of the women from the Dorcas Society shortly after he died, "At least the battle is over," a phrase she distinctly remembered her bother, Lawrence, using when Aaron had died just three years earlier.

And even though the battle was over for Richard, that certainly wasn't the case for Ruth. The vigil at her husband's bedside had taken its toll on the now-fifty-eight-year-old widow, and even her health, which had always been considered above normal, was now showing signs of decline. Only three weeks before Richard's initial diagnosis, her own nonagenarian mother, who was starting to show signs of dementia, had set the kitchen in the family home in Webster Groves on fire, an event that significantly damaged both the kitchen and the adjacent dining room. Afraid to leave the old woman alone, and unwilling to park her mother in a nursing care facility, Ruth opened up her home, and Emma Saroh was situated in one of the guest bedrooms that had a full bath attached, just down the hall from the master suite. Within only a few months of her arrival, Richard's failing health and ultimate cancer diagnosis had propelled Ruth to the role of dual caretaker, and much like her biblical namesake, she made no attempt to back away from the endless day-to-day work and responsibility that the situation presented. Family members, on numerous occasions, had suggested that Ruth bring in a part-time professional care assistant to help with all that was required, but Ruth steadfastly insisted that "family should be cared for by family," as thoughts of her old aunt Matilda ran through her mind; and she single-handedly cared for her dying husband until hospice was brought in and provided some much-needed assistance.

"I just don't think this is going to work," Ruthie grunted as she unsuccessfully tugged at the zipper of Ruth's black dress again. Ruth walked to a full-length mirror that was on the inside of a closet door and looked at herself from top to bottom and then turned and looked at the back. "Oh, I hate this!" she exclaimed, her voice filled with frustration. "I was hoping to wear this tomorrow."

"Here," Ruthie chimed in, holding up a dark navy-blue dress with capped sleeves that was pushed to the back of the closet. "I like this one better, anyway. And you can wear that beige cashmere sweater over it if it's too cold."

"Oh yeah, I forgot about that one," Ruth replied with a renewed sense of optimism. "I bought that to go to Allison's mother's funeral." She walked over and examined the blue dress that Ruthie was holding up, felt the material between her fingers, and then stood back and looked at it again. "I guess you're right," Ruth relinquished with a sigh. "This looks like our only option." She walked back to the mirror and took off the black dress, exposing a full slip, and then held it up to her face and breathed in heavily. "You know, I wore this to

Aaron's funeral," she remarked pensively, staring into the mirror. "It's funny how things can trigger your memory," she added prophetically as she walked across the room and sat down on the side of the twin bed.

Ruthie laid the blue dress over the railing of the hospital bed and took a seat next to her. "You still miss him that much?" she asked as she grabbed Ruth by the hand. "It's been three years."

"Oh, more than you know," Ruth replied wistfully. "I guess the loss of a child is a pain that never really goes away. And now Richard's death has brought it all back up again." She paused, and her mood seemed to lighten a little. "I was cleaning out a drawer in the main guest room last week—I was making room for some of Mom's stuff—and I came across this little plaque that he made for me, probably about when he was around seven or so." Ruth paused and looked out the large back window. "It was a Bible verse that he had written out by hand, and then he had laminated it on this piece of wood. It must have been something that he made at Bible school." She paused a moment, as if trying to remember the exact words. "It said, 'Where you go, I will go, and where you stay, I will stay.'"

"That's from the book of Ruth," Ruthie replied, squeezing her friend's hand a little tighter. "That child knew more than anyone ever gave him credit for," she added thoughtfully and then chuckled.

"Boy, ain't that the truth," Ruth replied as she lifted up her friend's hand in the air and gave it a shake. "You know, come to think of it, when he was little, I used to read to him from the Bible all the time, and whenever I asked him what book he wanted me to read from, he always said 'Ruth!' Now, that was probably because that was my name, but still, he seemed to love that story."

"Oh, I think he was smarter than most people ever gave him credit for," Ruthie chimed in.

"I think in some ways he was smarter than any of us!" Ruth responded adamantly. Ruthie nodded and then reached down for her handbag. "You know, I thought about him, too, a couple weeks ago," she started out, rummaging through her purse. "I was reading this book at the library about Aaron and Moses, and there were pictures of this small white mosque on top of Mount Hor that was supposedly built on the place where Aaron was buried. It was really fascinating, and of course, the book talked about his life and his relationship with Moses, and I found this Bible verse from Numbers. Here, I wrote it down to show you." She finally found what she was searching for, pulled out a slip of paper, and then started to read. "And when all the congregation saw that Aaron had perished, all the house of Israel wept for Aaron thirty days."

"Oh, I love that," Ruth replied. "What book did you say that was from?"

"It's from Numbers. Numbers 20, verse 29."

Ruth took the slip of paper and studied it closely. "I always loved the story of Aaron in the Old Testament," she stated after a few moments of silence. "And that's why I picked that name. He always just seemed to be very human to me. He made mistakes, he stumbled many times, just like we all do, but his heart was always aimed in the right direction. And he always, through it all, stood by his brother. He was always loyal to Moses." Ruth paused and let out a small laugh. "And Richard's family wanted to name him William or Edward or the names of one of those kings of England, but I stood my ground!"

"Oh, so that's where the Charles came from!"

"Yes, I guess I couldn't win them all," Ruth joked back. "And if I remember my history, the first Charles didn't fare too well!" Ruth joked, and both women let out a large laugh.

"Now," Ruth proclaimed with a new sense of determination, "where's this blue dress you want me to try and squeeze into?" Ruthie pointed over toward the hospital bed. "Over there." She motioned. Ruth grabbed the dress and walked back to the mirror and held it up against her body. "So this is it," she proclaimed while checking the length of the hemline. Just as she was ready to try it on, the door swung open, and her mother, Emma, entered into the room.

Emma Naomi Saroh had originally started her life in Germany as Emma Dorthea Naomi Schmidt, a surname that was derived from the German word *Schmied*, which meant blacksmith or metalworker, a name that suited her middle-class upbringing, and she had immigrated to the United States at the age of nine to live with an aunt who had come to St. Louis just a few years earlier. As she had often detailed, she entered the country through the port of New Orleans after leaving her hometown of Detmold in the principality of Lippe. The old woman, who had always had an interest in history, had at many family gatherings narrated that her hometown had been formed out of land acquired by the destruction of the Duchy of Saxony following the demise of Henry the Lion in 1180, a history lesson that Emma had even researched on one of her three trips back to her home country. From New Orleans, she had traveled up the Mississippi River and settled in the bustling city of St. Louis. Although her integration into her new country had been complete, she would still, after over seventy years of American citizenship, lapse into German when she got excited or angry. One of her favorite sayings, which she reeled off at any provocation, was "Goldene jahre mein arsch," which when translated meant "golden years my ass," a statement that delighted her grandchildren and embarrassed her children in equal measure. Her advancing years had brought about countless infirmities, the worst being the beginning signs of Alzheimer's, but she was still able to move around on a very limited basis with the use of a walker, and she required attending at all meals, bathroom visits, and bedtime.

"Cora. Cora!" the old woman yelled out as she plodded her way into the room with her walker. Ruth, always worried about her mother falling, jumped up and stood beside her. "Cora's not here!" she yelled back to her mother, who had lost almost 50 percent of her hearing. "Cora's not coming until tonight, remember?" she added as she placed her arm around her mother for added support.

"Oh, that's right," the old woman acknowledged. "You did tell me that, didn't you?" She sluggishly crossed the room, her daughter at her side, and then took a seat in one of the dressing chairs that had been placed next to the hospital bed.

"You remember my friend Ruthie, don't you?" Ruth asked her mother, moving the walker to the side of the room.

"Oh yes!" the old woman spoke up as she precariously settled into the chair. "She married a Kaermor, didn't she?" she queried, as if checking herself.

"Yes, that's right, Mother!" Ruth exclaimed, looking at Ruthie with a shocked expression, glad to see her mother having one of her more coherent days. "You first met her when Regina was born. Remember, she and Clyde came down to the hospital to visit."

"If you say so," Emma countered with a befuddled-looking smile on her face. She reached up and tugged at a loose-fitting shawl that was sliding off her shoulders.

Ruthie walked up to the old woman and reached down and patted her on the hand. "Oh, that's been so long ago nobody can remember that!" Ruthie stated, hoping to lessen Emma's embarrassment. "It's sure nice to see you again," she enunciated loudly. "How do you like living here in Ox Bend?"

"Where?" Emma countered.

"Ox Bend. How do you like living here in Ox Bend?"

"Oh, it's all right. My life is confined to two rooms now, anyway. I guess I might as well be here as anywhere else!"

"And is Ruth treating you all right?" she asked jokingly. She looked up and winked at Ruth still standing by her mother's side.

"Whatever you say, dear," Emma answered and then looked away, a response that had become her go-to reply when she either didn't hear or didn't understand what was being said.

"She's doing fine," Ruth assured her friend. "You like it here, don't you, Mother?" she joked as she patted her mother on the arm.

"Well, I'll let you guys catch up," Ruthie spoke up, grabbing her purse and making her way for the door. "My daughter is dropping off one of the triplets this afternoon. She says they prefer a man-to-man defense over a zone!"

Ruth waved goodbye to her dear friend as she left the room and then sat down in the second dressing chair next to her mother. "Mom, can I get you anything?" she asked as she patted her mother on the arm again.

"No, I'm good now. Just sit here by me for a while," the old woman retorted. "Tell me, how are the plans going? Has everything been made ready?"

"Yes, I've pretty much turned over everything to John and Vickie, and we're planning on doing a lot of things just the way we did for Aaron. I remember how much Richard liked his coffin, so I got the same one for him, and I let Regina and Vickie take care of all the flowers and the guest book and the pallbearers and all that stuff. And I think Regina's girls are going to sing again." Ruth paused, as if some important fact had just entered her mind. "Oh, that's right, you didn't make it to Aaron's funeral, did you?" She paused again, and her brow furrowed as she thought back to the funeral three years earlier. "That's right, Daddy had pneumonia, and I think you were half-sick too. It was a beautiful service, though. You would have approved," she added. She jumped up and pulled her mother's shawl back up around her shoulders.

"So Cora is coming tonight?" Emma asked as Ruth retook her seat.

"Yes, but it's going to be later on. Highway 40 is underwater, so they have to go way down to the interstate to get around it."

"What!" the old woman bellowed. "Forty's underwater? Where?"

"That whole stretch there in the old Gumbo Bottoms along the Missouri is all underwater."

"Oh mein gott," Emma retorted, lapsing into German. "Will Cora be able to make it?"

"She will. It's just going to take longer, that's all," Ruth said reassuringly.

The two women sat quietly for a while as Ruth listened to a pair of cardinals chattering just outside the bedroom window. "Is Cora here?" Emma yelled out again, as if she had just come out of a nap.

"No, Mother," Ruth answered with the patience of Job. She got up and opened the top drawer of the cherry dresser and pulled out the little plaque that Aaron had made. "Here, look at this, Mom. Aaron made this when he was seven."

"Aaron made this?" she asked as she took ahold of the small keepsake. She held it up in front of her face, lifted her glasses up on her forehead, and tried to read it.

"Yes. I came across it when I was cleaning out the dresser in your room. It's a Bible verse from the book of Ruth," her daughter qualified. The old woman intensely studied the small memento and then started to rub the sides of the object with her paper-thin hands.

"You know, it wasn't all her fault," she let out as the plaque slipped from her hands and fell to the floor. Ruth quickly jumped up and grabbed the precious memento off the floor.

"Whose fault?" she asked as she looked up at her mother.

"The whole Aaron thing!" Emma yelled out. "It wasn't all Cora's fault. I blame Richard the most!" she snapped.

Ruth stood up and peered down at her mother. "What wasn't Cora's fault?" she asked. "What are you talking about, Mom?"

"The whole mess," Emma whispered and then stopped. She frantically started to rummage through her housecoat pockets. "Where's my Kleenex?" she mumbled, sounding a million miles away.

Ruth sat back down in the overstuffed dressing chair, laid her head back into the soft upper cushion, and stared up at the old tin ceiling that had somehow survived since 1888.

"Is Cora here yet?" the old woman asked yet again.

"No, Cora isn't here yet, Mother," Ruth replied softly as she laid her head back and closed her eyes.

CHAPTER
9

The funeral arrangements were all in order when Ruth came downstairs to do her final check, a task that she and her husband had been performing for the past thirty-plus years. The old Pembroke Renroth grandfather clock with gilded-metal foliate face and Chippendale-style mahogany case that Werner Clarkson had shipped over from England had just chimed out five times, and she found the viewing room completely deserted. Only a few things had changed in the funeral home since Aaron had been laid out three years earlier: the hallway leading into the main viewing room had been repainted a rose-colored beige with eggshell finish, the main solid-oak showroom bier, which had been in continuous use since 1888, had started to crack down the center and had been exchanged with the one in the smaller viewing room, and a newer, more up-to-date women's bathroom that could accommodate up to four had been added toward the back of the smaller viewing chamber.

Regina Battenhorst, who had actually been at Richard's side when he passed away, and her two daughters bore the brunt of the important personal tasks necessary to move the funeral service forward, giving Ruth a much-need break. Vickie Harrison, who had gradually assumed more and more of the office duties, had arranged for the embalming, ordered the necessary death certificates, published the obituary, ordered the guest book, called the company that prepared the grave site, and under the direction of Ruth herself, ordered the casket and flowers. Regina, worried about her mother's health, had actually stayed at the funeral home in one of the guest bedrooms until after the body had been completely prepared for burial, and had even helped her mother select the tie, shirt, and suit that would be needed for the showing. She had also helped with the music selection, offering up her daughters to sing another duet, and had acted as a buffer between her mother and the day-to-day challenges of keeping the business going.

The number of flowers that lined the front of the room on each side of the casket was considerable, and they went a long way in expressing the small town's bereavement at the loss of one of its leading citizens; and at the request of Ruth, a large amount of money had also been collected in lieu of flowers, all the money earmarked for the Lippstadt Church and Cemetery Fund, which subsidized the upkeep of the old church and graveyard. Because he had been born and raised in the small town, there wasn't a resident who didn't know the name of Richard Clarkson. His work with the city, the local chamber of commerce, and the church and his philanthropic endeavors over the years had placed him in high esteem with many of the townspeople, and four large poster boards, covered in photos sent in by local residents that documented the town's appreciation, were placed at the entranceway to the main viewing chamber.

As Ruth walked up to the casket, she found her husband of thirty-seven years, dressed in his dark-blue suit, lying peacefully, his reading glasses, which he had been perpetually searching for his entire adult life, placed in the grasp of his large folded hands. The three surviving Clarkson children had ordered a small heart-shaped wreath, made of red roses and white carnations, that read, "Dearest Father," and it was pinned on the inside of the coffin by his head. She reached down and softly touched the embroidered satin squares of the casket lining and then reached up and straightened his lapel; she felt the soft worsted wool between her fingers and could smell the subtle scent of the carnations and roses wafting down from the heart-shaped wreath, and her mind began to drift back to the origin of it all. She remembered their first meeting on the campus of St. Louis University, the awkward nervousness and innocence of their first date, and the overpowering carnal attraction that had originally consumed her. She remembered the boundless energy that Richard had initially brought into her life, the youthful visage of unrestrained vitality and self-assurance, that precious, carefree spirit of youth, unbounded by the gravitational pulls of obligation and burden, untouched by the remorseless vagaries of life itself. She could see him standing in his formal suit at the altar on their wedding day, she could see his sanguine smile, she could almost hear his original laughter, a rasping, guttural sound that sometimes seemed to have no origin, and she wondered how it all had slipped away. It seemed that the passage of time, the very act of entropy, like the relentless pounding of waves on a shore, had levied an exacting toll, had slowly worn away the sharp, crisp edges of youth and promise, and had left them both exhausted, but on very different shores. Was this the fate of every marriage? she wondered. Or was this just the cost of age itself? She stood back and looked at the long rows of flowers, all emblems of the spring of life: orange and white roses, yellow gladiolas, purple daisies, pink carnations, white chrysanthemums, and purple asters that surrounded the bier, the fragrance almost overpowering. Millay's prophetic words, which her son had recited just three years ago, drifted through her mind as she stood over her husband's body: *Into the darkness they go; the wise and lovely, crowned with lilies and laurel they go; but I am not resigned.*

Suddenly, as if by some divine intervention, Richard Jr. walked up and placed his arms around his mother and gave her a gentle, loving squeeze. "I thought I'd find you here," he whispered in his youthful way. He turned her around and kissed her tenderly on the forehead.

"When did you get here?" Ruth gasped as she grabbed him by the arms, pushed him back a step, and then looked him up and down.

"I just got in. I would have been here sooner, but I had to go around and come out 70. It's a mess out here now."

"Oh, I heard that," Ruth replied, her spirits rising. "They say the whole Gumbo Bottoms are underwater!" she added animatedly.

"Yes, and it's even worse over on the east side," Richard Jr. reported.

"Yes, the papers are calling it a five-hundred-year flood," Ruth volleyed back, then smiled up at her son. "So how are you? Are you hungry? Do you want me to fix you something to eat?" she rattled off before Richard Jr. could say a single word.

"No, Mother! No! I'm fine. I grabbed something on the way out."

"Well, there's tons of food in the fridge. So many people have been dropping off stuff. I can sure heat something up for you."

"Mom," Richard said calmly, "relax. I don't need anything to eat."

"Well, if you change your mind," Ruth added in a motherly way. "Mom and I will never get it all eaten."

"So everything is ready to go, then?" Richard Jr. asked thoughtfully, a nervous tension etched in his voice. He glanced around the old viewing parlor, where he had spent so much of his childhood, and then looked back at his mother. "Everything looks good," he added reassuringly, remembering his father's penchant for perfection. "I'm glad you finally painted the entrance hallway. It looks much better—a much better color." He finally looked down at his father and paused as a strange look came over his face, almost as if he were seeing him for the first time. "It's always weird, that initial look at the body after someone has died," he whispered. "You see someone your whole life, and then the day comes when you take your last look." He paused and took a deep breath and seemed to be overcome with sentiment. "Nothing lasts forever, does it?"

"Yes, I know," Ruth responded pensively, sensing her son's fragile emotional state. "And no matter how many times you do it, it never gets any easier," she added prophetically. Ruth again looked up at her son and sensed his uneasiness. "What is that line from Hamlet?" she asked, hoping to distract him. "You know, when they're digging in the graveyard and they find Yorick's skull. 'Alas, poor Yorick!'" Ruth started to recite. "'I knew him, Horatio, a fellow of infinite jest, of most excellent fancy,'" she added with a smile.

"'He hath bore me on his back a thousand times,'" Richard Jr. picked up as he looked at his mother's face, "'and now how abhorred in my imagination it is!'" He paused and looked back down at his father and fell silent.

"You know, for all of Hamlet's brooding and sulking on the subject of death," Ruth went on thoughtfully, "I think that was the first time that he really faced it. He had always talked about it in all his rambling soliloquies, but it was just some intangible thing, some topic of discussion, but seeing that skull of his old friend Yorick suddenly made it all very real."

"I guess that's kind of how I feel now too," Richard Jr. replied as the point of his mother's comments hit home. "You know, I spent the first eighteen years of my life right here in this funeral home, in this very room. And I was surrounded by death and dead bodies that whole time. You'd think I would be used to it by now." He paused briefly and let out an uneasy sigh. "But I guess it's always different when it's someone you loved."

"So you did love him, then?" Ruth asked hopefully as she placed her arm around her son.

"Yeah, but I don't think I always *liked* him," Richard Jr. replied candidly. "I didn't like the kind of man he was. I didn't like the way that he treated you."

"But that's just it," Ruth jumped in. "You just said it. He was just a man. Burdened with the same realities and weaknesses that all men face, that all of us face." She reached into the casket and placed her hand on his shoulder. "Whatever shortcomings he might have had, I came to accept them a long time ago, and I'm sure he accepted mine as well. And my forgiveness, my letting go of everything, has done more for me than it ever did for him."

"But I don't know if I can ever forgive him, Mother," Richard Jr. whispered thoughtfully as he seemed to struggle with some deep inner conflict. "I just don't know."

"That's something that will come with time, Richie," Ruth consoled. She reached over and rubbed her son's back, and they both stood silently and just looked down at the body in the casket.

"He looks old, Mom," Richard Jr. finally said after a few moments.

"That's just the cancer, Richie."

"I know, but still, it looks like he's lost at least thirty pounds. And this suit looks like it's three sizes too big for him," he added. He leaned over the body and touched the lapel.

"I know," Ruth replied with a heavy tone of regret. "John tried his best to pin it all together in the back, but it was just too much material." She paused a moment, as if reliving some event from the past. "This was his favorite, though. I remember him jokingly telling me one day that this was the one that he wanted to be buried in." Ruth leaned forward and brushed the right sleeve of his suit coat. "Who knew it would all play out that way so soon."

Richard Jr.'s mood changed suddenly, and he grabbed his mother by the hand and looked her in the eye. "Mom, did you still *love* him?" he asked with a youthful innocence that cut right to his mother's heart.

Ruth, surprised by the question, thought for a moment before she answered. "I think I did," she finally replied tentatively. "But you have to understand that love between old people changes. It's tempered, it's not like when you're young, especially if you've been married a long time, like your father and I were." Ruth paused and looked down at her husband again. "And it was never the same after…" She stopped talking abruptly.

"After the affairs, you mean. Right?"

Ruth looked back at her son, surprised by the directness of his question. "Ah, so you knew about that?" she asked. She reached over and grabbed him by the hand and led him to one of the viewing couches on the front row.

"Of course I knew, Mother," Richard Jr. said as he took a seat next to his mother. "We all knew."

"I hate that you had to know about all that. I tried so hard to protect you kids from a lot of what went on."

"When did it all start?" Richard pressed.

Ruth sat quietly for a moment, as if deciding whether to answer truthfully or not. "Right from the start, actually," she finally answered straightforwardly with an embarrassed slant in her voice.

"Oh, Mom, that's terrible! I had no idea it had been going on for that long."

"Well, I never really knew for sure, but things just happened that made me suspect. I would get calls, and then there'd be nobody on the line. And then as the years went on, he made more and more of his trips out of town: conventions, fishing trips, and conferences. There was just this feeling that I got…I don't know."

"Like what?" Richard Jr. probed.

"Well, at first, I thought maybe it was just me feeling insecure, but as the years went on, I could just tell. I think he felt guilty about it, though, I really do, and he would overcompensate and try to make it up to me. And in some ways—and I know you probably won't understand this—I was actually sort of glad when he was gone."

"So why did you stay with him, then?" her son asked thoughtfully.

Ruth crossed her legs and then looked toward the coffin. "You know that we got married right after Richard graduated from college," she started out thoughtfully, "and he was really the first boy I ever dated, so I didn't really have much experience in that area." She paused a moment, and her tone of voice changed. "And marriage and family and my faith have always meant something to me," she added pensively. "And divorce back in those days was very different from today. It was not well received at all. And I knew that my parents would be opposed to any talk of any type of separation."

"What *did* Grandpa Saroh think of him?"

"Oh, a lot," Ruth uttered back half-jokingly. "I remember the day that I told him that Richard and I were planning on getting married. He sat me down and told me to think long and hard before I attached myself to a man like Richard. Those were his exact words, attached myself to a man *like* Richard. Maybe he had some insight that I didn't. I don't know."

"Or maybe it takes one to know one," Richard Jr. taunted.

"Ah, you may be onto something there!" Ruth countered with a laugh. "He just never really thought that Richard was good enough for me, I guess. Or maybe, as you say, he knew exactly what type of man he really was. And I listened to him, but I was just so much in love with Richard, and really, what else did I know? I had nothing to compare it to. It just seemed…" She paused, as if looking for just the right word. "Right. When I was with him it just seemed right. That's the only way I know how to explain it."

"What about Grandma?" her son asked, enthralled by his mother's heartfelt disclosure.

"Oh, my mother just wanted to get things settled. I think that's the exact word I heard her use on the phone when she was talking to her sister in New York a few weeks before the wedding, *settled.*"

"What did she mean by that?"

"Well, you have to understand that my mother thought that marriage was the only real option for a woman—that's just the way it was back then. And Cora was running wild at that time and definitely not settled, and Lawrence was off in his own world, and she just wanted me married and out of the way. Settled!" Ruth laughed under her breath and then went on. "So the night before the rehearsal dinner, she called me down to her bedroom to talk to me one last time before the wedding. We were living in that big house on Elm Street in Webster, and their bedroom was down on the main floor. And she told me that this was it, after tomorrow the die was set!"

"Wow, I've always heard about the famous mother-daughter prewedding talk," Richard Jr. responded with a smirk on his face. "I just never knew what actually transpired there."

"Oh, I'm sure no one has had a wedding talk like that before, or since," Ruth shot back. "And maybe she was just trying to warn me about the realities of married life! I don't know."

"So that's why you stayed with him?"

"I seriously thought about leaving during those first few years. But then before I knew it, Aaron came into the picture, and that just changed everything completely." Ruth stopped and looked closely at her son sitting beside her. "Aaron changed everything. He just transformed my life and gave me a new focus and a new purpose. And then your sister came along, and Charles, and then you, and time just moved on. And where would I go if I had left? What would I have done? I mean, things were different back in the sixties. And as I said, there was still a lot of stigma associated with divorce."

"Well, I would have left him!" Richard Jr. snapped defensively.

"You can't say that until you've been in the situation yourself." Ruth stopped and turned her body around so that she was almost directly facing her son. "You can't expect too much from people, Richie. We're all just human. Just like Aaron in the Bible."

"But to forgive infidelity!" Richard Jr. retorted.

Ruth paused and looked back up toward the casket and looked at the extended rows of flowers that flanked it on each side. "You know, infidelity in a marriage is a lot like the floodwaters that are out there now. You really don't hear it. You *know* that the water is rising, but you really can't actually see it happening. It just comes up more and more, ever so slowly, almost imperceptibly. And then all of a sudden you look around and everything's underwater and the damage is done."

Richard grabbed his mother's hands and looked her in the eyes. "'But a marriage, that began without harm, scatters into debris on the shore, and a friend from school drops cold on a rocky strand.'"

"Ah, Donald Hall. You understand more than you know," she added, patting her son on the leg. "So how does that end? Something about delicious and fitting?"

"'Let us stifle under mud at the pond's edge and affirm that it is fitting and delicious to lose everything.'"

CHAPTER 10

The funeral went off with the same deliberate organization and military precision that Richard himself had always demanded, and Ruth had told her daughter that she was sure her husband would have been pleased with the way it all transpired. All of Ruth's children were there, with most of their children as well. Regina and her husband, Scott, who also served as a pallbearer, arrived with their three children, Alex, Abby, and Anna, and the two girls were again pressed into service and sang "Amazing Grace," a cappella, a rendition that didn't leave a dry eye in the room. Charles, who everyone thought looked exactly like his father, was there with his wife and their two children. Lawrence Saroh, who had recently met a retired teacher, Christie Thompson, from University City, arrived in a newly purchased handicap van with a chairlift on the back and had been personally chauffeured by his new girlfriend's son. Old Louis Clarkson, who had attended Aaron's funeral in his wheelchair at age ninety-seven, had died just two months later, but his daughter Olivia and her second husband had flown in from Cleveland to attend the service, one of the few remaining relatives on the Clarkson side of the family, with the exception of Beatrice Lerrib, the granddaughter of old Louis Clarkson. Beatrice arrived with a hired caretaker in a wheelchair, unable to walk, and she was rumored to weigh more than six hundred pounds, an assumption that few in attendance doubted. Cora Lasciter, who had kept in touch with her sister since their reconciliation at Aaron's funeral, attended, but without her fourth husband, Henry, and the couple were rumored to be "taking a break," a fact that Cora had categorically denied to her sister by telephone just three nights earlier. Alex Battenhorst and Reverend Vollbrecht's eldest son had helped get Emma Saroh downstairs from the third-floor guest room and seated her on one of the couches at the front of the viewing parlor. Clyde and Ruthie Kaermor attended and, as they had done at Aaron's funeral, served as greeters at the entrance to the home, and Ruthie had also been put in charge of the church luncheon, a task that she handled without fault. But the bulk of the crowd in attendance consisted of fellow church members, business acquaintances, family friends, and local residents of the small town and surrounding county that had all, at one time or another, brought their own departed loved ones to the Clarkson Funeral Home and left them in the capable hands of Richard Clarkson.

Reverend Vollbrecht, who had worked with Richard for many years on church affairs, gave a heartfelt sermon based on scriptures from 1 Corinthians verses 51–52: "Listen I tell you a mystery: We will not all sleep, but we will all be changed in a flash, in the twinkling of an eye, at the last trumpet." A verse that Ruth had heard on countless occasions, but never with such prescience. He also oversaw the short grave site ceremony that followed at the old Lippstadt Cemetery, where Richard was laid to rest next to Aaron, and, at the special request of Ruth, closed out the internment with a verse from Revelation 21: "He will wipe away every tear from their eyes, and death shall be no more, neither shall there be mourning, nor crying, nor pain anymore, for the former things have passed away."

The church luncheon was all laid out when the funeral party arrived, and Ruthie Kaermor took charge of marshalling the crowd through the food line that ran the entire length of the main dining room and out into the hallway. The local Rotary chapter had purchased three large Kretschmar hams in honor of their fallen member, and the local chamber of commerce had sent over fifteen pounds of mustard potato salad and four large sheet cakes, giving the local women's society some much-welcomed assistance in the food preparation.

Ruth and Cora had found an empty table up close to the coffee and dessert stand, and they had positioned Emma's wheelchair so she was facing out, looking over the dining room, and Regina and her two daughters were seated there as well. The mood was surprisingly light; Emma seemed to be having one of her better days, and the discussion of flowers had taken over the conversation.

"I think the one with the orange and white roses was the prettiest," Abby said as she shooed away her cousins, Clifford and Eli, who had taken a sudden, predictable interest in the young girl.

"Well, I think the one with chrysanthemums was prettier than that," Anna shot back with a mouthful of potato salad.

"Oh, they're all pretty," Ruth interjected, hoping to cut off any squabble. "And don't talk with your mouth full!" she added in a grandmotherly way.

Regina looked across the table at her daughters and shook her head. "Those two could argue about anything! The other day I heard them arguing about wearing white after Labor Day!"

"I say wear what you want," Cora chimed in as she cut a piece of gristle from her ham and then daintily placed it in her mouth.

"Listen to your aunt," Ruth rejoined, then laughed. "She's so seldom right!" The comment got everyone around the table laughing, except for Emma, who seemed to be in a world of her own.

Ruth, hoping to get her mother involved, leaned over and placed her hand on her arm. "Which one did you like the best, Mom?"

"They all looked pretty to me," Emma answered and then let out a small laugh.

"No, you have to pick, Grandma!" Anna shouted out from across the table, always wanting to keep things stirred up.

"How can one thing of beauty be better than another thing of beauty?" Ruth interceded, knowing that her mother hadn't heard the question. "Beauty is truth; truth, beauty," she added. She got up and pulled her mother's shawl back up on her shoulders.

"Oh, look, look," Abby said in a hushed voice, pointing across the room. "Who's that girl talking to Alex?" she asked mischievously.

"Well, let's go find out," Anna replied, gulping down a last bite of potato salad and then darting across the room.

"I'm right behind you!" Abby yelled as she took off after her.

"Oh, those girls!" Regina laughed, watching them rush away from the table. "Like bulls in a china shop sometimes!"

"To have that much energy again," Ruth joined in with a slight tone of regret.

"Oh, Ruth, you never had that much energy," Cora contradicted, a comment that had them both chuckling to themselves.

Emma reached up and tapped her hearing aid. "What's so funny?"

"Cora says that I never had any real energy when I was young," Ruth repeated loudly as she sat back down.

"You had energy enough!" the old woman replied sharply. "And anyway, energy is overrated. Too much of it leads to nothing but trouble," she added. She glanced over at her daughter Cora, who had suddenly gone quiet.

Regina jumped up and started to gather the dirty plates and napkins from the table, hoping to redirect the conversation. "Are you done with these?"

"Yes! Take them away," Ruth and Cora both chimed in in unison.

"I'm going to run back to the kitchen and see if Ruthie needs any help," Regina announced. She picked up a few more items and then scurried away.

"She's really a help to you, isn't she?" Cora asked, watching Regina walk across the crowded dining room.

"Yes. I really don't think I would have made it through all this without her." Ruth looked up at Regina standing in the food line next to her brother Charles. "There is no gift like a daughter."

Just as Ruth turned back around, an old man with a pronounced limp walked up to the table. He was dressed in an old dark-brown wool suit that had small moth holes in both of the sleeves, a white dress shirt that had started to turn yellow with age around the collar, and he was holding a weather-beaten fedora in his left hand. "I am so sorry for your loss, Ruth," the old man stated in a broken German accent. "Your husband was a great man," he added, extending his hand to Ruth.

"Oh, thank you so much," Ruth replied, touched by the old man's sincerity. "I appreciate that." She stood up and clutched his outstretched hand tightly. "But I don't think I know you, do I?" she asked. Her brow wrinkled, and she looked closely at the old man's weather-beaten face.

"Oh, don't be embarrassed," the old man replied as he shook her hand aggressively. "I know you probably don't remember an old man like me. But I did meet you once, but it was a long time ago." He paused, and heaviness entered his voice as he went on. "Years ago, when my wife died, your husband came to my rescue. I didn't have enough money for a proper burial, and your husband…well, he took care of things for my Sophie." The old man paused, and a faraway look came over his face. "He was a great man, your husband. Ein heiliger," he added in German.

"Well, thank you so much for the kind words about my husband," Ruth replied softly as thoughts of her husband ran through her mind. She reached over and gave him a hug and couldn't help but notice the heavy smell of wood smoke that permeated his clothing. "That means more to me than you can ever imagine," she added genuinely. She pulled back and shook the man's hand again. "Have you had something to eat?" she asked. "There's plenty of food up there."

"Oh, thank you, Mrs. Clarkson, but I have to go. My daughter is waiting for me in the car. I just wanted to say how sorry I am." With that, the old man bowed self-consciously a couple times, as if he might have been walking away from royalty, and left the church basement.

"Did I hear that right?" Cora asked after the old man had made his departure. "Did he say Richard was a great man?"

"Yes," Ruth answered with an unexpected sense of pride. "And he even called him a saint!" Ruth paused and waited for Cora to come back with some snide remark.

"I never will understand the male species," Cora finally uttered with a confused look on her face.

"Well, I think it's safe to bet that men say the same thing about us sometimes!" Ruth mused out loud.

The remainder of the luncheon turned out to be a whirlwind of activity as more than one hundred people made their way through the lunch line. Emma, worn out by it all only thirty minutes in, had asked to be taken back to her room at the apartment, and the two young gentlemen who had initially deposited her there had seen to it that she was safely restored to her third-floor suite. The mayor and his wife, most of the old chamber members who had worked with Richard through the years, almost every business owner in the small town, fellow church members, friends, and even several colleagues from the National Funeral Home Alliance had all made their way to Ruth's table to express their condolences. Countless heartfelt stories and reminiscences that had spread out over a lifetime were recounted and retold as each guest shared a noteworthy connection they had to Ruth's husband, and she was truly touched by the intimacy and affection that they lavished on him, a cathartic process that brought her a great sense of peace and a new perspective of her husband. It seemed as if the old adage "You can't see the forest for the trees" had a ring of truth to it, and she came to understand that her mysterious husband had lived a busy life of influence that had had a profound impact on the small town, and she was genuinely touched by the newfound realization.

After most of the crowd had already gone home, Ruth was rummaging through her purse in search of her checkbook and Cora was busy applying a thin layer of pinkish-looking lipstick when Charles, dressed in his full police uniform, with his wife, and their two young boys, dressed in matching blue suits, came walking up to the table. Charles reached down and kissed his mother lovingly on the forehead and placed his large right hand on her shoulder. "We're heading out now, Mom," he whispered, his voice filled with affection. "You need us to do anything else before we go?" he asked. He looked at Cora and tipped his cap.

"No, I'm fine, and Cora is going to stay overnight. Thanks again for all you've done, Charles. I really do appreciate it."

"Go on," Allison prodded. She gently pushed her two young boys in Ruth's direction. "Give it to her," she whispered. She knelt down behind them, then smiled up at Ruth as Eli stepped forward and handed his grandmother a card made out of red and white construction paper.

"Here, Grandma, we made this for you."

Ruth took ahold of the card and then looked down at her two grandchildren. "Oh, what's this?" she beamed. "Let me see…oh, how pretty!" she exclaimed as she opened it and started to read:

Rejoice with those who rejoice, and
weep with those who weep.

She stopped and clutched it to her breast. "This is the most wonderful gift you could have ever given me!" she exclaimed. She laid the card down and grabbed the two boys, one in each arm. "I love you both so much!" she whispered as she clutched them tightly.

"Okay, boys, give Grandma a kiss now," Charles said as he put his arm around Allison. "We have to go. I have to go to work."

"Goodbye, you two," Ruth gushed. Both of the young boys reached up and gave her a kiss. "I love you both so much!" she added.

Charles wrangled the two boys and grabbed each one by the hand. "If you need anything, you call me, Mom. Anything!" he added, leading the boys toward the exit.

"He's wonderful, Ruth!" Cora exclaimed as the young family walked away. "Strong and silent, but when he does say something, it's worth listening to."

"I know," Ruth agreed. "And about twenty people told me how much he looks likes his father!" Ruth paused, and a contemplative look came over her. "But he's really nothing like Richard at all. He has more capacity…no, I don't know if that's the right word."

"He has the capacity for intimacy," Cora articulated.

"Yes, that's what I was trying to say," Ruth countered. She looked at her sister with a shocked look on her face. "You continue to astonish me, Cora."

"One hundred dollars an hour at Whitman's, I better get something out of it," she joked. Cora turned to take one last look at Charles and his family, and she noticed a young man loitering around the entranceway to the dining room. "Who is that?" she asked, pointing to the young man.

Ruth, who had been busy writing out a check to the minister, slipped it into her purse and turned around and looked. "I don't know. I don't recognize him either." Just as she turned back around, the young man walked right up to the table and stood timidly across from the two women.

"Are you Ruth Clarkson?" the young man, who was dressed in a black polyester suit that was a full two sizes larger than he needed, asked very politely.

"Yes. Yes, I am," Ruth answered. She quickly started to rise to shake his hand. "And this is my sister, Cora," she added, pointing at her sister. "And who are you?"

The young man said nothing and just gawked at Ruth from across the table. "Do you mind if I sit down?" he finally asked awkwardly.

"No, please have a seat," Cora interjected before her sister could reply. The young man sat down and self-consciously placed his hands on his lap under the table.

"Do we know you?" Ruth asked again politely. She looked over at her sister and then back at the young man.

"No," he replied, "I don't think we were ever supposed to meet."

"What do you mean by that?" Ruth asked, her interest piqued.

"I don't think Richard wanted me to meet you," he answered mysteriously.

"So you knew my husband?"

"Yes, I knew Richard," he countered, his voice fading.

"Through work?" Ruth asked curiously. She looked at her sister again and then back at the young man.

"Look," he blurted out clumsily as he looked up across the table, "I don't really know of any easy way to say this." He stopped and looked down, and his eyes started to tear up.

Ruth got up and walked around and stood next to the young man. "It's okay," she consoled, putting her arm around his shoulders. "I've always found that the best practice is to just say what you have to say."

The young man looked up at Ruth standing above him. "My name is Mark, and I'm Richard's son."

CHAPTER

11

B y the time Ruth finally got back to her bedroom that night, it was half past nine. Her brother, Lawrence, and his new girlfriend, Christie Thompson, had stopped by after the luncheon to visit, but her son Sean, who was acting as chauffer, had plans for the evening, and the trio had left around five. The steady stream of well-wishers, who continued to drop off dishes for the bereaved family, had finally come to an end, and all the employees had long since gone home. Cora, who had decided to stay on a few days to help out with her mother, had been put up in the small bedroom adjacent to the guest suite where Emma was staying, and Richard Jr., who had taken a few weeks of vacation time from this job, was staying in another guest bedroom at the very front of the building, across the grand living room, a space that was seldom used because of a large flashing Western Auto sign directly across from the funeral home that blinked incessantly throughout the night.

Ruth was seated at an antique cherry vanity that matched the rest of the bedroom set, staring at her worn-out-looking reflection in a large beveled mirror, which was surrounded by small snapshots of her children and grandchildren tucked between the mirror and the frame. Just as she pulled down a small black-and-white photo of Aaron sitting in an old pedal car made out of metal that Werner Clarkson had bought for his grandson, Richard Jr. knocked lightly and then entered the room.

"So how are you surviving it all?" he asked, his voice filled with concern. He walked up and kissed his mother on the head and then noticed the small photo clutched in her hand. "Oh, who's that?" he asked curiously. He bent down behind his mother and looked closer at the small snapshot.

"I think this was taken in 1960, when Aaron was about four years old," Ruth answered and then held the picture up for her son to see. "He always loved that little car."

"I remember that car!" Richard Jr. acknowledged animatedly. He took the photo and held it up before his face. "Look how cute he was back then."

"Oh, all you kids were cute," Ruth replied as only a mother could. She got up, took one last look at the picture and gently placed it back on the mirror. "Come and have a seat over here by me," she added and then pointed to one of the two matching dressing chairs.

Richard plopped down cavalierly and rubbed the stubble on his chin and neck. "Well, I think it all went very well," he stated as he sat down, knowing his mother would want his input. "I think the Black Prince would have been proud," he added playfully as his mother took a seat next to him.

"I agree," Ruth replied with a restrained grin. "I think the Black Prince would have been extremely proud!" she added jokingly, picking up on her son's clever word play. "And I thought the service was good, and Reverend Vollbrecht always does such a great job. And the grave site ceremony went off without incident, so that was good too." She paused and looked out the rear window of the bedroom. "And I couldn't believe how many of the townspeople showed up. I really think Richard would have been shocked."

"That didn't surprise me at all. He was great to everyone in this town!" Richard Jr. slipped in. "It was his own family, his close relationships that he struggled with."

Ruth looked back at her son, pursed her lips, and shook her head in subtle disapproval. "He had his moments," she finally added defensively. "And I actually learned a lot about him today. So many people had wonderful stories about him, about how he had helped them, and how much he had meant to them."

"He was a politician, Mother," Richard Jr. chirped satirically. "Remember, he even ran for mayor!"

"No, this was different," Ruth corrected him politely. "This was much more heartfelt than just his typical glad-handing and sound bites. And it was good to hear. I was really touched by a lot of it." Ruth paused, and a reflective look came over her. "At least for today, the light outweighed the shadows?" she added, with a contented look on her face.

"Well, maybe you're right," Richard Jr. responded, seemingly touched by his mother's outpouring. Ruth paused and looked closely at her son still slouched down in the dressing chair. "It's going to be so different now, going forward, with the business and everything." She paused, and a sudden look of panic came across her face. "Do you think I can handle it all?" she asked desperately.

"Of course you can, Mother!" Richard Jr. assured her, his voice rising. "It's been mostly you running it for the past fifteen years, anyway!"

"Ah, I guess you're right," she finally agreed after a moment of silence, her sudden panic attack subsiding. "I guess I'll just take a day at a time and see how it all goes," she added with a forced sense of optimism.

"I have every faith in you, Mother. You've always been stronger than Dad, anyway!"

"Well, there's many different types of strength, Richie," Ruth speculated, "but that does makes me feel better, to know that at least somebody has confidence in me."

"And you're a natural when it comes to this type of business, the way you can empathize with people. You were the one that really held it all together. I mean, look at today! Look at the great job you did with Dad's funeral!"

"So you think everything was okay?" Ruth asked desperately, as if her husband's approval was still foremost in her mind. "You think your dad would have liked it?"

"Oh, of course he would—he would have loved it! And everything went off without incident, and that was always his Achilles' heel, always afraid that something would go wrong!" Richard Jr. paused and started chuckling to himself. "Remember Grandma Clarkson's funeral?" he asked, hoping to get his mother laughing.

"Oh my, poor Marcella!" Ruth responded as she shook her head in disbelief. "Why Richard ever let her brother do the eulogy. He had to be in his early nineties, and I don't think he even knew where he was!" she added and then let out a small laugh.

"Well, thank God for small mercies!" Richard Jr. shot back as he let out an even larger one.

As the laughter died down, Richard Jr., still rubbing at his back, got up and walked over to one of the large windows that faced the alley at the back of the funeral home. "Has Cora already gone to bed?" he asked with a faraway tone as he stared out the window, a full moon casting ghostly shadows on the alley down below.

"Yes, she helped Mother get ready for bed tonight, helped her with her bath and gave her all her medications, and I think she's pretty tired." Ruth paused and looked back toward the door to see if anyone was entering. "You know, she's better with Mother than I thought she'd be," she half-whispered. "Can you believe that?"

"Very few things about my aunt Cora surprise me anymore," Richard Jr. quipped.

"And even though she won't admit it, I think this whole Henry thing has her pretty upset."

Richard Jr. turned and looked back at his mother. "Yeah, what's going on with that?"

"Ah, who knows," Ruth responded reflectively. "You know, I don't think she's ever been able to really let her guard down with men, if that makes any sense. She's always kept them at arm's length." Ruth paused, as if she were trying to analyze her sister's complicated past. "Maybe she just hasn't found the right one. I was hoping that Henry would be different."

"Well, she's had four times at the plate. The law of averages should have worked in her favor with at least one of them!"

"I think she did really love Jasper, Jasper Stockdale," Ruth interjected with a thoughtful tenor.

"Which one was that?" Richard volleyed back and then held up four fingers on his right hand. "Was he the star football player?"

"No. That was Trenton, the first one. That was right after she graduated. And that was doomed from the start!" Ruth paused, and an embarrassed slant came over her face. "I hate to even say this, but he was one of those guys who seemingly peaked in high school," she added in a hushed voice.

"Did you like this Trenton guy?" Richard Jr. asked as his interest seemed to pick up a little.

"Yeah, he was a nice boy, but definitely not the brightest. He was in my French class—oh my, what an assault on a language! But he was very good-looking. That's powerful currency at that age! And of course, he was the star quarterback for the football team, which seemed to compensate for a multitude of deficiencies." Ruth paused and looked curiously at her son. "The quarterback's the one who throws the ball, right?"

Richard smiled, glanced back at his mother, and nodded.

"Oh, I got that right," she mused out loud. "But the one I think she really loved, though, the one I really liked, was her second husband, Jasper Stockdale. He was probably the best of them all. He was cut from a better material, and I think they could have made it, but of course, he was killed in Korea."

"I remember Dad talking about him," Richard Jr. replied, a sudden serious look on his face. "They never did find his body, did they?"

"No," Ruth answered regretfully. "And how does one deal with that?" she asked rhetorically. "Cora really hasn't had it that easy, you know. She always insists that I'm the strong one in the family, but I think, in a lot of ways, she's a lot more resilient than I am!"

"Well, what was Cora like in high school?" Richard Jr. asked as he turned around and looked back toward his mother, his interest in his mysterious aunt piqued.

"She was a very independent person and sort of moody, which for some reason seemed to attract all the boys. And she was more of a tomboy, and she certainly was always the center of attention when we were kids, especially in high school." Ruth paused and shook her head and smiled. "And she always had some boy chasing after her, but she never could really get serious with them."

"Well, I've seen pictures of her from back then," Richard Jr. interjected, "and she was very beautiful!"

"Oh, no doubt about that," Ruth agreed. "But that never seemed to work in her favor. She dated a lot of different guys, but she just never seemed to trust them, and so we were all shocked when she announced that she was marrying Trenton." Ruth paused again, and a thoughtful look came over her. "I sometimes think she married him to just get out of the house, to finally start her life, and to maybe make Mother happy. I don't know. But she always seemed to have a short attention span when it came to men. Maybe she just got bored with them."

"Maybe it was all just a mask," Richard Jr. stated as he walked back and sat down next to his mother again. "Maybe it was some way to protect herself from something." He paused, and a curious look appeared on his face. "Do you think she's ever really been happy?"

"I don't really think so," Ruth replied after giving the question some serious thought. "And now she's on husband number 4, and that looks like that's headed for a quick end."

"Why don't you talk to her about it?" Richard probed. "Maybe there's something going on with her. Maybe she's hiding some secret or something and it's bothering her."

"Well, she's gone back to seeing a psychiatrist now, a Dr. Whitman, and I think it's helping. She first started seeing him back shortly before Aaron died, and then she quit going for a few years. But for some reason, she started to see him again. And I've asked her about it, but she just seems guarded about the whole thing."

"So Cora's seeing a shrink?" Richard asked half-jokingly. "It's about time!" he added and then let out another large laugh.

"Oh, go ahead and laugh," Ruth shot back disapprovingly, "but I think it's actually helping her. And she's even trying to get me to meet with him!"

"No, Mom, I'm just kidding," Richard Jr. added with a heavy dose of repentance. "I think it's a great thing." Richard Jr. got back up, arched his back as if it were still hurting, and went to stand in front of the back window again and just stared out into the darkness. "Seeing someone certainly helped me," he finally confessed and then glanced back at his mother for her reaction.

"What?" Ruth exclaimed. "You've seen a psychiatrist?"

"No. But I did see a counselor right after I got out of college."

"What's the difference?"

"A psychiatrist is a medical doctor, whereas counselors are generally master's-level psychotherapists. They focus more on things like mild depression, relationships, and things like that."

"But why would you need to see someone like that?" Ruth asked with all the emotions of a concerned mother. Richard Jr. didn't say anything and just continued to stare off into the moonlit night. "Do you really love me, Mother?" he finally asked cryptically without looking back, his voice suddenly filled with a profound tension that seemed to come from some place deep inside.

"Well, of course I do," Ruth countered, sounding a little put off by the question.

"But what if I wasn't who you really thought I was?" he asked as his voice started to quiver. "What if I had this whole other secret life that you knew nothing about?" He stopped and dropped his head, and an eerie silence spread across the room.

Ruth got up and walked over to stand next to her son, who had started to visibly tremble. "Are you talking about your being gay?" she finally countered.

Richard Jr. looked up in surprise and seemed unable to speak as a single tear started to run down his cheek.

"What, you thought I didn't know?" Ruth whispered to her son. She put her arm around him and gently started to rub his back. "In some way, I think I've always known."

"And you're not disappointed in me?" he asked as he looked directly at his mother, his voice barely audible.

"No, I'm not disappointed," Ruth gushed, her voice filled with a love that only a mother could express. "No! Absolutely not!" She grabbed her son by the chin and gave it a squeeze. "You're my son, and I love you unconditionally. In some ways I love you more, because I know what you're going to have to face in this world—that's the only thing that I really regret." Ruth paused and waited for her son to respond to her comments.

"I've been so afraid to tell anyone," Richard Jr. finally whispered, his voice starting to relax, as if he had just stepped back from some unearthly precipice.

"Why?" Ruth asked as she put her arm around her son.

"It's just not an easy thing to talk about," Richard Jr. replied.

"But you've always been able to talk to *me*!" Ruth answered, a sense of worry entering her voice.

"I know, I know, but I have this friend from college—his name is Ernie—and he told his parents last Christmas." Richard stopped, and a shudder ran through his body. "And when he told them, they didn't say anything, they just walked out of the room. They just left him standing there. And the next morning, when he woke up, he found a letter that they had typed out to him, telling him that they never wanted to see him again."

"And is that why you were afraid to tell me?" Ruth asked compassionately, feeling the weight that her son had been carrying.

"I guess…I mean, look at what happened to Ernie! I think it takes an amount of courage and trust that I just really didn't have before."

"What do you mean?" Ruth asked.

"Oh, Mother, you have to have a family that you trust and love, and you have to feel love, you have to feel unconditional love—that's the only way you can feel safe enough to let people know who you really are, no matter what your secret is." He paused and looked his mother in the eye. "And that's why I can tell you. But not everybody has that." Richard Jr. paused and looked back out the window again. "And I know how the world really is. Words and actions are two different things. Most people never really philosophically accept it. They say they're fine with it, but the reality of it is just too much." Richard Jr. paused and thought a few moments before he went on. "And an even bigger problem is accepting it yourself. I mean, everybody keeps talking about being gay like it's some choice that people make! I mean, that's all you ever hear."

"But you seem to be okay with it, aren't you?" Ruth asked, a deep tinge of fear couched in her question.

"I don't know," Richard Jr. answered honestly, his eyes drifting off into the shadows outside the window. "The problem is, you hear it all so much, the taunts and the negative comments, and you start to believe it yourself. And you start thinking that maybe you *can* change, that maybe everybody's right, that there is a choice." He paused and looked back at his mother, who was looking down, standing like a statute at his side. "But there isn't. The only choice is whether you face it or not!"

Ruth looked up at her son with a kind of terror. "And you, have you faced it?" she asked, her voice filled with a new level of fear.

"I'm starting to, I think. I don't know. Most of the time, I try to just ignore the feelings, to suppress them, to intellectually come to terms with it all! But Adrienne Rich is right—all our high-toned questions breed in a lively animal, and no amount of thought or analysis is ever going to change that."

"Then you just need to accept it," Ruth uttered with a depth of sincerity that Richard Jr. had never heard from his mother before. "You need to embrace it. You can't let the actions of two parents, or the actions of other people, affect how you move forward. We'll all be here to support you."

"I appreciate that, Mother, I really do. And maybe you're right. Maybe I just need to stop thinking I can change things and just accept it."

"Well, what about your close friends?" Ruth asked, her voice still filled with worry. "How have they responded?"

"I have this one friend that I told a couple of years ago. We actually met in college, and I thought he was really a good friend, you know. And when I told him, the very first thing he said was, 'I'm okay with it just as long you don't have anything to do with my brothers.'" Richard Jr. stopped and looked up at his mother. "He had a couple of brothers that would visit him on occasion, and we'd all hang out. And that's all he said. I can accept what you are, just keep it away from my family, like I was some kind of predator or something."

"What did you say to him after he said that?"

"Nothing. I mean, what could I say? He thought he was being some open-minded, compassionate person."

"Are you still friends with him?"

"Not really. Everything with him has to be on his terms."

"Well, you've just described about every man that I've ever met!" Ruth added with a chuckle, attempting to lighten the mood.

"Oh, Mom, you're probably right." Richard laughed as he grabbed his mother and gave her an embrace. "You know, all these years I've kept this a secret because I was afraid of what would happen, afraid of what might happen if I let down the mask." He paused and looked back out the window. "You know, you wear a mask long enough and before you know it, that's what you become." Richard Jr. paused and looked back closely at his mother, who was standing silently by her son. "Did Dad know?" he asked timidly.

"I don't think so. He said some things at times that led me to believe that he suspected, but I don't think he really wanted to know. Men just can't deal with the realities of life like women can. It's all so black-and-white with men." She pushed her son back a step and grabbed his arms and looked him in the face. "The shadows are as important as the light," she chanted and then smiled.

"Oh, I doubt if this is what Brontë had in mind when she wrote those words!" Richard joked back.

"Oh, I don't know. You never know," Ruth answered.

CHAPTER

12

The following morning, a large storm front had made its way into the Midwest, and heavy rains were soaking the region, with flash flood warning posted across the entire greater St. Louis area, only exacerbating the already-historic flooding. Cora had gotten up early and dressed and fed her mother, allowing Ruth a rare opportunity to just relax and enjoy the morning paper. Richard Jr. had been dispatched to the church, at the request of Reverend Vollbrecht, to collect the leftover ham and potato salad from the funeral luncheon the day before, with explicit instructions to take them to the local food shelter, along with an entire uncut chocolate mousse sheet cake.

Cora and Ruth were seated in the front living room of the third-floor apartment, a large formal space with a twelve-foot-high ceiling that was separated from the dining room by a grand archway, a room that Ruth had always found too drafty in the winter and too hot in the summer. The imposing room had two floor-to-ceiling bookcases that flanked a large masonry fireplace and was furnished with a nineteenth-century French living room set in carved, lacquered wood from the 1890s, which included a small divan and four matching chairs that Marcella Clarkson had reupholstered in the early seventies, a set that was said to have been purchased by Alfred and Edna Sprick, the original owners of the building. But the most prominent feature in the room, what caught everyone's attention almost immediately, was a large reproduction of Vermeer's *Woman in Blue Reading a Letter* that Ruth had commissioned from a company out of Budapest after she fell in love with the original in Amsterdam. The large six-foot-by-five painting, framed in carved mahogany wood with gilded trim, hung above the large fireplace on the outside wall opposite the main entrance and was the focal point of the entire room. When Ruth had first laid eyes on the original, she had fallen in love with the subtle blue tones and muted colors of the painting that were highlighted by the soft morning light that was entering the scene, and she had become almost obsessed with it after she studied the work more thoroughly. On closer examination, she noticed that the chair and map rail in the painting were casting shadows, but the woman herself, reading a mysterious letter, was not; it was a subtle detail, and a play with light and shadow, that seemed to highlight the female figure in a very unique way. Through a tour guide at the museum, she also learned that the back wall in the painting contained a map of the counties of Holland and West Friesland in the Netherlands, which led many critics to suggest that the mysterious letter that the woman was reading was written by a traveling husband, a detail that, as Ruth had written to her mother in a postcard, had endeared her to the painting forever.

"Cora, I have something to tell you," Ruth started out as she took a delicate sip from her coffee cup, part of the family's Royal Albert coffee service that had originally been given as a wedding present to Werner and Marcella Clarkson. "Richie and I had quite a revealing conversation last night," she started out tentatively, unsure of exactly how her sister would react to her news. "He finally had the courage to tell me that he's gay," she added, half-expecting her sister to react negatively.

"Oh my god," Cora gasped. "You know, I did wonder about him, though. He's always reminded me of Henry's eldest son from his first marriage." Cora paused, let out a low sigh. "He's gay too, I think."

"Oh, I didn't know that," Ruth stated, shocked by the news. "How did Henry react to it?"

"He doesn't know, I don't think. And if he does, I'm sure he doesn't want to talk about it. You know how men are about such things. But I actually like him better than his other children, especially the youngest one, and it's never really made any difference to me one way or another." She paused and looked at her sister and kept her eyes fixed on her as she started to speak again. "So what do you think about it all?" she asked, trying to sound like Dr. Whitman.

"Oh, I think it's fine, but I've known ever since he was in high school, so I've had plenty of time to come to terms with it. And I told him that it made no difference to me whatsoever." Ruth paused and let out a motherly sigh. "I am worried about him, though. I don't think he's really accepted it all yet."

"Did he say that?" Cora asked.

"Not is so many words, but I can tell that he's struggling with it. I just hope he'll be okay."

"You really are something, Ruth. The way you're able to handle things. I just wish I had your…" She paused, as if searching for just the right word. "Constitution," she finally offered up.

"Sometimes the choices that are made for us turn out to be the best ones," Ruth said softly as she looked directly at her sister and took another sip of coffee.

"I think I'm starting to realize that," Cora answered. "Does the rest of the family know?"

"Not yet, but I encouraged him to go ahead and tell them. It is the nineties, after all," she countered.

"Yeah, the 1890s!" Cora batted back and then laughed. "You don't really understand how people can be, Ruth! Let me tell you, as a whole, we're a pretty nasty, closed-minded species."

"Oh, don't say that!" Ruth yelled out. "I was up all night last night, worrying about it, and now you're getting me all worked up again."

"Ah, he's a strong kid," Cora consoled, regretting her honesty. "He'll survive. He'll be okay."

"Well, I hope he does more than just survive!" Ruth proclaimed.

"Oh, you know what I mean. He's a good kid. He'll be okay." Cora stopped talking and reached down for her purse. "You don't mind if I smoke, do you?" she asked self-consciously.

"Yes, I mind!" Ruth countered. "I thought that you had quit!"

"Well, the only time I really need one now is when I get nervous or I'm at Dr. Whitman's office."

"Well, there's something very wrong with that statement!" Ruth replied, cutting her sister off.

"Oh, you're right. Of course, you are," Cora replied as she set her purse back down. "You're always right."

"But I have other things on my mind too," Ruth stated, hoping to move the conversation along. "What am I to do about this whole Mark thing?"

"Ah, yes, Mark, our shadowy visitor at the luncheon. That was certainly a surprise entrance he made!" Cora picked up her coffee, took a drink, set it back down, and then looked up at the old oil painting. "Do you really believe him? Do you really think he's Richard's son?" she asked incredulously.

"Actually, I do," Ruth answered very matter-of-factly as she set her cup down. "I guess I am just a little concerned about why he wants to meet with me."

"And is that such a good idea?" Cora questioned, looking back down at her sister. "I mean, you don't know the first thing about this boy."

"I don't know. But he just seemed so sad and so alone. I don't know…I just feel this sense of empathy and compassion for him."

"Well, even if you do meet with him, what good is it going to do?" Cora queried.

"Well, I don't exactly know, but what if he really is Richard's son? I mean, put yourself in his position. He just lost the man he believes is his father, and even if Richard isn't, Mark believes it. And that's a terrible thing for a young man. Especially if he hardly knew him. And if I can help him through that, then maybe that's what I should do."

"But I'm more worried about you!" Cora exclaimed, her voice filling with apprehension. "Lord knows where this will take you if you start down this path. Do you really want to know about it, about all the details?" Cora picked up her cup and took a sip, her eyes peering closely at her sister over the top of the cup. "Trust me, extramarital details can be quite…how should I word this…sordid," she added, for effect.

Ruth blushed a little and set her cup down and looked closely at her sister. "You know, I've sat back my entire life and sort of lived in the shadows. Maybe I didn't want to know the *sordid* truth about my marriage to Richard. But maybe I should have! Maybe I should have asked more questions!"

"But knowing something in general terms is one thing, and knowing all the details is quite another!"

"But he's gone now, and I'm tired of being in the shadows!" Ruth yelled, as if some sense of liberation had just taken ahold of her. "Can the reality of the situation be any worse than what I might conjure up in my mind? Maybe I should have stood up and tackled all this years ago. Isn't that what your Dr. Whitman is always telling you to do? I think I need to face whatever comes out of it."

"My god, you do sound like Dr. Whitman!" Cora confirmed. "And that's exactly what he's always telling me."

"And maybe he's right. I've played the role of the doting wife for the past thirty-six years, and now I don't have to do that anymore."

Just as Cora started to answer back, Regina and her daughters, Anna and Abby, came bounding down the hallway.

"We've come to help get the thank-you notes started!" Regina yelled as she popped her head into the large living room.

"Oh yes!" Ruth responded. "See, I told you Regina was a great assistant at helping me get things done," she whispered to Cora.

"More like a slave driver!" Cora quipped, and both women broke out laughing.

CHAPTER 13

"The first time I remember him coming to my room, I was probably around seven years old," Cora related, her voice reportorial, almost completely devoid of emotion. "At first, I didn't really think anything about it. He told me that this was going to be our special time, and I was glad about it at first." She paused and crossed her arms tightly and stated to rub her outer arms, as if some chill had just run through her. "He had always told me that I was his favorite, and I just thought this was his way of showing that." Cora stopped talking and just sat motionless, as if unable to go any further.

"Go on," Dr. Whitman encouraged.

"And then as time went on," Cora finally started up again, "he started asking me to do more and more things." Cora stopped and froze, her breaths short and light.

"Cora," Dr. Whitman whispered, "you have to go on. You have to walk through this."

Cora took a few deep breaths in acknowledgment and started to speak again with the same detached tone of voice. "So after a few times, he started to get on the bed with me and lie beside me. And then after a few more times, he just did whatever he wanted." She stopped and looked to the side of the room where the fish tank was putting out a gurgling cadence across the room. "And I told him that I didn't want to do it, that he was hurting me, but that never stopped him."

"What would he say when you told him to stop?" Dr. Whitman asked.

Cora looked back directly at the doctor and then lowered her eyes. "He told me that I had to do it and that if I ever told anyone,

I would be sent away, that I would lose my mother and my family." She paused, and an angry look came over her. "He said if anyone found out, it would destroy the family, that it would be all my fault." Cora stopped talking and fell into a deep silence.

"Cora, go on," the doctor finally prodded after a few moments of intense quiet.

"I just wanted him to stop!" she yelled out, emotion finally entering her voice as she seemed to come back to life. "I just wanted it all to stop!" she shouted out again.

"And when did it stop?" Dr. Whitman asked.

Cora again looked over at the fish swimming back and forth in the confined rectangular tank and seemed ready to move forward, her voice picking up volume as she proceeded. "When I was thirteen, my mother walked in the room. It was right at the end of one of his visits, and he was just leaving." Cora stiffened and seemed to be reliving the event all over again. "And Daddy just froze and stood there and didn't say a thing. He never said a word, and I didn't either."

"And what did your mother do?" Dr. Whitman asked, trying to keep the conversation going.

Cora looked back in the direction of the doctor, but somehow past him. "She just looked at me. She never looked at him, she just looked at me, and then she just closed the door."

"And what did you feel at that time?"

"Well, I was afraid that I would be sent away!" Cora yelled out, as if she could still feel the original fear. "That's what he always threatened me with, and I felt this overpowering guilt about what was going on. In some ways, I felt like it was all my fault."

"And do you still feel that way?"

"I don't know what I feel. How does anyone feel about such things?" She paused, and a curious look came over her face. "Maybe I had just stopped thinking and feeling. It was like I had disconnected—yes, that's the right word—disconnected years earlier from all of it."

"And how do you think your father's actions have affected how you see yourself?"

"I think he took away my sense of myself." Cora paused, and a thoughtful look came over her, as if she had just made some important self-realization. "He took away my ability to value myself in any way."

"And do you think that's had an effect on the relationships you've had in your life?"

"Oh, I'm sure it has," Cora replied with a self-loathing tone. "How could I really love anyone else when I couldn't love myself?" she added and then lowered her head.

"You said a few moments ago that you felt disconnected from it. Do you feel disconnected from it now?"

"I still feel ashamed, it that's what you're asking."

"And your mother never came to you or said anything about what she had seen?" Dr. Whitman asked as he tilted his head to the right.

"No. She never said a word."

"And you never approached her about it either?"

"No."

"So how did you interpret your mother's silence?"

"I guess I felt like she was disappointed in me," Cora answered, her emotions starting to surface again. "I felt like she saw me the same way that I saw myself! And I could tell by the way she looked at me that day that she thought it was my fault."

"And why did you think that?"

"She never treated me the same way after that day. I mean, we really never had a close relationship to begin with. Ironically, I was always closer to my father than my mother. But this just changed things. I don't know." Cora paused and looked back toward the fish tank. "As I've thought back on it years later, she must have said something to him, though, because he never came to my room again after that. After that day, after she walked in, that was the end of it."

"So you thought it was all over?"

"Yes. And we all just went on like it had never happened." Cora paused again and let out a small gasp. "That's the way it always was in our family. We always just went on like nothing ever happened."

"And do you think it's all over now?" Dr. Whitman asked as he leaned forward in his chair and tilted his head to the right again.

"What do you mean?" Cora asked.

"Oh, I think you know what I mean," Dr. Whitman responded.

Cora thought for a moment before she answered, then suddenly looked up. "Oh, I see. Is it over?" she responded as she understood what the doctor was asking. She leaned forward on the couch and finally looked the doctor in the eye for the first time in the session. "I don't think it will ever be over," she finally responded coldly.

"Yes!" Dr. Whitman echoed. "It's not over for you because you've never dealt with any of it. You've never said a word to your father or your mother about any of it. You've just kept it all bottled up inside, and emotions like that, that are kept inside, will surface in some other way, usually in some negative way, until you deal with it." Dr. Whitman pointed to the fish tank on the side of the room. "You're like those fish in that tank. You're confined in this world of guilt and repressed feelings, and you can't move forward. There's always a silence that surrounds this type of abuse. And that silence can be as harmful as the actual event."

"So how do I free myself from all this," Cora asked as she looked at the tank again as if seeing it for the first time.

Dr. Whitman leaned forward and looked directly at his patient with a new sense of urgency. "Listen closely to me, Cora. You never had a choice in what happened to you as a child. You had no control over that. But you do have a choice now. This is a seminal moment in your life when *you* can make the choice to move forward." Dr. Whitman paused and sat back in his chair. "And you're absolutely right, your father's actions have affected how you value yourself. In a sense, he blocked your ability to value yourself in any real way. But demons only live in the dark, Cora. That's the only place they can thrive! And we need to bring this out of the shadows and into the light."

"But I don't know how to do that!" Cora replied in desperation.

"Well, that's what we're going to work on in here. And it's not going to be easy. We're going to have to bring it all up and face it, so you can finally put it behind you."

"What do you mean?" Cora asked anxiously, her heart beating heavily in her chest.

"Both of your parents are still alive, aren't they?"

"Yes," Cora responded, looking back at the doctor. "But one is starting to get dementia, and the other is in a full-care nursing home!"

"Well, that's okay, because what we're going to do is not for them," Dr. Whitman proclaimed powerfully, "or about them. This is all for you."

"Okay," Cora replied with a great deal of skepticism. "So how do we start?" she asked, her voice lacking any true conviction.

"Before we meet again, I want you to write a letter to your mother and your father explaining to them exactly how you felt about what happened to you."

"What?" Cora snapped, as if horrified by the very thought of it.

"Just put in your own words how you felt, how what they did has affected you throughout your life. Just the act of writing it down is therapeutic in and of itself."

"Oh, you have no idea what you're asking of me, Doctor." Cora paused, and a look of fear came over her, and she started to tremble. "I can't face my parents, especially my father. I don't know how to do that. I've never stood up to them before."

"Then it's time to change that, and I am going to help you."

"But they're too old now. Isn't it too late to bring this all up again?" Cora responded pleadingly.

"It's not for them," Dr. Whitman exclaimed decisively. "These letters will be for you. And even if you never confront either of them, it's the starting point."

"What do you mean?" Cora asked skeptically.

"Even if you think you can't do something, you have to try to do it. You have to try it and practice the behaviors even if you don't believe in them. And then, eventually, the emotions will catch up with the behaviors."

"But that's not me," Cora defended.

"When people create an image of themselves, a lot of times they come to believe that image. I want you to do that. I want you to see yourself as a strong woman who can stand up for herself."

"You have much more faith in me than I do in myself," Cora answered. She sat back into the couch and crossed her arms tightly, her eyes fixed on some distant point, as if she were struggling internally, attempting to find the courage to move forward with the doctor's plan. "Maybe you're right," she finally whispered as she looked back at the doctor. "Maybe I do need to face this. Maybe it's time I stop avoiding everything, hiding from everything." She hesitated one more time and then sat up straight. "And if you think I can do it, well, then I'll try."

"Do you mean that?" Dr. Whitman asked very seriously.

"Yes," Cora responded, her lips barely moving.

"Then you've already made the first important step."

CHAPTER 14

Cora and Ruth were walking down the hall to the third-floor apartment living room to have coffee just as the Howard Miller Windsor mantel clock was striking nine. Cora had arrived the night before, circumventing the ever-increasing flooded areas, to discuss future options for their mother, Emma, who was continuing on her downhill slide, a decline that had forced the two women to talk about a more permanent long-term care option. A local Helping Hands organization that would come to Ruth's house for three hours daily and assist in any number of care-based duties was discussed, as well as a full-care nursing home, typically the final option, but the ultimate decision was tabled in hopes of finding additional alternatives, and they wanted to bring Lawrence in on any final decision-making.

Cora had also, as part of her therapy with Dr. Whitman, disclosed to her sister the dark secret that she had carried since childhood, a therapeutic process that had kept the two women up most of the prior night as they struggled with the harsh realities of the ultimate family betrayal. In unequivocal truthfulness, Cora had told her sister the unbelievable details of her sexual abuse at the hands of her father. At times she spoke without connection, as one might report a casual event or occurrence, at other times she was filled with rage and anger, and at other points she was gripped with painful emotion, as if the events were still happening, but at no time did she ever stop from moving forward. And just as Dr. Whitman had predicted, the process had proved to be a liberating one, and she had actually felt better after unburdening herself with the unspeakable secret.

Ruth, who had never really had a close relationship with her father, was devastated by his supreme betrayal, and as the night unfolded and Ruth suffered with her sister, a new sense of acceptance and understanding had been fostered between the two women. Ruth, who had always looked at her younger sister as a vapid adolescent, concerned only with frivolous appetites, was suddenly presented with a new reality, and a veil that had separated them throughout most of their lives had been suddenly, and irrevocably, removed. The shadowy shroud of disgrace and betrayal that had always surrounded Cora, that had always lurked just beyond the edges of reality, was somehow lifted, and Ruth could see her sister as she had never seen her before. The confusing puzzle that had always been Cora's life had suddenly been filled in with one very important piece, and the true picture of her life was coming into focus.

"So are you going to be all right, Cora?" Ruth asked her sister as she handed her a small pitcher of cream. "Why don't you plan on staying on here a little longer?"

"Oh, I appreciate the offer, but I don't know. Henry is expecting me back. He has some banquet coming up, so I really need to get back to the city." She paused and grabbed her sister's hand. "But I think I am going to be okay," she replied, her eyes red and blurry from a night of crying. "You know, I do feel a lot better having told you," she quickly added, giving her sister's hand a tight squeeze. "Dr. Whitman told me that that would happen. He always told me that time doesn't really cure anything, only actions do."

"What did he mean by that?" Ruth asked.

"I just always thought that as time went on and I was further removed from my childhood, it would all just eventually be okay. That time would heal everything. But I see now that nothing could have been further from the truth."

"I just wish I had known what was going on," Ruth responded regretfully. "I can't believe that I didn't see it! Maybe there would have been something that I could have done." She paused and looked closely at her sister. "I just feel like such a fool. All this going on right in front of me, and I didn't know a thing."

"There was nothing you could have done, Ruth. And I was just so ashamed of it all. Believe me, I didn't want anyone to know, least of all you."

"But all the unhappiness and grief that you went through," Ruth lamented. "And all alone!"

Cora reached forward and grabbed her coffee. "Dr. Whitman says that Jung believes that we have to embrace our grief, that that's how we grow," she responded out of the blue. "And that's what we are working on now."

"Grief makes one hour ten," Ruth recited back to her sister, picking up the word *grief.*

"Jung?" Cora asked as she sat back and blew on her coffee.

"Shakespeare. *Richard II*," Ruth answered and then let out a small laugh.

"Ah, you and Richard Jr., you guys always did like Shakespeare. I just never could get through it," Cora added and then made a funny face. "I remember Brian, my third husband, he took me to see *Richard III* at this college production at Washington University!" Cora paused and chuckled to herself, as if she could see the tragedy playing out in her mind. "Oh my god, I couldn't keep track of all the people he had killed. And then those little princes! I was completely lost!"

"Oh, I am familiar with *Richard III*, and after last night, I have a whole new understanding of him now!" Ruth joked back.

"Yes, and now I have to write our dear sweet *Richard* a letter and go see him," Cora responded derisively as her mood took on a sullen tone. "Maybe I will stay on an extra day. Henry will understand. And you can help me write those letters to Mom and Cole." Cora paused and looked at the painting of the *Woman in Blue Reading a Letter* peering down from over the fireplace and was struck by the irony of the situation. "It's much easier reading letters than writing them! And you're good at writing—you love to write!"

"Oh, I think you need to do that," Ruth replied. "I think that's the purpose of the exercise." Cora looked over at her sister, and her face filled with disappointment. "But I'll do what I can," Ruth augmented and then gave her sister a quick smile. "Let me run and grab the coffeepot," she said as she jumped up, hoping to move beyond the letters. "You will drink another cup, won't you?" she asked, disappearing down the hall to the kitchen.

Cora got up and walked up to one of the two floor-to-ceiling bookcases that flanked the large fireplace and started reading through the titles, fingering the spines as she made her way down each shelf. "I didn't know you liked Edith Wharton!" she yelled. She pulled out a copy of *The Custom on the Country* and started to page through it.

"She's my favorite!" Ruth yelled back, popping her head from the kitchen and looking down the hall. "Find *The Custom of the Country*!" she shouted again. She grabbed the coffeepot and started to make her way back to the living room.

"I have it here," Cora started to yell, then stopped as her sister entered the room. "I have it here," she repeated, holding the book up.

"Take it with you and read it. Mother told me that your name came from that book. The main heroine is a girl named Undine Sprague, and that's where she got your middle name."

Cora picked up her purse and slipped the book inside. "Oh, I have to read it now! Is she a great leading lady?" Cora asked curiously, her vanity engaged.

"Well, that depends on your definition of *great*," Ruth responded and then laughed. "In fact, there are some similarities between you two," Ruth stated and then thought the better of it. "Just read it. But I will say this: once you've read it, you'll never forget Undine Sprague!"

"Now you really have me curious!" Cora exclaimed. She reached down and grabbed the book out of her purse and started to read the back cover.

"Put that away! You're going to spoil it!" Ruth demanded as she refilled their cups and then set the pot down. Just as Cora was placing the book back in her purse, the telephone in the hallway rang out.

"Oh, I bet that's Regina," Ruth said cheerily as she got up and walked out into the hallway. "She always calls about this time of day."

"Hello," Ruth answered. She sat down on a chair positioned right next to the phone stand and started to twirl the spiral cord around her free hand.

"It's great to hear from you too."

"I'm doing much better now. Really, I am."

"And thanks again for the beautiful flower arrangement. That was really thoughtful."

A long silence occurred, and Ruth nodded, as if agreeing wholeheartedly with the caller.

"Okay, then. Monday morning it is. I'll see you here at 9:00 a.m. I'll meet you in the office. Yes. Yes. Okay. Goodbye."

"Well, you're never going to believe who that was," Ruth said as she made her way back into the living room and sat down next to her sister. "It was Milton Pape, our banker," she added with a curious look on her face.

"What does he want?"

"He wants to meet with me this coming Monday. He said the loan board met and he needs to talk to me about our lines of credit."

"Have you dealt with him before?" Cora queried as she picked up her cup and blew on it.

"Well, I've met him, but Richard handled all the finances. He never would let me interfere with any of that."

"Just like a man," Cora shot back. She set her cup down, crossed her arms, and looked up at the painting above the fireplace again. "I just hope it's not bad news like our pregnant friend up there is getting in that letter," she added sardonically, pointing to the painting.

"How do you know it's bad news?" Ruth quipped back playfully.

"There's a man involved, I'd wager. So what else would it be?"

"Oh, Cora!" Ruth reacted. "You're terrible!"

"Think what you will, but men and finance, that's my area of expertise," she added cleverly.

CHAPTER
15

The Clarkson Funeral Home office, just off the main entrance to the building, had originally been added to the blueprint in the 1947 restoration. Werner and Marcella Clarkson, who were both at that time reaching middle age, had decided that the idea of an updated office on the main floor, a suggestion that had been brought up increasingly more by the funeral home staff, had become a necessity. They had originally been using a small office on the second floor and had been hesitant to give up furniture showroom space, but with increased regulations around both the funeral and the furniture businesses, running up a flight of stairs each time a special document was needed had become too much for the aging couple, and a spacious office was created just to the right of the main entrance to the old building. A large antique oak rolltop desk that Werner Clarkson found in the basement of the Commerce Bank building he had acquired in 1933 had been restored and placed as the centerpiece of the new office space, and as the years had gone by, additional technologies, fax machines, electric typewriters, central phone systems, had been added, which somehow clashed with the large old desk, an antique that Richard Clarkson had grown quite fond of and flatly refused to part with.

When Milton Pape walked into the office, Ruth was sitting at a smaller reception desk that sat beside the large rolltop typically used when new clients first came to the funeral home and was attempting to look over the books, something she had rarely done in the past. He was an elderly gentleman, born in the same year as Richard Clarkson, but had not aged as well as the deceased funeral home owner, and he looked fifteen years older than his actual age, a fact that didn't bother the old banker in the least. Milton and Richard had served on numerous committees and local civic projects over the years and had created a strong relationship, one that Richard had relied on when facing the annual loan review process. Based on the length of his tenure with the bank and a deed of trust to the building and all the business assets, Richard had been able to secure two substantial lines of credit: one that was used to cover cash flow shortages, and the other for business expenses. Although Ruth knew that the loans existed, since she had been forced to sign the original lending documents and all the subsequent renewal paperwork on numerous occasions, her understanding of exactly how the funds were used and, more importantly, repaid was severely lacking.

"Ah, Milton, come in and have a seat," she greeted as she got up to shake his hand. "How are you doing?"

The old man, dressed in a tight-fitting double-knit suit that was stretched to its limit, gingerly took a seat in a chair next to the desk and set his briefcase down by his feet. "Oh, better than some, I guess. My hip is killing me, though," he mumbled, arching his back and grimacing. "The gifts of old age, I guess," he added with a chuckle. "So how are *you* doing?" the old man asked as he finally seemed to settled in and looked up at Ruth, his chest heaving in and out as he struggled for air. "*That's* the question."

"I'm doing okay," Ruth offered up with a sense of forced optimism. "Things are finally getting back to normal at home, I guess. But I am struggling a little with the business side of it," she admitted. "But John and Vickie have really been lifesavers these past few months. Richard had really turned a lot of the day-to-day operations over to them."

"Well, that's good. I know Richard always wanted to keep involved in everything, but I guess with all his traveling, he finally realized that one person just can't do it all." He took a long pause and glanced at Ruth over the top of his glasses. "Are Charles and Regina involved in the business in any way?" he probed curiously.

"Not anymore," Ruth reported back, a little confused by the question. "Regina comes in and helps out if we get backed up with funerals, but she spends most of her time with her kids now, and

Charles is a deputy sheriff now over in Lincoln County, and he farms part-time too. So they're really pretty much out of it now."

"Oh yeah, yeah, kids these days go their own way, don't they?" He took a large gulp of air and looked over his glasses again. "So what's your plan going forward?"

"I guess we'll just plug along as best as we can," she answered sheepishly. She recognized that her answer was not a very good financial one as soon as the words left her mouth, and her face gave full disclosure of her sudden realization.

"So you mean to hold on to the business, then?" Milton puffed in total disbelief.

"Well, I have been giving it a lot of thought, and I was planning on it."

"It's a tough job for a man, much less a woman," the old banker replied unabashedly. "I just don't know," he said, slowing down and choosing his words carefully, "how the loan board is going to take to that idea." He reached down and pulled a folder out of his briefcase and plopped it on the desk.

"Oh my," Ruth remarked, as Cora's words, *Men and finance are my area of expertise,* ran though her mind.

"Here're copies of both of your lines of credit," Milton stated very matter-of-factly as he slid the papers over to Ruth. "One is due for review in three months, the other in six."

"Well, how much is drawn against these lines?" Ruth asked, unable to think of any other question.

"The cash flow line is maxed out," the old man answered, pulling another paper from his briefcase. "And the other, here, only has five thousand available."

Ruth glanced at the documents and saw that each line was capped at 100,000 dollars, and her heart sank.

"Well, let me look this all over and take it under advisement," Ruth said as she realized she was too ill-equipped to go on with the discussion. "I guess I have some decisions to make," she added with a counterfeit optimism. She quickly got up, hoping the old man would follow suit, but he remained seated, seemingly ignoring Ruth's overt gestures.

"Yes, yes, a lot of things to think about, Ruth. It's just not a good situation, is it?" he asked rhetorically. Ruth walked from behind the desk and tried again to marshal the old man toward the door.

"You be sure and give my best to your wife when you see her," she stated cordially.

Milton Pape finally pulled himself up from the chair, picked up his briefcase, and started to make his way out of the office.

"I sure will," he puffed out, then stopped his exit and turned and looked back at Ruth. "She's down in the city for the week. Our daughter is having a little marital problem, if you know what I mean, and she's down there to get things straightened out."

"Oh my," Ruth replied as the old banker limped out of the office.

CHAPTER 16

R uth was shopping the aisles of the neighborhood IGA store, a
locally owned market that had been open for business in the
little town of Ox Bend for over thirty years. Originally housed in a
turn-of-the-century downtown building that was destroyed in the
1963 tornado, the store had been moved to a new shopping center
that had been developed on the grounds of an old college, Central
Wesleyan, which had flourished in the county from 1864 through
1941. The small institution, which had been opened by the German
and English College of Quincy, Illinois, was dedicated to "provide a
home for orphans of the Civil War" and to "supply a higher educational institute for the youth of the German Church in the West,"
as defined in their very specific initial mission statement. Werner
Clarkson, Richard's father, had attended the small college and had
often gone into long harangues about the needless destruction of
the old abandoned campus buildings: the orphans' home, the ladies'
dormitory, and the main college building. One by one, with the
exception of the college church, they had all been unceremoniously
demolished as the grounds had been redeveloped for commercial
growth, and he flatly refused to shop at the IGA after it reopened on
what he considered hallowed ground, a decision that had made the
local market Ruth's favorite grocery.

As Ruth was reaching down for a cut of meat at the bottom of
a large freezer at the very back of the store, Mark Callier, the young
man that had first approached Ruth at Richard's funeral luncheon,
walked up behind her with a large manila envelope in his hand.
"Mrs. Clarkson," he interrupted, his voice timid and unsure. "Ruth
Clarkson," he repeated a little louder.

"Ah, you scared me!" Ruth exclaimed as she popped her head up from the freezer and looked around in surprise. "Oh, it's you," she added, finally recognizing the young man standing beside her. She observed that he was dressed in the same oversized dark suit that he had been wearing the first time she met him at Richard's funeral, and she noticed the large manila envelope clutched in his right hand; and although it had only been a little over a month since she had first met him, he looked different in some almost-undefinable way. His face seemed to be drawn in more and had a gaunt appearance under the unforgiving overhead fluorescent lighting, and he had dark circles under his light-blue eyes, which seemed to dart around nervously as he talked. His thick dark black hair appeared to be wet and was slicked back off his face, and he had a light beard shadow around his dimpled chin and squared-off jaw.

"I wondered if I'd ever see you again," Ruth stated pensively. "You know, you gave me quite a surprise that day."

"That wasn't my intent," the young man replied softly. "I didn't mean to upset you."

"Oh, I know you didn't, and I wasn't so much as upset as I was shocked," Ruth confessed honestly. "But you did give me a lot to think about." Ruth paused, and the young man said nothing. "So how did you find me here?" she asked apprehensively.

"I saw you leaving the funeral home, and I followed you," the young man confessed and then realized how cryptic his comment sounded. "But please don't be afraid of me," he added, sensing that Ruth was feeling uncomfortable. "I just want to talk to you, that's all." He reached over and gently grabbed Ruth by the arm.

Ruth looked down and then quickly pulled her arm away from the young man's grip. "I don't know if that's such a good idea," she answered uneasily.

"But I just want to talk to you," Mark implored with a sincerity that seemed to soften Ruth's resolve. "And Richard was my father!" he stated boldly. "You believe me, don't you?"

"Oh, I really don't know what to believe anymore." Ruth paused and seemed to be carefully considering what she wanted to say. "My husband and I had an unusual marriage, and there's so much that I really didn't know about him." She quickly stepped behind her shopping cart, grabbed the handle, and slowly started to move farther down the freezer aisle.

"Why are you afraid of me?" the young man pleaded as his shoulders drooped and his head bent forward. "Why is everyone afraid of me?" he repeated under his breath. "What have *I* done? What have *I* done to any of you?" Without saying another word, the young man slowly turned and started to walk away.

A great rush of compassion came over Ruth, and she turned and started walking back toward the young man. "Mark, wait!" she called out, as if controlled by some sense of compulsion. Mark stopped and turned around. "And let's say that we did talk," Ruth stated as the young man turned and faced her. "What could I possibly offer to you?" she asked with a deep tone of sincerity.

"The truth," the young man whispered. "The truth about my father. You know more about him than anyone, and I don't know anything about him at all, really. I only knew him as this shadow that would enter our lives and then leave just as quickly." He paused and looked down. "I guess I just want to know who my father really was."

Ruth reached out and grabbed the young man by the arm. "I sometimes think I hardly knew him either," she confessed honestly.

"Just give me a few minutes. Please," he begged, picking up on Ruth's subtle emotional change. "Just a few minutes."

"Okay," Ruth finally agreed. "Let's head up to the front of the store. There's a bench outside the store. We can sit there and talk." Ruth got behind her cart, and she and the young man started walking to the front of the store. "You probably told me when we first met, but I don't remember your last name," Ruth stated as they made their way down the aisle, a loose wheel on the shopping cart screeching the entire way.

"Callier," the young man answered respectfully.

"Ah, Mark Callier. Mark is a beautiful name. It means 'warrior like' in Latin, and of course, it has great biblical significance too." Ruth paused and looked over at the young man. "I'm sorry, I ramble when I get nervous."

"I make you nervous?"

"No, not really, but you do have to admit this is a unique situation."

"Yeah, I guess it is," the young man replied and flashed a brief smile for the first time.

"So do you live around here?" Ruth asked, feeling a little more relaxed.

"No. I'm staying with an aunt over in St. Charles County. My mother and I used to live in the city in the Shaw Park area," he added with a regretful tone.

"Oh, I'm familiar with that area. I was raised in Lafayette Square."

"Yeah, I know that area well," Mark countered.

"You sure are dressed up for grocery shopping," Ruth observed as they turned a corner at the end of the bread-and-bakery aisle and headed toward the checkout area.

"Oh yeah," the young man replied awkwardly. He looked down at his worn-out suit coat and tugged at the lapel with his left hand. "I have a job interview this morning."

"Here, let me check out and I'll meet you outside in a few minutes," Ruth suggested as they approached the front of the store. Ruth went through the checkout line, and the young man went outside, sat down on the bench, and laid the envelope that he had been clutching by his side.

"It's actually really nice out here today," Ruth stated as she approached the young man sitting on the bench outside the store.

"Yeah, I guess it is," the young man responded as he moved over to the far end of the bench.

"Yes. Now, you said that you lived in the Shaw area, and I know that neighborhood very well," Ruth started out nervously as she sat down on the bench next to him and placed her bag of groceries at her side. "Beautiful homes, a little sketchy though," she added. "So where does your mother live now?" she asked, both her curiosity and her parental instincts taking over.

The young man looked out at the College Methodist Church just across the street from the market, the final remnant of the old

Wesleyan College. "She's dead," he answered with little emotion as he continued to stare at the old brick church.

"Oh, I'm sorry to hear that," Ruth responded. Without thinking, she placed her hand on the young man's arm and gave it a gentle squeeze, and he looked back at Ruth and then bowed his head. "There's little in this world worse than the loss of a mother," Ruth added parentally. "When did she die?"

The young man said nothing and started to wring his hands together on his lap.

Ruth clutched his trembling hands in her own. "I'm sorry, Mark, I didn't mean to bring up a lot of bad memories. We don't have to talk about this if you don't want to."

"I blame him for her death," the young man finally blurted out unexpectedly, after a long pause. "I blame him!"

"Who?" Ruth asked.

"Richard!" Mark half-shouted as he looked back up at Ruth.

"Why would you think that?" Ruth asked in her most sincere voice.

"Because…," the young man started out and then just fell silent.

"Mark, let's just start over. Let's start from the beginning. Okay?" she asked, giving his clenched hands another squeeze. "First of all, why do you believe that Richard is your father?"

"Because he is!" Mark responded frantically. "Because I spent my childhood with him!"

"Are you sure it was *my* Richard? Richard Clarkson?"

Without saying a word, the young man picked up the envelope that was lying on the bench next to him and pulled out a small collection of black-and-white photos and handed them to Ruth. She started to thumb through the stack and then stopped at one particular photo. "Oh my god," she uttered under her breath. She held it up before her face, and the rest of pictures slipped off her lap.

"Here, I got them," the young man responded quickly. He got down on one knee and started to collect the photos from the pavement. "I'm sorry that you had to find out this way," the young man said as he looked up at Ruth. Ruth, who was still staring at the photo in her hand, said nothing, and the young man retook his seat next to her.

"You're right, this is Richard," Ruth finally confessed, her heart beating rapidly, her mind drifting back on her time with Richard. She continued to stare at a black-and-white photo of her husband laughing at the camera, sitting in front of the Elephant House at the St. Louis Zoo, a small curly-headed young boy perched on his lap. "It's Richard. That's my husband," she admitted. She looked out across the street at the old church and then back down at the small photo, and tears started to roll down her face. "And look how happy he looks." She turned and looked at the young man who was sitting silently by her side. "I don't ever remember seeing him that happy."

CHAPTER 17

Cole and Emma Saroh's three children were looking over the lunch menu on the patio at Romains, a trendy restaurant in Lafayette Square, just a block from where Cora and Henry Lasciter were living on Rutger Street. The Lasciters had, at the insistence of Cora, completely restored an old home on what the locals referred to as "short" Rutger, a tree-lined avenue of exceptional, turn-of-the-century homes only a block off the trendy business district of the area that included several very prominent restaurants. And what made the street so unique to the old neighborhood was the fact that half of the street contained "mirrored homes," so as residents entered the street and looked at a house to the left, they would find an identical "mirrored image" just like it across the street, an idea that somehow had always intrigued Cora. Their massive three-story home, which included a miniature swimming pool, was only a few streets up from the original Saroh homeplace on Hickory Street, a Second Empire-style Victorian home that was in desperate need of restoration. Romains, where Cora and Henry often found themselves on weeknights, was located in an older brick structure with a massive mahogany bar at the entranceway that had a stained glass window as its centerpiece that looked out onto the patio.

"How is Christie doing?" Ruth asked as the waiter walked away with the drink orders.

"Yes, tell us," Cora chimed in before Lawrence could respond.

"Things are going great," Lawrence answered with an unexpected twinkle in his eye. He paused and set his menu down. "You know that she lost her husband to heart disease just about two years ago now, and I often think that I'm just another burden for her. But she seems happy. I hope she really is."

Cora looked directly at her brother with a discerning smirk. "Women fake a lot of things, but happiness is seldom one of them," she retorted with a subtle laugh.

"Oh, I'm sure she's happy," Ruth jumped in, giving her sister a stern look.

"And she has her children and her grandchildren now," Lawrence went on, ignoring Cora's remark completely. "So we each maintain a lot of our freedom. And I think that's best. We're even keeping our finances separate. What's hers is hers, and what's mine is mine!" he added.

"Is that the trend now?" Cora mocked. She lifted her glass, as if to propose a toast. "Let's just hope it doesn't become a permanent thing," she added as she gazed out across the crowd. "Oh, look, there's a poster from last year's house tour!" she exclaimed. She pointed across the patio, and Ruth and Lawrence turned to take a look for themselves. "You all must join me next year when they have it again. I think you'd like it."

"Three-story homes with long flights of steps just don't work from where I'm seated," Lawrence threw out as he patted the handles on his wheelchair.

"Well, not just wheelchairs," Ruth chimed in. "What do older people do down here? Could you imagine if Mother still lived here? At least in Webster she was able to set herself up in that bedroom suite on the main floor."

"Yes, until she burned it down," Cora teased sarcastically.

"Oh, Cora!" Ruth admonished. She reached over and gently slapped her sister on the arm.

"Well, so what are we going to do?" the pragmatic Lawrence asked as he attempted to refocus the direction of the discussion. "I think that she's just become too much for you, Ruth. I know you think that you can handle it, but it's just too much."

"He's right," Cora joined in. "And even if you could, I think you need to take some time for yourself. Between mother and that funeral home, you hardly have a chance to do anything for you anymore!"

"What about the Shepherds Crossing Home, where Dad is?" Lawrence threw out.

"Yes, that's a good option," Cora agreed.

"And they'd be together again," Lawrence countered.

Ruth just sat back in her chair and said nothing, and Lawrence looked at Ruth imploringly. "This has to be a joint decision," he added. "We all have to be in agreement."

"So you really think that's the best decision?" Ruth finally asked. She was looking back and forth between her brother and sister, trying to read their expressions.

"Yes, yes, we do," they both jumped in together.

"It's just so final," Ruth whispered, as if the thought of it was more than she could bear. She set her menu down on the table and sat back in her chair, and her face took on a melancholy slant. "I was there the day they came for Richard's mother," she started out somberly, "and took her to the home out there in Ox Bend." Ruth stopped talking and crossed her arms tightly and started to nervously rub the outside of her arms. "I'll never forget that day as long as I live. She was living in this beautiful home about four miles outside of town. She and Werner had built it back in the early fifties, and it was a two-story home with a lot of steps, and it had a lot of ground with it, and she was getting too old, and she just couldn't stay there by herself anymore. So Richard made the decision to put her in the nursing home." Ruth paused and looked down as if she were seeing it all play out again. "And the day they came out to get her, Richard and I were both there. She had gotten really bad at the end, and we had actually been taking turns staying overnight so she wouldn't be alone. And this van pulled up, and two men came in and put her in a wheelchair and took her out of the house. Just like that. She didn't say anything, she didn't yell, or even cry, for that matter. She just got in the chair and they rolled her out." Ruth paused again and grabbed a tissue from her pocket and wiped her nose. "And I knew that she'd never be in her house again. That that was the last time she'd see her home." Ruth paused and looked down. "And I kept wondering what she was thinking as they took her away. I wondered what it must be like to be at that point in your life, when the end is so near, when you're leaving your home forever." Ruth paused and looked back up at Cora and Lawrence sitting silently across the table. "And I walked outside as they drove off with her. I can still see her, just like it was yesterday, perched in the back of that van as they drove her away."

"Do you think she knew that she was leaving her home for the last time?" Lawrence asked.

"Oh, I think she knew, and I guess that she had just accepted it, was ready to face the end."

"But how do you accept that?" Cora interjected, sounding unexpectedly melancholy. "How do you accept it?"

"I guess that's a question that we'll all have an answer before too long," Lawrence countered as he looked at his sisters affectionately.

Cora reached for a tissue of her own. "How did Richard take it?" she asked.

"You know, Richard never cried at his mother's funeral, or at his dad's, for that matter. But that day they took his mother away, he cried violently. Almost to the point that I was starting to worry about him. It was something I had never seen him do before, or after, as far as that goes."

"Never underestimate the bond between a son and his mother," Lawrence whispered.

Cora grabbed her sister's forearm and gave it a tight squeeze. "Mom is so lucky to have you caring for her. Most children don't want their parents around when they get old. Hell, most of them don't even want them when they're young!" she added and then let out a small laugh as she attempted to lighten the mood. "But let us help you with this. We'll get through it all together."

"Okay," Ruth acquiesced. "Decision made."

"This old-age business is not for the faint of heart!" Cora snapped as she took a drink of water and sat back in her chair. The waiter walked by with a tray full of drinks and motioned that he would be right back.

"The old Tibetan proverb is true," Ruth said wistfully. "After the mountain, more mountains."

CHAPTER 18

Shepherds Crossing Nursing Home was only about three miles from Cora Lasciter's home in Lafayette Square, in a commercially zoned area close to St. Louis University. The building had originally housed a rehabilitation facility that acted as a bridge between the hospital and home and had been staffed with a large number of physical therapists, many of them graduates of St. Louis University's physical therapy program, and the institution had even acted as a field training site for those close to graduation. But the age of the building and the costs to bring it up to the current standards required by a modern physiotherapy institution forced the owners to relocate to a newer structure on the other side of the university, and Shepherds Crossing bought it shortly thereafter.

Cora and Ruth, seated in the waiting area just off the main entrance, were waiting for their two o'clock appointment with the facility admissions adviser.

"God, it smells in here," Cora whispered to her sister as she looked around, the realities of old age pressing in around her.

"I don't think that can be helped in places like this," Ruth replied defensively. "Old people don't keep so well," she uttered. She flushed with embarrassment and looked down as she realized what she had said.

"Lawrence was right, you have been spending too much time with me lately!" Cora teased.

"I know! What is it about you that seems to remove everyone's filters?"

"Who needs filters?" Cora thundered. "When you get to our age, you just need to say what you have to say. You may not get another chance."

Ruth gave her sister a slight grin of recognition. "Maybe you're right. Maybe you're right," she repeated, as if trying to convince herself.

"Write that down!" Cora joked.

"Oh, here he comes now," Ruth whispered to her sister. "Please try to behave yourself."

The facility admissions adviser, Thurston Bellows, a rotund man in his midfifties with long tufts of hair sticking out his ears and a completely bald head, ushered the two ladies into his office and offered them a choice of coffee or water, which was denied by both, and then dismissed himself as he went to get the set of admission papers that was required of all new patients.

"My god, did you see his ears?" Cora whispered mischievously to her sister. "I guess men don't really lose hair, it just comes out somewhere else," she added, then giggled.

"Stop that!" Ruth commanded, as she flushed with embarrassment. "And sit back and just relax. He's going to hear you."

"I doubt that!" Cora retorted and then thought the better of it when her sister gave her a disapproving stare. "This is the most uncomfortable chair I've ever sat in," Cora whispered with a conciliatory tone, hoping to move the conversation away from her jokes about Mr. Bellows. She placed her hands on her lower back and arched her spine. "My back is killing me!"

"Yeah. You can tell they want us to visit but not stay too long," Ruth quipped just before Mr. Bellows returned with an application in hand.

The medical part of the interview process was quite lengthy, as Mr. Bellows went through a rather-long list of pertinent questions about the patient's overall health, medications, special needs, physical impairments, dietary restrictions, etc., but the financial part of the process was significantly truncated because of the fact that a "financial worksheet" had already been compiled when Cole was admitted to the home, and that information was simply copied and attached to Emma's admission file. The interview was followed by a grand tour of the place, which had been constructed in a large square with an outside garden located in the center. The fifteen-minute tour took them through a typical single-occupancy room, the general dining area, the facility recreation room, the in-house beauty parlor and barbershop, one of the central nursing stations that was located at the end of each of the halls, and the centralized showering area, with newly purchased, special lift machinery. As they finished up, they found themselves back at the front office, having completed the three-sixty tour.

"We'll need payment for the first month up front and at least a two-week notice to secure a room," Thurston Bellows explained as they headed back into the office, and the sisters retook their seats. "We have your father's information here on file already, and we'll work with Dr. Prelutsky—I know he's been your parents' physician for some years now, so we'll have him send over your mother's information as well. We also have a staff physician on call here at the facility, and of course, he will work in tandem with your family physician on the patients' overall health plan. In case of an emergency, we send all our residents to the St. Louis University Hospital, which is located just down the street." Mr. Bellows paused a moment to let his mind catch up with his memorized monologue. "There really aren't any set visiting hours, as you probably already know, but if you do visit after 8:00 p.m., you will have to use the side entrance that I pointed out to you on the tour. The front entrance is number-coded for entry and is completely closed after that time for the security and protection of all our residents. Any questions?" he asked, finally taking a generous breath.

"No, I think that answers all our questions," Cora stated as she got up, glad to be off the uncomfortable chair. "We'll talk to our brother, Lawrence, about it—we want to bring him in on the final decision—and I will call you later today."

"Very well," Mr. Bellows said. He rose and shook hands with each sister and handed each of them an advertising brochure from a marketing case that he had prominently displayed on his desk. "Welcome to the Shepherds Crossing family!" he added with a large, uncomfortable-looking grin.

Ruth grabbed her sister by the arm as they were walking out of the office. "Okay, Cora, you need to go down and have your visit with Daddy," she stated firmly. "You have your letter with you, don't you?"

"Yes," Cora answered reluctantly.

"Well, then you have no more excuses. You've been putting this off long enough, and you just need to do it."

"What if he's not even awake?" Cora threw out as an excuse, her face turning white. "What if he doesn't even know who I am anymore?"

"Oh, I'm sure he knows you—he knew who I was a few days ago!" Ruth paused and tried to think of a more convincing argument. "And you know what Dr. Whitman said: this is for you, not him!"

Cora just stood motionless and started to tremble, and Ruth grabbed her sister by the forearm.

"Do you want me to go with you?" she asked, somewhat reluctantly.

"No," Cora finally countered, her sense of purpose returning. She straightened up and looked down the long corridor that led to her father's room, as if she might have been staring into some dark abyss. "You're right, you're right," she repeated, as if trying to convince herself. "I just need to go ahead and do this."

"Just remain calm and think about what you're saying." Ruth paused and threw her arms around her sister. "Words without thought never to heaven go," she whispered in her ear.

$$C \; H \; A \; P \; T \; E \; R$$
19

S hepherds Crossing Nursing Home had originally been suggested by an old, longtime friend and oncologist who had treated several members of the Saroh family over the years, Dr. David Butler, who had used the institution for both of his aging parents, a decision that he had never come to regret. Based on his recommendation and the fact that it was a certified skilled nursing home, the Saroh children admitted their father when his health issues had simply made caring for him at home an impossibility, a decision that was met with ferocious resistance from the aging patriarch, at least initially. Emma Saroh, his wife of over fifty years, had originally opposed the move as well, but the frontline reality of being the one in charge of his day-to-day care, monitoring his ever-changing lists of medications, arranging for transportation to three separate specialists, dealing with unending insurance forms and papers, and his constant mood changes soon altered her stance on the matter, and she had gladly relinquished her ever-growing list of obligations.

Cole Saroh had originally been diagnosed with frontotemporal dementia at age eighty, after he had started showing symptoms that strangely affected his language, and the diagnosis had been later confirmed when changes in his conduct, judgment, empathy, and foresight were also noticed. The family had initially thought he displayed signs of Alzheimer's, but as the doctors had been quick to explain, Alzheimer's patients typically have trouble thinking of the right word or the right name but have much less difficulty making sense when they speak, listen, or read, which certainly wasn't the case with Mr. Saroh.

The room was a small single-occupancy space with a window looking out on the Serenity Garden, as it had been referred to in the home's brochure, with a small bathroom located at the front entrance. A tightly plaited, commercial-grade beige carpet covered the entire area, with the exception of the bathroom, which had been fitted with a special slip-resistant tile. A small heating-and-cooling unit, wedged under the back window, was blowing an almost-intolerable stream of hot air across the room. The bed, an adjustable, fully electric hospital bed with a plastic-coated air mattress that had been specifically designed for long-term-care patients, was located against the side wall at the front of the room, allowing easy access to the toilet area. An oxygen machine placed beside the bed was putting out a muted drone, and one of the nurses on staff, who had just administered the morning rounds of medications, was emptying a urinal as Cora entered the room.

"Just a minute!" the nurse yelled out over the loud swishing noise of a flushing toilet. "He needs his bed changed," she added. She took a can of Lysol off the back of the toilet and gave the small room a quick spray. "Oh, I'm sorry!" She blushed as she almost ran into Cora as she rushed out of the bathroom. "I thought you were someone from housekeeping." She stopped and brushed her forehead with her wrist.

"Oh, that's all right," Cora answered sheepishly, her nerves even more frazzled.

"Are you family?" the nurse asked, sensing the visitor's apprehensive feelings.

"Yes. I am his daughter," Cora whispered with hollow words. She inched her way farther into the room and nervously looked around, as if she were entering a foreign world.

"Oh, I guess I just haven't seen you here before," the nurse replied with a perfunctory half-smile. She removed her rubber gloves and placed them in a wastebasket next to the bed.

"Well, I don't get over here as much as I should," Cora said half-heartedly, feeling some unexplained compulsion to defend herself. She finally got up enough nerve to go and stand next to her father. "How is he doing?" she asked as she finally looked down at her father for the first time.

"He was pretty good this morning," the nurse reported, her voice reportorial and upbeat at the same time. "We had him up earlier, and he even went down to the dining room for his breakfast." She grabbed the patient's file off the dresser and started to make a few notes. "He usually just wants to take his meals here in the room, but we always try to encourage him to get out more."

Cora noticed a wheelchair parked in the corner of the room. "Can he still walk?" she asked as she looked back at the nurse.

"Barely. We still try to get him to stand a little and go to the bathroom, but he's so wobbly now we're afraid he'll fall."

"Oh, I see," Cora replied, looking back down and noticing a bright-red "fall risk" bracelet around his dark-blue wrist.

"He's quite a character," the nurse retorted as she continued to fill out the patient's file. "He's a sweetie, though, but he does keep us on our toes."

"I can only imagine," Cora responded cryptically as she tried to analyze the nurse's comments. She set her purse down and pulled up a small folding chair next to the bed and sat down.

"Go ahead, try to wake him!" the nurse bellowed out, used to raising her voice to be heard. "He was awake just a few minutes ago, but he can doze off at the drop of a hat, and he's been sleeping all morning, and he needs to stay awake for a while." The nurse grabbed the old man's file and hurried out of the room in response to a buzzer echoing out in the hallway.

Cora just sat silently for a few minutes and watched her father lying on the bed, his breaths shallow and irregular. She looked down at the oxygen machine putting out a dull drone across the room and noticed the rubber hoses wrapped around his ears and inserted into his nose.

"Daddy," she whispered. "Daddy," she uttered again after receiving no response. She leaned forward on the chair and looked down closely at the old man lying in the bed. His face was gaunt and thin, with deep hollows around his eyes, and his head was tilted back, his mouth open as he struggled for air, his breathing labored and irregular. His hands, which were on top of the covers, were cracked and grossly misshapen from arthritis and covered in dark age spots, and his fingernails were long and in desperate need of trimming. "Daddy, it's Cora," she tried again, a little louder. Suddenly, his eyes started to flutter and twitch, as if he might have been waking up, and for just a moment she thought of escaping, running away, avoiding the uncomfortable realities of her past; but then memories of Dr. Whitman flooded her consciousness, and she stood her ground. "Daddy, wake up! It's Cora," she finally commanded again as she regained her courage. She sat back into the chair, folded her arms, and just stared out the back window, as if worn out by all, the hot, dry air of the heater blowing on her face.

"Daddy, I don't know if you can hear me or not," she finally started up again, her voice surprisingly clear and direct. "But I guess that doesn't really make any difference now. Dr. Whitman says that I am doing this for me. Not you." She paused and looked back down at her father seemingly oblivious to his visitor. "Oh, I guess you're wondering who Dr. Whitman is?" she asked disdainfully, as if she were carrying on a two-way conversation with herself. "Well, he's the psychiatrist that I have been seeing on and off for the past few years who's trying to fix all the things in my life that are broken." She hesitated and took a deep breath, as if looking for the strength to go on. "I guess it's hard to believe that Daddy's little girl has problems," she finally uttered in a sarcastic tone that seemed to come from some deep, inner place. She paused again, uncrossed her arms, and leaned forward in the chair toward her father, her courage increasing by the moment. "You know, I tried for years to figure out why you did all those things to me. I always wondered if it was something that I had done or something that I had said that started it all. I think now that's why I always kept our little secret, why I lived in silence. It was because I sort of blamed myself."

Cora took a short pause, as if she were reloading a gun. "But you have no idea what you did to me!" she fired out in defiance. "You have no idea how what you did affected my childhood, my relationships, my marriages." She stopped and let out a guttural, repressed laugh. "Did you know that I am on lucky number four now? I've become *Daddy's little girl* to a lot of different men," she continued, her voice rising. She stood up from the chair and glared down at her father, her anger reaching its apex. "But I'm done with all that now. I'm done with you! I'm done with feeling guilty! I'm done blaming myself! I'm just done!" she yelled out, as if she were emptying the chamber. She paused, her body trembling. "And I know hating you is only hurting and controlling me, but I will never forgive you," she added. Just as she started to turn away from the bed, the old man's eyes opened. "Oh, so there you are, Daddy," she whispered, turning back around, her eyes dancing wildly. She bent down over the bed again and looked him in the eyes. The old man said nothing and just looked up at her, his deep-set eyes wide and alert, filled with fear, his breathing suddenly deep and rapid.

"So what do have to say to me?" Cora demanded. She continued looking down at the hollow shell of the man she had always known as her father, and for one brief moment, she almost felt sorry for him, could almost feel the love she once held in her heart.

Cole Saroh again, true to his lifelong practice of silence, said nothing and just continued to stare up at his daughter, his body quivering with fear.

Finally, Cora bent down and whispered in his ear, "I used to love you, Daddy. I loved you more than anything in this world."

She stood up, grabbed her purse from the floor, and walked out of the room.

CHAPTER
20

C ora and Ruth were sitting out on the back portico of Cora's three-story home on Rutger Street in Lafayette Square just as the sun was starting to set. The remnants of two large salads from Calico's Restaurant were lying on the patio coffee table, along with half of a lemon layer cake from Miss Hulling's Bakery, and a half-empty pot of coffee.

"Well, you got your Calico's salad," Cora gibed as she closed the lid on her to-go box. "All the great restaurants here in this city and you always want another Calico's salad," she added and then laughed.

"I can't help it," Ruth defended. "I've loved them since I was kid!"

Cora cut a large slice of the lemon layer cake and placed it on a small saucer. "Ah, so you have," she replied, licking her fingers.

Ruth took the piece of cake and looked keenly at her sister, who was starting to cut a second piece. "So do you want to talk about it?" Ruth asked. "I can understand if you don't. I just want to make sure that you're okay."

"No, actually I do want to tell you about it," Cora answered calmly. She laid the cake knife down and then took a seat across from her sister. "It was quite a visit."

"Well, do you feel any better about it now?" Ruth asked, with a little hesitancy in her voice.

"You know I do," Cora replied positively. "I do feel a little better, just like Dr. Whitman always said I would. Of course, I wouldn't want to go through anything like that again, but I do feel better now that I faced him."

Ruth took another bite of cake and then nodded as she reached for her coffee. "What did he have to say for himself?"

"That's just it—he never said a word."

"What?" Ruth grilled inquisitively.

"He never said a word!" Cora replied firmly. "When I first walked in, there was a nurse in the room, and she seemed to know him very well—she was a tall thin woman in her midforties, with long brown hair. She even said he was quite a character." Cora paused and thought back for a moment. "Yes, I think that's exactly how she put it: quite a character. And right before she left, she told me to go ahead and try to wake him up because he was sleeping too much."

"Yes, I know which nurse you're talking about. She's always there during the mornings. And I had the same problem with him a few weeks ago when I was there!" Ruth concurred.

"So I sat down at the side of the bed and tried to get him to wake up. But he didn't respond when I called out his name. His eyes sort of fluttered, but he never seemed to really wake up. And I tried a couple more times, but still no response." Cora stopped and placed her hands on her cheeks and shook her head back and forth. "And he had that heater in the room going full blast! Oh my god, it had to be close to ninety degrees in there!"

"It's like that every time I go in there too!" Ruth commiserated as she, too, started shaking her head. "He's always so cold. It has to do with the blood circulation, I guess, or the medications he's on."

"Well, his must be circulating only once a day now!" Cora joked as she let out a nervous laugh.

"So you never got him awake?"

"Not at first, but just like Dr. Whitman suggested, I went ahead and confronted him about what I was feeling. I mean, I just let it all out."

"And he said nothing!" Ruth rejoined in surprise.

"No. He just lay there. At first, I thought he was sleeping, but I don't know. I just had this feeling that he was really awake. And I think he heard every word I said, because at the end, right as I started to leave, he finally opened his eyes, and he looked up at me, and I just knew that he had heard everything that I said." She paused and thought for a moment, a chill running through her body. "And I could see fear in his eyes too. He never said a word, but he was afraid."

"Oh my," Ruth countered. "I can only imagine what he was thinking."

"And I told him that I would never forgive him," Cora replied with a stamp of finality. "And I never will!"

"Never say never," Ruth replied. "You never know what the future might bring or how your heart might change."

"What? Have you forgiven Richard?" Cora barked back, trying to change the subject.

Ruth set her cake down on the table and leaned back in her chair. "You know, I think I have," she responded with a sense of heartfelt sincerity. "It didn't happen overnight, but I've known for years about my husband's shortcomings. And after his funeral and all the wonderful things that people said about him, my feelings toward him changed in some way. It's so strange, you can live with somebody your whole life and yet they still remain a mystery!" She stopped and looked closely at her sister. "For if you forgive men when they sin against you, your heavenly Father will also forgive you."

"That's why you're the good one," Cora retorted half-jokingly. "And I'm the bad one!"

"Oh, nonsense, Cora! You always sell yourself short. But give it time. Daddy's in that horrible place, and who really knows the reality of being where he is, on that unforgiving precipice, until you're at that point yourself? So give yourself some time, and I believe that you will eventually forgive him." Ruth paused. "No, I know that over time you will forgive him." Ruth reached forward and picked up her cup off the table and poured herself another cup of coffee. "Are you going to talk to Mother too?" she asked tentatively, adding cream to her coffee.

"Yes, I think I have to. In some ways I'm dreading that talk just as much as the one with Daddy."

"Oh, I don't think it will be that bad. Why don't you come out next weekend?" Ruth suggested. "You can stay over again. You can talk to her then."

"Okay, that's our plan, but I don't want to talk about me anymore." Cora paused, and a roguish smile came over her. "I know that's hard to believe!" she added with a guttural laugh. "But let's change the subject," she demanded, taking a huge bite of cake. "I have an appointment with Dr. Whitman tomorrow, and I'm sure he'll have me rehashing this all over again, anyway!"

"Well, there is something else I have been wanting to talk to you about," Ruth started out. "It's about the funeral home and my keeping the business. How are things going between you and Henry? I know you said that things were rough for a while."

"You know, I think things are going to be okay. We've actually been focusing on it in therapy, and I don't know. Dr. Whitman thinks it might help if he joined me in a couple of sessions, and he's agreed to do that. And I'm starting to see a different side of him now." Cora stopped and seemed to be thinking carefully about her next statement. "He's changing," she finally blurted out.

"Oh, I think it's more likely that you're changing," Ruth volleyed back. "I think this therapy is helping and you're finally getting to know yourself."

"You sound like Dr. Whitman." Cora puffed with a smirk. "That's what he keeps saying. He says that I'm finally starting to *value* myself."

"Well, I think he's probably right!" Ruth interjected. "And I think Daddy had a huge impact on how you see yourself, how you value yourself."

"Well, maybe so, but I wonder sometimes if I'm really making any progress. Sometimes I feel like I'm just wasting my time in therapy."

"When skies are hanged and oceans drowned, the single secret will still be man," Ruth replied with a grin. "It takes a while to understand your fellow man, and even longer to understand yourself!"

"Ah, you may be right. If you had just pointed that out to me two husbands ago!" Cora joked.

"Seriously, Cora, I don't think Henry is changing at all." Ruth stopped and looked intensely at her sister. "I think *you* are. I think you're changing into someone who's more comfortable with herself.

You're changing into a person with a strong self-image. You're becoming the person you should have always been."

"Well, you're as responsible for that as anyone!" Cora countered. "And you may be right. I am getting comfortable with Henry's pragmatic way of looking at things. I think he sort of balances me out."

"That brings me back to why I asked about him. I know that Henry has a lot of expertise with business and finance. Do you think he could take a look at the funeral home books and help me decide what to do?"

"I'm sure he would," Cora mumbled, her mouth full of cake. "But he's cutthroat. He'll tell you exactly what he thinks, whether you want to hear it or not."

"Well, maybe that kind of honesty is exactly what I need."

"So I take it that your visit with your banker didn't go as planned?"

"No, it definitely didn't." Ruth leaned forward and crossed her arms. "And I think the idea of a woman running a business like a funeral home is way beyond him."

"He said that?" Cora barked back defiantly as she set her cake down.

"Not in so many words, but I'm good at reading between the lines. And now I'm more determined than ever to keep the business going!"

"And I have no doubt that you can!" Cora replied.

"So do you think Henry would help?" Ruth asked again, going back to the original question.

"Of course he will," Cora answered with absolute assurance. "Henry likes being right much more than he likes being loved. I'll just make him think it's the right thing to do!" she added, then laughed out loud.

"And how do you do that?" Ruth asked, a befuddled look coming over her.

"His expertise is business. Mine is getting men to do what I want them to do!" she thundered with a smirk.

"Oh, Cora!" Ruth exclaimed. "You don't talk like this to other people, do you?"

CHAPTER
21

The weather had turned wet again, and the local flood warnings that had only been discontinued a few weeks prior were back on the television, the massive amounts of water from up north continuing to flood the lower Mississippi and Missouri River basins. The local farming communities had hardly been able to plant even a third of the fields, since many lay soaked under as much as a foot of water and the ground was just too waterlogged to support heavy farm machinery. Ruth was waiting for her daughter to come and pick her up for a day game at Busch Stadium, and Cora had arrived a few hours earlier, with plans to stay overnight and complete her therapy assignment by confronting her mother, Emma. Ruth was standing in front of the closet mirror, trying on Cardinal sweatshirts and windbreakers, trying to find something suitable to wear.

"That looks fine," Cora barked from the bedroom dressing chair as Ruth was busy trying on her third Cardinal sweatshirt. "You're just going to a ball game, and it's probably going to get rained out, anyway," she added with a laugh.

"I know, but none of them fit me right," Ruth griped. She stepped back from the mirror and tugged at a tight-fitting sweatshirt with the name Musial on the back. "They're either too long or too short or too loose or too tight!"

"Just wear that one," Cora ordered. "Who's this Musial guy, anyway?" she added, hoping to infuriate her sister.

"Oh! You're hopeless!" Ruth shot back. Just as she started to try on another sweatshirt, she heard the elevator creaking up to the third floor. "That's them now. I have to go. Don't forget, Mom's medication and her Ensure shakes are in the bottom of the fridge," she rattled off as she headed for the door. Just as she was ready to depart, she stopped and looked back at her sister. "Don't back out of this now. If you're going to do it, now's the time. She's going to Shepherds next Monday."

"I know, I know," Cora responded, her mood changing suddenly. "I guess tonight it is, then," she added as Ruth disappeared down the hall.

Cora went to the back window and looked out at the light rain that was beating against the windowpane and attempted to formulate a first sentence, a starting point for the difficult discussion she needed to have with her mother. She had initially thought that she might just read the letter that she had written for her therapy session, but she opted to start out speaking from her heart, with the letter in hand as a backup if necessary. No time like the present, she thought to herself as she turned and headed down the hall.

"Mom, are you awake?" she yelled, slowly opening the door to the middle guest room. "I'm coming in."

"No, I'm not sleeping, dear," Emma responded with a faint voice as she adjusted her hearing aid. "Just lying here with my eyes closed."

"Well, get some light in here," Cora replied, half-disgusted. She tucked her letter in her dress pocket, went to the window, pulled back the curtains, and pulled up the shades. "It's raining, but you can still get a little light."

"Has Ruth left already?" the old woman asked feebly.

"Yes! You're stuck with me now!" Cora replied kiddingly.

Emma put her arm up to cover her eyes, as if the light from outside was blinding her, and Cora walked to the foot of the bed and started cranking the head of the bed up. "You need some daylight in here, and you need to sit up a little while too," she barked. "Is that enough, or do you want it a little higher?"

"That's good. That's good," the old woman answered, meekly pulling her covers up around her shoulders. "It's always so cold in here." She shuddered.

"Cold! It's almost eighty in here!" Cora fired back. She pointed to a thermostat sitting on the bed stand that Emma had insisted Ruth purchase.

"I know, but I just never feel warm anymore." She stopped moving, and a silence came over her. "I would just like to feel warm again," she finally said as she looked her daughter in the eye.

"Okay, let's get you another blanket, Mom," Cora responded with a slight tone of repentance. She went to a large cedar chest in the corner of the room, pulled out another blanket, and then placed it over the two that were already on the bed. "There, is that better now?" she asked. The old woman said nothing and just pulled the third blanket up tight around her neck.

"Mom, I need to talk to you," Cora started out very intently. She sat down on a small folding chair beside the bed that was used when visitors came. "I need to talk about when I was a little girl."

"Ah, who can remember that far back?" Emma grunted with a disinterested tone. She glanced down at the thermostat on the bed stand and then looked away toward the window.

"Unfortunately, there're certain things that I remember that I wish I *could* forget," Cora replied as her confidence increased. "But I can't. And Dr. Whitman thinks that the only way I can deal with them is by revisiting them. Bringing them back up and facing them."

"So what exactly do you want to talk about?" the old woman asked with a slight tone of irritation. "And what good does dredging up old memories do, anyway?" she added as she sat up a little straighter in her bed. "Retrospection has its price, you know. It takes its toll."

"Well, believe it or not, retrospection, as you call it, has done more for me than you could ever imagine," Cora shot back. The old woman just clenched her jaw and said nothing. "As you know, I started to see my psychiatrist again, a Dr. Whitman, and he's been helping me deal with a lot of things that happened to me when I was a little girl."

"What things?" the mother asked as she finally looked back at her daughter.

"I think you know what things!" Cora replied, holding her mother's gaze.

"Oh, Cora, what are you talking about? Turn on the radio. Let's see if the game's started," she demanded. She pulled her left hand out from under the covers and pointed to the radio on the table beside the bed.

Cora stood up from her chair, bent down over her mother, and just looked her in the eye. "We are going to talk about this, Mother," she proclaimed in a tone of resolute determination. "And we're going to talk about it now."

"To what end? Why bring it all up now?" Emma snorted, realizing that her daughter would not be dissuaded.

"Because I am the one who's suffered from it!" Cora fired back, her emotions boiling. "I'm the one who's lived with it my whole life. I'm the one who lost her childhood!"

"Oh, don't be so dramatic," Emma replied. She leaned forward in the bed and pulled the covers up tight around her neck again.

"Dramatic!" Cora yelled out. "Dramatic! You know what he did to me back then! I know you do!"

Suddenly, the old woman laid her head back into her pillow and closed her eyes and started to tremble, as if some horrific memory had just overcome her, and her entire mood seemed to change dramatically. "I know," she muttered under her breath. "I know," she repeated, her voice fading away.

"Why didn't you do something?" Cora pleaded as she realized that her mother knew exactly what she was talking about.

"And what did you want me to do?" Emma asked as she opened her eyes and looked at her daughter. "You don't think that I didn't suffer from it too!"

"I wanted you to protect me," Cora snapped, with a desperation that seemed to have no origin. "I wanted you to make me feel safe. I wanted you to be my mother!"

"And do you think that he did any less to me?" Emma asked, her voice filling with remorse. Tears started to stream down her face, and she looked off out the back window. "How could I protect you when I could hardly protect myself?"

"But you walked into the room that day!" Cora yelled out in pain. "You saw what he was doing! And you did nothing!"

"I know! I know!" Emma shouted back with agony etched deeply in her voice. "I tried to stop him, but..." She hesitated, looked back at her daughter, and reached her left hand out from under the covers again and grabbed her by the hand. "I didn't know what to do," she started out as she clutched her daughter's hand. "I couldn't stop him!" she yelled out like a wounded animal. "And there were no options for women at that time. There was no possibility of a divorce. And if I did, where would I go? What would I do? I had no money. I had no choice but to…" She paused and thought for a moment. "Bear it," she finally added.

"Oh, Mom!" Cora exclaimed in disgust, standing up and walking to the window on the side of the room, staring out at the overcast sky. "Don't you see? Through all these years of silence, I thought you blamed me for it happening!" she shouted. "I thought you blamed me!" She stood at the window for a few moments and watched the raindrops hitting the windowpane, her heart beating frantically in her chest. She said nothing for a few moments, as if she might have suddenly just escaped to some distant place, far away from reality.

"Cora, come here," Emma finally responded as the silence became too much for her. "Please come here," she begged again. Cora finally walked back to the side of the bed and looked down at her frail mother sitting rigidly up in the bed, her eyes filled with anguish. "Cora, listen to me," the old woman implored. "I never blamed you. If I blamed anybody, it was myself. I just hated that I had no control over anything, no control over what he did." She leaned forward in her bed and motioned for her daughter to take her seat again. "There's nothing fair about this world, Cora, especially a woman's place in it. I learned that from my own father-in-law." The old woman sat back in her bed and let out a low sigh, as if she were remembering something that had caused her a great deal of pain, and Cora sat back down next to her mother. "You remember Cole's mother, don't you? Grandma Elsie?" she asked.

"Yes, of course I do," Cora answered.

"When Cole and I were first married, we used to go out to an old farm that was owned by Cole's father, Frederich. It was where he was raised as a child. No one lived in the old house anymore, but one of Cole's brothers, Thomas, still farmed a good part of the land. And we'd go out there on the weekends during the summer sometimes and help out, especially during the hay season, and then the men would go hunting there too." Emma paused and seemed to be seeing the whole scene play out in her mind. "And one day, the men were all out working in the hayfields—Frederich, Cole, and Thomas, they were all out there—and Elsie and I were to bring lunch out to them at noon so they could keep on working and not lose any daylight." Emma paused again, and a shudder went through her; she pulled the blankets up tighter around her neck. "And we had all the food packed up and ready, and we were right on time, but Elsie couldn't get the old tractor started, so we had to put it all in a wheelbarrow and walk it out to the field, way out at the back of the farm, where they were." Again, Emma paused, as if she might not go on, the scene playing out in her mind. "Anyway, we finally got out there, and we were about twenty minutes late." She stopped again and looked off out the back window, her eyes fixed on some point beyond. "And Frederich walked up to Elsie, and he took his fist, and he knocked her to the ground. He almost knocked her out because she was twenty minutes late."

"Oh my god!" Cora exclaimed as she imagined the scene playing out. "What did you do?"

"I ran over to Elsie, who was still on her hands and knees on the ground, and I asked her what I should do, how I could help." Emma stopped and looked back at her daughter, her eyes burdened with the memory. "And all she said to me was, 'Set the food out.' She grabbed my hand, and she looked me right in the eye, and she pleaded with me, 'If you really want to help me, please just get the food ready.'"

"Oh, Mother, that's horrible!" Cora exclaimed as the reality of the situation surrounded her. "Was Elsie okay? What did you do?" Cora fired off before her mother could answer.

"I quickly set the food out, then I went back to Elsie, who was still on the ground, and I tried to help her get back up, but I couldn't." Emma stopped talking, and it seemed as if the burden she had been carrying had suddenly become too much. "And I wanted to say something to her. I wanted to tell her to just run away from him, to just leave him and find some safe place to go. But then she gave me this look." The old woman paused, and her voice softened a little as she went on, as if she had finally come to terms with what she had seen. "I'll never forget that look she gave me. She looked me in the eye, and I didn't really see her anymore. It was like she was gone, and I just saw this defeated shell of a woman, some apparition filled with desperation and fear. Her eyes said everything that she couldn't."

"Did you ever talk to her about it? Did you ever say anything to Cole about it?" Cora fired off in rapid succession.

"No," Emma responded as she looked back out the window. "No one ever said another word about that day. I've never said a word about it either, until this moment. I guess I was too afraid. I don't know. But I can only imagine what else poor Elsie had to deal with. And your father was cut from that same bolt of material."

Cora just sat back in her chair and looked off out the back window too.

"A woman's job in this world is far harder than any man's," Emma went on. "But if I ever started to weaken, if I ever thought about just giving up, I'd just think of Elsie down on the ground on all fours, and that would somehow give me the strength to go on." Emma stopped and looked back at her daughter, who was still just staring out the window. "Why do think it was Mary Magdalene who first found the empty tomb? You don't think a man could have handled that, do you?" she added and let out a rare laugh.

"And all these years I've blamed you for everything," Cora cried out in desperation as she looked back toward her mother. "I was so wrapped in my own world I never realized what you were going through."

"Ah, it's a woman's job to always take the blame. And I knew you blamed me for it all, but I was fine with that as long as he stopped."

"So you *did* confront him about it? Didn't you?" Cora asked desperately.

"Yes," the old woman replied with a resolute tone. "I told him that if he ever did it again, I would divorce him and I would tell everyone exactly why. Maybe in some way, Elsie gave me the strength to finally just do it."

"So you never knew until that day? When you walked into the room?"

"I didn't really know, but I had my suspicions. I just had this strange feeling that something was going on. Maybe it was a mother's intuition. I don't know. But I stopped it." She looked closely at Cora and pulled her other hand out from under the blankets and held it out to her daughter. "Can you ever forgive me?" she asked.

"Oh, Mother, I've been such a fool!" Cora whispered, clutching her mother's hands. "All these years we've kept silent about everything. We did exactly what Cole wanted us to do, what he *needed* us to do. But we don't have to live that way anymore. We can move past it all now." Cora stopped and looked strangely at her mother, as if it might have been the first time she really saw her. "There's nothing to forgive, Mother, nothing at all."

"**N**ow, pay attention, Alex! Go ahead and read it again, but read it aloud this time," Ruth insisted as she pushed Alex's eighth-grade Patterns in Literature text back in front of him.

"Why do I have to read it aloud?" Alex quipped.

"Because that's how you get to the rhythm of it." Ruth paused and then gave him a grandmotherly look that seemed to have little effect. "Just read it," she finally commanded, pointing toward the text.

> It dropped so low—in my Regard—
> I heard it hit the Ground—
> And go to pieces on the Stones
> At bottom of my Mind—
>
> Yet blamed the Fate that flung it—less
> Than I denounced Myself,
> For entertaining Plated Wares
> Upon my Silver Shelf—

"Oh, this is the original version!" Ruth exclaimed after Alex finished. "It's just the way Emily initially wrote it."

"What do you mean?" Alex asked, more confused than ever.

"When she died in 1886, her family found all these bound-up pages of poems that she had written throughout her life, and they had a lot of dashes and what some would consider improper grammar in them, so her family reworded them and had them published.

And then after everyone realized her genius, they went back to publishing them in their original form. That's what this one is."

"So what's the difference?" Alex asked.

"Well, see here, this one. The family took out these dashes, and 'flung it' was changed to 'fractured,' and this word, *denounced*, was changed to *reviled*."

"Which is better?" Alex asked, as if he were finally actually interested.

"Oh, I prefer the original," Ruth responded as she sat back in her chair. "So what do you think the poem means?" she asked, attempting to get her grandson refocused.

"We have to find out what 'it' is, don't we, Grandma?"

"Ah, that's right. That's the key to it."

"Well, how do we figure that out?" Alex fired back.

"Let me ask you this, When you 'denounce' yourself, what does that mean?"

"That maybe I did something wrong?" Alex asked with an interrogative inflection.

"Yes! That's it!" Ruth exclaimed, as if she had just reached some significant milestone. "So what does 'it' mean, then?"

"I don't know," Alex answered, dropping his head down.

"If you've done something wrong, how does that effect your opinion of yourself?"

"I guess it wouldn't be very good?" he stated with a tone of uncertainty.

"Yes!" Ruth encouraged. "So what does 'it' mean then?"

"My opinion of myself?" Alex asked.

"Yes! *It*, my opinion of myself, dropped so low I heard it hit the ground. But she doesn't blame fate, she blames herself." Ruth paused and pointed to the last line of the poem. "Here. Do you know what a *silver shelf* is?" Alex just looked at Ruth with a dumfounded look and shook his head. "Well, you're a little young to know what that is. Back in the old days, people would put their valuable silver up on the top shelf so kids like you didn't mess with it!" She reached over and playfully jabbed her grandson in the ribs. "What does it mean when something is plated?"

"Oh, I know this one," Alex chimed in, glad to have an answer. "That means that it's not solid. It just has a thin coating on top of it."

"And is that as valuable as solid silver?" Ruth asked.

"No!" Alex exclaimed. "I get it now! She put something on her top shelf that wasn't really valuable."

"Like all of us do at times, we make something that really isn't important in life seem way more important than it really is. And I think here she's saying that she realizes that and she's mad at herself for making something that really wasn't very important seem like it was. And she blames herself more than anyone else. And that's rare these days! Everyone always wants to blame somebody else for all their problems."

"So will you help me write that all down?" Alex asked as he grinned at his grandmother, a ploy that had worked on prior occasions.

"No! And don't give me that grin! You have to do that yourself. You know what it's about now. Just write it down."

"Why do we have to read all this stupid poem stuff, anyway?" Alex mumbled under his breath, mad that his assistant was bailing.

"Someone once told me that you study poetry so that you have it when you need it. You learn it now, and then when you get older and you need it, it will mean something, it will help you."

"And has any of this stuff ever helped you?"

"More than you will ever know!" Ruth gushed. She reached over and gave her grandson a squeeze. "Now, get busy before your mom gets home."

Ruth was at the home of her daughter and son-in-law, Regina and Scott, who lived on a ninety-acre tract of land that Scott had inherited from his parents' estate shortly after the couple were first married. The ground included a large two-story farmhouse-cottage-style home that the couple had built shortly after they were married, several outbuildings, and a large barn that Scott, a car mechanic, would use to work on vehicles on the weekend. Ruth had come out to watch over the three children, something she did on occasion when there wasn't a body at the funeral home, until Regina got home from a shopping excursion to St. Louis.

"Anybody home?" Regina yelled out as she walked in from the garage, her arms laden with packages. "Anybody home?"

"We're in the dining room!" Ruth shouted back. "Alex is doing his homework, and the girls are upstairs. I think they're on the phone."

"They're always on that phone," Regina quipped in a disapproving tone. She set her packages down on a large center island in the middle of the large kitchen. "Did Alex finish that homework?" she asked as Ruth walked in.

"Yes, he's doing it now," Ruth answered. "And they're reading Emily Dickinson. I'm glad to see they still teach her in the classroom."

"Well, that's why I wanted you to come out and help him with it. That stuff's like reading Greek to me!"

"He's got it now, so he should be all right." Ruth walked over and turned off a coffeepot that had just finished brewing. "I made some coffee. Let's go sit out on the patio and drink it before I head back into town. You can put all that stuff away later."

"Yes, Mother," Regina answered compliantly. Ruth grabbed a couple coffee cups, filled them up with decaf coffee, and walked out to the patio.

"Oh, look over there," Ruth whispered just as Regina was sitting down. "See, three deer over there. Oh, and look, there's a baby one too!"

Regina said nothing initially and just blew on her coffee and then took a sip. "They're all over the place," she finally replied, unimpressed. "And you should see what they do to my garden! Between them and the rabbits, it's a wonder I have anything left at the end of the summer."

"But they're so cute," Ruth defended.

"You sound just like Anna! She loves them too!" Regina leaned forward in her chair and looked closely at her mother. "Listen, I was wondering what happened when Henry came out and looked over the business," she asked, taking the conversation in a completely different direction. "What does he think you should do?"

"Yes, he came out just last week, and he went over everything. He even had this young accountant that works at his firm with him. And I mean, they went over everything."

"What did John and Vickie and the rest of the employees think?" Regina asked with a great deal of concern.

"Well, of course they were apprehensive. They have no idea how much debt the company has taken on, and of course they're worried about their jobs. And I just told them the truth. That until Henry could look it all over and give me some direction, everything was up in the air."

"Well, do you even want to keep the business?" Regina asked reflectively.

"You know, I always thought that if anything ever happened to Richard, I wouldn't want to keep it. But now that it's a reality, I just don't know. What else would I do?"

"Sell the damn thing and enjoy yourself!" Regina countered as her voice jumped a half-octave. "That was his family's business!"

"Ah, but it's mine now. And it's my responsibility. And there's a lot of jobs at stake too!"

"So what was Henry's suggestion?" Regina asked, going back to her original question.

"He said that it's still a viable business and that he couldn't understand how it had taken on so much debt, especially considering that the building was paid off. He said it just didn't make sense. And he said there was a lot of money being drained out of the business and a lot of creative accounting practices going on too." Ruth paused and shook her head, as if she still couldn't believe it all. "He said it was quite a mess!"

"Well, was he paying the taxes?" Regina asked as the reality of the situation started to sink in.

"We don't know. He's still looking into that, and I may have to get an attorney who specializes in tax law."

"Well, where was all the money going?"

"He had a special account at a bank in St. Louis that he was depositing money into monthly." Ruth paused, and she leaned over toward her daughter. "He said he thought it was money used to support another household or person."

"What!" Regina bellowed. "What other person?"

"Well, I would guess that it was Mark and his mother, but he's still looking into that. He's going to get the bank records and try to figure out where the money was ultimately going." Ruth paused and looked away from her daughter. "And there's more. It appears that he was spending a lot of money on gambling."

"You have to be kidding me!" Regina replied in disbelief. "So what was Henry's suggestion?" Regina asked, trying to cut to the end as she took a sip of coffee.

"I need a cash injection into the business," Ruth said self-consciously, unsure just how her news would be taken. "And I'm going to bring Cora in as a silent partner."

"What!" Regina yelled out as she choked on her coffee. "Cora! A partner!" she added. She picked up a napkin and dabbed at her blouse.

"Silent partner," Ruth answered sheepishly. "Silent partner."

"That woman hasn't been silent a day in her life!" Regina shot back.

"Now, settle down, Regina," Ruth replied calmly as she shooed a fly away. "I need this cash injection. And Cora has cash."

"You mean Henry has cash!" Regina interjected.

"No. No," Ruth repeated very definitely. "We talked about that very thing. Evidently, Cora has quite a bit of money of her own. I think she got some type of a large settlement when Jasper was killed. And it's not going to be in Henry's name. He was very clear about that. It would be Cora that would be doing it. It would be her money. It would be her investment."

"What if she changes her mind and wants to get involved more in the business?" Regina countered as she started to settle down after the initial shock.

"Well, I asked her that very thing. And she said she didn't want to be that close to that kind of business." Ruth paused, and a big grin appeared across her face. "She said she'd be afraid that she'd end up in one of those coffins!" Ruth added with a wry smirk.

"Oh my god! And I can hear her saying it!" Regina added, as they both roared with laughter.

CHAPTER 23

A strange relationship had started to develop in the small town of Ox Bend, and the locals, who had always dutifully kept track of all such occurrences, had taken notice. After Ruth's encounter with Mark Callier at the local IGA store, she had somehow felt an overpowering empathy for the young man and had decided to meet with him again, a decision that set into place a series of subsequent meetings and phone calls between the two that dramatically changed the course of their connection. At first, the get-togethers were few and far between, as Ruth gradually attempted to learn about the life of the young man, but as time went on and she came to realize the difficult childhood that he had endured, she developed an almost-obsessive fascination with the young man. Her sister, Cora, fresh from a session with Dr. Whitman, had suggested she was attempting to replace the loss of her husband with his progeny, a suggestion that Ruth had simply dismissed as "utter nonsense."

During the course of their meetings, Ruth had discovered that his mother, Sarah Callier, had started seeing Richard in the spring of 1960, after they had met at the home of one of Richard's old college roommates and started to see each other whenever Richard could orchestrate some pretense to be away from home: a chamber-related trip, a funeral directors' convention, an accounting seminar, a fishing excursion. She learned that her husband's affair had gone on in one form or another for years and that Mark was born just a few years after the affair had started and that Richard, just as Henry had uncovered, had been forwarding a monthly pension to the young mother under the expense category "miscellaneous" on the business ledger. As the meetings continued and Ruth learned more and more about the young man's life, the locals started to enhance and abridge the true facts of the situation, adding a dash of local color or an editorial slant to give it more of a tabloid perspective, a process that Ruth Clarkson simply chose to ignore, despite the constant concerns voiced by her children. She had decided that the young man was an innocent in the whole matter, as much a victim of Richard's lifestyle as she had been, and she made the conscious decision to help him in any way she could.

The rains that had been drenching the area for weeks had finally moved out of the area, and a bright, unimpeded sun was finally drying out the county that had been flooded for months. Ruth Clarkson had picked up Mark Callier at his home in St. Charles County and was driving him down to St. Louis to attend an outdoor job fair that was being held at Forest Park, a thirteen-hundred-acre tract of land just off the downtown corridor that had hosted the Louisiana Purchase Expo of 1904.

"Mark, can I ask you something?" Ruth queried as she checked her rearview mirror and switched over to the passing lane.

"I guess so," Mark replied in his typical taciturn way.

"You've told me a lot about yourself, and I appreciate that, but you've never told me what happened to your mother." Ruth stopped and glanced to her right to see Mark's reaction, but he said nothing and just looked out the passenger-side window. "Every time I bring her up, you change the subject," she probed a little further. "That time we met at the IGA, you said that it was Richard's fault that your mother was dead. What did you mean by that?"

Mark initially said nothing, but then he leaned his head back into the headrest and looked out, straight ahead, over the dashboard, and seemed to be letting down the wall of separation that always kept everyone at arm's length. "I think Richard was the worst thing that ever happened to my mother," he responded coldly. "Of course, she didn't see it that way," he continued, his voice tinted with disgust. "And yet he was the only thing she ever really thought about or cared about—she just became obsessed with him. And she spent her whole life waiting around for him to make his next visit."

"And how often did you all see him?" Ruth asked, unsure if she really wanted to know the answer.

"At first, I think it was more often—at least that's what my mother said, anyway. But by the time I was around two or three, he really wasn't coming around that much anymore, and when he did come, I think that was only because of me. I don't think he really wanted to see her anymore." Ruth said nothing and just thought back to the countless trips that her husband had made over the years, and a nervous heaviness came over her. "And I really believe she thought that he was going to get a divorce and marry her one day," Mark went on.

"Now, I don't know if he ever really said that to her in so many words, but I think that's what she thought. And I tried to tell her that that was never going to happen." Mark paused and stuck his arm out the open passenger-side window and leaned up against the door. "I knew very little about my father growing up, but I did finally figure out one thing: I knew he'd never marry her." He stopped and looked over at Ruth behind the wheel, his hair blowing in the wind. "But I could never get her to see it, and so her whole life centered on her waiting for him to show up."

"Did she have any close friends or family?" Ruth asked as she reached up and adjusted the rearview mirror, an eighteen-wheeler close on her tail.

"Not really. Both of her parents were killed when she was very young, and she was taken in by a foster family when she was around seven, I think, and they finally adopted her. But they were an older couple, and they died when she was in high school. And then she got involved with the wrong people. And I think that had a lot to do with her emotional state. She never really had any self-esteem. She had looks, but no self-esteem. And I think that's why she just waited around for Richard."

"Sounds like she had a rough life," Ruth responded, surprised by how forthcoming Mark had suddenly become.

"She always told me that you can really only love once in your life, and for her that was Richard. And I guess in her own codependent way she did really love him."

"Well, in some ways I can understand that," Ruth replied with a direct honesty that took Mark off guard. "In a lot of ways, Richard was an easy man to love."

"Oh, but this was more of an obsession than love, and then you mix that with alcohol and drugs and that's a deadly combination."

"Oh, I hate to hear that," Ruth chimed in, her heart breaking.

"As far back as I can remember, she always had a drink in her hand. And I think that's probably why she couldn't keep a job." Mark stopped and quickly rolled the window up, as if a chill had just come over him. "And then she started taking these nerve pills she got from the doctor. And when she took them along with the booze, she just disappeared. I can remember coming home and she would just be gone. She was sitting there. She could still talk and answer questions, but her eyes were hollow and she wasn't really there anymore, and I was just on my own—that was my life!"

"There's nothing worse than addiction, Mark," Ruth said as she looked over at him staring out the window. "In so many ways, it just takes over a person's life."

"I know, I know," Mark whispered, his voice softening. "And what's so sick about it all, I really didn't know what kind of life we were living when I was a little kid. I had no idea. But then, Richard paid for me to go to this church camp one summer." Mark hesitated and looked directly at Ruth. "That's when everything changed, that's when my eyes were opened."

"What do you mean?" Ruth asked, feeling that Mark was finally starting to open up.

"I must have been about eight years old at that time, I guess, and Richard arranged for me to go to this weeklong church camp out in the country. I can still remember my roommate. His name was Larry. He was the nicest little kid. I had never met anyone like him before, you know, and we just hit it off right away. And that whole week, everything was about us. They had all this stuff planned out just for us, for me. Everybody was so nice and caring, and it was all about me!"

Mark paused and looked back out the side window again, as if he might have been seeing it all pass before his eyes. "I never had that before, you know. There was never any time in my childhood that I felt like anything was about me, or for me." He paused again and let out an inarticulate murmur. "And I can remember coming back home after that week, and I was standing in my room, looking out the window, and I just started to cry. I didn't know why at first, but I just couldn't stop crying. And then it just come over me all at once. My eyes were opened, and I suddenly realized how messed up my life was, how wrong everything was. I never, until that very moment, realized it."

"I am so sorry, Mark." Ruth reacted consolingly. "That's the problem with an addict: It all becomes about them. They just get wrapped up in their own addiction."

"And nothing was ever the same after that week, and for a long time, I hated Richard for sending me there, for opening my eyes."

"I had no idea you went through all that," Ruth empathized, her heart breaking.

Mark sat up straight and leaned forward in the seat, and his mood changed dramatically. "And then one day I came home and she was just gone. Some of her clothes were still there, but she was gone. And she just never came back."

"Well, did you call the police? Did someone try to find her?" Ruth asked in rapid-fire fashion.

"I called them, but they said she probably just decided to leave. I mean, they all knew her. She had been arrested numerous times for drugs and alcohol, and she wasn't a priority, and there wasn't any evidence of any crime or anything. And they said their hands were tied. They said she had every right to just leave if she wanted to." Mark paused and looked over directly at Ruth sitting behind the wheel. "But I know that she's dead."

"Oh, Mark, how can you know that for sure?"

"I just know," Mark answered firmly. "I just know," he repeated, as if attempting to convince himself as much as Ruth.

"So how long ago was this?" Ruth asked as she pulled the car off the highway into a rest stop. Mark waited to answer until Ruth had put the car in park and looked over at him.

"It was the day that she found out that Richard had died," he finally answered.

"Oh, no!" Ruth exclaimed in anguish. "Why didn't you tell me this when you first met me?"

"What?" he yelled at Ruth sarcastically. "Tell you that I'm your husband's bastard son, and 'Oh, by the way, my mother just disappeared and probably killed herself because she didn't want to live without him!'" He got out of the car, slammed the door, and walked over to a shaded park area with benches and sat down. Ruth walked up to the young man, sat down next to him, and clutched his hands in hers.

"I don't know what all you've been through, Mark. I don't think anyone can imagine that kind of thing unless they've experienced it themselves. But I do know this much: you're an innocent in all this. None of this was ever your fault." Ruth sat back into the bench and looked out over the highway, the traffic whizzing by, each vehicle caught up in its own little isolated world.

"Do you know the story of Ruth in the Bible?" she asked. The young man said nothing and only glanced at her coldly and then looked away again. "Well, Ruth married a man that lived far away from all her family and friends, and then her husband died and her mother-in-law, Naomi, told her to go back to her own home and to be with her own people. But Ruth said no. 'Don't urge me to leave you or turn back from you. Where you go, I will go, and where you stay, I will stay.'"

"Sounds like a dumb idea to me," Mark responded coldly. He sat back into the bench, stretched his legs out, and crossed his arms tightly. "What does it mean, anyway?" he finally asked with a hint of remorse.

"Well, she stayed with her mother-in-law and she was working in the fields when a man saw her and asked about her because he wanted to meet her. And he ended up marrying her. She ended up finding happiness again in this foreign land, and things worked out for her. Her staying with her mother-in-law was rewarded."

"Well, that certainly doesn't have anything to do with my life!" Mark grunted. "There is no happy ending in this story," he added mordantly.

Ruth paused and looked at the young man closely. "But, Mark, your story is far from over. And I think that the book of Ruth illustrates that we can suffer losses in our life and we can be taken to very dark, lonely places, but we can find joy and happiness and prosperity again."

Mark sat up straight and looked over at Ruth sitting at his side. "Why are you so nice to me?" he asked with a sincerity that Ruth had never seen in him before. "I mean, I came to you looking for answers about my father, about who he was, and you've been so good to me about it all. And I know how uncomfortable this whole situation must be for you." Mark paused and looked down. "No one has ever shown me kindness like this before."

"Oh, Mark, the world is filled with good people who want nothing more than to give and to love." Ruth paused and looked closely at Mark still gazing out at the highway. "I once had someone in my life who taught me that," she finally added as she thought of Aaron.

"But I don't even know where to start to look for happiness," the young man whispered as he looked down, his harsh exterior slipping away. "I don't know where to start," he repeated desperately.

Ruth stood up and reached her hand down to Mark. "Well, maybe I can help you with that," she said sympathetically as Mark reached up and took her hand. "Come on! We're going back to Ox Bend. I have just the job for you!"

Part 3

Boaz replied, "I've been told all about what you have done for your mother-in-law since the death of your husband—how you left your father and mother and your homeland and came to live with a people you did not know before. May the Lord repay you for what you have done. May you be richly rewarded by the Lord, the God of Israel, under whose wings you have come to take refuge."

—Ruth 2:11–12

CHAPTER
24

The Edge was on the north side of Lafayette Square, about two blocks off Chouteau Avenue, in what many of the locals still considered a "sketchy" part of the neighborhood, as the name seemed to imply; and the ownership group had long been rumored to have questionable antecedents, but such a reputation only seemed to increase the interest in the long-running Italian eatery, and it had become a favorite of Henry and Cora Lasciter since they first purchased the large house on Rutger Street. The flat-roofed one-story restaurant looked almost run-down and shabby from the street but had been professionally decorated and lushly appointed on the inside, and their caprese salad with pesto sauce, a selection that had become Cora Lasciter's favorite, had been recognized on numerous occasions in the local *Riverfront Times* urban weekly. She and her husband, Henry, were seated way in the back of the restaurant, at a candlelit table close to a baby grand piano that was typically played every Friday and Saturday night by a hired musician to entertain the crowds with easy-listening fare and traditional Italian favorites. Seated with the couple were Ruth Clarkson and Quinten Denver, better known to all his friends as Quin, a longtime friend and coworker of Henry's at Boatman's Investments. Quinten stood just over six feet tall and had curly light-brown hair that had started to thin on the top and piercing light-brown eyes, which sort of quivered when he looked at someone, as if he might have been seeing things, observing moments and behaviors, that others might have looked right past. He had recently buried his wife of thirty-plus years, and like Ruth, he had been born on August 8, 1935, a personal fact that Cora had discovered late one evening at an after-hours office party.

Cora viewed the coincidence as some type of "divine intervention," and she had immediately started to cajole her husband into arranging a meeting between the two singles.

As one waiter was removing the remains of mushroom risotto and pasta carbonara, another was opening the second bottle of Beaujolais and refilling the crystal wineglasses.

"So how did you find this place, Cora?" Quinten asked as he shook off the waiter and placed his hand over his wineglass.

"Henry brought me here right after the first time we looked at the house on Rutger," Cora replied, giving her husband a loving glance. "And we've been coming back ever since. And it's really one of my favorite places to go in the city now." She took a sip from her refilled wineglass and gave a nod. "And we like to support local businesses, so we end up here a lot."

Quinten turned toward Ruth and smiled, showing off his set of perfect white teeth, his eyes sparkling in the iridescent candlelight. "And what about you, Ruth, have you been here before?" he asked.

"Yes, but only once," Ruth responded as she gazed around the busy restaurant in amazement, a jazzy version of "Volare" coming from the baby grand. "But I really do enjoy coming here. I love to people-watch, and this is a great place for that," she added and then blushed slightly.

"I try to get her into the city every chance I can," Cora interrupted. She glanced across the table and affectionately smiled at her sister and winked. "But she seems doomed to spend her life at that funeral home!"

"Well, as an investor in *that* funeral home," Henry interjected with forced emphasis, "you should be out there more yourself!"

"Oh, I trust my sister to keep it all running," Cora rejoined with a big, carefree smile. She grabbed her husband's forearm and gave it a gentle squeeze, a move that always seemed to win him over.

"Well, that's your first mistake!" Ruth fired back with a mischievous smile, a comment that got everyone around the table laughing.

"So you're a businesswoman, then?" Quinten asked, his eyes focusing on Ruth.

"And a damn good one too!" Henry threw in as he tossed back a large gulp of wine.

"Well, I never really think of myself that way," Ruth explained, seemingly embarrassed by the attention. "My husband and I always worked as a team taking care of the business, and then all that fell to me after his death." She paused and took another sip of wine. "You see, this funeral home was my husband's family business, and I was sort of pushed to the helm when he died a few years ago."

"I'm sorry to hear that," Quinten replied respectfully. "Henry did tell me that you had lost your husband. Not an easy thing to go through," he added with a compassionate tone. He looked down and nervously fingered the stem of his empty wineglass as thoughts of his dead wife entered his mind.

"Quin's wife died just a few years ago too," Cora interjected, always hating any lull in the conversation. She looked at her sister and raised her eyebrows and then waved to a passing waiter, hoping to grab his attention. "You two certainly have a lot in common!" she added as the waiter passed by, ignoring Cora completely.

"Well, then you know the difficulties of losing a spouse, don't you?" Ruth interjected in her typical caring way. She fluffed the napkin on her lap and then looked closely at Quinten. "How did she die, if I may ask?"

"I need to use the ladies' room," Cora suddenly interjected, attempting to brush past Ruth's question.

"No. No. It's all right," Quinten jumped in just as Cora started to rise. "It's fine." He looked directly at Ruth again. "Everyone is so afraid to say anything about her around me, and I don't like that. I want to talk about her. Maybe not the terrible way she died, but that's not what I choose to remember. I don't want our relationship to be defined by the worst moment of our lives!" He stopped and looked down at his wineglass again.

"My wife was gunned down in a parking garage downtown after a Cardinal ball game two years ago." He paused and put his elbows on the table and lowered his head into his hands. "The headline in the paper read, 'Random Carjacking Goes Wrong.'" He stopped and looked back up, and a faraway look came over him. "I always found it amazing that they could sum up the end of her life that way, that they were able to encapsulate it into one neat news bite, all in just four little words."

"And they've never caught the guys who did it either!" Henry jumped in as Cora awkwardly sat back down.

"I am so sorry for your loss," Ruth returned, a deep tone of empathy etched in every word. She reached over and touched his arm that was resting on the table. "That must have been a terrible experience to have to go through. I mean, I can't even imagine."

Quinten looked up at Ruth. "Thank you," he replied, touched by her comments.

"So where did you have the funeral?" Ruth asked, more out of professional habit than anything else.

"We had it at Benson's Funeral Home over on Kingshighway. And she was buried at New St. Marcus on Gravois."

"Oh, Richard knew the Bensons," Ruth replied, attempting to lift the mood. "He worked with Mr. Benson on several committees over the years, and I met his wife once years ago too. That's a great funeral home with a great reputation." Ruth took a sip of wine and sat back in her chair. "And my grandmother and a lot of my family on the Saroh side are buried at New St. Marcus."

"It's a beautiful old cemetery, isn't it?" Quinten responded, his spirits seeming to rise a little. He sat back in his chair, too, and seemed to relax a little. "And the Bensons did do a great job. Everything was as good as it could be, considering the circumstances."

"Over four hundred people attended," Henry blurted out, keeping true to his numbers-based approach to things.

"It *was* lovely," Cora interjected. She gave her husband's arm another subtle squeeze and then started to rise. "Gentlemen, if you will excuse me," she announced with an air of sophistication. "I'll be right back." As she started to walk away, she gave her sister the "join me" look across the table.

"Wait, I'm coming too," Ruth responded right on cue. She placed her napkin on the table and followed her sister into the restroom.

"What are you doing?" Cora jumped in as the door was closing behind them. "I don't really think all this *funeral* talk is appropriate for a first date!" She placed her purse on the countertop and started preening herself in the mirror. "Who wants to talk about funerals?"

"So this is a first date?" Ruth asked, addressing her sister's reflection.

"No, of course not," Cora backtracked. "That's not what I meant. And it'll probably be the last, anyway!" Cora stopped and turned around to face her sister. "And what if it were! I just think that you two might be right for each other. You were born on the exact same day, for God's sake!" She paused and took her sister's hands into her own. "If that isn't some type of sign, I don't know what is! And I don't want you to ruin it with all this morbid funeral talk!"

"But I think he wanted to talk about it," Ruth defended. "I think he wants to talk about his wife."

"Yes. Because you brought it all up!"

"Well, I'm sorry, but that is the business that I'm in, and you're in it now too! And we're not sixteen anymore. We didn't meet in study hall, and we're not stopping to eat on our way to the prom!"

"Well, you're probably right," Cora replied and then broke out into a round of uproarious laughter.

"Stop that! Shush!" Ruth whispered as she started to giggle herself. "No more wine for you! They're going think we've lost our minds in here!" she added. Just as they finally started to get themselves under control, a large-framed woman with a Thatcher hairstyle came bursting into the restroom disapprovingly, and the two sisters quickly made their escape.

"Are we leaving already?" Cora inquired as they approached the table and found both Quinten and Henry standing, talking to one of the managers.

"Yes, my dear," Henry answered with his usual official tone of voice. He reached down and swallowed the last drink from his wineglass. "And Anthony here just told us that Princess Diana has been in some kind of wreck or accident or something over in Paris." He threw a hundred-dollar bill down on the table. "It's all over the news," he went on. Henry placed his arm around his wife, who seemed upset about the tragic news, and led her to the front door.

Quinten walked up behind Ruth and grabbed her gently by the arm. "It was wonderful meeting you tonight," he whispered, his voice filled with anxious tension. "And I want to thank you for talking to me about my wife. I really do appreciate it. No one ever wants to talk about her around me."

"That's because they don't know what to say," Ruth countered with a subtle smile.

"But you do," Quin replied profoundly.

"I've had a little more experience than the normal person when it comes to such things."

"Yeah, I guess you do," Quinten replied with a nervous laugh. "I would love to see you again," he blurted out with the uneasy energy of a sixteen-year-old boy asking for a first date. "I hope I'm not being too forward." He blushed and looked down at the floor. "I haven't asked a girl out on a date since I was seventeen."

"You know, I think I would like that," Ruth answered kindly, smiling from ear to ear. "I would like that very much," she repeated.

Quinten looked up, and an even larger smile spread across his face.

25

"We're not done using that!" Henry Lasciter barked out as a young twenty-year-old man wearing a tank top with "Work Angry" written on the back attempted to jump onto the seated low-row lat machine that he was standing next to.

"Sorry, dude," the young man mumbled back under his breath. He grabbed his water bottle and towel and promenaded across the room with his chest stuck out like a bantam rooster.

"You get in your sixties and it's like you're invisible," Henry whispered to Quinten Denver, who had just finished super-setting a set of bicep curls with twenty-pound dumbbells.

"Don't kid yourself," Quinten whispered. "You've been invisible in this place since you turned forty!" he added, wiping his face. "And I think they're probably afraid to look too closely at us. We represent a little too much reality for men in their twenties."

"You're probably right," Henry agreed. He straddled the lat machine bench, sat down, and started a set. "This is the second set, right?"

"Yes," Quinten replied, wiping down his face and neck.

Henry Lasciter and Quinten Denver had been working out together at the local Club Fitness, a St. Louis-based gym that was geared toward a more serious fitness clientele, for over four years. Their place of employment, Boatman's Investments, had a small in-house workout area, but the close proximity of Club Fitness and the large number of different weight machines, free weights, exercise classes, and on-staff trainers made the gym a much better alternative, and they would often slip out of the office around midday to avoid the large crowds that filled the place after the regular workday.

"So how are things going with you and Ruth?" Henry asked as the two made their way from the free weight area to the cardio section at the far back of the gym.

"Yeah, I think things are going pretty good. I've seen her quite a few times since our dinner at the Edge. We talk almost daily on the phone, and I actually went out to Ox Bend a couple of times, and she gave me the grand tour of the funeral home."

"Yes, it's quite a building," Henry echoed. "And it has two rentals on the second floor too," he added, always with an eye for the bottom line. "That really helps."

"It's architecturally very interesting too, and the apartment on the third floor is really nice."

"Yeah, she and Richard have lived there ever since they first married."

"She said it was built in 1888."

"Well, that's about right, but it's had some major overhauls over the years." Henry paused, and his face took on a serious look. "I can't imagine the cost of keeping up an old building like that! It's got to be a money drain!"

"She seems to be doing okay with it all. And she has the apartment really fixed up nice. Seems like she really likes it out there."

"Too far out," Henry criticized.

"And then last weekend, she actually came down here, and we went to the art museum."

"Sounds like you guys *are* hitting it off," Henry concurred, mounting a Precor elliptical running machine. "Of course, you were doomed from the moment you told Cora your birth date, and she got it in her mind that you and her sister were destined to be together!" he added teasingly. "We'll all have to get together again soon. Maybe go to the symphony or something."

"I bet Ruth would really like that," Quinten concurred while jumping on an adjacent elliptical.

"Especially if it's anything Rachmaninoff!" Henry disclosed. "She loves his *Second Symphony*."

"Good to know," Quinten replied as his breathing started to pick up. "So what's the story on her husband, anyway?"

"Ah, that was quite a business." Henry puffed, picking up his speed a little. "The two of them started seeing each other in college and married shortly after he graduated back in the late fifties. He was actually raised out there in Ox Bend."

"And Ruth was raised here, wasn't she?" Quinten asked.

"Yes. Over in the Lafayette Square area. And then I think the family moved out to the Webster Groves area when she was in her teens."

"Yeah, Ruth said they both went to St. Louis University. What did he major in?"

"Oh, I have no idea. Probably some type of degree in business," Henry replied. "And then I assume he had to get his mortuary science degree after that, to run the funeral home."

"And what about Ruth?"

"I don't think she ever finished her degree. I think she was in some kind of liberal arts program—I think that's what Cora said. But after he graduated, they just got married and moved out to Ox Bend. That was probably a big mistake on Ruth's part!"

"What do you mean by that?"

"Well, not finishing her degree, giving it all up for him! And from what Cora tells me, he wasn't worth it!" Henry paused again, and he glanced over his glasses at Quinten. "He had a roaming eye right from the start. I guess that's the best way to put it. From what I can piece together of the whole thing, he had numerous affairs with a lot of different women, and he even had a long-term relationship with some woman that lasted for years! They even had a child together!"

"Is that Mark?" Quinten asked curiously.

"Yes. Mark Callier. Have you met him?"

"Yes," Quinten replied. "I met him when I first went out to see Ruth. When she gave me the grand tour of the place, he was there. He works there now!"

"Seems like a pretty good young man, from what Cora tells me. He runs a lot of the unskilled day-to-day logistics of the business: seeing that the vehicles are kept up and ready, overseeing the grave site preparation, marshalling the parking, and lining up the funeral possession, stuff like that."

"Well, how did she ever come to hire her husband's illegitimate son?" Quinten fired back in curious disbelief.

"You just have to know Ruth to really understand that one!" Henry panted. "Supposedly, he told Ruth that his mother died around the same time that Richard did, and of course that really pulled at Ruth's heartstrings." Henry brushed his forehead with the back of his hand, and his voice lowered as he went on. "But I have my doubts about that whole story. It was all very mysterious, and I don't think that's ever really been cleared up satisfactorily, at least not for me."

"Why's that?" Quinten asked. He stopped pedaling, wiped down his forehead, and looked directly at Henry.

"Too many unanswered questions about the whole thing!" Henry fired back, looking over the top of his glasses again. "And there's never been any proof provided that she's dead. And I looked, and I never could find an obituary in any of the local papers. For all we know, she just left and started a new life somewhere else."

"Did Mark report her as a missing person?" Quinten asked.

"Says he did! But who knows for sure? And he just keeps insisting that she's dead."

"Did you tell Ruth all this?"

"Of course I did! And Cora told her too, but she just brushed it off. She says he just doesn't like talking about his mother or the past. So she doesn't push the issue. You know how women are."

"The young man certainly has been through a lot. Did he have any kind of relationship with Richard?"

"Oh, yes!" Henry retorted as he adjusted the incline from four to five. "Evidently, when he was small, Richard would come and spend a few days with them regularly over the years. And he would take him places all over the city. That's why Ruth believed the young man when he showed her a picture of himself and Richard at the zoo when the kid was only about five years old!"

"That's almost unbelievable," Quinten responded with a shocked look on his face.

"The man was living some kind of double life or something!" Henry snorted. "All very strange," he added, then smirked. "Hell, I can barely keep up with one woman, much less two!"

"But that still doesn't explain how he came to work for Ruth," Quinten pointed out.

"Cora says Ruth never could pass up bringing home a stray. And when she found out about all this, well, she brought him home and gave him a job."

"Well, you know, I can kind of understand that," Quinten replied as he started to pedal again. "The kid's an innocent in it all. And I guess Ruth saw that." Quinten paused and adjusted the resistance and incline. "She really is quite a woman."

"Well, the kid's actually been a great asset to the company too. Richard had just about run that company into the ground! Saddled it with a lot of debt, and now they're left with trying to turn it all around."

"I would think the funeral business was pretty profitable," Quinten interjected with a smile. "It's definitely recession-proof!"

"And you would be right in thinking that, but Richard had more than one demon. He had a really bad gambling addiction, and I think that's where a lot of the profits from the business went."

"I never realized how much Ruth had gone through with him. She really is a remarkable lady."

Suddenly, Henry stopped pedaling and looked over at Quinten. "Are you getting serious about Ruth?" he asked point-blank.

"I think I am," Quinten answered. "I think I am," he repeated as he turned and smiled at Henry.

"Are you thinking about asking her to marry you?" Henry asked.

Quinten stopped pedaling, too, and looked closely at his friend. "You know, I think I am," he replied in amazement, as if he just at that moment realized it.

"Well, I don't know whether to warn you or congratulate you!" Henry thundered. "Being with a Saroh woman is quite a ride!"

"Oh, wow, this is absolutely breathtaking!" Quinten said as he looked up at a large forty-foot-tall rock precipice towering above him. "This area and that bluff in particular are just beautiful. You know, it's almost like being in a foreign land and we've discovered a secret, hidden island."

"I know!" Ruth concurred as she looked around at the picturesque scenery. "It's got to be one of the most beautiful areas in the state."

"How do you know about this place?" he asked enthusiastically. Ruth, who had just sat down on a blanket that was spread out on a sandy beach area just below the bluff, motioned for Quinten to take a seat beside her. "An old family friend and his sister own this farm, and this is Charrette Creek that runs right through the property. The creek goes on from here and then dumps into the Missouri River about four miles east."

"Can you imagine owning a piece of paradise like this?" Quinten mused out loud, sounding like an envious schoolboy.

"Well, it's been in the same family here for generations! And when Richard was a kid, he used to come out here all the time with one of the owners. It was a well-known place back in those days. And then when Richard and I got married, he would bring me out here sometimes too. He was good friends with the Krueger family." Ruth paused and brushed some sand off the side of her skirt. "And when Richard was a young man, he used to dive from the top of that bluff!"

Quinten sat down and then lay back and placed his hands behind his head and stared up at the top of the bluff. "Well, he had more guts than what I ever had!"

"He always did seem to have more guts than sense!" Ruth chirped back and then blushed.

"So what's the name of this creek again?"

"Charrette."

"How do you spell that?"

Ruth spelled the name out for him.

"And where did the name of the creek come from?" Quinten asked.

"From what I've been told, it most likely got its name from a French frontiersman, Joseph Chorette." She spelled that name out, pointing out the differences in the spelling. "And all the locals around here call that Krueger's Bluff," she added, pointing to the giant rock precipice that was just across the creek.

"Well, it's absolutely unbelievable," Quinten gushed. "It's hard to believe that places like this exist!"

"It is beautiful," Ruth concurred. "And it's really breathtaking in the spring, when the creek is up and really running."

"Let's go in the water!" Quinten yelled out as he rose to his feet and held his hand out to Ruth, his eyes quivering with excitement.

"Oh my lord," Ruth quipped, "I haven't been in that creek for years!"

"Well, then, it's about time!" Quinten chimed in indefatigably. "Come on," he implored with a huge smile. "We'll just take our shoes off and wade in a little ways."

"Well, you're going to have to help me get up from here," Ruth interjected. "I'm still pretty good at sitting down on the ground. It's the getting up that's getting difficult!"

"Come on, I'll get you up!" Quinten laughed, reaching down and grabbing Ruth by the hand.

After wading in the creek for over an hour, the two of them returned to the sandy beach and just sat in silence and looked around at the idyllic, pastoral beauty that surrounded them on all sides. The afternoon sun was heading west, and long, cool shadows started to cover the valley, and a gentle breeze was blowing off the creek. The only sound was the rushing babble of the stream as it made the turn in front of the bluff and then rushed over the rocks as the creek bottom became shallow again. Quinten had lain down on the blanket with his right arm outstretched, and Ruth was lying next to him, with her head resting on his arm.

"Ruth, is it right that I can feel this happy again?" Quinten asked boyishly after a few minutes of silence.

Ruth, surprised by the question and unsure of exactly what it meant, sat and up and looked down at Quinten. "What do you mean?" she asked tenderly. Quinten took his right hand and placed it on Ruth's lower back. "After I lost Francine, I just never thought I'd be happy like this again. But now, being here with you, I just feel happy. I never imagined that this would happen or that I would ever feel this way again."

"And you feel a little guilty about it, don't you?" Ruth volleyed back.

Quinten said nothing for a moment, as if he were struggling to formulate an answer. "Yes," he finally admitted. "I do. I don't want to, but I do."

"You really loved her, didn't you?"

Quinten sat up and placed his arms around his legs and rested his head on his knees. "I always thought I did, but I don't really know now."

"Well, that sounds ominous," Ruth countered, with a perplexed look on her face.

"Oh no, no, I worded that wrong. I loved her with all my heart," Quinten defended, "but I just don't know if I ever really showed her that. I don't know if I ever really appreciated her while she was here."

"Like the folks in Grover's Corner?" Ruth whispered under her breath.

"Where?" Quin asked inquisitively.

"It's not important. It's just this fictional town from the play *Our Town*, where everyone just takes life for granted and never really experiences it until it's too late."

"Yes!" Quin exclaimed as he looked over at Ruth. "Just like that! It's like this Japanese poem I came across shortly after Francine died." He paused, looking up at the bluff. "I was struck by the lightning of seeing you after you were gone." Quinten lowered his head back onto his knees. "After she was killed, I suddenly realized that I never really saw her when she was here. She was there in front of me all the time, but I just feel like I never really ever saw her in any way that really mattered, until it was too late." Quinten paused and let out a long sigh.

"Well, it sounds like a lot of marriages that I know," Ruth interjected, hoping to assuage some of Quinten's guilt.

"And you're right," Quinten stated with a new sense of energy. "It was just like your Grover's Corner. It was like I was asleep. I was just sleep-walking through life, and it was all right in front of me, and I just looked past it all." He stopped and looked up at Ruth sitting quietly at his side. "Why couldn't I really see her when she was here?"

"Oh, Quinten, you're being too hard on yourself," Ruth responded lovingly. "And I think all of us are guilty of taking our loved ones for granted at times, taking the world for granted."

"But did you ever feel that way about Richard?"

"Oh, it sounds like you had a much different kind of marriage than I had," Ruth admitted with an unusual degree of honesty. "Mine was more of a marriage of convenience." She paused and chose her words thoughtfully as she went on. "I realized after Richard was gone that I really didn't want to *see* him. Maybe I was afraid of what I'd see if I really looked too closely. I don't know." Ruth paused again, as if some profundity had just come over her, and she looked closely at Quinten. "I was the one who was invisible in our marriage."

"But I see you now," Quin interrupted. He reached over and placed his arm around Ruth's shoulders and pulled her in close. "And I want to see more of you. I've wanted to see more of you since that first time we met down at the Edge." He paused and looked down. "I was so nervous that night. I felt like an awkward sixteen-year-old boy again."

"Well, you were no more nervous than I was," Ruth said reassuringly.

"But you didn't seem nervous at all to me!" He paused and looked back up at Ruth. "You seemed perfect. And I was captivated by you right from the start." He paused again and looked down, as if he were working up the nerve to say something important. "And at our time in life, I don't want to wait around," he said boldly. "I don't want to hold back on what I really feel. I don't want any more regrets about the things I *didn't* do." He paused and looked back up at Ruth. "I love you, Ruth," he uttered with deep emotion. He stood up, pulled a small box out of his pocket, and then bent down on one knee and grabbed Ruth's left hand. "Ruth, I was going to ask you this tonight at dinner, but I just can't wait any longer. Will you marry me?"

Ruth, shocked by the sudden proposal, just sat motionless as tears started to well up in her eyes.

CHAPTER 27

" 'll have the Cobb salad with your house dressing, and we're going to split an order of the grilled shrimp appetizer. But bring it out with the salad," Cora added as she handed her menu to the waiter.

"And you?" the waiter asked. He placed Cora's menu under his left arm and looked directly at Ruth.

"You know what, I think I'll try the Cobb salad too, with the house dressing on the side." Almost before Ruth could finish her order, the waiter snatched the menu from her hands and was off to a table in the back, where an unhappy customer was doing an exaggerated "check mark" in the air with his right hand.

"Boy, they're busy today," Ruth whispered to her sister as she gazed around the patio at Romains Restaurant in Lafayette Square.

"It's always like this around noon," Cora explained. "A lot of the businessmen from downtown head over here and take an extended lunch hour." She stopped a moment, and a smile came over her face. "How do you think I met Henry?"

"You're kidding?" Ruth exclaimed as she placed her napkin on her lap.

"Absolutely not! Right over there. I was eating a Cobb salad," she added. Ruth looked closely at her sister to see if she was kidding, and then both of them broke out into laughter.

"Oh, Cora, you do continue to amaze me sometimes. I wish I had your way with men!" Ruth stopped, and a shocked look appeared across her face. "Did I just say that?" she joked.

"Yes! Yes, you did! Where's a witness when you need one?"

"Seriously, though, I do envy how comfortable you are around men. You always seem so relaxed. So natural. I always feel like I'm tripping over my words when I'm around them."

"Relaxed!" Cora barked out. "Oh, you never relax around a man. You never really let your guard down. Men are hunting animals by instinct, and they love the chase. You relax too much and they'll think the chase is over, and they're off to the next conquest!"

Ruth stopped and really thought about what Cora just said, and a strange look came over her.

"Oh my god," she finally exclaimed. "You're starting to make sense to me. I'm starting to think like you!"

"Well, it's about time!" Cora thundered back. "Now, since we're on the subject of men, what's going on with you and Quinten? I heard that he spent almost the whole weekend out there last week and that you went to some creek or something."

"Yes, but how did you hear about that?"

"Henry told me! He ran into Quinten at the gym."

"Oh," Ruth responded with an inquisitive look on her face.

"What, you think women are the only ones who gossip?" Cora exclaimed. "Get a man working out, doing something physical, and he'll tell you anything!" She paused and looked to her right and then to her left. "This one time, when Trenton and I were in his car parked down at Lafayette Park—"

Before Cora could finish the statement, the frazzled waiter returned with some bad news from the kitchen. "I'm sorry," he said with faked sincerity, "but we just sold out of the shrimp. I can bring you an order of calamari, at no additional cost."

Cora looked at her sister, who gave a nod. "Yes, that's fine. Thank you," Cora replied.

"Can I get you ladies anything else?" he asked, placing his pen behind his right ear.

"Yes," Cora said as she looked mischievously at her sister and then back up at the waiter. "Let me ask you something. Do you men tell your friends everything that goes on in your life?" The waiter looked totally dumfounded, and his face gave full disclosure of his confusion. "I mean, when men get together, do they gossip? You know, do they tell their friends everything?"

The waiter looked back over his shoulder and then looked back at the women just as a big smile appeared across his face. "Honey, I couldn't keep a secret if my life depended on it," he blurted out and then turned and walked away. Both women broke out into laughter.

"I guess we have our answer," Cora whispered, which started the women laughing even harder.

After the salad plates were cleared away and the sisters were finishing up their coffee, Ruth leaned forward, placed her arms on the table, and looked intensely at her sister. "You asked me what was going on with Quinten, and actually, I do have some news on that front." She paused as Cora set down her coffee cup and gave her sister her full attention. "Quinten asked me to marry him last weekend."

"Oh my god!" Cora exclaimed. "I *knew* something was going on! I *knew* Henry was keeping something from me!"

"Yeah, we went down to Charrette Creek to this farm that's owned by a family friend out in Ox Bend, and he asked me there on a sandy beach under this beautiful bluff. It was so romantic!"

"Well, what did you tell him? Did you accept?" Cora fired off before her sister could respond.

"I told him I would think about it," Ruth replied as she sat back in her chair. "I'm really nervous about it all, though. Maybe I'm just too old to get married again. And I'm afraid I'll make another mistake. You know what they say, there's no fool like an old fool!"

"Oh, nonsense!" Cora barked. "Saying yes to a wedding proposal and having a wedding is the easy part. It's the marriage after that causes all the problems."

"I'm serious, Cora. I've only been with one man in my whole life, and that was Richard." She paused, and a confused look came over her. "I just don't want to make another wrong decision. And marriage is such a final thing."

"Not necessarily," Cora interjected with a wink.

"Well, maybe not in your world!" Ruth responded, shaking her head and smiling at the same time. "But I just have to be 100 percent sure that it's the right thing, that it's the logical thing to do."

Cora suddenly slouched down in her chair, as if some heavy weight had just been placed on her, and she looked at Ruth. "See. You're always the wise one. What's that song say? 'Only fools rush in'? I just wish I had half your sense. I always ran into everything like I was killing snakes!"

"Mom used to always say that!" Ruth exclaimed with a laugh.

"Yeah, I know. That's where I got it! You don't know how many times she told me I went after things like I was killing snakes. And she was probably right." Suddenly, Cora sat back up and leaned in toward her sister. "But I just don't know if you can apply logic to something as illogical as love. I think that's how you approached things with Richard. You always thought it was logical to stay with him. It made logical sense to keep the family together for the sake of the children." She paused and reached out across the table and grabbed her sister's hands. "Maybe this time around you need to follow your heart, however illogical it might seem."

"Oh my god, you're making sense again," Ruth replied with a nervous grin. "But it's just such a big step."

"Well, let me ask you this, Are you attracted to him? Does he turn you on?"

Ruth blushed and looked down. After a few moments of silence, she looked back up. "Yes," she finally admitted. "Very much so."

"Well, there you go!" Cora replied as she squeezed her sister's hands. "That's half the battle! Believe me, it's a tough go if you don't. And you need to get past that number one!"

Ruth blushed again but smiled at the same time. "Maybe you're right." She stopped and looked around the busy restaurant and then looked back at her sister. "I'm going to marry him!" she uttered. She picked up her coffee cup and raised it in the air. "I am going to marry Quinten Denver," she repeated just to see how it sounded.

"Oh my god!" Cora exclaimed with delight. "Someone in the family is getting married, and it's not me for a change! I am so happy for you!"

"Daumen drücken!" Ruth uttered under her breath.

"What?" Cora asked as she leaned forward. "What was that?"

"Daumen drücken. Don't you remember Grandma Elsie saying that?"

"Yeah, sort of," Cora responded. "It does sound kind of familiar."

"It translates literally to mean 'press' or 'hold your thumbs.' But Elsie always said it meant to keep your fingers crossed."

"Daumen drücken," Cora whispered.

CHAPTER
28

C ora and her sister, Ruth, found themselves in a familiar place as they sat at the bedside of Emma Saroh at the Shepherds Crossing Nursing Home in downtown St. Louis. Only a month earlier, a call had come in during the middle of the night with news that their father, Cole Saroh, had died at 12:03 a.m., in the very room that the women now sat, of complications from COPD and congestive heart failure. A small funeral had been held at the Shepherds Funeral Home, a sister company of the nursing home that was located only three miles from the New St. Marcus Cemetery, where the old man was laid to rest. And only three weeks to the day after his internment, Emma Saroh's doctors had called Cora with the heartbreaking news that it was time to prepare for the final days of her ailing mother, and Emma was transferred to the special hospice room at the back of the nursing home.

Once Emma Saroh came to the lonely comprehension that she was going to die, that her illness was terminal, she began the slow, inevitable process of withdrawing from the world around her. She lost interest in many of the things that she had enjoyed throughout her life, she no longer read her romance novels or watched her favorite television shows and seemed to show little interest in anything that was going on around her, and she had even started to refuse to see loved ones who came for visits. The most telling of all her symptoms, and the one that had caused the most concern for Emma's children, was her refusal to eat as she continued to withdraw into her illness. The children had initially attempted to force her to eat and had even suggested the use of a feeding tube, but at the direction of the hospice caretaker, they had finally decided to allow their mother to make the decision herself, to let nature take its course, a particularly counterintuitive conclusion for the kindhearted Ruth. Emma's breathing had become irregular as the days had passed, and at times a sort of "rattling" could be heard as she struggled for air, and her extremities had started to take on a purplish, blotchy appearance that the hospice nurse referred to as mottling.

The family had been taking turns sitting at the bedside of the old woman, in hopes that she would not have to die alone, that at least one family member would be at her side as she "plunged again into the inane," as Ruth remembered Carlyle putting it. Regina and her three children had originally made arrangements to be at the nursing home on Mondays and Wednesdays, a schedule that was soon truncated as the old woman's health declined rapidly and she started to refuse to see guests. Lawrence came as often as he could but was limited by his wheelchair and was dependent on finding a driver to transport him to and from the location. Charles had worked out a schedule with the police department in Lincoln County that allowed him to visit on the weekends, and several local neighbors had volunteered to cover his farming duties on those particular days; and he made transporting his mother to and from the nursing home his principal objective. Richard Jr., who had just recently moved to Houston, Texas, would fly in whenever his job allowed and was put up in a third-floor bedroom of the Lasciter home in Lafayette Square when he was in town. Ruth, who at the direct request of her children had limited her driving to the local IGA store and back to her home in Ox Bend, relied on Charles and other family members for rides into the city and would often stay over a few days at her sister's house, in a spare bedroom that was just one room down from where her son would stay.

Cora and Ruth were sitting in chairs next to the bed in the specially designated "hospice room" at the Shepherds Nursing Home, and Charles, who had arrived a few hours earlier, was standing just outside the door in the hall, as if serving as a sentry for his dying grandmother.

"So you don't think yesterday was a good sign, then?" Cora asked her sister, who was sitting to her right, next to their mother's bed.

"I really don't know what to think, but I'm just afraid that yesterday was her rally."

"Oh, that 'last rally' business," Cora fired back unbelievingly. "I remember Aunt Jewel always going about that," she grunted in skeptical disbelief. "You don't really put any stock in that, do you?"

"Well, say what you want, but it does seem to happen," Ruth countered. "Both of Richard's parents went through a similar thing, and I've seen it many times in our family."

"When?" Cora barked out in disbelief.

"Don't you remember? Mom told us that old Aunt Matilda went through something like this right before she died. They said they went into her room the morning before she died, and she was sitting up and alert and demanded that they take her outside, to let her sit on the back porch for a while. And they did that and thought maybe she was getting better." Ruth paused, and her face took on a serious look. "But they found her dead in my bed that very next morning!"

"Oh my," Cora whispered as she vaguely remembered hearing the story.

"I know that it sounds strange," Ruth went on, "but it really happens."

"So what exactly was she like yesterday?" Cora asked as her interest in the strange phenomena increased.

"I came in at my usual time around six thirty, and she was sitting up in her bed, which she hadn't done all week. And she was very talkative and engaging, which was very unusual, and she said she was ready to go home. She even had her small travel suitcase out, like she was planning on leaving that day."

"So what did you say to her?"

"I just told her that they still had to run a few more tests on her and that maybe later in the week she could go home for a visit." Ruth stopped, and tears started to well up in her eyes. "It was just so sad. I kept thinking back to the day they took Marcella away." Ruth paused again to collect herself, then went on. "And then she finally just let go of the idea of going home. She just accepted it. And when the night nurse came in, she told her that there was a change of plans, that she wouldn't be going home after all." Ruth dropped her head into her hands and started to sob. Cora just sat silently, not knowing what to say, and then started to rub her sister's back. After a few moments, Ruth lifted up her head and wiped the tears from her cheeks. "There is an old African proverb that says that the death of an old person is like the burning of a library. And that's true."

"What do you mean?" Cora asked.

"When someone dies, they live on for at least a few generations in the minds of those they met and knew: their children, grand-children, friends, and coworkers. But then when they die and there is no one left alive who knew them, or remembers them, they die all over again. And that's what's going to happen when she's gone." Ruth looked affectionately at her sleeping mother. "She knew old Frederich Saroh, Cole's father, and she knew all his brothers and sisters too, and her parents and grandparents and all their brothers and sisters and cousins—they all disappear with her. She's the last one of that generation. And everyone that lived in her memory will be gone forever."

Just as Cora started to respond, Charles walked in from out in the hall. "How's she doing?" he asked awkwardly, never knowing exactly what to say in such situations.

"No change," Ruth answered as she reached up and took her son by the hand. "You don't have to stay here any longer. I know you have work to do at home, and I bet the boys are missing you. Cora and I are going to be here, and I'm going to stay over tonight."

"Yeah, I know, but I want to stay a little longer." He paused and then walked to the foot of the bed. "You know, Grandpa died just a month ago, and now if Grandma goes, that will be number two."

Ruth looked back at her son. "Don't even think it," she countered quickly.

"Think what?" Cora jumped in.

"That deaths always happen in threes," Charles answered soberly.

"Oh, baloney!" Cora replied with the wave of her hand.

"No, that's true," Ruth jumped in. "That's always the way it's been in our family."

"Oh, that's not true!" Cora retorted with a sound of panic in her voice.

"Yes, it is," Ruth assured her. "Don't you remember? Aunt Jewel's son was killed in that car accident in New York, and then her husband died just a few months later. And then Jewel just a few months after that."

"Oh my god," Cora gushed. "I wish you hadn't reminded me of that!"

About an hour later, just as Charles was getting ready to walk out the door, Emma started to stir. At first, it was almost imperceptible, but Ruth had been adjusting her oxygen tubes at that time and noticed that she was starting to move ever so slightly. Then, all of a sudden, Emma's eyes opened. Cora went around to the other side of her mother, and Charles stood at the foot of the bed. Her eyes, now wide open and looking toward the ceiling, dilated and seemed to turn a bluish-gray color as her breathing shallowed, and became less and less noticeable. Her eyes remained steadily fixed on some distant point, as if she could see all that lay before her and she was reaching out to it, embracing the mystery that was just beyond. Ruth grabbed her mother's tissue-thin hand, which was cool to the touch, and she clasped her hands around it tightly. No one said a word as a hushed aura fell over the small room. After a few moments, her breaths, which had become almost unnoticeable, finally just stopped, like the ticking of a clock that needed to be rewound. A quiet tranquility came over the room, and the old woman's face, which had borne the pain of over ninety years of living, seemed to relax; and she looked almost like a small child lying in a bed, her eyes wide open. The three family members, like mute, ghostly apparitions hovering around a grave site, just looked at one another in utter silence, as if there were no words worthy of the scene.

CHAPTER
29

"**S**o it looks like it's again been a while since our last visit," Dr. Whitman stated, a little judgmentally, as he paged through Cora's rather-lengthy file. "But I am glad to see you back." The doctor set the file aside, pulled his reading glasses down to the end of his nose, and looked closely at his patient. "First, let me start off by saying how sorry I am to hear about your mother. Saying goodbye to a parent can be one of the hardest things we have to do in life. There is no loss quite like that."

Cora, who looked unusually thin, was dressed in a peach-colored pantsuit, and she nervously crossed her legs as she started to speak. "Thank you. I appreciate that. I had no idea how hard it was going to be."

"You've lost a loved one before, haven't you?"

"Yes, Jasper, and of course Daddy, but this was different in some way. I don't know. I just feel this emptiness inside. I think about her, I think about my childhood, I think about her life with Daddy, and these almost-unbearable waves of anxiety come over me."

"Are you keeping up with your journaling?"

"I'm trying to, but..." Cora stopped talking abruptly and looked to the side of the room and saw that the fish tank was gone. "Where's the fish tank?" she all but yelled.

"It developed a small leak in the back, so I had to dismantle it."

"But you're bringing them back, right?" Cora asked with a hint of desperation in her voice.

"Oh, they'll be back," Dr. Whitman assured her. "Now, let's refocus. I want to talk more about the death of your mother and how you've been dealing with it."

"I figured you would," Cora replied as she seemed to settle down a little. "Actually, I was fine the first few days after it happened. Maybe it just hadn't sunk in yet, I don't know. I was keeping busy with making plans with the funeral home for the service and everything. And Ruth was staying there with me at first, and that helped. But she had to go back home. She had to check in on the business." Cora paused and crossed her arms tightly as she thought back to the day her mother died. "I was with her when she passed, you know. I was holding her hand. It was one of the hardest things I've done in my life."

"It sounds like you had forgiven your mother."

"Oh, yes. And I was so thankful for that. I'm so glad she knew that."

"So," Dr. Whitman started out, tilting his head to the right, "tell me more about how you feel now."

"I've been better these past few days, but about a week after the funeral, I had this terrible experience. Henry was on a business trip, and I was alone at the house, and I had just lain down to go to bed, and then all of sudden these waves of anxiety came over me, and I felt like I literally couldn't breathe. I felt like I was suffocating!"

"So what did you do?"

"I had to get up! I had to sit up to get a breath. I guess it was some kind of panic attack, I don't know. So I took a Xanax, but even that didn't seem to help, so I called Henry and talked to him until it passed."

"How long did it last?"

"Probably about twenty minutes or so, and the whole time I just stayed on the phone with Henry."

"So how are things going between you two?"

"Ah, we still have our issues, and he's in his world and I'm in mine. But I will say that he really was a support to me during all this." Cora stopped, and a curious look came over her face. "He really was," she repeated as a subtle smile appeared on her face. "I think I am starting to really understand him more. I'm getting better at seeing things through his perspective."

"What do you mean by that?"

"He has such a logical approach to everything—you know how bankers are. Everything with him is so black-and-white, everything has to *balance out* at the end of the day." Cora stopped, reached into her purse, and pulled out a cigarette. "And I almost envy that in him at times. That uniquely masculine ability to make a decision and then just accept it, never looking back, never questioning it." She lit the cigarette and then reached forward and grabbed an ashtray off the side table and balanced it on her lap. "And these days, all I seem to do is question everything."

"Do you see questioning as a bad thing?"

"I don't know," Cora answered quite seriously. "Henry doesn't seem to question anything, and I envy that in him sometimes."

"And do you think this type of unexamined approach brings him happiness?" the doctor asked very deliberately.

"Such a word, *happiness*!" Cora remarked, a look of disgust coming over her face. "Anyway, I don't think he really sees the world in that context. I don't think he's ever sad, I don't think he's ever happy, and I don't think he ever thinks about being sad or happy." She paused, as if she couldn't think of just the rights words. "He's just Henry!"

"What do you mean by that?"

"I don't know!" Cora yelled. "Who knows? Has any woman every really known a man?" she added abruptly. "I don't think there's a man on earth who isn't harboring at least one dark secret."

"Well, now you speak in generalizations. Maybe the issue isn't with Henry or with men in general. Maybe he knows who he is and he's content with that. Maybe the issue is with you."

"Oh yes, of course, it's all my fault," Cora jibbed sarcastically.

"You know I'm not saying that," the doctor responded parentally. "And I think it's good that you're trying to see things from his perspective. I don't think you've ever done that before, in any of your relationships. And any successful marriage has to be a two-way street." Dr. Whitman stopped and tilted his head to the right again and leaned forward in his chair. "Let me ask you this, and I want you to really think about it before you answer." He took a short pause for effect. "Do you *love* Henry?"

The question took Cora completely off guard, and she laid her head back into the couch cushion and stared up toward the ceiling. "I think I've spent the better part of my life trying to find love, but I don't even know if I know what that is." She looked back down and took a deep drag of her cigarette. "You know, when I first met Henry," she started out with smoke escaping on each syllable, "I was the first one to use the *love* word." She paused and flicked the ash off her cigarette. "And that was first time that ever happened. I never said it first to any of my earlier husbands."

"Well, that's an interesting observation. Tell me about it," Dr. Whitman volleyed back.

"It was probably about eight or nine months after we had first started dating. We had gone down to the Arch, and we were standing up at the top and were looking out of those little windows, looking down on the city below. And it really was breathtaking, and I guess the excitement of being up there just came over me, and I reached over and gave him a kiss and told him that I thought I was falling in love with him."

Cora paused and took another deep drag off her cigarette. "And you know what he said to me? He said it was his experience that those who *invested* in love typically didn't get a good return." Cora stopped again and flicked her cigarette into the ashtray. "Those who invested in love typically didn't get a good return," she repeated mockingly. "That's my Henry! Always an eye for the investment!" she added mordantly.

"And how did you feel about that?"

"Well, at least he was honest," Cora whispered in a hushed voice, attempting to sidestep the question. "That's more than I can say about most of the men in my life."

"But he asked you to marry him, didn't he?"

"I guess he saw a good investment," Cora quipped back with an artificial smirk.

"And is that how you see yourself, an investment?"

Cora paused and seemed to be analyzing the question very closely. "In some ways I think I am," she finally responded with complete honesty. "In Henry's business—really, in any business environment—a man needs the accessory of a woman at his side to be successful." She hesitated a moment, as if she might have lost her train of thought. "The right shoes, the right handbag," she added with a laugh.

The doctor lowered his head and glared reproachfully at Cora over the top of his reading glasses.

"Hey, Henry told me that himself!" Cora defended. "He told me that to be successful in the business world, he needed a wife, someone to attend the office parties with and to entertain the occasional out-of-town business guests!" Cora paused and nervously flicked the ash off her cigarette. "And if you're good-looking, that's even better."

"And that's how you see yourself?"

"In a way, I guess I do. But at least it's a role that I'm good at!" Cora shot back assertively.

"Oh, Cora," the doctor exclaimed as he shook his head in disbelief, "do you really think that the only reason Henry married you was to have some accessory at this side? Do you really believe that?"

Cora didn't respond, and she lay back into the couch again and crushed her cigarette out in the ashtray, and the harsh exterior that always seemed to surround her suddenly vanished, and she appeared almost fragile and exposed.

"Cora, listen to me. And I want you to really hear what I am saying. I think this goes back to how you value yourself. Henry is not your father," Dr. Whitman stated with firm resolve, "or Trenton or Brian or even Jasper, as far as that goes. Don't let the actions of those men, especially your father, cloud the feelings you have for your husband. Don't give them that power over you. You say you're starting to see things from his perspective—I think *perspective* was the word you used—and that's a move in the right direction. I think that shows growth and progress. And when you get right down to it, he's just a man. And he probably has the same insecurities and apprehensions that you have. You may not see them in him, but I bet they're there." Dr. Whitman paused and looked at his watch, then grabbed Cora's file and opened it. "I am going to have you do an exercise between now and our next meeting. It's sort of a blind-study questionnaire around future goals that I want each of you to fill out independently."

Cora suddenly sat up straight, and a sense of honesty came over her face. "Dr. Whitman," she said, interrupting, "you asked me if I loved my husband, and I never really gave you an answer." The doctor looked up from the file and focused on his patient. "I don't know if I do or not," Cora whispered. "I honestly just don't know."

CHAPTER 30

"So you're sure you want to have your wedding at the old Lippstadt Church?" Cora barked out. "It doesn't even have electricity in it," she added, to reinforce her point.

"Yes," Ruth responded adamantly. "We're not having a royal wedding or a concert!" she added jokingly and then looked at her sister for some type of reaction.

"Not bad," Cora replied with a huge grin. "But leave the jokes to me!" she snapped and then took a sip of her coffee. She stopped abruptly and then took another even smaller sip from the plastic cup. "Does your coffee taste right?" she asked as she set her cup down and her face puckered up in disgust. "This much for a cup of coffee and it tastes like this!"

Ruth, who was sitting across from her sister on a tall stool, had just taken the top off her cup and was blowing on it. "Well, let me try it here. It smells all right," she said as she took a small sip. "It's not that bad. It's a little strong, but I like it that way."

"Well, I'm taking mine back!" Cora announced. She replaced the plastic lid on her cup and stormed off toward the counter of the small coffee shop, Coffee-Squared, which was just around the corner from Cora's Lafayette Square home. Ruth shook her head as her sister took her place in the back of a rather-long line and started to look around the small establishment. The coffee shop was on the ground floor of an old three-story brick building that had been recently renovated on Park Street, the small business district in the square. The eight-hundred-square-foot area still had the original oak hardwood floors, the original artisan tin ceiling in silver whitewashed metal, ten-foot-tall exposed brick walls, and two large bay windows, with room for a small table and two chairs in each covey, which flanked the inset entrance door to the business. Ruth was seated in the bay window to the right of the front door, and two women, an older woman with bright red hair and a younger girl who looked to be in her teens, were seated in the left bay window. As Ruth was waiting for her sister to return, she noticed the red-haired woman staring at her through the side windows of the entranceway. Ruth nodded cordially to the woman and then looked away, but the old woman just kept staring. After a few minutes, she got up and walked over toward Ruth.

"There's a young man standing beside you," the red-haired woman announced, as she boldly walked up to Ruth. "He wants me to talk to you." Ruth was shocked by the comments, and she nervously glanced over at her sister at the counter. "Pardon me. What did you say?" Ruth asked politely, uneasily picking up her cup and blowing on it.

"There's a young man standing beside you," she repeated. "And he wants me to speak to you." Ruth didn't know what to say, and she just looked at the woman in total confusion.

"Don't be afraid," the old woman went on with a reassuring tone as she picked up on Ruth's uneasiness with the situation. "Do you believe in mediums?" she asked. Ruth, still in shock by the sudden declaration, again said nothing and just shook her head slightly. "My name is Marla, and I am a medium. I can communicate with people on the other side. And there is a young man wanting me to communicate for him."

"Well, I don't know if I really understand all that," Ruth responded politely, finally finding her voice. "I think there must be some kind of mistake."

"I am seeing two As," the old woman went on, ignoring Ruth's prior comments completely. "That's how they communicate. That's how I work. I see images and outlines in my mind, and I am seeing two As." Just as Ruth was getting ready to respond, Cora walked up with her replacement coffee and took a seat across from her sister.

"This is Marla," Ruth started out as she secretly rolled her eyes. "She says that there is a young man standing beside me and that he wants to talk to me."

"Look," Cora stated as she took her seat, slipped the lid of her replacement coffee, and took a small sip. "We don't do crazy!"

"Oh, I assure you, I'm not crazy," the old woman fired back, completely unfazed by Cora's crass remark. "There is a young man standing beside you. And he is showing me two *As*. And I'm seeing two images that usually represent a mother to me." She paused and looked confused. "But I see two of them. Two mothers. Does that make any sense?" she asked, her face contorted with curiosity.

Suddenly, Cora set her cup down and looked at the woman in shock. "Two *As*?" she asked. She looked across the small table at Ruth, whose face had suddenly gone white. "Like in the name Aaron?"

"Yes," the old woman stated excitedly. "That's it! But what does the 'two mothers' thing mean?"

Cora clasped her hands together and placed them under her chin. "I gave birth to a son named Aaron, but my sister here, she raised him. She was really more his mother than I was. So in a way he always had two mothers."

"That makes sense," the old woman said, nodding. "And he wants you to know that he's fine. And that he's with his father."

Ruth, who up to this point had said nothing, gently grabbed the woman's arm as tears started to stream down her face.

"And he's okay?" she asked imploringly. "He's okay?" she repeated in desperation.

"Yes, he's fine, and he's with a father figure."

Ruth looked over at Cora, who had suddenly gone silent. "He must be with Richard!" Ruth exclaimed. She looked back at the old woman. "My sister here had him when she was very young, and then my husband, Richard, and I, we adopted him."

The old woman pulled her arm back. "I'm seeing blood, a father, not a stepfather."

"But what does he want to tell us?" Cora blurted out, nervously cutting the old woman off.

"I see he was a veiled child," the old woman responded, again ignoring Cora's direct question. "He was born with a veil over his head. It's a very rare occurrence. Do you understand what this means?" she asked.

Suddenly, Cora placed her hands over her cheeks, as if she had just seen a ghost. "Oh my god," she whispered. "One of the old nuns at the hospital told me that he had been born with a veil over his head. And I didn't know what that meant at that time. But she told me that the child was special, that he would have a special purpose in life." Cora stopped talking abruptly and looked over at her sister. "I don't know. I don't know," she mumbled, as if she had suddenly become disoriented.

Ruth reached over and grabbed her sister by the arm. "He was special," she uttered to her sister. "He was."

"And I'm seeing the number 3, but I don't know what that means. He's worried about the number 3, or the third day, or the third event, or something to do with the number 3." The old woman stopped. "Does the number 3 mean anything to you?" she asked poignantly.

Cora and Ruth just looked at each and shook their heads.

"He also wants me to show you a plaque or a card or something with writing on it. And it has to do with the name Ruth. What's the significance of Ruth?" she queried.

"My name is Ruth," Ruth interjected in disbelief.

"Maybe, but I sense something more historical, something older," the woman countered.

Ruth looked at the old woman keenly as a few more tears started to run down her face. "He gave me this little plaque that he made when he was little with a Bible verse from the book of Ruth on it. And I still have it! I think that's what he's referring to." She paused as she tried to remember the exact verse. "Where you go, I will go, and where you stay, I will stay," she recited. She paused and looked back at her sister. "You know, I can almost feel his presence when I'm at home. Just out of the blue sometimes, I'll think about him, or I'll sort of feel him standing beside me."

"That's him!" the old woman interjected excitedly. "He's always watching over you."

Cora and Ruth looked at each other in amazement as any final doubts or skepticism about the authenticity of the old woman's abilities dissolved.

"And there is another man coming forward. But he's way in the back. He doesn't want to come too close." The old woman grabbed her chest and looked as if some real pain had just entered her body. "I am feeling a terrible pain in my chest. That's my symbol for some type of chest wound, and I can feel blood rushing. He was very young, and his death was very violent." The old woman stopped suddenly and looked closely at Cora. "And I am seeing the letter *J*. And a bell, or the name Belle, or something to do with a bell."

Suddenly, Cora stood up and looked at her sister in amazement. "Oh my god!" she exclaimed. "Jasper Stockdale, that's the *J*, and his nickname for me was Cora Belle!"

"And he died violently?" the old woman queried.

"Yes, he was shot in Korea when he was twenty-seven years old."

"And he's showing me a dog or something. It's like a dog, but not really a dog. A symbol, maybe, of a dog."

Cora reached into her purse and pulled out a small pendant in the shape of a small bulldog fashioned in pewter that was attached to her key ring. "This must be it!" she exclaimed. "Jasper's nickname was Bull Dog. It was a nickname that he got when he played football in high school." She paused and looked down at the small adornment that she had kept on her key ring ever since she first received it. "He gave this to me just before he shipped out that last time. It was the last thing he ever gave me."

CHAPTER
31

There were two bodies laid out at the Clarkson Funeral Home as the last week of October approached, and the winds that had started to come out of the north with more and more regularity had ushered in the first cool night of the fall season. In the large main viewing chamber was a young high school student who had been killed in an unfortunate motorcycle accident, and the outpouring of cards and flowers and sympathy notes that flooded the small funeral home had been almost overwhelming for the staff, as they prepared for what was sure to be the largest funeral since Richard Clarkson had been laid out four years earlier. In the smaller room, at the back of the funeral home, Erna Koelling, who had reached the ripe old age of 102, was laid out in a peony-blue cotton brocade suit that she had purchased for her great-grandson's wedding only two months earlier. She had been a lifelong resident of the small town of Ox Bend, and she was thought to be the last surviving resident in the county that had been born before 1900. The unusual dichotomy between the two situations was not lost on the people of the small town as they mourned the loss of two of its citizens, but in drastically different fashions.

Ruth Clarkson and Quinten Denver were sitting in the funeral home office, at the front of the building, discussing last-minute wedding plans, and Quinten was attempting to talk Ruth into flying to Hawaii as soon as the service was over, an idea that Ruth was not completely sold on.

"I just don't know if I feel comfortable leaving the business for that long," Ruth countered to Quinten as the Hawaii discussion continued on. "And it's such a long flight!"

"Ah, live a little, Ruth," Quinten countered with a twinkle in his eye. "Vickie and John can take care of the place for a couple of weeks." He paused and flashed his irresistible trademark grin to his bride-to-be, and his eyes quivered back and forth with excitement. "Let's get out of Grover's Corner for a while," he added with a laugh.

"I should have never told you about that place!" Ruth shot back with an even bigger laugh.

"Come on, live a little!"

"Now you sound like Cora," Ruth fired back.

"Hey, you should listen to your sister!" Quinten retorted. "I really like her."

"Most men do," Ruth replied with a smirk. "But do we have enough time to get flights and reservations and everything? The wedding day is only a few weeks away."

"I have all that taken care of," Quinten answered cryptically.

Ruth looked at him closely. "What do you mean by that?"

"I already have everything reserved!" he exclaimed and then handed her a brochure on Kauai. "All you have to do is get on board!"

"Oh, Quinten! You're always one step ahead of me!"

Before Ruth could add another impediment to the trip, they heard a light knocking on the office door. "Come on in!" Ruth yelled out cavalierly. "And we'll pick this conversation up later," she whispered to Quinten, who was looking at another brochure on Pearl Harbor. She rose and started making her way across the office, her Hawaiian brochure still clutched tightly in her hand. Just as she reached the middle of the room, a thin weather-beaten-looking woman, with dyed jet-black hair that made her look almost like a cartoon character, came walking into the office. She was extremely thin, and her face was drawn and wrinkled, and her dark, almost-black eyes looked tired and bloodshot and gave her the appearance of someone who had grown accustomed to unhappiness and suffering.

"Hello. My name is Ruth Clarkson," Ruth said as she cautiously approached the woman, "and this is Quinten Denver. Please come in and have a seat." She reached out and attempted to shake the strange woman's hand, but she would not acknowledge Ruth's gesture, and she just looked blankly at Ruth and tugged at an old gray sweater that was drooping off her shoulders. "Here, please have a seat," Ruth said. She walked back behind her desk, the brochure still clutched in her left hand, and waved toward a chair just across from her.

"What can we do for you?" she asked in her best business voice as she sat back down behind the desk. The strange woman sat down and placed a large black purse on her lap.

"So you're Ruth Clarkson," she said mysteriously with a large voice that didn't seem to match her demure appearance. "Do you not know who I am?" she asked before Ruth could respond.

"No," Ruth answered. She glanced back toward Quinten, who was standing just behind her.

"Mark never told you about me?" she asked, her eyes watching Ruth's every move.

"Mark who? Mark Callier? Our Mark Callier?" Ruth grilled, attempting to get to the identity.

"Yes, Mark Callier," the woman finally shot back bitterly. She hesitated, and her eyes darted back and forth between Ruth and Quinten. "I'm his mother," she finally pronounced in a shadowy way.

Ruth's mouth dropped open, and she again quickly glanced back at Quinten with a shocked look on her face. "Mark told me that his mother was dead," Ruth countered after the initial shock of the woman's declaration wore off.

"Oh, is that what he told you?" the woman yelled out with a pain that seemed to be attached to nothing. "I might as well be!" she added with words laced with agony.

"I don't understand this," Ruth replied as she started to get an uneasy feeling about the woman. "The Mark Callier that works here, he's convinced that his mother died over four years ago."

"Well, I might as well have been dead in that institution!" the woman fired back, her dark eyes fixed on Ruth. Suddenly, Ruth remembered the misgivings that her sister and Henry had voiced over the supposed death of Mark's mother, and she started to grapple with the possibility that the woman was indeed telling the truth, that sitting in front of her was her dead husband's longtime secret lover.

"So what do you want?" Ruth asked, her voice filled with trepidation. "Why are you here?" she asked, nervously rolling up the brochure.

"You know he loved *me!*" the woman yelled out with a voice that seemed disconnected from reality, completely ignoring Ruth's direct question. "He never really loved you!" she added coldly. She sat forward and placed her hand in the large purse sitting on her lap. "He told me as much on many different occasions, and he would have been with me, if it weren't for you!" she bellowed out, her voice continuing to rise. "His perfect little wife and his perfect little family. But what about us? What about me? What about the child he had with me? And now you've taken him from me too!"

Ruth stood up and started to walk from around the back of the desk. And then, without warning, the woman pulled a small revolver from her purse and fired a direct shot into Ruth's left shoulder. Quinten lunged forward, attempting to block Ruth from the gun-fire, and the woman unloaded the gun in rapid-fire succession, hitting Ruth again in the arm, and then striking Quinten Denver four times before he finally fell to the floor. The final shot was a direct hit to the center of his forehead. The woman calmly, as if in some somnambulant state, walked behind the desk and looked down at Ruth, who was lying on the floor next to Quinten, and she started to pull the trigger again, but it only clicked—the chamber was empty. She pulled the trigger again and again and then finally just dropped the gun and walked out of the office.

Ruth rolled over and saw Quinten's lifeless body covered in blood lying next to her. She reached over and cradled his head in her lap and started to rock back and forth with him clutched in her embrace.

"Oh my god," she wailed. "What have I done? Quinten! Quinten! What have I done to you!" Suddenly she stopped, and a silence came over her. She looked down and saw the Kauai pamphlet lying at her side, covered in blood; she could hear the old Pembroke Renroth grandfather clock chiming the half-hour in the distance. She could smell the subtle scent of chrysanthemums wafting across the room, and the metallic scent of iron in the blood that covered the scene. She looked down at Quinten. His eyes were open wide, as if he could still see her. It was the same distant, mysterious look that she had seen in her mother's eyes. "Oh my god," she cried. "Number 3!

Number 3!" A bright light surrounded her, and she felt herself falling back toward the floor. She grabbed her shoulder and could feel the warm blood rushing over her hand. She looked up one last time and then slowly closed her eyes.

CHAPTER
32

"Mommy! Mommy!" the young boy yelled from the oldest section of the small Lippstadt Graveyard. "Mommy, I can't read this one!" he added with an infectious boyish enthusiasm that only youth could produce.

"All right, let me come look!" Ruth yelled back. She stood up with the assistance of Werner and Marcella Clarkson's gravestone, a clump of crabgrass clutched loosely in her left hand. A clear blue sky was shining overhead, and the sun was streaming down soft, ethereal rays through the vernal canopy of oaks and hickories that surrounded the small church and cemetery, and Ruth Clarkson was just finishing up her monthly weeding duties around the family headstones.

"Mommy! Mommy!" Aaron yelled out again in youthful impatience.

"I'm coming!" Ruth replied quickly. "You don't want weeds growing around Granny's grave, do you?" she added as she finally reached her son, who was looking down at one of the older sandstone markers that was starting to fade away from years of erosion.

"Look, Mommy, I can't read this one!" the young boy shouted out. He dropped to his knees and then looked back up at his mother.

"Ah, that's in German," Ruth replied. She reached down and affectionately placed her hand on the boy's head.

"What's German?" Aaron asked.

"Well, that's the language that my family used to speak when they were in Germany."

"Why?" the young boy asked with unlimited youthful curiosity.

"It's just a different language," Ruth explained as she tousled the boy's curly brown hair. "There are lots of different languages in the

221

world." The boy said nothing and just started to pick at some moss that had partially obscured the death date on the old stone. "You know Grandma Emma, don't you?" Ruth asked. "She speaks German all the time."

"Why?" the young boy asked again with a huge grin.

"Because she was actually born in Germany and then came over here on a boat when she was a young girl."

"Is Germany far from here?"

"Oh, yes, it's across the Atlantic Ocean." Ruth bent down next to her son. "See here it says, 'Liebster vater.' That mean 'dearest father,' I think."

"So this was someone's father?" the young boy asked inquisitively.

"Yes. This was someone's father. And see here, he died in 1899."

"Whose father was it?" Aaron asked as he looked up at his mother curiously.

"Oh, I don't know. He died a long time ago. His children are probably already gone too."

"So nobody remembers him anymore?" the young boy asked as he jumped up and ran to a small stone that was just two spaces down.

"Well, we just did," Ruth replied reassuringly. "That's why I like coming out here. It gives me a chance to remember them." Ruth looked lovingly at her young son, who was hunched over a very small, very old sandstone marker. "Do you think you'll remember me when I'm gone?" she whispered as she walked up behind the young boy.

He looked up at his mother standing behind him, and he shaded his eyes as a bright beam of sun peeked out from behind the canopy. "I will never forget you, Mommy. I could never forget you," he added as he looked back down at the small stone in front of him. "Who is this?" he asked. He pulled a dandelion that had taken root at the base of the small marker. Ruth bent down and tried to read the faint lettering.

"Oh my," she finally uttered. "This is Irene Sprick. This is Marcella's older sister." She paused and pointed to the dates. "See, she was born and died in the same year. She was only a few weeks old when she passed."

"Why did she die, Mommy?"

"Back in those days, they didn't have a lot of the medicines and hospitals like we have now, so sometimes little babies just couldn't make it. And I can remember Marcella telling me that this little girl was born at home and then died just a few days later. They even had her funeral service at the house where she was born."

"Was Grandma sad?" Aaron asked as a concerned look came over his face.

"Well, honey, she died before Grandma Marcella was even born."

"Why does she have a different name from Grandma?" the inquiring young boy asked.

"Well, Grandma Marcella was born with the last name of Sprick. She was actually a cousin to the Spricks that built our funeral home. But when she got married to Grandpa, she took his last name of Clarkson."

"Why?" the young boy asked almost indignantly.

"That's a good question," Ruth answered with laugh.

Suddenly, the young boy got up and started to run as fast he could to the other side of the graveyard. "Aaron!" Ruth yelled. "Don't run off too far now!" The young boy suddenly just disappeared, evanesced into one of the beams of light that dotted the small graveyard. Ruth dropped the clump of weeds from her hand and started running toward the small church, where she had last seen him. "Aaron!" she screamed as she started to run in a panic. "Aaron! Aaron! Aaron!"

"Mom! Mom! Wake up!" Regina beckoned. She reached down and grabbed her mother by the hand. "Wake up, Mom." She paused and looked back toward a nurse who had just re-entered the small emergency room stall. "She's starting to wake up. She's been yelling out for Aaron."

"And who is Aaron?" the nurse asked as she slung her stethoscope around the back of her neck.

"That was her eldest child. He died years ago."

The nurse went to the side of the bed and leaned over her patient. "Mrs. Clarkson, you have been in an accident, and you are

223

in the hospital. Do you hear me? You've been shot two times, and I need you to try to open your eyes."

Slowly Ruth opened her eyes and looked up at the nurse's gentle face towering above her. "Mom?" Ruth mumbled under her breath.

"Good, good!" the nurse yelled down at Ruth. "I am Nurse Whitten. We're going to be taking you to surgery in just a few minutes. Your daughter is here with you." She paused and quickly glanced up at Regina and then back at her patient. "Do you understand what I am saying?"

"Quinten," Ruth whispered. "Quinten," she uttered again as her eyes darted over to her daughter. "Where is Quinten?" she mumbled. "Is Quentin okay?" she asked again pleadingly.

"He's fine," the nurse replied firmly. She stopped and checked a heart monitor that was beeping at the side of the bed. "Don't you worry about him. You just need to focus on getting better." Before she could finish adjusting the monitor, a group of young men in full scrubs came in and wheeled the bed out and down the hallway.

Just as she was being transported to the operating room, Charles came running up to his sister, Regina. "I heard it on the scanner. I heard that there was a shooting at the funeral home, and I went by the scene, and I came down here as fast as I could. Is she going to be okay?" he asked desperately, his usual calm demeanor all but gone.

"I don't know. She's been shot twice, and she's lost a lot of blood. Once in the chest and shoulder area and once in the arm. They just now took her off to surgery." Regina paused and walked up to her brother and threw her arms around him. "Who would do this?" she asked as tears started to run down her face.

"It was that Mark Callier's mother," Charles responded very matter-of-factly.

Regina pulled back and looked up at her bother. "Mark that works at the funeral home? There has to be some kind of mistake. He told us that his mother was dead!"

"Well, they caught her standing at a payphone just a few blocks down from the funeral home. They said she never tried to escape or anything, and she freely admitted to the shooting. She told them that her name was Sarah Callier and that she was Mark's mother."

"But why?" Regina fired back.

"Oh, who knows?" Charles answered with a disgusted tone. "She's been in a mental institution the past few years, and she's just an unstable person." Charles paused and grabbed his sister by the arm and led her out of the emergency area to a small waiting room. "You know that she was Dad's lover for years, don't you?"

"Oh yes, I know all about it. But to try to kill my mother like she had anything to do with it." Regina stopped suddenly, and a frightened look came over her face. "And what about Quinten? Mom kept asking about him when she finally came around. Was he there? Is he okay?" she rattled off in rapid-fire fashion.

Charles looked kindly at his sister, his usual sense of levelheadedness returning. "He's dead Regina. He was shot four times, once in the head. They said he was dead before he hit the ground."

"Oh no!" Regina moaned. "Oh no!"

CHAPTER 33

"Cora, you really need to go home for a while," Ruth pleaded with her sister. "You can't stay out here in Ox Bend indefinitely. I'm going to be fine. I have the physical therapist coming by three times a week, and Regina and Charles are stopping in all the time." She paused and looked directly at her sister, who was sitting next to her bed, reading a copy of *The Awakening*. "And what about poor Henry? He's going to think he's lost his wife!" she added, hoping to grab her sister's attention.

"Henry is an absence-makes-the-heart-grow-fonder kind of guy," Cora quipped back with a grin. She laid her book down on the arm of the dressing chair and gave her sister her full attention. "And the more I'm away from him, the more attentive he seems to be when I do see him!"

"Cora, I'm serious. I'm worried about him."

"Well, you can worry about him all you want!" Cora exclaimed with a stamp of finality. "I'm worried about you, and I'm not leaving here until I'm sure that you're going to be okay. It's only been two months since you were shot!" She stopped, and her face took on a serious countenance. "You have no idea how upset we all were when we heard the news. And in some ways, I still can't believe that it all happened." Cora paused and took a deep breath, and her face took on a solemn look. "I just thought, maybe for once, it was your turn at happiness."

"Little good really comes from happiness," Ruth answered philosophically as thoughts of Quinten ran through her mind.

"Oh, don't give me that!" Cora barked back. "You and your platitudes!"

"No, I'm serious," Ruth defended as her mood took on a serious tone. "Anything of great value, any real progress in the world, or great work of art usually comes from suffering and pain. It's the anguish in the world, the pain in the world that really moves it forward."

"Well, then, you've done more than your share of moving things forward! Let somebody else move it for a while," Cora remarked sarcastically. "I just thought that maybe it was your turn to have a little happiness," she added. "Would that be so horrible?"

She leaned forward and grabbed her sister by the hand. "Have you ever really been happy?" she asked with a serious tone that Ruth was not used to seeing in her sister. "I mean really happy?"

"You know, Richie asked me that same question about you one time," Ruth deflected. "It was the night of Richard's funeral."

The intense look on Cora's face disappeared, and she sat back into her chair and looked off out the back window. "I think I chased that rabbit long enough when I was younger, and with very little success, I might add. I'd settle for contentment now."

"And are you content now?" Ruth asked with a new level of sincerity.

"Well, maybe," Cora answered as she slipped into a rare philosophical disposition. "Old age takes so many things from you sometimes we forget that it actually brings a few things too, and I think a sense of contentment is one of those."

"And I agree, but old age can bring a lot more than just contentment!" Ruth remarked back.

"Well, don't analyze that too closely—you might be disappointed in the results!"

"Ah, you're probably right," Ruth confessed with a sigh.

"And anyway!" Cora blurted out as she resumed her usual temperament. "We're not talking about me!" she yelled. "You always do that. You answer one of my questions with a question of your own, and we end up talking about me. You're worse than Dr. Whitman!" she added with a laugh. "Now, answer the question. Have you ever really been happy?"

Before Ruth could answer, Richard Jr. walked in the bedroom with a huge bouquet of dark-pink roses in hand. "Well, speak of the devil!" Cora yelled out as he entered. Richard Jr. placed the roses on the dresser and then walked over and gave his aunt a kiss, and then his mother.

Ruth reached up and grabbed him with her good arm and pulled him in close. "It's so good to see you," she whispered. "And you've come just in time to save me from Cora, who thinks she's Dr. Whitman now!" she added, just loudly enough for her sister to hear.

"I think my aunt would have made a great therapist," Richard Jr. retorted, a devious smile spread across his face. "And as I understand it, life's best teacher is experience."

"Well, I know that's not a compliment," Cora volleyed back with a smile of her own. "But I am going to take it as such!"

"That's what I love about you, Aunt Cora, your ability to see the world exactly as you want it!"

"Hey, if it's my party, I might as well decorate it the way I want!" Cora fired back. "And being a therapist would be the last thing I'd ever want to do—hearing people go on and on about all their problems!" She paused and gave her nephew another playful look. "What about my problems?" she bellowed as everyone started to laugh.

Richard Jr. paused, sat down in a folding chair next to the bed, and let out a huge guttural laugh. "I surrender! I surrender! I know when I'm defeated," he added with another huge laugh.

"So what have you two young ladies been discussing that has Cora so keyed up this morning?" Richard Jr. asked playfully. He leaned back in his chair and locked his hands behind his head.

"I'm trying to convince Cora that I am well enough now for her to go home for a while," Ruth explained. "I'm worried about poor Henry all alone down there in that huge old house!"

Richard looked at Cora and winked. "How is old Henry doing?" he asked, ignoring his mother's remark completely.

"He's fine," Cora answered with a tone of confidence. "Your mother thinks that all men just fall apart without a woman around, but Henry is perfectly fine by himself."

"Well, I'm going to have to agree with Cora on this one, Mom," Richard Jr. stated as he leaned forward and grabbed his mother's hand. "The only thing most men like more than routine is quiet.

As long as they have at least one of those things in their life, they're happy."

"So what exactly are you saying, Richard?" Cora quipped back cheekily before Ruth could get a response in.

"Oh, I think I said it!" Richard Jr. replied as all three started to laugh again.

"But Cora is right, Mom," Richard Jr. picked up after the laughter died down. "We're all worried about you. And those were serious wounds you suffered." Richard Jr. leaned in over the bed and looked closely at the bandages around Ruth's right shoulder. "What did the doctor say the last time you saw him, anyway?" he asked as a concerned tone entered his voice.

"He says my shoulder will never be like it was before, but if I keep up with my therapy, I should get at least some of the range of motion back, as well as some of the strength. And he said I might need a shoulder replacement at some point too."

"And I'm seeing to it that she does her exercises daily," Cora chimed in.

"And what about going back to work?" Richard Jr. probed. "I don't want you to overdo it too soon."

"John and Vickie are taking care of everything just fine, and Vickie has her license now too. And if they have any concerns, I told them to check with me. So really, all I'm doing is signing checks and approving expenses."

"And what about Mark?" Richard asked uneasily as he sat back into his chair again. He glanced over at Cora and then back at his mother. "Has he ever shown up here again?"

"No," Cora answered for her sister. "And I don't know if Ruth should be seeing him anymore or not, considering the way things have turned out."

"Well, I'm worried about Mark," Ruth interjected, her voice filled with concern.

"Of course you are!" Cora replied harshly before Ruth could finish her thought.

Ruth ignored her sister and reached over and grabbed her son's hand again. "Cora thinks this is all his fault. But I feel sorry for him.

He's probably horrified at what his mother has done." Ruth paused, and a sense of genuine concern entered her voice as she went on. "I mean, I can't even imagine what he's going through."

"But why would he tell you that his mother was dead?" Richard asked. "That's the one thing I just don't understand. Why would he lie about that?"

"I don't know," Ruth answered, shaking her head. "I don't know. Maybe he thought she was dead. I just don't know. But this is not his fault," Ruth added adamantly.

"Well, the good news is that I have been granted a leave of absence from my job, so I can stay here with you for at least the next month," Richard Jr. announced.

"Oh, that's great news, but are you sure it won't affect your job?" Ruth responded, sounding like a worried mother.

"It's fine, Mom," he answered reassuringly. He paused and looked over at Cora. "And that means that Cora here can go home for a while!"

"Well, I guess I know when I'm not wanted!" Cora joked back. "I'll go make us all some coffee, and I'll call Henry and tell him I'm coming home," she added as she left the bedroom. "And don't talk about me while I'm gone either!" she yelled back from the hallway.

Ruth pulled herself up a little in her bed and then gave her son a motherly look of concern. "Are you sure about this? You sure it's okay to be away from work?"

"Yes, Mother," Richard Jr. replied convincingly. "And I'm looking forward to it. And we need to get you out of this house for a while. Where do you want to go? I'll take you anywhere!"

"Well, I would like to go the New St. Marcus Cemetery." Ruth stopped and looked down. "That's where Quin is buried, and I never got to go to his funeral or anything. And I want to at least see where he's buried."

"That's way down on Gravois. You sure you're okay to go that far?" Richard Jr. asked with a deep sense of concern.

"Yes!" Ruth fired back without hesitation. "I need to go there. I need to see him. I need to see where he's buried."

Richard Jr. stood up and then sat down on the bed next to his mother and put his arm around her. "You really loved him, didn't you mom?"

"I did," Ruth responded, her voice dropping almost to a whisper. "And it was different from the way I felt about your dad. I mean, I loved him in the beginning, and I still loved him in some way at the end. But it was different with Quinten." Ruth paused, and her spirit seemed to deflate a little. "Maybe it was just because it was all new. Maybe it, too, would have been ground down by the inertia of life. I don't know." She paused and looked up at her son sitting next to her. "Maybe this way it stays perfect, like some work of art."

"Oh, you don't believe that," her son replied as he gave his mother a squeeze.

"You know, Aaron tried to warn me that this was going to happen," Ruth announced out of the blue. Richard Jr. leaned forward and looked his mother in the eye.

"What do you mean? What are you talking about?" he asked with a great sense of concern.

"Cora and I were down at this little coffee shop just a few days before the shooting, and there was a medium there." Ruth paused. "Do you know what a medium is?" she asked her son.

"Yes, Mom, I know. They say they can communicate with the dead. I've actually read a couple of books about them."

"Yes. So we were down at this coffee shop just around the corner from Cora's house, and this woman came up to me, and she said that there was a young man standing next to me and that he wanted to talk to me." Ruth stopped again as a shudder ran through her body. "She kept saying that she saw two *As* and that she was seeing an image of two mothers."

"But you don't really believe in that kind of thing, do you, Mother?" Richard Jr. asked with a concerned look on his face.

"Well, I didn't at first, but the two *As*, that was Aaron, and the two mothers, Cora and I! And I believe it was Aaron. It had to be him! She knew way too many things that only he would have known. She even knew about the little plaque that he had made for me in Bible school with the verse from Ruth."

"That is strange," Richard Jr. finally chimed in as his skepticism seemed to be lessening. "And I think sometimes that the mysteries in life still outnumber the truths."

"And the last thing she said was that he wanted to warm me about the number 3. She kept asking me if I knew what the number 3 meant." She paused, and her face took on a painful look. "He was trying to warm about the third death. Cole, then Mom, and then Quin."

"But, Mom, do you really think it was him?" Richard Jr. asked, sounding almost like a small child.

"Oh yes, and I'm even more sure about it now than I was then. And I can feel him around me at times. It's like I can feel his presence. Just like Aaron in the Bible watched over his brother, Moses, my Aaron is watching over me."

"Wow," Richard Jr. exclaimed as the reality of what his mother was saying started to settle in. "You always did like the story of Aaron. Is that why you picked that name?" he asked after a moment.

"Well, the name in Hebrew means 'mountain of strength,' and you're right, I was always fascinated by Aaron in the Old Testament. He was so human, so imperfect in so many ways, and yet so strong." Ruth paused and looked directly at her son sitting next to her. "Do you remember the story of Aaron in the Bible?" she asked intently.

"Yeah, parts of it. Didn't he make a golden calf or something?"

"Yes, that's it. When his brother Moses ascended Mount Sinai and was gone for those forty days, the people came to Aaron and asked for some type of observable God that they could pray to, and so he collected gold and made a golden calf that they started to worship. And of course, that was wrong. And he made other mistakes too, but that's what I like about him, that human side of him. But through it all, he never lost his devotion and dedication to his brother and to his faith."

"And weren't his two sons burned at the stake too?" Richard Jr. asked as he thought back on the story.

"Yes, and he never spoke out against it. He believed in God's righteous judgment, and he never questioned it. He had faithful silence while facing the worst tragedy imaginable." Ruth stopped and grabbed her son by the arm. "We can never know God's ways. We just have to accept them in faith. That's what Aaron did. And that's what I have to do now too."

"What do you mean?" Richard Jr. asked, his mind filled with memories or his older brother.

"I don't know why Quinten is gone. I wish more than anything in the world that he were still here, but I've not lost any of my faith by his loss. And now I have my own Aaron watching over me. And that gives me peace."

"Oh, Mother, I never realized how important your faith is to you. And after all that you've been through."

"It's *because* of all that I've been through that makes me who I am today. And I would never have been able to survive it all without faith."

"But don't you ever just get mad?" Richard Jr. asked, looking out the back window of the old bedroom apartment. "Don't you just wonder sometimes how any God could let what happens in this world go on?"

"Well, that's the difference between us, my son. You see God through theology and study. I see him through faith."

"Coffee's ready!" Cora yelled from the kitchen. "Richie! Come give me a hand!"

Richard Jr. stood up and looked down at his mother. "Will I ever have faith like you do, Mom?" he asked in an-almost desperate tone.

"Oh, I think you will," she answered. She reached up and grabbed his hand again and squeezed it. "You have a long way to go. You're still rowing on that midsummer pond, ignorant and content." Richard Jr. smiled as he thought of Donald Hall's poem. "You'll find your faith in your own way," she reassured him.

"Richie!" Cora yelled again from the kitchen.

"Oh, you better go, or I'll be planning another funeral!" Ruth joked. She let go of her son's hand and watched him walk out of the room.

Part 4

"The Lord bless you, my daughter," he replied. "This kindness is greater than that which you showed earlier: You have not run after the younger men, whether rich or poor. And now, my daughter, don't be afraid. I will do for you all you ask. All my fellow townsmen know that you are a woman of noble character."

—Ruth 3:10–13

CHAPTER 34

The Clarkson Funeral Home, which had served the small community of Ox Bend, Missouri, since 1888, had been out of business for over a decade. The residents of the small town had never quite been able to move past the gruesome murder that had taken place in the town's oldest business, and Ruth, as she had finally come to comprehend, had never been able to give it the energetic attention and care that she had before the loss of Quinten, and she had slowly detached herself from it all. Cora Lasciter's cash injection had enabled Ruth to pay off the debt that Richard had left her, and she had been able to repay her sister back over time, but the company continued to struggle, and breaking even had become the ultimate goal each year. Her unconscious lack of attention, and the high cost of maintaining a building that was over one hundred years old, along with the northward expansion of the local commercial district away from the aging downtown area, had all, in some way or another, finally brought an end to the family business. After much discussion with Cora and her family, Ruth Clarkson made the conscious decision to just "let the business go," as she had couched it to a reporter for the *Ox Bend Journal*. With very little fanfare in December of 2004, after 116 years in business, the Clarkson Funeral Home logged its final day in existence. T. S. Eliot's famous line "This is the way the world ends, not with a bang, but with a whimper" ran through Ruth Clarkson's mind as she made her final ledger entries in the company books.

Another important fact that had a direct bearing on the closing of the business was the gradual decline in the health of its primary owner. Ruth Clarkson had never completely regained the use of her right arm after the tragic shooting and murder of Quinten Denver, and the strength in her shoulder had never returned, and she had experienced extended bouts of pain in the years that followed the shooting. And only five years after Quinten's death, while completing an annual checkup, she had been rushed to Barnes Hospital in downtown St. Louis when some issues with her heart were discovered. She had been diagnosed with arterial fibrillation, a problem with the heart's electrical system that caused irregular heartbeats, and had even undergone an "ablation" surgery to correct the problem, a process that proved to be only partially successful. But the surgery, in conjunction with a prescribed beta blocker, had kept her heart in a regular "sinus rhythm," the ultimate goal of the doctors, most of the time, with only occasional episodes of irregular heartbeats. To protect her from possible stroke during these intermittent bouts of "A-fib," as the doctors had referred to it, she had also been prescribed a blood thinner medication to protect her from the possibility of blood clots forming in the heart, a medication that caused her to consciously watch and monitor her food intake, with certain foods completely removed from the diet. Two years after her ablation surgery, it was detected that she had higher-than-normal levels of cholesterol and was given medication therapy for that as well, which had the unfortunate side effect of muscle pain and weakness, as well as frequent spells of stomach pain. As her health continued its predestined decline and her list of medications increased, closing the business seemed to be her only course of action.

Her reaction to the closing of the company that had been forced upon her as a young bride had surprised even herself, and she fondly looked on the historic ending as one might look upon the extinction of an animal, the end of not only her own small business but also of many such entities that had struggled to survive in a world rushing forward with mergers and acquisitions, and she felt an unexpected posthumous affinity and closeness to her husband, Richard, and the Clarkson family, who had brought her into their world so long ago. The irony that she, the outsider in the family, was now left with what remained of their legacy was not lost on her, and she felt a compulsion to "hang on to the old lady," as she had worded it to her sister, and decided to remain in the third-floor apartment that had been her home for over sixty years.

The lower level had been summarily emptied by an auction service that quickly disposed of the furniture and fixtures of the business. The old solid oak bier that had been in the building since Alfred and Edna Sprick first opened the business in 1888 had been given to a struggling family-run funeral home in neighboring Jonesburg, Missouri, and the newer one was sold off with a collection of other miscellaneous funeral supplies to an investment group out of the St. Louis area. Most of the equipment from the embalming area was too old to be of any real value, and it was sold off as scrap. All the first-floor contents—the outdated sound system, old church organ, coffee makers, tables, chairs, desks, refrigerators, everything that was used in the business—were auctioned off at rock-bottom prices. Even a few miscellaneous desks, chairs, and file cabinets that were left in the vacated second-floor rental spaces were disposed of.

Ruth, wanting to maintain at least a few artifacts from the business, kept one of the two old Ballard Designs viewing couches and placed it in the small front guest room on the third floor, and the other was sold at auction to a young couple who was hoping to open up a coffee shop in nearby Wentzville, Missouri. The large oak roll-top desk that came from the Commerce Bank closure in 1930 was auctioned off for four thousand dollars, a price that Ruth assumed Richard, who had always refused to let go of the old desk, would have been happy with. The antique Pembroke Renroth grandfather clock that old Werner Clarkson had shipped over from Bristol, England, was sold for a little over twelve thousand dollars, a sale that had many in the small town looking through their attics for similar priceless treasures.

Once the sale was complete, and the two lower levels were entirely emptied, a construction company was hired to "secure" the building, as Ruth had explained it when questioned about the ongoing construction, by closing up the front and side entrances and placing plywood over the first-level windows until the space could be rented out. With the funds from the sale of the furniture and fixtures of the business and the old grandfather clock, the back entrance was secured and additional lighting was installed along with a handicap ramp, and the old Otis Elevator was given a thorough overhaul. Two years after the funeral home closed, a local real estate firm, wanting to capitalize on the trend of restoring architecturally significant buildings, leased out the entire lower level and remodeled the space, creating three separate leasable units.

The aging wall-to-wall carpets throughout the third-floor apartment, which were put down in 1957 as a wedding present for Ruth and Richard by Richard's parents, were ripped up, and beautiful oak hardwood floors were discovered, and a crew had been brought in to sand them down and restore them to their original luster. An antique Ethan Allen walnut dining table and chairs that had originally been in Ruth's family home in Lafayette Square had been brought up out of storage in the basement, refinished, and placed in the dining room. Ruth had all three of the bathrooms updated and even had an American Standard walk-in soaking bathtub with power jets installed in her main bathroom. New appliances were bought for the kitchen, and for the first time in her life, she had an ice-maker that she bragged about to anyone who would listen. Under the direction of Regina, Ruth's daughter, new curtains were hung in all the rooms, and the entire apartment was given a fresh coat of paint.

A three-acre tract of land that Ruth had purchased as a building site just two weeks before Quinten's death was eventually sold to Alex Battenhorst, Ruth's grandson, who had plans of building a log house on the site. The ground, adjacent to the Charrette Creek farm where Quinten had proposed marriage, had a breathtaking view of Krueger's Bluff from the back line of the property, a fact that figured heavily in Ruth's decision to keep the acreage in the family, and she had often, over the years, gone to the site as a respite from the vicissitudes of daily life.

Sarah Callier, Richard Clarkson's longtime lover, had been apprehended and arrested for the murder of Quinten Denver only moments after she left the scene of the crime, and she sat for over two years in the local county jail as the legal system struggled to figure out her punishment. After years of legal maneuvering based around the woman's sanity and ability to stand trial, she was finally placed in a secure mental institution in Jefferson City, Missouri, where she stayed until her death four years later. Her son, Mark Callier, who all his life had only wanted the love of his father, had survived the vagaries of a fractured childhood as well as the mental instability of a woman obsessed with a man she could never have, but his mother's murdering of Quinten Denver proved to be his breaking point. When asked why he told everyone that his mother was dead, he simply stated, "To me she was dead," and he had felt little remorse about the deception until she had reappeared and changed Ruth Clarkson's life forever. He had never been able to comprehend what his mother had done, never quite recovered from her final break from sanity, and he soon left the Ox Bend area and was thought to have moved to Portland, Oregon, based on a postcard that Ruth received five years after Quinten's death. It pictured the famous tourist attraction Portland Center Stage at the Armory, with a Bible verse, Matthew 5:4, "Blessed are those who mourn, for they will be comforted," scribbled on the back in what looked like a child's handwriting. It proved to be the final correspondence Ruth ever received from the young man.

Cora, who continued her therapy sessions with Dr. Whitman until he closed his practice in 2010, remained married to her fourth husband, Henry Lasciter, until his death in 2011, and finally found the balance and stability that she had always longed for in a relationship. As the couple aged, she had come to appreciate and value Henry's pragmatic view of reality, and she relied on the stability and equanimity that he always provided, however "boring" he might have appeared to the rest of the world. Through him she had come to accept the betrayals of her childhood, had been able to demystify her disintegrated view of men, and had even, as her sister Ruth had once predicted, been able to finally forgive her father and walk away from the heavy burden of hatred.

When Henry had first been diagnosed with lung cancer in 2010, she faithfully remained at his side through nine months of treatment, pain, and decline and had been given a firsthand look at the ugliness and finality of infirmity and old age. At his side on his final day, she had watched her husband, once filled with life and health, pass into eternity, and she had, for the second time in her life, experienced a genuine sense of loss and suffering that had left her almost inconsolable. And as "the beast in the jungle" had finally made its leap, as she remembered Henry James putting it, she finally knew the answer to the question that Dr. Whitman had asked her so many years before. She had been capable of love; she had deeply loved her husband.

After Henry's passing, Cora came into possession of a small estate as dictated by Henry's final trust agreement. His fortune, severely lessened by his battle with cancer, was divided between Cora and his three surviving children, two from his first wife and one from his second. Although the compensation was less than Cora had expected, it had allowed her to monetarily keep the old house on Rutger Street in Lafayette Square, but as age began to takes its toll, the unforgiving flights of stairs in the old structure became more than she could handle and she had been forced to close off the top two floors. Sentimentally unwilling to just walk away from the house, she had set up her main living area in the first-floor parlor and had even converted the dining room into a makeshift bedroom, much to the chagrin of nosy neighbors. As her struggles in the old mansion grew, she started to spend a good portion of each month in Ox Bend with her sister, Ruth, who had also grown frail over the years, and the two old sisters gradually started a process of "looking out for each other," as Ruth had put it to her daughter in a letter; although each sister privately insisted that she was really the main caregiver! As Cora's visits increased, the spare bedroom where their mother, Emma, had stayed for a while had been turned into her own permanent guest suite, and she moved in the majority of her clothes and personal effects to make staying for lengthy visits possible without constantly packing and unpacking and only made periodic day trips back to Lafayette Square to check on the property. The two widows, now advancing in age, had come to rely on each other in ever-increasing ways and were able to repair the sisterly bond that had been lost in their earlier years. As progressing age took more and more away from them and they grappled with the hostile realities of old age, where practicality outweighs abandon, they still attempted to enjoy life as much as they could, knowing that, as Ruth had so poignantly quoted Frost at her eightieth birthday party, "nothing gold can stay."

$$\overset{\displaystyle C^{H^{A^{P^{T}}}}{}_{E}{}_{R}}{\textbf{35}}$$

The old apartment on Main Street in Ox Bend was filled with the muffled roar of laughter and conversation as the smells of baked turkey, ham, casserole dishes, freshly baked biscuits, and pumpkin pies wafted to every corner of the old dwelling. The Clarkson clan had gathered for their annual Thanksgiving Day celebration, and a good number of the family were present and accounted for. Regina, who had lost her husband just four years earlier, had flown in from Tampa, Florida, where she now lived, and her eldest daughter, Anna, was there with her fifteen-year-old son, Michael, who had been born on Anna's twenty-fourth birthday. Michael's father, a man that Regina had called morally bankrupt after only two meetings, had refused any involvement in the process, and the family had rallied around Anna as she undertook the arduous task of raising a child on her own. She had even stayed for several years with Ruth, until she married a young military man, Thorton Nordwald, from adjoining Lincoln County, who was currently stationed at USAG Baumholder Army Base in Germany. Charles, Ruth's still dashing-looking son, who was now the county sheriff in Lincoln County, was there with his wife, Allison, as well as their son Eli and his wife and their three-month-old baby, Clifford, named after Eli's brother who had been killed a few years earlier while serving in the Army. Richard Jr., now a successful editor in New York, was there with his boyfriend of sixteen years, Steven, as well as one of Steven's bothers, Kirk, who had driven out from St. Louis. Also in attendance was old Clyde Kaermor, now just a few weeks shy of his eighty-seventh birthday, who had lost his wife, Ruthie, just six months earlier. The old man, now confined to a wheelchair and living in the local nursing home, had been checked out of the facility and brought across town to the apartment by Charles and his brother, Richard Jr.

The large number of attendees made a sit-down dinner impossible, and the old walnut dining room table was set up in buffet fashion as the family started the drawn-out process of circling the table and filling their plates and then finding a place to eat in the large apartment. The front bedroom, where the old Ballard Designs couch had been sitting since the business had been shut down, was fitted with a large portable table and a few extra folding chairs, and two more tables were wedged into the living room area, one placed directly below the *Woman in Blue Reading a Letter* reproduction that Ruth had always steadfastly refused to part with. A fourth table was placed in the main entranceway from the hall, half of it in the dining room, and half of it in the hallway, and the kitchen table was pulled out from the wall, allowing for three additional folding chairs to be added.

The young women with small children were the first to go through the line as they juggled multiple plates at one time and continually asked, "Do you want any of this?" as their children followed along like openmouthed baby birds at their side. As each person completed the line, they found a place at one of the tables throughout the apartment, and some even sat at the living room couch, their plates precariously perched on their laps.

After most of the family had gone through and were finding their seats, Ruth walked over to Clyde Kaermor, who was sitting by himself next to the front window in the living room. After his wife's death just six months earlier, his own health had taken a turn for the worse as he fell into a deep depression, and he had been moved from an assisted-living care facility to the local nursing home, where he continued to decline rapidly.

"How are you doing, Clyde?" Ruth whispered as she walked up behind him and placed her hands on his shoulders, knowing that he was legally blind now. "I'm so glad you could make it."

"Oh, not so good," the old man whispered feebly. "I just wish Ruthie were here," he added in a broken voice, a sentiment that he had repeated in every conversation since the death of his wife.

"Yeah, we lost the best of us when we lost her, didn't we?" Ruth replied wistfully. She walked around to the front of his wheelchair and straightened the blanket that was draped over his lap. She looked at the old man's weathered face and vacant-looking eyes and patted him on the arm. "I miss her too," she whispered. "More than you know."

"Oh, I know you do," Clyde responded. He reached up, his hand shaking from what the doctors had diagnosed as "active tremors," and grabbed Ruth by the hand. "I just wish it had been me instead of her," he added in a broken voice.

"You can't think like that, Clyde," Ruth countered firmly. "God has his own plans for us here on earth. And anyway, she needed you there at the end. You helped her through it." He clutched Ruth's hand a little tighter.

"Well, I hope so," he answered wishfully. He paused and looked up toward Ruth's voice. "You know, my mother always told me that the only guarantee that old people can give is that they'll die."

"Well, I can't argue with that," Ruth whispered as she reached down and kissed the old man on the head. "But it's how they go that we can control. The kindness that we can give them."

"Well, you did more in that regard than anyone. The way you took her in when none of the children would."

"They all had busy lives, and I understood that. And it's not easy caring for the elderly." Ruth paused and seemed to be remembering some distant place and time. "We don't keep so well," she finally added with a little laugh.

"No argument with that," the old man responded with a distant smile. "That's why it takes a special kind of person to do it." The old man paused, and his voice took on a serious tone. "It takes a person like you, Ruth. How can I ever repay you?"

"Oh, don't even think about that. She would have done the same for me!" Ruth said reassuringly. "After all the help she gave me over the years, and the babysitting she did, and helping out at the funeral home. Both of you, I owe you both so much."

"Well, she loved being here with you. I hope you know that."

"I was just returning an old favor!"

The old man paused and seemed to be drifting back in time. "I remember when you all first moved here. Remember, it was back in 1957." He paused, and a rare smile appeared on his face. "Ruth and Ruthie! You two sure have gone through some things over the years!"

"Oh my god, who can remember back that far?" Ruth deflected with a melancholy tone.

"Hell, that's all I can remember anymore!" he spouted and then let out a small laugh. "I don't know what I did yesterday, but I remember what happened in 1957!"

"Ruth! Ruth, come here!" Cora shouted out from across the room. "We need you to clarify something," she added with a mischievous tone.

"Don't listen to her, Mom!" Richard Jr. called out as he placed his arms around his aunt and gave her a squeeze. Richard Jr.'s comment was followed by a round of laughter from everyone crowded around the dining table.

"Come on, Clyde," Ruth said in a very animated way. She got behind his wheelchair and grabbed the handles. "Let's go see what Cora's up to now and get you something to eat!"

After Ruth helped Clyde get his plate together and then filled her own, she ended up sitting at the table that was set up under the watchful eye of the *Woman in Blue Reading a Letter*. Regina was seated at the head of the table, and her daughter Anna, and her son, Michael, a junior in high school, and his new girlfriend, Treasure, were seated beside her.

"Grandma, come over here and sit by me!" Anna yelled out as Ruth walked up to the table, a dinner plate in one hand and a glass of wine in the other. "I want you to meet Treasure. She's Michael's new girlfriend." Ruth, just three months removed from a total left hip replacement, slowly made her way around the table and took a seat next to her granddaughter.

"This is my grandmother," Anna spouted out proudly to Treasure as Ruth settled into her seat, "Ruth Matilda Saroh Clarkson!"

"Oh my, such a big introduction!" Ruth blushed. She looked over at her great-grandson and his girlfriend sitting across from her and shook her head, astonished at how young they looked. "And my granddaughter knows that I hate the name Matilda!" she amended with a laugh.

"I love the name Ruth, though," Treasure interjected unexpectedly. "That's my middle name," she added proudly. She looked at Michael and flashed an innocent blush that seemed to have a visceral effect on him. "I was named that after my mom's sister."

"It's a pretty big name to have to live up to," Ruth kidded. She smiled and looked closely at the young couple again. "It's an important biblical name too," she added.

"Tell us again how you got that name, tell us about the story of Ruth," Anna demanded as she set her fork down. She nodded and looked around the table for supporters.

"Oh, no one wants to hear about that," Ruth countered. She picked up her napkin and placed it on her lap, hoping that she had put an end to it.

"No, it's a fascinating story, Mom!" Regina interjected with an even more determined tone than her daughter. "And Anna's not going to let it go until you do!" she added with a laugh.

"She's right!" Michael concurred.

"And we all would love to hear it!" Anna yelled out as everyone around the table agreed.

Ruth, bowing to the pressure, sat back into her chair, looked around the table, and started to speak with an air of mystery about her. "Well, years ago, my great-great-great—oh, I don't know how many greats we're up to now—grandmother was said to have been visited on her deathbed by Ruth the Moabite from the Old Testament."

"And this really happed too!" Anna chimed in an attempt to give credence to the story. "This really happened!" she repeated in a very animated way.

"Let her go on," Regina jumped in, giving her daughter a "motherly" look that Anna had seen on many prior occasions.

"Well, as the story was told to me," Ruth went on, "in 1819 my ancestor Ruth Lissette Petersmeyer was living in Germany in a little town called Detmold. Now, of course, this was before the unification in 1871, but it's a small town up in the northern part of the country in a county called Lippe. It was probably up close to the Weser River and the Teutoburg Forest." Ruth paused and cleared her throat and then took a little sip of wine. "Now, Ruth had been sick for a long time, and her daughter had taken her to her house and put her up in a small garret at the back of the home. They didn't really expect her to live that much longer."

"What was she sick from, Grandma?" Michael interrupted.

"Well, I don't know if anyone really knows for sure, but my mother told me that her mother told her that it was probably cancer because she was suffering through a lot of pain with her illness." Ruth paused and folded her arthritic hands on the end of the table as a solemnity came over her. "And one morning her daughter came in and found her mother sitting up in the bed, all the pain and suffering that she had been going through gone! And Ruth told her daughter that a woman had visited her during the night. She said that this woman had appeared beside her bed and had reached down and touched her on the forehead and all her pain just suddenly disappeared."

Charles, who had walked up to check on his mother, was now standing quietly at her side as she went on with the story.

"And so Ruth asked the woman who she was and why she was there, and the woman told her that she was Ruth the Moabite and that she was preparing a place for her, that she wouldn't have to suffer any longer." Ruth paused a moment and looked at the frozen faces around the table, and a chill ran through her. "And she lived another month totally pain-free and then passed away in her sleep on Easter Sunday of that year." Ruth paused again and then leaned forward and readjusted the napkin on her lap. "And ever since, the story has been passed down from generation to generation, and the name Ruth has been revered by the family, and they've been naming their children Ruth ever since." She glanced up at her handsome son standing quietly above her and grabbed his hand. "And that's how I got my name."

"But, Grandma, how do you know that really happened?" Michael asked skeptically. He glanced at Treasure and then secretly grabbed her hand under the table.

"He's just a skeptic!" Anna chimed in with a wry smile as she looked at her son. "Don't listen to him!"

"I am not, Mom," Michael defended, embarrassed at being called a skeptic.

"No," Ruth interjected, "that's a good thing. If you look up the definition of the word *skeptic*, it means someone inclined to question accepted opinions and beliefs. And that's a good thing, because your mind isn't already made up. You're still questioning."

"But how do you really know it happened?" Michael asked with a sudden burst of sincerity in his words that could only come from the innocence of youth.

"Knowledge and truth are not easy things to understand," Ruth countered thoughtfully. "Philosophers have been grappling with that question for centuries. But where does anything really exist beyond the mind of man? Shakespeare says there is nothing good or bad that thinking makes it so! And if I believe in my mind that something happened, then how can that not be true. How can that not be my truth!"

"Well, I believe it!" Anna chimed in, always trying to be her grandmother's favorite.

Ruth looked at her great-grandson and winked. "It's all a matter of faith, Michael," she said. "You just continue to be skeptical and keep asking your questions. You'll find your own answers in your own good time. Now, enough talk about Ruth! Let enjoy this meal before it gets cold!"

By eight o'clock that evening, the last remnants of the all-day feast were finally packed away, the dishes were all done, the folding tables and chairs had been taken down to the second floor, and the two old sisters were sitting alone in the front living room on the antique French couch from the 1890s, the Vermeer reproduction of *Woman in Blue Reading a Letter* silently peering down upon them.

"Doesn't that drive you crazy?" Cora started out as she looked up at the painting and waved. "Seeing that pregnant woman reading that letter all these years and never knowing what's in it!"

"Why do you always insist she's pregnant," Ruth responded with a predictable laugh. "We've gone through this a hundred times before!"

"Oh, please, no woman wants her waist to look bigger than it really is! And I doubt if the women from Vermeer's day were any different."

Ruth looked over at her sister and just shook her head. "Well, I actually like not knowing what's in the letter," Ruth said with a sense of conviction, hoping to move away from the ongoing pregnancy debate. "Then I can fill it in any way that I want. And who knows, maybe Vermeer was trying to imply that we, women, we need our secrets. We need a little mystery around us."

"Well, it's not much of a secret! She's pregnant!" Cora goaded back with a laugh.

"Oh, Cora!"

"And I bet that's some surreptitious letter from a boyfriend or the father of the baby."

"Oh, Cora!" Ruth uttered again, both amused and infuriated at her sister's comments. "You're hopeless! And just what did you look like when you were pregnant?" she asked with a laugh.

"I made sure that no one ever saw me that way!" Cora barked out. "Aunt Jewel wanted to take pictures to send back to Mom, but I wouldn't let her!"

"Oh, I have one," Ruth corrected her. "I found it going through Mom's things after she died. It must have been one that slipped through."

"No, you don't!" Cora bellowed back with confidence, sure that no such evidence existed.

"Oh, but I do, dear sister," Ruth replied with a smirk as she got up and left the room.

Cora turned around and looked behind her as her sister left the living room. "You better not be dragging out those old pictures again!" she yelled.

Within a few minutes, Ruth returned with a large box containing old pictures and letters and several timeworn picture albums. She sat down, opened the album on the top, and went right to the page she was looking for. "See here, see," she said, pointing to a small black-and-white photo in the upper right-hand corner. "That's you and Aunt Jewel! And it looks like you're at least eight months pregnant here."

"Oh my god!" Cora exclaimed. She removed her thick glasses and bent down over the picture. "I don't think this was taken when I was pregnant!" she added, then let out a laugh. "It's probably just the fashions of the day that make me look that way!" she added with a heavy dose of sarcasm.

"Oh, Cora!" Ruth exclaimed again. "Clever to the very end!"

"But look at this," Cora said as she turned the page, hoping to move past the unfortunate-looking photo. "Here's a bunch of pictures of Aaron! Just look at that face."

Ruth reached over and grabbed the album back. "He sure was cute," Ruth exclaimed as she bent down over the album. "And look, in this one, he looks just like you, Cora. Around the eyes, he looks just like you did when you were little."

"Oh no, he doesn't," Cora fired back. She reached over and grabbed the album back and bent down to get a closer look. "He looks just like his father! See, he even has that little cleft in his chin, just like Richard did." Suddenly, Cora stopped talking and quickly tried to turn the page in the album.

Ruth pushed Cora's arm aside, grabbed the album back from her sister, and pulled the small black-and-white photo out of its plastic covering and examined it closely. "You know, now that you mention it, he does look like Richard. He has Richard's squared-off chin with that little dimple in the middle. It was more noticeable when he got older, but I can still see it here."

Suddenly, Ruth stopped talking, as if some profound realization had just come over her, and she looked at her sister, who was sitting motionless at her side. "Wait a minute," Ruth whispered as she turned toward Cora, her mind spinning in a thousand different directions. "What did you just say?" Cora said nothing and just looked up at the woman in blue, who suddenly seemed to be sneering down at Cora with a contemptuous look. "Cora, what did you just say?" Ruth asked again, her voice rising as she spoke.

"Nothing," Cora muttered back, her lips barely moving.

"I heard you! You said that he had the same little cleft chin, just like his father, Richard, did!"

"I know! I know!" Cora suddenly confessed as she lowered her head into her hands. "There's something that I have been wanting to tell you for years." She stopped and started massaging her temples, as if some great headache had just overtaken her. "And I have tried to tell you on several occasions, but you know how secrets become comfortable over time. It just seems like they somehow take on a life of their own." She paused again and clutched her hands at her breast. "And I wanted to tell you so many times, but—"

"What are you trying to say, Cora?" Ruth interrupted as she reached over and grabbed her sister by the arm.

Cora looked down at her sister's hand resting on her arm, and a rush of adrenaline came over her, and she looked back up at Ruth. "Richard *was* Aaron's father," she finally whispered, her voice filled with infinite remorse as she uttered the secret that she had carried for over sixty years.

Ruth sat back into the couch and let out a long, slow sigh, as if she were physically struggling for air. After a few moments of intense silence, Ruth looked over at her sister still sitting motionless on the couch next to her. "Are you sure?" she asked.

"Yes, it's true, Ruth," Cora confessed again with the sense of conviction that Ruth was looking for. "Richard *was* Aaron's father."

Ruth said nothing for a few moments, and her eyes drifted back up toward the painting hanging above the fireplace, and she felt as if she, too, had just received some disclosing letter from the past, had been blindsided by some dark, secret truth that had lurked in the shadows for years.

"I always wanted to tell you," Cora went on as her voice started to tremble. "But I just…"

A deep sigh stopped her from going on, and she felt as if she couldn't breathe. Ruth, who had been staring up at the painting, looked back down at her sister. "I always wondered why Richard knew about the child before I did," she finally said as the reality of the statement started to settle in. "Now it all makes sense."

Cora remained silent, visibly shaken, and buried her head in her hands again.

"And Mom and Daddy knew too, I guess?" Ruth asked.

"Yes," Cora confirmed without looking up.

"So everyone knew but me?" Ruth asked, making a visible effort at self-control.

Cora raised her head sharply and looked back up at her sister, her eyes filled with years of suffocating guilt. She wiped the tears from her eyes, got up from the couch, and walked over to the large front window and stared out into the darkness below, as if she were looking into some portal to the past, the old Western Auto sign across the street flashing rhythmic tints of yellow light against her shadowy face.

"Only Richard, Mom and Daddy, and I were supposed to know," she finally answered as she regained her composure. "But I think Richard told his parents." She paused a moment as she thought back, searching for any details that she might have overlooked. "And I think old Louis Clarkson knew too," she finally confessed without looking back.

"Oh my god," Ruth replied, her grip on the photo album tightening. "Louis said something to me at Aaron's funeral! And I wondered what he meant." Ruth paused, and her face reddened. "At the luncheon, he said that I should have been told the truth. But I didn't know what he was talking about at that time." Ruth set the photo album on the coffee table, crossed her arms tightly, and looked over at her sister, still standing quietly in front of the window, with a kind of terror. "And what about Lawrence? Did he know?" she asked.

"No," Cora responded adamantly. "Daddy wouldn't let us tell him. I didn't even tell Aunt Jewell the truth!"

"But why not tell me?" Ruth implored, as if her life depended upon knowing the answer.

"Oh, Ruth," Cora replied and then let out an incoherent murmur. "You had just gotten married! You were only married a few months! And Richard begged me to not tell you about it. He was so afraid that you'd leave him."

"But then why decide to keep the baby at all?" Ruth asked without thinking.

Cora turned quickly from the window and looked her sister in the eye. "That was my decision," she proclaimed emphatically. "I didn't really have any control over what was going on at that time in my life, and a lot of that was my own fault, but I did know one thing! I didn't want to give up my baby. I couldn't bear the thought of never seeing the child again." Cora stopped, as if the pain she had experienced all those years ago had suddenly reappeared, and she turned around and looked back out the window.

"Oh, Cora," Ruth mumbled to herself as she wrapped her mind around the truth.

"But of course, Daddy told me that keeping the child was out of the question," Cora went on, her voice gaining strength. "So it was decided that Richard would adopt the baby and that I would still be able to see him. I would at least be able to be a little part of his life. And so that's how it was decided." A deep sigh stopped Cora from going on.

"Then you did love the child, didn't you?" Ruth asked as she internalized what she had just heard.

"Of course I did," Cora responded with an emotional tone that Ruth had never heard from her sister. "Of course I did," she repeated desperately. "But Daddy warned me that I would have to keep my distance, that I would never be able to let anyone know that the child was Richard's. And Richard agreed with that, and so did I. And I was willing to do that just as long as I knew that the child was okay, that he was being loved."

Cora looked back over her shoulder at her sister. "And I knew that if there was anyone in the world that I would trust with my child, it was you."

Ruth felt the depth and pain in Cora's comments, and it was echoed back in her reply. "But why didn't you tell me this sooner?" she asked with a forgiving tone. "You could have been a bigger part of his life!"

"I wanted to," Cora answered, truth imprinted on every syllable. "I always wanted to tell you the truth, but I couldn't as long as

Richard was alive. I had promised him that. And then after he was gone, the lie had become so ingrained, so comfortable. And I knew the relationship that you and Aaron had. I knew how much you loved him, and I was afraid that the truth might affect that in some way, might change how you felt about him." Cora looked back out the window, the dim yellow light flashing on her face like a slow, methodic heartbeat.

Ruth remained silent and looked back up at the strange woman looming above the fireplace, as if she might have known the secret all along. "Remember when we met that medium down in Lafayette Square," Ruth finally started out quietly, "and she kept saying that she saw a father figure with Aaron?"

Cora looked back at her sister with a confused look on her face.

"Don't you remember? She kept saying that she saw a father figure with Aaron," Ruth repeated. "And I said it must be Richard but that he was his stepfather, and she corrected me. She specifically said that it was not a stepfather, it was a father figure."

"Ah, I remember," Cora finally admitted, turning back toward the darkness.

"That all makes sense now," Ruth went on. "But I just wish you would have told me sooner, Cora."

"You know, Dr. Whitman tried to get me to tell you the truth for years," Cora admitted, "but I was always so afraid that I would lose you. That you'd never be able to forgive me." She paused and let out a long, inarticulate moan. "Oh, I've made so many mistakes in my life, but none bigger than this one!"

"So when did this happen?" Ruth asked as she stood up from the couch and faced her sister.

"Do you remember the fire?" Cora asked without turning around. "The fire at the nursing home?"

"Yes," Ruth answered as she thought back, her mind picturing the horrific details of the scene. "It was that week?" she asked incredulously. "The week we had just gotten back from our honeymoon?"

Cora didn't respond and just continued to look out the window.

"Answer me, Cora," Ruth demanded. "Was it that week?"

"Yes," Cora finally answered, her voice trembling. "It was that day. It was that morning of the fire, when it first broke out."

"But I was there with you that morning!" Ruth yelled out. "We were all there in the apartment together!"

"Don't you remember?" Cora interjected frantically. "After we first heard the sirens in the distance, Ruthie called and asked if we knew what was going on." Cora paused and clasped her hands together, as if she were praying. "And then she came over and you and her decided to walk across town and see for yourselves." She paused again momentarily, as if she might have been seeing the scene playing out in her mind. "And I was going to go with you, but then at the last minute, I decided to stay. I decided to go back and lie down again and take a nap." She stopped and looked back over her shoulder at her sister. "That one decision…"

She paused, and her lips stirred faintly, and she looked back out the window. "If I had just gone with you two," she moaned, "none of this would have happened."

"So what happened after we left?" Ruth prodded.

"I was sitting on the edge of the bed, just a few minutes after you had left, listening to the sirens in the distance. And then"—her voice started to break up slightly—"he just came into the room, and he walked right up to me, and he put his arms around me and started to kiss me." She quickly looked back at Ruth, who was still standing motionless by the couch. "And before I knew it, he was on top of me."

"Oh my god!" Ruth yelled. "He attacked you?" she asked in horror.

Cora didn't respond initially and looked back out the window, as if she really didn't know the truth herself. "I don't know. I don't know," she echoed agonizingly. "I wish I could say that he had, but I don't really know. I was attracted to him, and I had been flirting with him ever since you guys got back from New York. You know how I was back then—I flirted with everybody. And maybe he read it the wrong way. I don't know." She stopped and turned around and directly faced her sister for the first time.

"But I tried to stop him, I did, but then I just gave in." Cora hesitated, and it sounded as if the words she uttered and her emotions had disconnected as she went on. "It was just like with Daddy. I just let him do what he wanted. It was always just easier that way." She paused and looked down, as if a heavy wave of guilt had just come over her. "I always just let them do what they wanted," she finally repeated.

Ruth walked over to her sister and placed her arms around her tightly. "And you kept this secret all these years. Do you know the price of keeping secrets?" she asked as Cora started to sob uncontrollably. Ruth grabbed ahold of her sister's trembling arms and pushed her back to arm's length and looked her directly in the eye.

"It's not your fault, Cora. I don't blame you. You're not to blame for this."

"Oh yes, I am," Cora answered, her voice breaking up. "You know how I was back then. It's all because of the way I was. It's my fault. It's my fault," she kept repeating.

Ruth started to gently shake her sister. "But look what came from it! Look at the gift that was given to us all! I know that it was a terrible thing to happen, it was a horrible thing to happen to you, but I wouldn't trade a single second of my time with Aaron for anything in this world." She paused, and a sense of serenity came over her. "Sometimes great things come from horrible circumstances. And who knows, maybe it was all supposed to happen this way. Maybe it was God's plan all along to give us Aaron."

Cora looked back at her eighty-four-year-old sister standing in front of her, and all the years of guilt and remorse that had built up suddenly started to leave her. The anguish brought on by years of subterfuge and lying started to flow away like a wave receding into the ocean, and she felt a calmness and connection to her sister that she had never experienced before. "Then you can forgive me?" she finally asked with the sincerity of child as the last wave of anxiety left her.

"There's nothing to forgive," Ruth answered, throwing her arms around her sister.

CHAPTER 36

D r. Millner's office was in the town of Marthasville, Missouri, a small township that was the original grave site of Daniel Boone and his wife before their bodies were disinterred and reburied in Kentucky, and it was just a short fifteen-mile drive from Ox Bend. Regina, back home for an extended visit to the area, was sitting in one of Dr. Millner's patient rooms with her mother and her aunt Cora. Cora, who was now living full-time in the upstairs apartment with her sister, had called Ruth's children the week before with some disturbing news about their mother's deteriorating health. She had told them that for the past few weeks, Ruth had not been acting at all like herself and had started to become withdrawn and tired and had even fallen several times in the apartment and had started to use a walker to maintain her balance. And her appetite, already diminished by the cholesterol and heart medications, had all but disappeared, and she was suffering from bouts of nausea and extended periods of confusion. Charles had immediately taken Ruth to an emergency room at a local hospital in Lake St. Louis, Missouri, where a series of tests had been run, and the results of those tests had been forwarded to Ruth's primary caregiver, Dr. Millner, and the three women were back at his office to get the results.

The sterile gray room was extremely cold, with only a large examination table centered in the middle, two chairs against the wall, and a small stool on wheels that was tucked under a desk in the corner of the room. An unobtrusive picture of a vase with red roses was hanging at a crooked angle just above the desk.

"My god, it is cold in here!" Cora exclaimed nervously as she took Ruth's walker and set it aside and then attempted to help her sister up on the examination table. "Here, Ruth, put your right foot up here on this step first, and then we can help you get up on the bench."

"Come on, Mom," Regina coached, "you can do it."

"This was not designed with old women like us in mind, was it?" Cora mumbled under her breath as Ruth finally made it upon the examination table. Ruth had no more than sat down when the door opened, and Dr. Millner walked in.

He was a younger, robust, energetic man with a prematurely receding hairline and a youthful-looking face with approachable large brown eyes. He had only recently taken over the practice from a retired doctor who had started the business back in the early seventies, but he had already endeared himself to his patients. The usually jovial young doctor, who was known for his magnetic personality and great bedside manner, was unusually quiet and reserved as he entered, and he had a file with him that he clutched tightly in his left hand.

"Hello," he greeted as he entered the room, his eyes darting back and forth between Cora and Regina, who were standing on each side of Ruth like muted figurines. "And you must be Cora, Ruth's sister." He stepped forward and shook hands with her but didn't look her in the eye, a detail that Cora interpreted as bad news. "And good to see you again, Regina," he added politely as he reached over and shook hands with her as well. He pulled the small stool on wheels from under the desk and rolled himself over to the foot of the examination table. He paused a moment and looked up at Ruth, perched quietly on the edge of the examination table, who seemed to be a million miles away.

"How are you feeling today, Ruth?" he asked caringly. He looked back down and opened the folder on his lap. Ruth said nothing, as if she might not have heard the question, and just shook her head slightly.

"She's been having a lot of nausea lately," Cora anxiously replied for her sister.

"And she hardly eats anything anymore," Regina added, placing her hand on her mother's shoulder.

The doctor looked up again closely at Ruth. "I have your results," he announced very seriously. "And I'm sorry, but I don't have very good news for you. With your recent weight loss and lack of appetite and stomach pain, I was worried that there might be some kind of cancer involved, and I'm afraid that that's what it is. And unfortunately, it's already pretty well advanced." Again, Ruth said nothing and just stared ahead in the direction of the doctor, her face seemingly devoid of all emotion. The doctor reached up and took ahold of Ruth's right hand and gave it a gentle squeeze. "Do you understand what I just told you, Ruth?" he asked kindly.

"Yes," Ruth finally muttered. She took a deep breath, as if some profound realization had just come over her, and her voice strengthened a little as she started to speak again. "I understand," she added as an image of her old aunt Matilda lying in her bed, gasping for air, formed in her mind.

"Now, there are treatments that we can pursue," the doctor said, then started his rehearsed list of options.

"No," Ruth interrupted adamantly. "No." She looked over at her sister and then down at the floor. "I don't want any treatment," she uttered, her voice filled with unwavering resolve. "It's just my time."

The doctor stopped and swung around and placed Ruth's file on the table behind him, then turned back around toward his patient. "And you're sure about this?" he asked tenderly, his voice breaking up.

"Yes," Ruth murmured. She reached down and grabbed the doctor's hand. "Don't worry about me," she whispered. "To everything there is a season." She let go of the doctor's hand and just looked down at the floor and seemed to disconnect from it all.

"Well, we need to get ahead of this," the doctor responded very seriously, seemingly touched by his patient's words. "Are you still staying at your home?" he asked. Ruth didn't answer, and the doctor glanced up at Regina and Cora, who were still standing like statuettes on each side of her.

"She is," Cora finally answered as tears started to steam down her face. "And I am staying with her. I've been living there for the past few years."

"And you stay there during the night as well?" he probed.

"Yes," Cora responded.

"And what about her medication?" he went on as if Ruth were no longer in the room. "Are you in charge of that too? Do you see that she takes everything as she should?"

"Yes," Cora answered again.

"And can she still use the bathroom by herself?"

"Sometimes, but I'm always worried about her falling," Cora replied.

"And what kind of bed is she currently using?"

"Well, she's on her regular bed now," Regina jumped in with a broken voice. "But we still have a bed that we got for Daddy when he was sick."

"Good, we'll need to get that set up again."

"We can see to that," both Cora and Regina replied in unison.

"Well, good, she really can't be on her own anymore." The doctor stopped and swung the stool back around toward the desk and started to make a few notes in Ruth's file. "And I would recommend that we start hospice as soon as possible," he announced as he looked back over his shoulder.

The word *hospice* created a visceral effect on both Regina and Cora, and they looked at each other in horror as the reality of the news started to really set in.

"Let me get you a list of local options. I'll be right back," the doctor said. He got up and quietly left the office.

As the doctor disappeared and the door went silently shut, it was as if all the air had been sucked out of the room and the women had been plunged into a vacuum, some alternate universe that no longer made any sense. It was as if time itself had suddenly stopped and no one could speak, the overpowering internal feelings of sadness and anguish almost more than they could bear. Each of the three women sat in silence and processed the situation as best as she could. After a few minutes, a nurse entered the room and asked Regina to join her in the office to sign some additional papers, leaving the two old women alone.

Cora looked down at her sister, frail and tired looking, still sitting frozen on the examination table, her eyes vacant, emotionless, seemingly detached from the horrifying reality of the situation, and she felt an overpowering sense of love and devotion for her sister, an overriding protective feeling that she had never felt before. Ruth had always been the strong one, the compassionate one, the loving one, the one taking care of everyone around her, but now Cora realized that Providence had turned the tables, that she now would have to step up and return the countless kindnesses that her sister had given her throughout her life. She realized that she now would have to be the strong one, that she would have to see her sister through the process of dying, and she felt as if her entire life had been leading up to this one event, that perhaps she had been given a chance at redemption, a chance to help the one person that had done so much for her. She walked around and faced her sister.

"I will see you through all this, Ruth. I promise," she whispered. She wrapped her arms around her sister's fragile frame. "Where you go, I will go, and where you stay, I will stay."

CHAPTER 37

"Be careful!" Regina barked, worn-out by two days of preparation and cleaning. "Put the head of the bed between the two windows at the back of the room!" she instructed as Charles and his son Eli were inching their way down the hall with the hospital bed toward Ruth's room. "And watch the walls!" she yelled over her shoulder as she walked out of the room.

"I think they have it now," Regina reported as she entered the living room, where Cora and Lawrence were sitting. "I had them take the bedroom set down to the second floor yesterday, and I cleaned the room really good too. We'll set the bed up just like we did for Daddy. And I'll bring in those folding chairs again for visitors, and of course we have the two dressing chairs."

"Well, what can we do?" Lawrence asked with a tone of desperation. "I know I'm stuck in this wheelchair, but surely, there's something I can do."

"Don't you worry about a thing, Uncle Lawrence," Regina assured him. "You've done more than enough already. I never would have been able to make my way through all those insurance policies and those letters from Medicare."

"Well, at least I'm still good for something," Lawrence replied with a subtle grin.

"Your just being here is more help than I can say," Regina added as she walked over to her uncle. She reached down and wrapped her arms around him and gave him a kiss on the cheek. "And I've taken a leave from work, so I'll be here," Regina assured him. "And Cora is here too, so if I have to go out, she's here with her. And the hospice nurse comes every other day, so we have things covered."

"Well, how long do you think she can stay here?" Lawrence asked, a serious look on his face.

"As long as we can lift her!" Cora chimed in. "And as long as we can keep her out of pain. I don't want her to die in some hospital."

"How is her pain?" Lawrence asked. "And the nausea, is that under control now?"

"For the most part," Cora answered hesitantly. "She's taking some medication that controls those things, and the hospice nurse checks on her pain levels and things like that."

"But she's just not eating anything," Regina jumped in. "And the hospice nurse says to just let her eat if she wants to, but not to force her."

"And does she still seem distant?" Lawrence queried. "Two days ago, when I was here, she was the worst that I had seen her. It was like she was just out of it."

"Well, the drugs probably have something to do with that," Cora jumped in. "But you're right, she just seems to be drifting away from us."

"Grandma!" Eli shouted from the master bedroom. "Where do you want this thing again?"

"I'm coming!" Regina shouted back, shaking her head.

Lawrence rolled his wheelchair over to where Cora was sitting on the living room couch, her copy of *The Custom of the Country* lying at her side.

"Are you up for this?" he asked his sister as he locked his wheels in place.

"Oh, I'm going to do everything that I can," Cora responded with conviction. "I promised her that. The problem is that we're both well into our eighties. It's like the blind leading the blind over here," she added with half a smile. "But Regina is here, and then the hospice nurse comes too. So we make it."

"Eighty's not so old," Lawrence replied with a smile of his own, attempting to lift the spirits of his sister.

"Oh god!" Cora bellowed back. "Funny how we keep putting off old age as we get older!" Cora paused and looked up at the *Woman in Blue Reading a Letter.* "When I was her age, I thought forty was old! And look at me now!"

Lawrence looked up at the old painting and pointed to the canvas. "Is she pregnant?" he asked, as if it might have been the first time that he really noticed the woman on the canvas.

"Yes!" Cora exclaimed. "Thank you! I've been telling Ruth that for over thirty years!" she added with a muted laugh. "And she always insisted it was just the style of the fashion that made her look fat!"

"She has always loved that reproduction," Lawrence replied nostalgically. "I was with her that summer in Amsterdam when she first saw the original!" He unlocked his chair and rolled over in front of the fireplace and looked up at the old oil portrait looming above him. "I must say, it is a beautiful reproduction," he stated. "The colors and the lighting are fascinating. And he seems to have really captured the private life of the young woman."

"And see that map in the background?" Cora asked, pointing up toward the picture. "Ruth says that's a map from the Netherlands, which has led many critics to speculate that her husband might have traveled for his job and that the letter she's reading was from him."

"Oh, I think I remember Ruth telling me that story once."

"She probably did, and with Richard always away from home, she related to that in some way."

Lawrence swung his chair around and faced Cora. "I guess we know now why he was gone so much," he stated as his mind drifted back. "Spending time with that Callier woman! The man was living a double life with another whole family, and we knew nothing about it. So many family secrets!" Lawrence paused and looked toward the hallway to see if Regina was returning.

"You know, old Louis Clarkson once told me another family secret." He paused and seemed to be cautiously deciding if he wanted to continue. "He told me that he thought Richard was Aaron's biological father." He paused again and kept his eye on Cora, looking for some type of reaction. "He told me this the day of Aaron's funeral."

Cora got up and walked over to her brother and placed her hand on his shoulder. "Well, there's a very good reason for that." She paused and took a deep breath, as if looking for some inner strength. "He was right. Richard was Aaron's father," she finally admitted.

"What!" Lawrence exclaimed. "I just thought the old man might have been losing it! You mean to tell me Richard really was Aaron's biological father?"

"Yes," Cora confirmed with a repentant tone.

"No…," Lawrence uttered. "You and Richard?"

"I wish it weren't true," Cora replied with an overriding tone of regret. "But it is."

"And does Ruth know this?" Lawrence asked as the rumor transformed from supposition to fact in his mind.

"Yes, she knows."

"So old Louis Clarkson was right!"

"It's true," Cora confirmed again, embarrassed by it all. "I kept it a secret for years at the beginning for Richard's sake, and then as the years went on, I just never could bring myself to tell Ruth the truth. I didn't know how it would affect her relationship with the child, and I was just so ashamed of everything that had happened." Cora paused and glanced back up at the painting. "And we had grown so close over the years, and I never thought that that would happen, and I didn't want to jeopardize that."

"Well, when did she find out, then?" Lawrence shot back, his interest piqued.

"It was a few years ago on Thanksgiving. I don't think you were here. You had gone to Christie's house that year. And that evening, Ruth pulled out the old picture albums, and as we were looking through them, I let it slip."

"What do you mean?" Lawrence asked.

"We were looking at some old photos of Aaron, and I said that he looked just like his father, Richard." Cora paused and seemed to be analyzing all that had happened. "Maybe it was some kind of Freudian slip. I don't know. I always wanted to tell her the truth, and Dr. Whitman was always trying to get me to tell her, but I just never could find the right time or the right words."

"And how did she react?" Lawrence questioned back.

"Better than I ever deserved," Cora whispered, her voice shaking with emotion. "And she was able to forgive me." Cora stopped and seemed to be reliving the conversation over in her mind. "She told me that sometimes great things come from terrible experiences."

"Well, it all makes a little more sense now," Lawrence replied as the shock of the news started to wear off. "I always just assumed it was Trenton's child. And I even asked Mother about it, and she said she didn't know who the father was."

"Oh, she knew all along," Cora confessed. "And Daddy did too."

"Ah, so many secrets on Elm Street," Lawrence replied, shaking his head. "You know, when you're raised in an environment of fear and intimidation, secrets become a way of life, and I guess that's just the way we always dealt with things back then." He paused and looked curiously at his sister. "But I can't image Richard wanting to keep the child, though. He never really seemed like the parental type."

"Oh, keeping the child was my choice," Cora announced with a great deal of conviction. "They all wanted me to give up the child for adoption, but I wanted to keep the baby! But the only way I could do that, the only way I could at least be a little part of his life, was by letting Ruth and Richard adopt the baby and then keeping it all a secret."

"Well, I guess that does makes sense," Lawrence agreed as he attempted to comprehend the situation.

"And Richard didn't want Ruth to know any of it, and I understood that. And I was just so ashamed of everything that happened I didn't want Ruth to know either. And Daddy certainly didn't want the truth to get out. God forbid we tarnish the image of Cole Saroh's perfect little family!"

Lawrence leaned forward in his wheelchair and grabbed ahold of his sister's hands and pulled her toward him. "Well, there was always one thing that I did know for sure, and that was that Ruth loved that child more than anything in this world. And of course, she would forgive you. That's just the way she's wired."

Cora bent down and put her arms around her brother. "What are we going to do without her?" she asked. "She was always the best of us."

"Oh, I can't even think about it," Lawrence replied as he patted Cora's arms. "I can't even think about it."

CHAPTER 38

The digital alarm clock on Ruth's bedside had just flipped to 3:07 a.m. when she first felt the presence of a mysterious figure standing at her bedside. At first, she thought she might be dreaming, and she rolled off her side and sat up in the bed, rubbed her eyes, and looked out across the dark room, but the unexplained visage, the otherworldly image, was still there, was still standing beside her bed. The female figure had a brilliant aureole encircling her, as if some type of energy was radiating from her body, and she was bending down, looking kindly at Ruth. Her bright eyes, the focal point of the image, were clear and warm, and she was smiling as she looked down, her right hand reaching toward the bed. She was robed in a long white gown, with a white tichel wrapped around her head, and she seemed to be floating just above the floor in some ethereal, unearthly way. And next to her was an eight-year-old Aaron, standing quietly, looking up at the lady by his side, the aura of youthful innocence and endless possibility etched on his childish face and mannerisms.

"Can Mommy see us?" he asked as he grabbed the figure by the hand. The woman only looked over at Aaron and then nodded.

"Mommy. Mommy, it's me, Aaron," the young boy whispered with a childish enthusiasm. He stepped forward and leaned down, his eyes dancing back and forth between the image and his mother. Ruth, acting only on instinct, tried to reach up toward her son and grab ahold of his hand, but she was unable to move and could only look upon the images hovering at her bedside.

"Mommy, this is Ruth," Aaron said as he leaned in even closer to his mother. "She says that you are sad now, but she's going to help you. She says that we're going to be together soon."

269

Ruth attempted to answer, but she was rendered mute, unable to articulate even a single syllable, and she just smiled up at the woman who seemed to be floating above her in some unearthly way. The woman reached down with her right hand and placed it on Ruth's forehead. Ruth could feel an overpowering sense of energy going through her body, and a brilliant light filled the room. Ruth closed her eyes and laid her head back as the pain and remnants of age and of illness started to slowly leave her body. She felt a tranquil, calming effect come over her, as if she were suddenly free from the earthly binds of age and suffering that had so thoroughly overtaken her. After only a moment, she opened her eyes again, but the images were gone, had vanished into the darkness. She sat up and swung her legs over the edge of her bed and cried out for Aaron, but he was no longer there.

"Aaron!" she yelled with emotions that came from deep inside. "Aaron, come back!"

Suddenly the door to the bedroom swung open, and Cora came rushing in.

"Ruth!" she yelled out as she came to her sister's bedside. "Ruth, wake up! You've been having a bad dream!" Cora turned on a small lamp in the corner of the room, which put an eerie yellow cast across the scene, and then sat down on the edge of the bed next to her sister.

"You've given me quite a scare," she said, her heart pounding in her chest. She placed her right hand on her sister's trembling shoulder. At first, Ruth said nothing, and she just looked at Cora sitting at her side.

"She came!" she finally announced as the reality of what had just happened started to settle in.

"Who came?" Cora asked.

"Ruth!" Ruth exclaimed incredulously. "And Aaron was with her!"

"Oh, you just had a bad dream," Cora assured her. "Let me get you half a sleeping pill. That should do the trick." Cora started to stand up, but Ruth grabbed her by the arm and pulled her back down.

"No, Cora. Ruth visited me!" she exclaimed, her voice quaking with eagerness. "Just like my mother told me that she came all those years ago. And she said that I will be joining Aaron soon."

"She *told* you that?" Cora asked very deliberately as she sat back down on the side of the bed, her mind racing in a thousand different directions.

"No. Aaron told me!" Ruth exclaimed.

"Aaron was with her?" Cora questioned skeptically.

"Yes! And he told me! She never said a word. She just placed her hand on my forehead. I could feel her touching me, and I could feel this strange energy radiating from her."

Cora reached up and tried to feel her sister's forehead.

"I don't have a fever, Cora. I know that you don't believe me, but she was real. They were real!"

"Well, I wish it were all true," Cora empathized. "Believe me, I wish it more than anything in this world, but your mind is playing tricks on you. You've heard that story and told it so many times you're dreaming about it now." Cora paused and turned to look closely at her sister. "But it's probably because they took you off all your regular medications. They always do that with hospice patients, but I told them I didn't think that was a good idea."

Ruth grabbed her sister's hands and clutched them in her own. "But don't you see? I don't need all that medication anymore. I don't need any more doctors or any more pills. I'm just like my old aunt Matilda now! And for the first time in my life, I feel content. I feel like I'm ready to go now. I know that it's my time."

Tears started to stream down Cora's face. "Oh, don't you dare give up yet!" Cora pleaded with emotions that came from some place deep inside. "Don't give up on everything. Don't give up," she repeated in a desperate tone. "I don't want you to go. I want you to stay here!"

Ruth reached over and put her arm around her sister. "It's all going to be okay now, Cora. You're going to be fine. You've always thought that I was the strong one, but you're so much stronger than me."

"Oh, don't patronize me, Ruth," Cora mumbled as she started to shudder. "Not now!"

"I'm not," Ruth replied with a renewed sense of honesty. "I wouldn't have been able to give up a child like you did, knowing you could never love it as its real mother. I wouldn't have been able to overcome what Daddy did to you. You're the strong one, Cora. And you are going to be just fine."

"But I can't bear the thought of you leaving!" Cora exclaimed as her eyes filled with tears again.

"Then don't think about it. Just think about today. Just take it one day at a time. There's a plan in place for all of it."

Cora stopped trembling, and a sudden calm came over her, and she looked her sister in the eye. "Where you go, I will go," she whispered, sounding almost childlike.

"And where you stay, I will stay," Ruth finished.

CHAPTER 39

"**A**re you sure you feel up to going today?" Cora asked as she helped her sister sit down on the old antique couch in the living room.

"Absolutely," Ruth responded unequivocally. "There's no way that I am going to miss Clyde's funeral. And if Charles is all right with it, I want to go Lippstadt too. I haven't been able to go out there for a long time."

"Well, he's planning on taking your wheelchair, but you'll have to see how you're feeling after the service. You don't want to overdo it." Cora took a seat on the couch next to her sister. "I am amazed, though, at how much better you're doing since…" She paused, as if she didn't want to say it. "The visit," she finally ended.

"Does it all still bother you so much?" Ruth asked.

"Oh, it all just scares me a little," Cora replied, sounding a little unnerved. "I'm not going to lie. But to see you sitting here, back with us again, without that unending pain, I guess it was nothing short of a miracle."

"I just hope I can make it till Easter Sunday," Ruth said. "You know, that's when the original Ruth died."

"Oh, I know. I've heard the story a thousand times. But let's not talk about it." She stopped and pointed up to the painting. "See, even she's a little freaked out about it all."

"Oh no, she isn't!" Ruth defended with a lighthearted laugh. "That's what I have always loved about her, her consistency." Ruth paused, and a serious look came over her face. "I think that's really the beauty of all art. The fact that it's unchanging, it's everlasting. It's beyond the frailties and changing whims of man."

Cora said nothing and then looked back up at the painting. "You amaze me sometimes, Ruth," she replied with an envious tone. "The way you view the world. I just see a picture of some woman reading a letter, but you, you see a young woman surrounded with mystery, and intrigue, and hope, and promise, a woman just starting out her life. You see it like no one else."

"It's like Keats's Grecian urn!" Ruth exclaimed joyously. "When old age shall this generation waste, thou shalt remain in midst of other woe, a friend to man," she added in a rhythmic tone. "And that reminds me, I want to you have that painting. I thought about giving it to one of the grandchildren, but she's done such a good job of watching over me all these years. I think you need her more than they do."

"Well, I guess that only fitting, since she's pregnant and all," Cora let out with a small, forced laugh, choking back tears. She looked at her sister, who was still staring up at the painting. "I just wish we could stay here, like this, forever," Cora whispered to her sister. "I just wish this moment never had to end." She paused, and tears started to well up in her eyes.

"Cora," Ruth stated very calmly, "go over there to that bookcase, on the second shelf from the top. Bring me that old leather Bible that's there." She was pointing to the bookcase on the right side of the fireplace. Cora got up, found what she was pointing to, and held it up.

"Yes! Yes, that's it. That was Mom's Bible. I found it when I was cleaning out her things. Bring it here to me."

Cora brought the Bible over and sat down next to her sister and started thumbing through the pages. "This was really Mom's?" she asked with a great sense of incredulity. "I've never seen it before." She paused, and a curious look came over her face. "And look, it's written in German."

"Pull out that folded piece of paper in the back," Ruth whispered as she leaned over toward her sister. Cora pulled out an aged dark-brown piece of paper that was wedged in the back, unfolded it, and then started to read. "Aber nicht heute," she read out loud as she struggled with the language.

"That's the title of the poem, and it means 'But Not Today,'" Ruth answered as she reached over and gently grabbed the paper from her sister. "It's this poem in German that I found."

"Well, who wrote it?" Cora asked, her interest piqued.

"I don't know," Ruth answered back as she slipped on a pair of reading glasses that was lying on the coffee table. "I have no idea who wrote it, or even when it was written. But for some reason, Mom hung on to it all these years."

"Can you read it?" Cora asked as she crowded in closer to her sister.

"'But Not Today,'" Ruth started out, pulling the page up in front of her face. "They visit with regularity now, these shadows, these ghostly *auftritte*." Ruth paused and looked toward her sister. "I think that means 'apparitions,'" she clarified and then looked back down. "These familiar vestiges from the past, dancing barefoot on the walls. I feel it—a breeze, a draft, a breath—assembling energies moving closer. I hear the prayerful echoes and voices, Words floating through the ages. The separation is less now. How comforting they are, how natural, how true. I need only reach out and grasp it. But not today."

After she finished, she placed the paper back into the old German Bible and looked over at her sister, who was sitting motionless next to her. "It's not always pretty, this world. I learned that a long time ago. But it has an order to it. And the end…well, the end is just as natural and true as any other part, maybe even more. And no one ever understands it until they're sitting right here where I am now."

"But aren't you afraid?" Cora asked desperately.

"Afraid of the inevitable? No, not anymore." Ruth paused and placed her hand on her sister's trembling arm. "I need only reach out and grasp it."

"But not today," Cora implored as she reached over and grabbed ahold of her sister's hands.

"No," Ruth whispered back. "Not today."

CHAPTER

40

"So how is she doing?" Anna asked as she anxiously entered the living room, threw her coat on the back of the couch, and looked around at the gathering. Regina glanced up and smiled at her daughter and motioned for her have a seat next to her. "The hospice nurse is in with her now," she replied. "She's giving her a bath. Come and have a seat by me." Regina was sitting on one of the antique French living room chairs and was talking to Richard Jr. and Cora, who were on the couch, drinking coffee. Anna walked around and gave her aunt and uncle a kiss and then sat down next to her mother. "So how has she been doing these past few days?" Anna asked. She set her purse down at her feet and leaned back in her chair. "I wanted to come by yesterday, but I had doctor's appointment in St. Louis."

"Well, it's nothing short of a miracle," Cora responded with incredulity. "Her pain is almost nonexistent, and she's so much more lucid than she was there for a while. She's back to the old Ruth again. It's really remarkable."

"And Dr. Millner was by here yesterday," Richard Jr. chimed in, "and he was surprised, too, by how well she's doing. And he was really at a loss to explain it all."

"Well, I think we all know how to explain it," Cora interjected in her typical straightforward fashion. "But would anyone believe us?"

"Well, what does the hospice nurse think?" Anna asked.

"She's never really seen anything quite like it either," Regina answered. "But she keeps telling us to not get our hopes up too much. And she says the fact remains that she has cancer throughout her body."

"But at least she's not in any pain," Richard Jr. added optimistically, "and it just seems like she's back with us now."

"Well, what about *you*, Anna?" Cora asked as she took a closer look at her great-niece sitting across from her. "You're starting to show a little! You're starting to look like the woman in the portrait up there!" she added with a laugh.

"Well, I had my doctor's appointment yesterday, and he said everything looks good. He said that he's always a little more cautious with women my age and that I need to be extra careful, but everything seems okay so far."

"Oh, dear, is thirty-nine considered old now?" Cora joked. "I'm in real trouble if it is!" she added as everyone laughed.

"Well, I personally don't consider it old," Anna defended, "but he said I'm doing great. And you know, I haven't really had any type of morning sickness like I had with Michael. This time it's really been much easier."

"That's a boy for you!" Cora quipped as she poked Richard Jr. with her elbow.

"I don't know what it is, but I'm just thankful for the way it's going," Anna proclaimed, patting herself on the stomach with both hands. She leaned forward in her chair and looked closely at her mother with a large smile. "Did you tell them?" she whispered to her mother.

"No," Regina answered mysteriously. She shook her head and then glanced over at Cora and Richard Jr. "That's your news to tell."

Cora set her cup down and looked at her great-niece. "So what kind of secret are you keeping from us?" she asked with a laugh. "That's my area of expertise!"

"Well, I just found this out yesterday for sure," Anna replied with a huge grin on her face. "And I called Thornton last night and told him." She paused a moment and glanced around at the eager faces surrounding her. I'm having a little girl!"

"Oh my lord!" Cora gasped as she looked at Richard Jr. sitting next to her. "You can name her Undine after me!"

"Oh god!" Richard Jr. spoke up. "One Undine in the family is enough!"

"And," Anna started out and then paused, "we've decided to name her after Grandma Ruth."

"Oh, that's a great idea!" Richard Jr. joined in.

"Yes, Ruth Undine!" Cora quipped back with a smirk.

"No," Anna replied. "We're going to name her Ruth Matilda!"

Richard Jr. looked at his aunt Cora, who was sitting quietly with her mouth open. "What, no comment about that!" he asked. "Cora is finally silenced!" he added playfully as everyone around the room chuckled.

"How can I add to that?" Cora finally responded. "I think it's an absolutely wonderful name!"

The hospice nurse, who was a large-framed woman with a kind face, a little turned-up nose, and large brown eyes that seemed to harbor some type of deep-bedded sorrow, quietly entered the living room. "She's sitting up in her bed now," she announced. "You can visit for a little while, but then I'd let her take a nap. She seems very alert today, but I still don't want her to get over tired."

Cora stood up and looked at Anna. "You go on back first. Tell her your news. I'm anxious to see how she takes it."

As Anna was leaving the room, Cora looked down at her nephew still sitting on the couch. "You know, she hates the name Matilda," she whispered and then shook her head.

When Anna entered the back bedroom, Ruth was sitting up, wide awake, the front of the hospital bed cranked almost all the way up. She was dressed in a freshly laundered light-blue nightgown with white trim around the collar, and her hair was neatly combed back off her face, and she almost looked like a freshly scrubbed little girl sitting in the bed.

"Grandma, how are you feeling?" Anna asked as she entered the room. She pulled one of the folding chairs up next to the bed and sat down. "Are you too tired for a visit?"

"Oh no," Ruth responded with a huge smile. "I'm feeling better today than I have for some time. And I always love talking to you." She paused and looked down at Anna's stomach. "So how are *you* feeling? It looks like you're starting to show a little."

"I was just telling everyone that this pregnancy was much easier than my first. I haven't had any of the morning sickness that I had with Michael." Anna paused, and a huge smile appeared on her face. "And of course, Cora said that was because he was a boy!"

"Oh, don't listen to your aunt Cora! She seldom thinks before she speaks, and the thinking part is only a part-time commission!"

"Well, actually, I do have some news for you," Anna started out mysteriously. "I found out yesterday that I am going to have a girl this time."

"Oh, that's great!" Ruth exclaimed. She pulled herself up a little straighter and clasped her hands together and pressed them against her breast. "That's just wonderful! Does Thornton know?"

"Yes! I talked to him last night, and he couldn't be more excited. And he has some leave coming up, so he'll be home within a few weeks."

"Oh, that's great news!"

"And because this pregnancy was such a surprise at this time in my life, such an unanticipated gift, I have decided to name her after you. I decided to name her Ruth Matilda."

Ruth pulled her clasped hands up under her chin and looked down, as if she didn't know what to say. After a few moments, she looked up at her granddaughter sitting by her bedside. "So you are going to carry on the family tradition. You know that the name Ruth has been used for generations on my mother's side of the family."

"Oh yes," Anna answered quickly. "And that's why I want to carry it on. I want to keep the name and story of Ruth alive in the family."

"Come here," Ruth demanded as she held open her arms. "Come here and give me a hug!"

Anna got up and threw her arms around Ruth and gave her a tight squeeze.

"But you know," Ruth whispered into her granddaughter's ear, "I have always hated the name Matilda."

CHAPTER 41

Cora was sitting on one of the overstuffed dressing chairs that had been moved to the foot of Ruth's hospital bed, her copy of *The Custom of the Country* lying open on her lap, and the hospice nurse was just finishing up her daily examination. Richard Jr. was standing at the back window, looking out over the rear of the funeral home, and Charles and Regina, who had been there all morning, had just stepped into the kitchen when the hospice nurse arrived.

"Her digestive system has started to shut down," the nurse announced solemnly, as if it were her own mother lying on the bed. She stood up by the side of the bed and took off her stethoscope and placed it around the back of her neck. "It won't be long now. I would suggest that you call any other family or anyone else who wants to make a final visit."

Cora nervously got and up and went to the side of the bed, her heart beating rapidly in her chest, and Richard Jr. walked over and stood at the foot.

"So how long do you think?" she asked, trying to hold her emotions in check. "She wants to make it to Easter Sunday."

"I don't know for sure, but I don't think it's going to be too long now." The nurse paused and looked down kindly at Ruth. "But it is Good Friday today, so she may make it, but you never really know for sure. I have another patient on the other side of town. I'll stop back by when I finish with him. We'll see how things are progressing by then."

"Okay, thank you so much," Cora replied sincerely. "You've been a godsend. I don't think we could have made it this far without you."

"Yes, you've been wonderful," Richard Jr. concurred.

"I appreciate that, but that's my job." The nurse paused and looked down again at Ruth lying silently on the bed. "But your sister has a special place in my heart. I don't know how to explain it, but I just had this connection with her, right from the start."

"Yes, that's my sister," Cora responded with a great sense of pride. "She definitely always had a way about her, and for some strange reason, people have always been drawn to her."

The nurse grabbed her bag and slung it over her shoulder and then paused and looked up at Cora and Richard Jr. standing helplessly beside the bed. "You know, the other day, she told me something really strange. She told me that she was visited by Ruth from the Bible," the nurse confessed incredulously. "Did she tell you that too?"

"Oh yes," Cora answered quickly. "And she's not the first one in the family to have said that!"

"And she also told me that her son is waiting for her on the other side."

"Oh yes," Richard Jr. stated emphatically. "That would be Aaron."

"You know, toward the end, people can experience all kinds of things in the mind," the nurse explained. "It's all part of the process. As the mind starts to disconnect, it starts experiencing things that don't really exist."

"Or maybe," Cora started out tentatively, "just maybe, it's the other way around. Maybe it's at the end when we can finally see things the way they really are."

"Well, I don't know about that," the nurse replied with a confused look on her face. "But she seemed to think it was all very real. And who are we to question it, anyway?" the nurse added as she touched Ruth's forehead and brushed her hair back. "I've only known her a few weeks, but I wouldn't put anything past her."

By three o'clock that afternoon, Lawrence had joined Cora, Regina, Richard Jr., and Charles in the bedroom as they all waited for the inevitable to happen. Lawrence, who had rolled his wheelchair up to the front of the bed, kept falling asleep, and his head was bobbing up and down as he tried to stay awake. Cora was seated in a folding chair next to her brother, and Charles had pulled over the two dressing chairs to the other side of the bed, and Regina and Richard Jr. were seated on them. Charles was standing quietly at the foot of Ruth's bed, looking down at his mother.

"Look at Lawrence," Cora whispered. "He can barely stay awake."

"Oh, I'm not sleeping," Lawrence quickly corrected her. "I'm just snoozing," he added as his head popped up and he looked around.

"You know, Mom used to do that too," Richard Jr. joined in. "I'd walk in and she'd be sitting upright on the couch, sound asleep. It always looked like she was just sitting there, looking up at the woman in the blue dress."

"That pregnant woman," Cora interjected with a short laugh.

"Oh, I remember you two going on about that poor woman," Regina joined in with a laugh of her own. "Always arguing about whether she was pregnant or not!"

"Well, she does look pregnant to me," Lawrence weighed in very matter-of-factly.

"Hear that, Ruth?" Cora spoke as she leaned in over her sleeping sister. "Lawrence agrees with me! That woman is pregnant."

"What in the world are you all talking about?" Charles finally asked, with a totally befuddled look on his face, a comment that got everyone around the bed laughing.

"Oh, don't even try to figure it all out," Lawrence spoke up as he looked at Charles and shook his head. "Entering a woman's mind is a dangerous adventure!"

"No," Regina answered smartly, "it's just a busier one!" Then she laughed.

"Well, I won't argue with that," Richard Jr. retorted. "Hey, where is this plaque that Aaron made for Mom? She told me that she wanted that to be buried with her."

"I have that," Regina answered. "I'll see to it that it's there when the time comes."

"And are you going to read Edna again?" Lawrence asked as he looked over at his nephew.

"Oh yes, and I actually wrote something myself. I think I'll read that too."

"What's it about?" Cora asked as she, too, focused on Richard Jr.

"Well, I've just been so inspired by her these past few years. The way she's just gracefully accepted old age. The way she's accepted everything. She never complained, and it was just the opposite with Daddy. And she never seemed to give up."

"And I don't care what anyone says," Cora jumped in. "Ever since she had that visit that night, she's been so much better. All that pain and nausea that she was experiencing before was gone after that."

"So then you think it's true?" Lawrence asked very seriously. "You really believe that she was visited by this representation of Ruth or an angel or whatever?"

"I do!" Charles answered before Cora could. "I believe it 100 percent."

"And I do too," Richard Jr. chimed in. "And that's what's been so amazing about all this. After all the things she's been through in her life and all that she's meant to everyone who's ever known her, it's her strength these past few months that has amazed me more than anything. The way she's bravely faced this part of her life, almost embraced it. And I don't know if I'll be able to do that…if I'll have the strength that she has."

"Oh, if Ruth has taught me anything," Cora interrupted, "it's not her strength that keeps her going. It's her faith."

"So how does this poem go, little brother?' Charles asked as he stood up straight and crossed his arms. Richard Jr. looked at the faces sitting around the bed and then started to recite his poem.

"Nature's bravest color doesn't filter through the flower. It chapters best the close of life, to celebrate that hour. When strong ancestral sap, that made it all begin, now lets the crimson, golden face turn loose upon the wind." Just as Richard Jr. finished the poem, Ruth's eyes started to open. Just a little at first, and then they opened up all the way, and she seemed to be staring up at Charles, who was still standing at the foot the bed.

"Look, her eyes have opened," Charles whispered in amazement. He placed his hands on the footrail of the bed and leaned in toward his mother. "Her eyes are open," he repeated softly, his voice laced with both wonder and torment. Cora grabbed ahold of Ruth's left hand, and Regina took ahold of her right, and they all leaned in closely around the bed and looked on in utter silence, not knowing exactly what to say, betrayed by the intimacy of language itself. Her breathing became light and shallow, and it started to slow down until it was almost imperceptible. Her green eyes dilated and took on a grayish color, and she appeared to be looking out somewhere past the confinements of the small room, out into the very mysteries of the universe itself, beyond the material remnants that still surrounded her. She took one last shallow breath, then it stopped, like all good things eventually do, and a hushed, peaceful stillness fell over the room, a quietness that defied human understanding. For just a moment, those illusionary, man-made constructs of time and space were all but gone, and they felt as if they were free-falling, plunging into a reality stripped down to its basic elemental form, far away from the comforting myths and philosophies of mankind, far beyond the midsummer pond, ignorant and content. The close-knit circle of family remained fixed in time, as if they were afraid to move, afraid to take that next breath that would signify that life was going on, that they were moving on, that Ruth was now a member of the ages, and the unrelenting burdens of life and living were beckoning them back, compelling them to let her go.

Finally, Cora let go of her sister's hand, stood up, and then leaned down and kissed her on the forehead, the all-too-human necessities of time and space returning, allowing her to put one foot in front of another, to return to the world of the living. "I'll go call the funeral home," she whispered, her heart cloaked in a deep-felt sorrow that she had never experienced before. "It's all over now," she said as tears streamed down her face. "She's finally back with Aaron."

CHAPTER 42

The sun was shining brightly, and soft rays of light were penetrating through the canopy of mature oak and hickory trees that surrounded the old Lippstadt Church and graveyard. The intense July heat and humidity that had been baking the area for days had suddenly been swept out of the area by a welcomed wave of cool northerly winds that created an almost resort-like feel. A woman and her two small boys were walking around the graveyard, looking for the headstone of the woman's aunt, who had been laid to rest only six months earlier.

"Get down off that gravestone!" she yelled to the older of the two boys, who was attempting to drag his younger brother up on the stone as well. "Get down from there!" she yelled again as she came running across the graveyard. The older boy jumped off quickly and then hunched down and started rubbing his fingers in the grooves of the lettering on the grave marker.

"Who's this?" the young boy asked with the endless curiosity of a child. "Who's buried here?"

The young woman stopped and bent down to read the gravestone. "Oh, it's just some old woman named Ruth. See, it says here that she was born on August 8, 1935."

"Did you know her, Mommy?" the curious boy asked innocently as he turned his head and looked up at his mother.

"No. No, she's been dead for some time now."

"So nobody remembers her now?" he asked with a childish naivete.

"I don't know, son. People come and go—that's the way of the world. Now come on, we have to go. Grandma's expecting us."

"But what's this funny name?" the child asked, refusing to go. The young mother turned back around and bent down and looked at the name her son was pointing to.

"Oh, that's Matilda." The woman chuckled. "That was her middle name." The woman paused and brushed a lock of auburn hair from her youthful-looking face. "And I bet she *loved* that name," she added sarcastically with a laugh as she grabbed her son by the hand and pulled him off the grave.

About the Author

Russell Clarke worked for over thirty years in the education field, teaching both high school and adult education in a large corporate setting, with a focus in the banking industry. Areas of study include two undergraduate degrees: a BS in psychology with a philosophy focus and a BS in education and a master's degree in adult education theory. His works typically examine the human condition, particularly as it relates to human relationships and the connections that people make. Now out of the corporate setting, he resides outside of St. Louis, Missouri, the setting of most of his works, and continues to write character studies with existential and philosophical currents.

CPSIA information can be obtained
at www.ICGtesting.com
Printed in the USA
LVHW050918031120
670566LV00006B/136/J